3B P9-CEK-444

LINES IN THE SAND

A NOVEL

THOMAS A. OHANIAN

Copyright © 2001 by Thomas A. Ohanian

All rights reserved. Printed in the United States of America. No part of this book may be used in any manner whatsoever, electronic, photo-copying, recording, or otherwise without written permission except in the case of brief quotations embodied in critical articles and reviews.

The characters and events in this book are fictitious. Any similarity to actual persons, living or dead, is coincidental and not intended by the author.

Published by Lines in the Sand Press.

Printed by Morris Publishing, Kearney, Nebraska.

For more information visit http://www.linesinthesand.com
First Edition

Library of Congress Control Number: 2001130053
Ohanian, Thomas A.
Lines in the Sand / Thomas A. Ohanian. — 1st ed.

ISBN 0-9709306-0-7

Cover Design by Peter Fasciano; Gina Lisa DiSpirito (Gladworks.com)
Cover Photo by Armin T. Wegner, courtesy Schiller-Nationalmuseum / Deutsches Literaturarchive Marbach.
Map by Mardy Minasian, cartographer, courtesy of Project Save Arme-nian Photograph Archives.

For Aram Aharonian Ohanian and Susan Masoian Ohanian

AUTHOR'S NOTE

Lines In The Sand is a work of fiction set in a background of history. Public personages both living and dead appear in the story under their rightful names. Their portraits are offered as essentially truthful, though scenes and dialogue involving them with historical and fictitious characters are of course invented. Any other usage of real people's names is coincidental and not intended by the author. Any resemblance of the imaginary characters to actual persons living or dead is unintended and fortuitous. Territorial regions and descriptions are easily subject to boundary issues, and are intended only to illustrate the narrative. Certain situations described in *Ambassador Morgenthau's Story* by Henry S. Morgenthau and published by Doubleday / Page in 1919 have been used within the narrative for dramatic purposes.

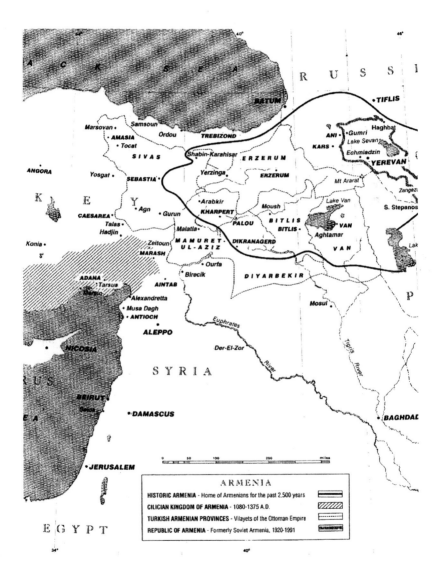

ARMENIA

HISTORIC ARMENIA - Home of Armenians for the past 2,500 years
CILICIAN KINGDOM OF ARMENIA - 1080-1375 A.D.
TURKISH ARMENIAN PROVINCES - Vilayets of the Ottoman Empire
REPUBLIC OF ARMENIA - Formerly Soviet Armenia, 1920-1991

LINES IN THE SAND

For the word of the cross is folly to those who are perishing,
but to us who are being saved, it is the power of God.
1 Corinthians 1:18

Part One

EAGLE'S NEST
THE BAVARIAN ALPS
OBERSALZBERG, AUSTRIA
22 August 1939

Berchtesgaden lay some one hundred fifty seven kilometers to the southeast of Munich and as the scenery sped by, Field Marshall Hermann Goering shifted uncomfortably. They had been in the cars for almost two hours and he was restless to get out and stretch his legs. Driving into the picturesque alpine town, the motorcade stopped. Goering, happy for the respite, stood and looked at the magnificent peaks surrounding them. Despite the waning days of summer, there were traces of snow still on the summits. He turned and looked at the men: Raeder, Von Brauchisch, Milch, Schniewind, and Halder. Each of them had been summoned quickly and all knew that the meeting would go well into the night.

The journey up was just seven kilometers, but the route was a steep, treacherous one, with curves that would bring instant death to the unsuspecting driver. The road itself had been cut through a mountainside of sheer solid rock, an achievement that was both extraordinary and inconceivable. The cars moved on, twisting, turning, following the road that led to their leader.

It had been built for his fiftieth birthday; and presented to him just four months earlier on the twentieth of April. It was called Kehlsteinhaus, teahouse, though the Americans had already coined a more dramatic name: Eagle's Nest.

The cars slowly moved up the last winding road and halted at the base of Kehlstein Mountain. The men got out, straightening their uniforms, carrying their satchels. They walked to the entrance of the tunnel. The German flag was flying in a gentle breeze and further up, on the summit, stood a large wooden cross. Over the tunnel's entrance, chiseled into the three-ton marble slab were the words "Erbaut 1938", built in 1938. The armed guard turned the lion-shaped door handle. The large oval doors swung open and the men stepped inside. They walked down the long tunnel, two abreast, their shoes clacking on the concrete floor. They moved quickly: he was waiting. Admiral Raeder shuddered; it was a good thirty degrees colder than outside and by the time they went up, they would be almost two thousand meters above Berchtesgaden.

The tunnel ended in a large circular waiting room, its large dome above them, and there was a musty smell, the natural reaction of moisture against rock. Iron crossbars were arrayed in precise two-meter increments along the wall. These held three candles each that burned brightly in the windowless holding room. The men entered the elevator, noting their reflections in the solid brass walls and mirrors that had been installed. Their leader suffered from claustrophobia, so Fick, the architect, had come up with the brilliant idea that the mirrors would lessen the feeling of confinement.

The men could hear the air whistling as the elevator moved quickly up the one-hundred-thirty-meter shaft. The door opened and they stepped out into brilliant sunlight, the lush yellowness of broom bush, accompanied by its sweet fragrance, catching their eyes. They moved past the arched open windows beyond the sun terrace, past deck chairs that had hardly been used. The view was spectacular. Slight cloud puffs dotted an otherwise brilliant blue sky as the sun glistened off the water of the Konigsee, surrounded on three sides by mountain ranges.

They were now high above Berchtesgaden and could easily make out Salzberg in the distance. The men turned, walking towards the octagonal main hall. As they did, Raeder caught a glimpse of him, looking out from the large arched window. The figure turned back, slipping into the darkness. The group came to the main doors and Goering reached out, touching the granite stone entresol.

"These came from a quarry near Passau," he said to the others.

They nodded, and entered the main hall. Despite the month, a small fire was burning in the black marble fireplace, a gift from Mussolini. Directly in front of the fireplace stood a huge circular table; the men put down their bags and took their seats.

Now they watched as their leader turned, scanning their faces. As he looked from man to man, his stare seemed to burn right through each of them. They felt the fire within their leader, and they had learned to take energy from him. They were nothing without this man; he was the reason the people still felt some shred of pride after they had been left with virtually nothing after the Great War. He was the reason the country had rebuilt itself after the retribution committees had seen to it that they would forever continue to pay for that war. And he was the reason that they would rise and die for him, no matter what he commanded.

He crossed his arms and continued pacing. And as he did, Adolph Hitler outlined the plan.

"Soon we will embark on the first stage of our great rebirth," he began. "This is the time for Germany to show her greatness. This is the time for Germany to take back what is rightfully hers." He paused, looking at them. They sat, erect, anticipating.

"Now, the great drama which we have put into motion is not only unfolding, it is approaching its climax. And what we embark upon is only the first step, but it is the necessary step."

He paused, all eyes riveted to him.

"If we are drawn into a conflict with Britain and France, Poland will not hesitate to move. She wants unobstructed access to the sea." He looked at the men, his anger rising. "They will never get it!" He pounded his fist on the desk. Raeder flinched.

"War," he said, looking at them. "War." He turned, pacing the length of the room. "We must act for the good of every German outside these walls. I tell you we cannot withstand the economic torture being done to us." He looked at the men and his voice took on a strangely plaintive tone.

"These Einschrankungen, these damned restrictions, are reeking havoc on our country. We have, at the very most, three years before we are completely ruined." He paused, looking from man to man. "If we let that happen, we will never rebuild this country. We will be lost." He smoothed back his hair, and the timbre of his voice once again became harsh.

"We will not let that happen. No, this is the time. There is disharmony between the British and the French. All that is necessary is to keep our intents secret from both the Italians and the Japanese. I will see to that."

The men looked at one another, nodding. Hitler crossed to the window and looked at the magnificent peaks in the distance. He clasped his hands behind his back and turned to them.

"It will take us no more than two weeks to take Poland. Neither the British nor the French will come to their aid. They are leaderless and they are tired." He clenched his fists.

"But we must strike fast and we must strike savagely. The world must be convinced that Poland has collapsed so that they will not be tempted to assist her. President Moscicki will not be able to run to Britain or to France. He will have to capitulate. Then we will tighten the noose. For this stand, we will draft over seven million fearless fighters."

"You all know Dr. Funk, the Economics Minister," Goering said. The men nodded. "I have personally instructed him to issue an order authorizing the use of prisoners of war to assist in our efforts."

"Nothing will be left to chance," Hitler said. "Once this begins, we will take on the West. To feed our machines, we will need labor."

"We will be ready," Goering said. "Once we move into the Czech territories, hundreds of thousands will be available to us. We can put them in the concentration huts, feed them scraps. We will have an infinite supply of labor to last the duration. Those that perish will be easily replaced. It costs us nothing."

"And use prisoners of war and inmates of concentration camps," Hitler said. "Put every last one of the Schwein to use."

"It will be done," Goering replied.

Hitler looked to his right.

"Admiral, the submarines?"

Rear Admiral Otto Schniewind stood. "Twenty-one of them. They are proceeding to their destinations in the Atlantic. With the Luftwaffe blockade of England, we will unleash a wider blockade with our submarines."

Hitler nodded, satisfied. General Von Brauchisch cleared his throat. The men turned in his direction.

"Yes, General?" Hitler said, staring at him.

"And the Russians?" Von Brauchisch asked. "Can we contain them?"

Hitler looked at him for a moment.

"The non-aggression pact will be our binding contract," he said. "Russia is not the least disposed to pull her chestnuts out of the fire.

Stalin knows that Poland must be destroyed!" He looked at them, the fire raging in his eyes.

"We are ready to divide Eastern Europe with them. Poland and the Balkan States will be carved up. This will give them what they desire. Our forces will not be tied up in the East like the last war. We will mass a million and a half men in one forward thrust at one time; we do not have to reserve three hundred thousand for the Eastern Front."

He paused, thinking.

"Regardless, we must plan on the eventuality of a war with the West. We will need as much land and territory to trade in the East. Everything depends on a massive, crippling strike against Poland. We will then capture Holland and Belgium. We use Russia to keep the West in check. After Belgium, we will demolish France, and then we will move against England."

He paused, making sure he had their complete and utter resolve.

"After that, we will turn and unleash our might against the Russians." His eyes glinted, black. "They will never again starve us out. The stockpiles we have created will see us through. I have ordered that the railways be mobilized. Our supplies will flow efficiently and endlessly. General Milch?"

General Erhard Milch, Inspector General of the Luftwaffe, stood.

"We are ready," he said. "The Luftwaffe will completely and totally blockade England. If given the order, we will level them."

"England has less than one hundred and fifty anti-aircraft guns!" Hitler exclaimed. "One hundred and fifty!" He looked at Goering, who nodded vigorously.

"The British Air Force has less than one hundred and thirty thousand men. Poland has less than fifteen thousand. We have over two hundred and fifty thousand!" He looked at the men and their expressions were as rabid as his manner.

"Now is the time," he cried. "Now. While they are weak." He looked at their eager, nodding faces. "Now. Not three weeks from now. Now, when they are fat, stupid, and tired of war. Now!"

He paused, his face a mask of sheer fervor. The men were caught up in that frenzy and they felt his invincibility.

"Make no mistake about this! Danzig is not the issue. We must have more Lebensraum!" he bellowed, using the German for living space. "We must secure food supplies and land. Invading Poland solves these problems. What were all of them doing when they took our possessions? They were laughing! Laughing at us!"

The men in the room, especially Goering, hung on every word. Hitler drew close to the center of the table and leaned on it, looking left to right.

"And they will laugh no longer," he said. "On the first of September, they will forget what it is to laugh. This is why I command you now. Wage this war against Poland brutally. Wage it without pity and without mercy. Eighty million Germans depend upon us to carry this out and to secure their rightful lands and future. We have already begun with our plans for the purity of our heritage."

He crossed his arms in front of him.

"When the war starts, there will be time. Then we will take care of our Jewish problem." He looked at them and calmness returned to his entire being.

"Now I should like to invite you on the sun terrace for a drink. Then we will discuss our plan of action."

The men nodded and walked out into the bright sunlight toward trays of refreshments. Raeder, the Grand Admiral of the Wermacht Marine, was last to leave. He closed his notebook and made his way toward the group. As he did, he saw Hitler signing several documents which he then gave to an aide who quickly departed.

"Pardon me, Mein Fuhrer."

"Admiral?" Hitler said, looking up.

"There is something troubling me," Raeder said. "Something that I must talk to you about."

"Please speak freely."

"Very well then," Raeder said. "Of this invasion, I assure you that you have my full support."

"Go ahead," Hitler said, examining him.

"I am concerned for Germany," Raeder began. "I am concerned about this final solution."

"There are no alternatives," Hitler said, crossing his arms in front of him. "You know how they are. You know that we must have purity."

"Yes, Mein Fuhrer," Raeder said. "But the world will judge us for this. Maybe not tomorrow but years from now..."

"They will judge nothing," Hitler said. He looked at Raeder. "We must take these steps. These Jews control too many of our businesses and universities. They are brash and arrogant. Given the chance, they will rise against us."

"Yes, Mein Fuhrer, but the world…"

"You know how desperate our situation is, Admiral!" Hitler said, growing exasperated. "You know that we need to expand. This is the only opportunity we will have. We control access to our territories. We control the press. We need labor and we cannot do it any other way. All that matters is that we win the war!" He looked at Raeder, who stood, stupefied.

"You are one of the most educated military men who serves me. But I am surprised that you have forgotten your history."

"I don't… what do you mean Mein Fuhrer?" Raeder asked.

"The Armenians."

"I don't understand."

Hitler looked at him, and a small smile crept onto his lips.

"No one will judge us because no one will care about these Jews. History has taught us that."

"Yes, but…"

"Study history, Admiral," Hitler said, interrupting him. "All the answers are there. War merely provides an opportunity for a solution." He walked toward the window and looked out into the vast mountains beyond. Raeder stood, watching him. Hitler turned.

"History has taught us that in times of war, anyone who is undesirable and a threat to the state can be eliminated."

"But, we must consider how history will treat us, how the world will treat Germany after…"

"Wer redet heute noch von der vernichtung der Armenier?" Hitler said, looking at him. Who after all is today speaking of the destruction of the Armenians?

PALOU, EASTERN TURKEY
June, 1914

The small hand reached up, picked plump, succulent grapes from the vine, and placed them in a wooden basket. Eight year old Ani Samuelian, her basket now full, ran along the dirt path into a small stone home. She placed the basket on the wooden table alongside some pomegranates. The house was a bustle of activity as Ani's family prepared for the wedding of her brother Vache.

"Ah, look at those grapes!" her mother Berjouhi, said.

"Help two old ladies," Ani's grandmother Agavni said. "Bring the mortar and pestle."

Ani dutifully complied, picked up the heavy stone mortar from the shelf, and nudged herself closer to her grandmother.

Agavni gave her a split pomegranate and Ani scooped out the fleshy meat and put it in a wooden bowl. When she was done, she began grinding the seeds into a liquid mass.

"Now turn for me," Ani's older sister, Margarite, said.

Azniv Khatchaturian, the bride-to-be, stood on a small wooden chair, dressed in a colorful overcoat that would serve as her wedding day outfit. She turned and Margarite pushed and primped, placing small pins to mark positions. Azniv was from Bitlis, southeast of Palou, and had traveled to the home of her intended husband for the wedding preparation. This was tradition; it was the way it was done.

"Mama, we are finished here," Margarite said.

Berjouhi and Agavni moved toward Azniv, who stood quietly. Berjouhi inspected the folds and tucks and wordlessly consulted with her mother, who nodded slightly.

"Turn for me," Berjouhi commanded.

Azniv promptly turned and flinched as Berjouhi pushed in various spots. Finally, she pronounced her decision.

"Ah! Margy, you have worked your magic again."

"Thank you, mama."

"It is a beautiful dress, Azniv," Berjouhi said.

"Thank you, Mrs. Samuelian," Azniv said, dropping her eyes. "I am very grateful."

Meanwhile, Vache Samuelian reclined in the barber's chair. His father, Ashod, sat silent, unfazed, reading the day's journal. Sam the Barber, his real name was Sam Golian, hummed a tune as he spread lather onto Vache's face. Drawing a straight razor several times against the well-worn thick leather strap, he sharpened the blade and began preparing the groom.

Agavni and Ani finished grinding the last of the pomegranate seeds and filtered the red liquid through a white sheet.

"We are ready here," Agavni said.

Margarite helped Azniv remove her wedding coat and they carefully folded it as Azniv stood in her long white under-dress.

"Come, sit down. This is the fun part," Margarite said, helping her.

Berjouhi opened a small bottle and poured the contents into the bowl of pomegranate juice.

"Now we put in the henna and you stir. See how it becomes darker?"

Ani nodded, stirring the mixture.

"That is good. We are ready."

Margarite gathered up the long white cloth of Azniv's under-dress, exposing her feet and lower legs. Berjouhi knelt down in front of Azniv. "As it was for my mother, may the stain of these sweet pomegranates bring you fertility and bountiful children," she said.

Azniv gently dipped her toes into the liquid. She giggled slightly, drawing smiles from the others. She dipped her feet in and slowly withdrew them. They were slightly stained and Ani put a white cloth beneath them.

"Now your hands," Berjouhi said.

Azniv stretched out her fingers, dipped them into the bowl, and withdrew them.

In the rear of Sam's shop, Vache looked in the mirror. Dressed in a long and colorful robe, he looked at his father. Ashod stepped forward and straightened the multicolored sash around Vache's waist. He nodded once to his son, turned, and nodded to Sam.

The sound of the zourna, the horn, and the dhol, the drum, accompanied the groom's procession as it wound its way through the small village. Dressed in their best clothes, Azniv's and Vache's families and relatives walked behind a rider-less horse. The procession reached Vache's home and the zourna and dhol stopped in unison.

The door opened and Azniv appeared, dressed in her long wedding coat. Her face was covered with a veil, underneath which dangled a rope of delicate small pearls which encompassed her face. A gold chain was draped around her forehead. Her mother, Elise, and her sister, Sona, stepped forward from their places in the procession. They kissed her on both cheeks and Azniv stepped forward to take the hand of her father, Nishan, who helped her climb onto the horse. Vache's mother, Berjouhi, nodded at Azniv's mother, Elise, who returned the nod and walked back into the house. She would not be allowed to see her daughter until she returned a married woman.

Again, tradition.

The procession filed slowly into the modest village church. The priest, Reverend Father Arsen DerArtinian, was assisted by two altar boys standing on either side of him. He was a big man, and was dressed completely in black vestments that he himself had sewn. His gray beard flowed long and despite his seventy-five years, he had a full head of perfectly white hair. The families took their positions at the front while the others filled the small pew-less church. Azniv's father, Nishan, kissed his daughter's forehead through the veil and joined his daughter Sona.

Father DerArtinian motioned for silence and beckoned Azniv and Vache to come together before him.

"Join hands, my children," he said.

Vache took Azniv's hands in his. Father DerArtinian motioned to his left and Vache's godfather, Levon, stepped forward. He held out a long wooden pole with a gold cross attached to the end, suspending it just above their heads.

"And God took the hand of Eve and placed it in the hand of Adam," Father DerArtinian began. "And Adam said, 'This is bone of my bones and flesh of my flesh. She shall be called woman because she was taken out of her man.' For this reason a man shall leave father and mother and go with his wife and the two shall become one flesh. Therefore, those whom God has joined together, let no man separate."

Hagop Melkonian stood with his father Sarkis, mother Lucine, and sister Anahid. His grandfather, Bedros, and grandmother, Takouhi, were just behind them. To the right, he saw his friends Souren and Armen.

Father DerArtinian looked at the assembly and paused for a moment.

"This is a solemn day, but it is also a joyous day. For it is a day when a son and a daughter leave the family to create a new family. It is a day of faith, and it is a day of love."

Azniv looked at Vache and he held her hands a bit more tightly. One of the altar boys, holding a gold tray, stepped forward. Atop the tray sat two gold crowns. Father DerArtinian placed one crown on Azniv's head, the other on Vache's. Then he turned them until their foreheads touched.

Hagop glimpsed his friends Souren and Armen and they silently acknowledged one another. As he shifted his weight from one leg to the other, through the crowd he caught a glimpse of Azniv's sister, Sona. Although he knew Vache well, he had not met Azniv or her family. Actually, he had never been outside of Palou, though he knew the surrounding villages: Kharpert, Moush, and Bitlis. He found it difficult to take his eyes from her. She was slightly shorter than he, with long, curly, and very dark black hair.

Hagop's sister, Anahid, at thirteen, two years his junior, nudged him in the ribs. For a younger sister, she already had strong powers of observation. Father DerArtinian opened the Bible.

"If I have a faith that can move mountains, but have not love, I am nothing. Love is patient, love is kind. It does not envy, it does not boast, it is not proud. It is not rude, it is not self-seeking, it is not easily angered, it keeps no record of wrongs. It always protects, always trusts, always hopes, always perseveres."

Hagop looked from Souren to Armen to Vache and Azniv. Sona's back was to him, and although she was masked from his direct view, he was able to see her profile.

Father DerArtinian continued. "Husbands, love your wives, just as Christ loved the church and gave himself up for her to make her holy, cleansing her by the washing with water through the word. And now these three remain: faith, hope, and love. But the greatest of these is love."

Father DerArtinian removed the crowns from their heads. He reached for a goblet filled with wine and offered it first to Vache and to Azniv who had to finish it. He then turned them to face the others.

"All of you are witnesses to this. All of you must do your part in welcoming this union into your homes and into your hearts. Let no person cross this. Let no one undermine it. Children, you are joined now, in the eyes of this church, and in the kingdom of God. Be humble to one another, and be humble in the eyes of the Lord." Father DerArtinian made the sign of the cross. "In the name of the Father, the Son, and the Holy Spirit. Amen."

"Amen" echoed through the church as Azniv and Vache walked to his family first and then to her family, save her absent mother.

Now the wedding procession moved through the small village, winding away from the church. Vache, resplendent in his ceremonial outfit, and with a shiny sword dangling in its scabbard at his waist, held the reins of the horse upon which Azniv was seated.

Reaching his home, the procession stopped and Vache helped Azniv descend. She stepped slowly towards the door and it opened. Her mother, Elise, stood as Asniv drew closer. The group looked on as they kissed and then Azniv gathered her coat close to her, bent down, and kissed the hearth of Vache's home. And with that, a cheer came up from the crowd and the group rushed in to congratulate each family.

In the village clearing, nothing more than a large grassy field, the wedding celebration was in grand progress. The sounds of the oud, the kanun, the duduk, and the dumbek brought forth a sweet, melodic sound as the musicians played. Children ate handfuls of grapes and raisins. A crowd of old men gathered around the fire and occasionally an impromptu argument would break out; the cooking of the fresh lamb meat always brought great discussion. It was inevitable. It was expected. It was part of what held this little village together.

"Turn it, turn it now. That's enough," said Sam the Barber.

"So now a barber is telling me how to cook?" retorted Souren's father, Dikran.

"So now a cobbler is telling me when the meat is done?" Sam replied.

"Ah, try this and then say something," Dikran said, handing him a thick slice of bread atop which sat a steaming piece of meat.

"Ah, I thought not," Dikran said, as Sam licked his fingers and, wordless, walked away.

Hagop, Souren, and Armen.

Hagop and Souren were both fifteen years old, while Armen, at thirteen, was the same age as Hagop's sister, Anahid. The three boys were inseparable. Sarkis, Hagop's father, had a small but arable piece of land where apricots, grapes, mulberries, figs, dates, and walnuts were grown. Hagop, his only son, was in charge of the lambs and other animals. Lucine, his mother, ran the house, assisted by Anahid. All lived together in the small home with Bedros and Takouhi, Sarkis's father and mother.

Souren's father, Dikran Jamgochian, was the village cobbler. Armen's father, Garbis Khatisian, was the village blacksmith. The village itself was a small area, situated in the Eastern region of Turkey, between Kharpert and Bitlis, roughly fifty kilometers to the east of Kharpert. From where they sat, the boys could see the newlyweds surrounded by well wishers.

"This lamb is good!" Armen said, gobbling up the meat.

"I should hope so," Hagop answered. "Those are my lambs!"

"And you are a good shepherd!" Souren offered.

"Ah, well, Vache is a friend of our family," Hagop said.

"And today, Vache is a fortunate man!" Souren replied.

"Are you going to talk or eat?" Armen said, licking his fingers.

"Have you finished that already? Where did it go?" Hagop asked.

Souren noticed Armen's stare and put one hand over his food.

"No. No. Look at him, Hagop. He has eyes like a jackal. This is my meal!"

Hagop watched all this with a slight smile: Armen, continually hungry despite his slender figure, and Souren, who savored every bite.

"Come, let's go down," he said.

The boys moved off the main clearing ground, stopped at a small incline, and sat in the shade of a large apricot tree. Older men and their wives, including Hagop's grandfather Bedros, and his grandmother Takouhi, their arms clasped behind their backs, moved elegantly to the music in a traditional dance. Each Armenian village was known for something particular: Kharpert was known for its kuftah, stuffed balls of meat. If you were from Constantinople, Bolis, it was fish. Especially mussels stuffed with rice and currants, seasoned with cumin.

Hagop's sister, Anahid, danced with Vache's little sister Ani. There were more dancers now, and the smell of freshly cooked lamb mingled with the sweetness of freshly picked grapes.

"I cannot believe how tall your sister is. Just yesterday she was a little girl," Souren remarked.

"Ah, she is a good sister. Much smarter than I," Hagop said.

"I think she is strange," Armen offered.

"Why do you say that?" Hagop questioned.

"Ah, I think all girls are strange," Armen responded.

Hagop and Souren exchanged glances and then Souren burst out laughing.

"Armen, boy. You are wise beyond your years!" Souren said.

"What do you mean? I think it is best not to think too much about them," Armen replied.

"You may be right," Hagop offered. "You may be right, after all."

Armen rose to his feet. "I will be back!"

"Where are you off to now?" Souren said.

"Ah, where do you think? I am hungry!"

Hagop looked back to the clearing. The musicians were playing louder now, increasing the tempo. Azniv's sister, Sona, entered the circle of dancers along with her mother Elise. They entwined their arms behind their backs and began dancing. Unlike the older woman, swathed in black, younger women who were not yet betrothed tended to wear more colorful garments. Sona wore a simple blue silk and cotton dress. Her bare arms and legs were dark, tanned, and firm. Long black curls framed her oval face. She moved gracefully and easily, smiling frequently. The tempo of the music increased and the dancers endeavored to maintain their pace.

Armen returned, carrying two handfuls of ripe grapes. He sat down and offered some to Souren. Armen nudged Hagop, but drew no reaction. The musicians again increased their pace, and the older dancers moved off, leaving the clearing to the younger ones. Sona twisted and turned and threw back her long hair. For a moment, it seemed as if she looked directly at Hagop.

Armen nudged him again.

"Hagop!"

"What? Ah, thank you," Hagop said, reaching for some grapes.

Souren noticed Hagop's preoccupation and traced his line of sight until it rested on Sona. The musicians finished, the dancers catching their breaths.

"Oh! Oh! Hagop?" Souren said.

"Ah... No. No more grapes," Hagop answered, looking towards the clearing.

Souren smiled and motioned to Armen, who sat, eating grapes.

"Souren, who is that?" Hagop asked.

"Who is who?" Souren replied, playfully.

"That one, there."

"Oh, that dark beauty?" Souren asked.

"That is Azniv's sister. Her name is Sona. They are from Bitlis," Armen said.

Both Hagop and Souren gave Armen an incredulous stare.

"How do you know all that?" Souren asked.

"I saw Hagop looking at her before I went to get the grapes. So I asked Anahid."

"You asked my sister?" Hagop said.

"Yes, sure, why not? She knows everything!"

Hagop and Souren looked at one another and shrugged their shoulders. Hagop looked over to where Sona stood.

"Hagop," Souren said. "Careful. That one will make your soul leap."

CONSTANTINOPLE, TURKEY
14 June 1914

Henry S. Morgenthau, United States Ambassador to Turkey, sat in an after-dinner room in the American Embassy. He was fifty-eight years old, tall, and of lean figure. His hair was cut short, high on the forehead, and he sported a mustache and goatee flecked with gray. He wore small wire rimmed pince-nez glasses and could have easily passed for a university professor or a man of industry. He had accepted the assignment directly from President Wilson and now resided in Constantinople with his wife, Josephine. His ambassadorial role was largely ceremonial: he attended state dinners, presided over official rituals, and entertained foreign dignitaries. The United States presence and interest in the Ottoman Empire were neutral; America had not yet developed the strategic interest in Turkey that was shared by Britain, France, and Russia.

He sat with British Ambassador Louis Mallet, French Ambassador Bompard, and the American Military Attaché Major John Taylor. Mallet was refreshing Bompard's glass of scotch. They tried to meet frequently to socialize and exchange information.

"Do tell us, Major," Mallet said. "What is the American position on all this?"

"We're still gathering our facts for President Wilson, Mr. Ambassador."

"Facts! Surely you must be joking! It's quite clear that war is imminent," Mallet said. "Willie is quite mad you know."

"One thing is certain," Taylor continued, "if war comes, Turkey could play a very important role."

He reached into his leather valise, withdrew a map, and unfolded it. He traced various locations as he spoke.

"Here, England, France, Germany, and Russia. To the South, Austria-Hungary, Bulgaria, and the Ottoman Empire."

Morgenthau and Bompard leaned forward to get a better view of the map.

"To the southwest, the Mediterranean. Above it the Aegean. And finally, the funnel, the Dardanelles."

Taylor's finger rested on the narrow strip of land, barely two miles in width. Morgenthau craned his neck forward slightly and rested his hands on both knees.

"They are, of course, extremely important," continued Taylor. "The Dardanelles form the connection between the Mediterranean and the Black Sea. And through that connection, supplies from England and France can travel freely to Russia. These trade routes have been exploited by all sides for years."

Mallet barely looked up from his drink. "Control the Dardanelles and materiel flowing into Russia will grind to a halt," he offered.

Morgenthau, Bompard, and Taylor looked at him.

"That's right," Taylor answered. "Control the Dardanelles and the Black Sea will become locked, as will the North Sea routes to the Baltic." Taylor traced the lines on the map. "If our allies must go around Norway and Sweden to reach Archangel's port at the White Sea, delays will be extensive."

Mallet put down his drink and lit a cigarette.

"Major, those seas are frozen over at least three to four months a year."

"Yes, Mr. Ambassador," Taylor replied. "As is Vladivostok."

Morgenthau looked at each of them "Major, I believe that when the war comes, Turkey will side with Germany," he said.

Bompard, Mallet, and Taylor fell silent for a few moments.

"Then we are in for a very long conflict," Taylor said.

Mallet blew a long puff of smoke.

"Let's hope that Mr. Wilson doesn't wait too long."

SARAJEVO, AUSTRIA-HUNGARY
28 June 1914

The young man was part of the Black Hand. He passed effortlessly through the crowd. The streets were lined with people waiting for the motorcade to pass. He took a position at the front of a dense pack of onlookers, lit a cigarette, and took a long and deliberate pull. There was still time. The motorcar would definitely pass this way.

Archduke Franz Ferdinand and the Duchess had come to Sarajevo as a gesture of good will. The continual struggle between Austria-Hungary and her subject, who wanted nothing more than to assert and attain her own distinct identity, had been flaring up. It was time for a visit.

The open-air motorcar worked its way slowly through the streets and as it did the Archduke and Duchess waved to the crowd. As the car turned, nineteen-year-old Gavrilo Princip let the cigarette drop to the ground. The motorcar drew closer and Princip stepped forward. He was only a few paces away. He raised his gun and looked directly into the eyes of the Archduke. The Duchess sat, horrified, her mouth agape.

The pistol fired once, hitting the Archduke directly in the neck. Blood splattered onto his white and gold uniform and covered his wife's dress. Screams rang up from the crowd. As Princip stepped forward, people scattered. He watched as the Archduke pressed his hand to his neck, the blood spurting out between his fingers. Princip looked from the Archduke to the Duchess. He pointed the gun at her stomach and fired. She gasped but no words came out. Princip ran into the crowd. The Archduke slumped slightly and reached out for his wife.

"Don't worry, my dear. Everything will be all right. Don't die… the children…"

And with his treasured passengers dying, the stunned driver snapped out of it, speeding off, searching desperately for a hospital.

CONSTANTINOPLE
4 July 1914

The American Embassy had been decorated in observance of the American holiday. Josephine, Morgenthau's wife, sat in a comfortable chair surrounded by the other wives of ambassadors and diplomats stationed in Constantinople. Morgenthau glanced briefly towards her.

"Well I would say that it has been a very economical day," Bompard offered.

"Ha! I should say so!" guffawed Mallet. "It's not often that we combine a funeral procession for an Archduke and his wife along with the liberty celebration of an itinerant son!"

"Now, now, Mr. Ambassador," Morgenthau said, smiling. "I believe we won our independence quite fairly."

"Well, I'll give you this," Mallet said, raising his glass. "I do like your Kentucky whisky! I'll take a Dewars over one of those terrible Buchanan Scotches any day!"

They shared a hearty laugh and Mallet raised his glass in a toast. He was older than Morgenthau and although Morgenthau had known Mallet only a short time, he greatly admired his intellect and experience. As Bompard, Mallet, and Morgenthau chinked their glasses together, firecrackers were set off.

"Curious, though," Morgenthau said. "Has anyone seen Wangenheim? I thought he would have made an appearance today."

"I haven't seen him for days," Bompard said, brushing back his long mustache.

"Oh, come, gentlemen," Mallet said, raising his eyebrows. "I think we all have a fairly good idea of where Herr Wangenheim is."

POTSDAM, GERMANY
5 July 1914

The long table was black and shiny and the men sat in high-backed steel and leather chairs. The businessmen were dressed in dark blue wool suits, the military personnel in standard uniform. Their attention was centered on a large map affixed to the far wall. Baron Hans Freiherr von Wangenheim, German Ambassador to Turkey, poured himself a glass of water. He offered to do the same for General Otto Liman von Sanders, who declined. The large man at the head of the table cleared his throat and all attention shifted toward the German Chief of the General Staff, General Count Helmuth von Moltke. He pushed forth a wooden pointer and began.

"Before his retirement, General Von Schlieffen devised what I am about to outline to you," he said. "Alas, he never received the opportunity to tests its merits, but I assure you, we will."

The business and military men leaned closer.

"The Schlieffen plan calls for a major assault directly on France," Von Moltke said, pointing. "We will then storm Belgium, arc downward, and enter Paris."

The businessmen looked at one another and then turned back to Von Moltke.

"We have calculated our efforts and their resistance and we will occupy Paris in six weeks. We will then move directly in the East and into Russia."

A brief wave of concern washed over Wangenheim's face. He was careful to conceal this from the businessmen and looked quickly toward Von Sanders, who gave no reaction.

"Gentlemen, our forces are ready," Von Moltke said." He looked at them. "Are you ready for the business of war?"

The businessman closest to Von Moltke checked quickly for any sign of dissension and found none. He shot his cuffs and straightened his Swiss watch.

"We require two weeks maximum to transfer our funds and make the necessary preparations for supplies," he said.

Von Moltke turned to Wangenheim. "Ambassador, what is your situation?"

Wangenheim's voice was a measure of confidence. He did not hesitate.

"Turkey is under control, General."

PALOU

The village square in Palou was just a small clearing. The church was to the east and a row of small shops stood to the west. Village homes, small and squat, were made from hardened clay and stone. Windows were cut directly into the frame and outfitted with wooden shutters or layers of heavy burlap sacks. The homes were adjacent to one another, and thus it was possible to move from home to home simply by opening common side doors. The July sun shone bright and hot and Azniv, Vache, and his entire family were gathered around Azniv's family.

"A safe journey," Azniv said, hugging them all at once. It would be some time before she would see them all again; travel was difficult in the winter months. Her family had stayed as long as they could after the wedding, but it was now time for them to return to Bitlis. Sona hopped into the back of the cart and as it pulled away Hagop approached, holding a small leather cord from which were tethered several small lambs.

Hagop, as the only son born to his parents, had been entrusted with the traditional responsibility of caring for the animals. It was a role that he came to love very early in life. He had a special affinity for the animals and he easily raised, cared, and healed them. But he always had difficulty when it was time to butcher them. His father, Sarkis, had to do it the first time.

"Keep this in your head when you get scared about doing this," he had said. "It is to feed your family."

When it came time for Hagop to act alone, he repeated his father's words and it was a bit easier. But he never told Sarkis how he had turned away, sick to his stomach that first time.

As the cart passed directly by him he met Sona's eyes. They were a beautiful chestnut brown and almond shaped. Sona glanced directly at him. She was the same age, fifteen, but in this village, in this time, it was not unusual for a girl to marry between the age of twelve and eighteen. Eighteen was being generous. Much depended upon the village and hands needed to work the land. Past eighteen years, however, and a girl was pretty well on her way to being an old maid.

"Doona Menatz."

"She's a stay-at-home."

"Old maid."

Hagop stood, staring at her. Sona quickly dropped her head, averting her eyes, and the cart passed. He watched for a moment, but she did not look back. He gathered up the little lambs and continued walking, oblivious to her glance back towards him.

CONSTANTINOPLE

From the window of his office, Minister of the Interior Talaat Pasha had an unfettered view of Constantinople. Physically, he was an imposing figure and his wide back and powerful biceps stretched tight the spread and sleeves of his black waistcoat. He wore a white, high collared shirt, and a gray silk tie. Atop his head was an ever-present red fez. He bore a thick, bushy black mustache, and could be at once intense and glaring and at the next moment charming and humorous.

The desk was sparse and his leather chair was framed in dark walnut and creaked loudly each time Talaat dropped himself into it. It was rumored that he was not Turkish at all but Bulgarian. Others said he was a Pomak, a Bulgarian whose ancestors had converted to Mohammedism. Talaat, himself, seemed to revel in this enigmatic role and would neither confirm nor deny a word.

He stepped away from the window and turned to Von Wangenheim. With Wangenheim, Talaat faced no less an imposing figure. He was over six feet tall and his physique was strong and firm. His short black and gray hair was parted just to the left of center, his mustache black, and his deep-set eyes were penetrating. He dressed impeccably, in a three-piece suit, round-collared shirt, and silk tie. Always silk.

Talaat moved to his desk and the chair creaked as he sunk into it.

"Herr Ambassador," he said. "I think you do not appreciate the difficulty of Turkey's position. We must have protection."

"There is nothing to worry about, Mr. Minister," Wangenheim said.

"You say that now, but tomorrow I wonder if you will be able to accommodate us. Turkey needs warships."

"I assure you, Mr. Minister," Wangenheim said. "Those ships will be delivered. You have only to open the Dardanelles and receive them. They will be there. Will you do that, Mr. Minister?" Wangenheim asked.

Talaat pursed his lips.

"Turkey will do what she must."

Ambassador Morgenthau walked up the steps to the American Embassy. It stood in the Pera section on the European side of Turkey, overlooking the Golden Horn and was a large, three-storied structure, with three tall arched entryways, surrounded by a high-stoned wall. The American flag flew in the gentle morning breeze.

Morgenthau stepped into the outer office and hung up his coat. His staff consisted of twenty men, all career civil servants. His closest assistant was James Mowbry and as Morgenthau entered, Mowbry already had the morning papers and overseas telexes ready for him to review.

"Good morning, Mr. Ambassador."

"Good morning, Mr. Mowbry."

"Morning telexes," Mowbry said. "The Austrians have done it, sir. It's on the top."

Morgenthau looked at Mowbry. The telex was from the American State Department. He read the headline and did not have to read the rest.

"28 July 1914. Austria-Hungary Declares War on Serbia."

BRUSSELS, BELGIUM
2 August 1914

King Albert's country was landlocked by France to the West, Germany to the East, and Holland to the North. Surrounded by his military and political advisors, he listened carefully to different viewpoints, scenarios, and strategies.

Foreign Minister Davignon tapped his pencil. "To allow Germany free passage through Belgium violates the Treaty of London. We will no longer be neutral."

King Albert rose from his chair, drawing the eyes of his loyal staff.

"Gentlemen, this is a perilous time for Belgium. And the weight of the decision made in this room must be mine and mine alone."

The men sat, transfixed. "For every country there comes a moment when she must stand for what she believes. For if she does not, then she surely will not survive. To choose anything less than one's ideals is to make a pact with something that will eventually devour us." He looked at Davignon. "Mr. Foreign Minister, you are to immediately deliver this to the German Ambassador: Belgium and every Belgian will not sacrifice the nation's honor by allowing your free passage. We will not violate our treaty of neutrality."

King Albert paused and sighed loudly.

"Gentlemen, let us prepare."

PALOU

The heat of early August beat down as Hagop worked in the small pen adjoining the house. This would be the last shearing of his sheep before the cold winter set in. He dropped the newly shorn wool into a canvas sack, wiped the sweat from his forehead, and rested. In the distance, his father Sarkis, and his grandfather Bedros worked in the wide front field, checking on the condition of the grapes hanging from plentiful vines.

Sarkis was fifty-one years old, short, compact, and rugged. He was always clean-shaven and had a full head of black hair without a trace of gray.

Sarkis was just seventeen when he married Lucine, the marriage arranged by their parents. Lucine was from Kharpert and Sarkis had not even seen her until the actual betrothal day. She was taller than he, thin, with a face more oval than round, delicate long eyelashes, and honey gold eyes. Many years after their marriage, Lucine one night told Sarkis just how scared she had been.

"You were so short," she said, laughing.

"And you were so thin!" he shot back. "I thought, how is this stick ever going to give me children?"

"We knew nothing about each other and my mother and father seemed to know everything! And now there are twenty-one years from that day. And it worked."

"Yes, twenty-one years. And it has worked well."

Bedros, his father, was seventy-eight years old and although his health had begun to fail in the last few years, he was still active. Occasionally, he had to use a cane to take the strain off his legs, but he hated the damned thing; he would rather put up with a small trace of a limp than be seen with it. His full white beard was immaculately trimmed and matched his short, white hair. He had been married to Takouhi for fifty-nine years and loved sitting with his friends, having a cup of thick, dark coffee and trading stories.

The sun was waning now, and Hagop stopped outside the cobbler shop and wiped his feet on the straw mat. He entered and saw Souren and his father Dikran working. Souren looked up and nodded, but he was cutting leather soles to fit a worn shoe and he had to concentrate: the blade was sharp.

"Hello Mr. Jamgochian," Hagop said.

"Hagop! Hello to you!"

"I am just finishing," Souren said.

Hagop stepped over to Souren's table and picked up one of the shoes that Souren had finished. He turned it over, inspecting it, admiring the soft brown leather.

"This is a very good job," Hagop said.

"Thank you. I think my fingers have finally warmed to it," Souren said, putting his tools away.

"Where are you boys going?" Dikran asked.

"We are going to meet Armen."

"Fine. Off you go. Goodbye Hagop."

"Goodbye, Mr. Jamgochian."

"Bye, papa."

Hagop, Souren, and Armen sat beneath the fig trees near Hagop's home. It was a clear evening and the daytime heat had given way to a more comfortable temperature. Around them, morakhs, grasshoppers, buzzed and clicked.

"Ah. These grapes are good," Armen said, licking his fingers.

"We will have to pick them soon for the feast," Hagop answered.

Souren couldn't resist. "Armen, boy, if you eat all of them, you'll save everyone a lot of work!" he said, laughing.

"That is all very funny," Armen said. "But the more that you both talk is less time for you to eat!"

The boys laughed and Hagop gazed out into the dark star-filled sky. The smell of fire-cooked chicken still hung in the air and it mixed with the sweetness of grapes, figs, mulberries, and apricots. He looked at his friends. Physically, he and Souren were similar: they were both just a few inches short of six feet in height. This was unusual, as most Armenians were, as Hagop's grandmother Takouhi once joked, 'short in height but long on faith.' Armen was smaller, compact, and despite his constant eating, trim. His father, Garbis, called him nabasdag, rabbit, because Armen was constantly scurrying about, unable to stay in one place for any length of time.

"Souren. You are a very talented cobbler," Hagop remarked.

"Ah. No. You think so?"

"Yes. It was very good work. How long did it take to master it?"

"My father began bringing me into his shop when I was three or four. There is something nice about a pair of clean and polished shoes. My father once told me that when a businessman meets another businessman he will always look down at his shoes first. Even if they are old, as long as they are polished, it shows attention and that is someone you want to do business with."

"It is a good trade to have," Hagop said.

They looked toward Armen.

"And you, Armen?" Souren asked.

Armen looked blankly at his friends. He reached for a pile of mulberries and gobbled them.

"Me?" he asked. "What do you mean?"

"He means what trade are you practicing?" asked Hagop.

"Besides eating, of course," Souren grinned.

Armen plucked the last grape off the bunch and twirled the stem.

"I like to eat. Eating is a good thing. You are next to God when you eat his fruit."

Souren let out a long, hearty laugh and Hagop sat there, grinning.

"Who told you that?" Souren said.

"No. It is true. I read it," Armen insisted.

"Where did you read that?" Hagop asked.

"In one of Father DerArtinian's books."

"Ah. I see," Souren nodded. "Armen, I believe that you will be a writer when you grow up."

Armen pondered the notion a few moments.

"A writer? Yes, sure, why not?"

"And what about you, Hagop?" he asked.

Hagop looked at Armen and then Souren. He looked out into the field. "Me? I am just a farmer's son. I have my lambs. We have our trees. I have my family. What else?"

"Ah. I can think of only one other thing," Souren said, glancing at Armen.

"And what is that, my wise old friend?" Hagop said, shaking his head. Souren did not answer. Instead, he turned his attention toward Armen and winked.

"Armen. What was the name of that dark beauty? You know, the one at Azniv's wedding..."

"Ah. Yes. What was her name?" Armen said. Hagop shook his head again and waited for the horse-play to stop.

"I think our friend Hagop can remember," Souren offered.

"Sona," Hagop said, quietly.

"What was that? We cannot hear you!" Souren chided.

"Sona. S-O-N-A," Hagop said, spelling it for them. "Are you satisfied now?" Souren and Armen broke into grins. Hagop paused for a moment and looked at the sides of Souren's head.

"With your big ears you should be able to hear anything!"

THE GOEBEN

On the deck of the German Battleship Goeben, location undisclosed, Admiral Wilhem Souchon read a communiqué from Admiral Von Tirpitz of the Imperial Navy Office. Souchon was a career officer and one of the most distinguished naval commanders that Germany would ever produce. His hair was close cropped and he was always clean-shaven, though in later years he would sport a thick, bushy black mustache. He was determined, disciplined, and not afraid to take the initiative.

"Cipher message to the Breslau, ensign. Proceed coordinates L-54."

"Yes, Admiral."

On the open ocean, the Goeben let out a cloud of black smoke from one of her enormous stacks and began her journey.

LONDON

In the secretive offices of the British Naval Planning Office, First Lord of the Admiralty, Lord Winston Churchill was seated at the long walnut table, surrounded by high ranking naval officers and strategists. Facing the group of men was a wall covered with large maps of the Mediterranean Ocean.

"Early this morning, we received reports of two German warships moving quickly in the Mediterranean," Lieutenant Commander Anthony Chisholm said.

"That's Milne and Troubridge, right?" Churchill asked.

"Yes," Chisholm replied. "Admiral Milne is the C-in-C in the Mediterranean. Admiral Troubridge is the S.C."

"Who else is close by?"

Chisholm walked to the large map. "The Indomitable and Indefatigable are best positioned. They're currently here and here," he said, tapping the locations.

Churchill paused, thinking.

"Very well. Signal to Milne that the Goeben is their main focus. Have him mobilize the Indomitable and the Indefatigable at once. Under international law, we are allowed only to pursue."

He stopped and looked at the members of his staff.

"That is, until Britain announces her official position, which, I believe, will be inevitable."

"This should elicit a bit of respect from the Germans, I should think," Chisholm said.

Churchill looked at him, pursed his lips, and said nothing.

JONCHEREY

The small group of French soldiers watched over the patch of land at Joncherey, on the border of Germany and Switzerland. It was just past ten o'clock at night and although they were young and willing, they had been hastily dispatched and their training was woefully inadequate.

A young French soldier, Hinault was his name, watched for any sign of movement along the brush of land that formed the invisible barrier between the two countries. He had been looking for hours. The bushes and tree branches moved slightly but he could not be sure: perhaps the wind.

But now the row of bushes suddenly turned into a line of men as German soldiers emerged from the woods. Hinault's eyes widened. There were hundreds of them. The Frenchmen raised their rifles and Hinault braced himself.

Two French soldiers to his left pushed aside branches that concealed the machine gun. The Germans drew closer and suddenly raised their rifles. The French opened fire. The machine gun began to turn and hurl bullet after bullet. The Germans dropped to the ground and returned fire. Hinault fired again and again. But there were too many of them. They kept coming. They were almost face to face. A shadow passed over him and he fired. The German line advanced. The gunfire was ferocious. They were being overrun. Within minutes, every French soldier lay dead.

LONDON
3 August 1914

In Paris, lines of men stretched out from the recruitment offices, spilling out onto the city streets. The morning newspapers were emblazoned with the headlines, "Germany Declares War on France." Now, in London, it was just past eleven o'clock at night and the lights burned brightly within 10 Downing Street. Seated at a large octagonal walnut table were the Prime Minister, the Right Honorable Henry Asquith, Secretary of State for War Lord Horatio Herbert Kitchener, Foreign Secretary Paul Grey, and Churchill. In front of each man was a packet of official documents.

"Mr. Foreign Secretary," Asquith began. "Dispatch to Berlin at the earliest possible. Advise her that this communiqué will serve as the final notice and must be treated as an ultimatum." The men looked at him. "Belgium is not to be attacked," he continued. "This notification will expire in twenty-four hours."

"I will draft and deliver it at once," Grey replied.

MEDITERRANEAN SEA

The British ship Indefatigable pushed forth through the calm Mediterranean Sea. The Indomitable, slightly to her stern, kept a close watch for the German warships Goeben and Breslau. Captain Francis Kennedy was in command of the Indomitable, and had under him an experienced crew. They had been searching for the German vessels for almost three days now. Kennedy had just finished looking at the ship's daily reports when he heard the rumble.

"Captain!" Ensign Albert Rodgers blurted. "The Goeben! On the port bow, seventeen thousand yards, speed twenty knots. The Breslau to her stern and veering to the north."

Kennedy brought the binoculars to his face and drew them across the horizon line. The Goeben filled his view.

"Ensign! Alert the Admiralty that we have sighted the German ships. Morse broadcast to the Goeben that they are to halt immediately. To the Indefatigable: general alarm, battle stations."

"Aye, aye, sir!"

The whoop-whoop-whoop signal that ordered the ship's crew to battle stations sounded and the men of the Indomitable scrambled to their positions. Aboard the Indefatigable, the men took up the battle guns.

"Position, Ensign!" Captain Kennedy said.

"Ten thousand yards, Captain. The Goeben's increased her speed. Twenty-four knots."

'Twenty-four knots!' Kennedy thought. 'If she can maintain that, we won't be able to stay with her.'

Aboard the Goeben, Ensign Franz Zimmer took the paper from the radio corpsman.

"Admiral, a Morse from The Indomitable."

Souchon quickly glanced at Zimmer. Souchon read the signal, smirked, and crushed it in his hands.

"Full ahead!" he ordered. "We will outrun their fat, tired ships."

The Goeben suddenly turned to her portside. As she did, the Breslau increased speed and turned north. The Goeben sped up, aimed directly towards the Indomitable and the Indefatigable.

"Captain, the Goeben's turned to port! She's increasing speed!" Rodgers said.

Kennedy took up his binoculars and saw that the German ship was bearing directly at and between the Indomitable and the Indefatigable.

"The Breslau's veered off; turned north, Captain," Rodgers reported.

Kennedy kept the binoculars to his eyes. "Maintain position, Ensign. Standing order to return fire if provoked!"

"Aye, aye, sir!"

The Goeben continued hurtling toward the two British ships, becoming larger in Kennedy's binoculars.

"Speed!" Kennedy demanded.

"Twenty-nine knots!" Rodgers said.

"Good God, twenty-nine knots! Position!"

"Three thousand yards. Captain, her crew is in battle position but her guns are fore and aft."

"Steady, Ensign. Fire only if fired upon."

"Aye, aye!"

The Indefatigable and her crew maintained their battle positions. On the Indomitable, the crew watched as the Goeben sped directly for them. 2,800 yards. 2,600. 2,200.

"Heading right between us, Captain," Rodgers called out.

"I see her, Ensign," Kennedy replied.

1,600. 1,500. 1,400.

"Guns still fore and aft, sir," Rodgers said, staring intently through his binoculars.

"Keep watching them."

1,100. 900. 700. The crews of the British ships raised their guns. The Goeben cut through the water at a rapacious pace.

"They have raised their guns, Admiral," Ensign Zimmer said.

Souchon peered through his binoculars.

"I see them. Speed!"

"Thirty-one knots, Sir!"

"Maintain speed and position!" Souchon commanded.

400. 300.

"Two hundred yards!" Rodgers cried out.

"Speed!"

"Thirty-one knots!"

100.

Kennedy looked at Rodgers. It was incredible. A ship that large going that fast and maintaining her direction as if following an invisible wire.

75.

The Goeben kept hurtling forward.

"They won't fire on us," Souchon said. We are not yet at war with them."

50.

45.

40.

Kennedy turned his head toward the starboard side. The Goeben tore by, passing directly between the two British ships. As it did, it threw huge whitecaps of water, splashing the two-inch thick glass window.

"Ensign!" Kennedy cried over the roar of engine and water. "Cipher to Admiral Troubridge on the Defence. Relay our coordinates. Advise additional ships be deployed. Lay in follow course not to exceed sixteen thousand yards. Her guns have too much range."

"Aye, aye, Captain!"

BELGIUM
4 August 1914

The warm summer sun beat brightly onto the lush field that was tall with the season's crops. Normally, it would have been a bustle of activity: horses, carts, row after row of workers bringing in the plentiful harvest. Within moments the tall corn stalks began to flutter and sway as hundreds of German soldiers crossed into the countryside.

LONDON

Prime Minister Asquith stood before the podium in the House of Lords.

"Despite, and in direct violation of, an ultimatum delivered by Britain on behalf of her allies," he began, "at sixteen hundred hours today, our intrepid neighbor, Belgium, was invaded by Germany."

He paused, measuring his words.

"Through her declarations of war on Russia and France, and now with this direct violation of Belgium, there can be no doubt as to the German intentions. I have dismissed the German ambassador and am removing our ambassador. Last evening, Germany was given a twenty-four hour period to reconsider its passage to Belgium. They have refused. At twenty-three hundred hours today, Britain will declare war on Germany. I ask those of you who are of able body to come to the assistance of your country at this most urgent time."

CONSTANTINOPLE

"Yes, but the fact remains that those ships were headed some-where," Bompard, the French ambassador, said.

"And in a hurry," added Taylor, the American military attaché.

Morgenthau looked at the men seated opposite him.

"And that somewhere is Turkey," he said, meeting Mallet's eyes.

"Christ, what in bloody hell is Churchill doing?" Mallet said. "If Germany has turned Turkey, those Dardanelles will become the richest real estate in the world."

Morgenthau nodded. "They have to capture the ships," he said. "Capture them or sink them."

PALOU
August, 1914

Grapes! Grapes everywhere!

The annual harvest was in full swing, and anyone who was capable was out in the fields. Hagop's, Souren's, and Armen's families worked side-by-side in the hot August sun. It was all part of the barter system: the cobbler provided shoes to the farmer, the farmer provided food to the blacksmith, and so on.

The vines were heavy with lush fruit. The grape leaves had already been taken beginning in early April until almost the middle of May; they would be used to make sarma, the leaves, derevs they were called, would be stuffed with rice, pine nuts, and, depending on the region, raisins, walnuts, or currants. Once the derevs were in, the women would go to work. First they were cleaned, then dropped into boiling water.

"Just to wilt them," Takouhi said, warning Anahid, who nodded vigorously.

"And now, the mixture," Lucine said, setting the big bowl on the table.

"Oof! Ba-baam," she said, "that is heavy!"

Anahid turned the wooden spoon over and over; smelling the mix-ture of cooked rice, roasted pine nuts, and soaked currants. Takouhi scooped the leaves out of the hot water and placed them on the table to cool.

Lucine looked at the mixture as if making some sort of mental calculation. Sometimes, when Takouhi wasn't looking, she would sneak in a little cumin, maybe even a little cinnamon. Takouhi could never figure out what the odd taste was, but they always seemed better.

"I say we are ready," Lucine announced.

They worked in threes, Lucine laying out the leaves, Anahid putting a dollop of the mixture in the middle, and Takouhi carefully rolling. Maritza, Souren's mother, came later to help.

For festivals, there could be as many as fifty women working together, always following Perouz Avakian's recipe. Regardless of what they were cooking, the women of Palou grudgingly conceded that Perouz held all the best recipes in her head. Though they would argue back and forth about each other's pilaf, Perouz's was the best. It was her sarma, dolma, kuftah, and tahn. Her simit, choereg, and boereg. When it came to a church gathering, it was Perouz who presided over the cooking.

What items or foodstuffs they could not produce themselves were obtained when travelling peddlers passed through Palou. Then, the bartering would begin. Nothing was ever the price first quoted and God forbid if a father or mother caught a son or daughter accepting the price after only one or two turns, a turn being defined by a price given and a response to that price. Three or four turns were standard. Six to eight were better. Past ten drew attention. Hagop could still remember the stories his mother told of the endless harangue that Takouhi visited upon her when she heard that her daughter-in-law had accepted the price of some raw silk after only three turns.

"What was in your mind? Please tell me what you were thinking!" Takouhi demanded. "You should never have given him that much for this! Look at the way it runs here and here! Sticking a needle through this will make our fingers bleed!"

That was ten years ago and Takouhi still brought it up from time to time. As the oldest woman in the household, she was the matriarch. Lucine was in Takouhi's home and she would adhere to her rules. She would never again make that mistake and she had become a vicious barterer.

"Watch out for the Melkonian woman," the peddlers would say as they rolled their carts into Palou.

"Which one? The older or the younger?"

"Both are terrible. But the younger is the worst!"

The families formed a human chain that extended from the fields to Hagop's home. Sarkis drew the sharp curled blade against the stem. He brought the bunch to his father and Bedros picked a grape from it. He rolled it between a thumb and forefinger. It was plump and firm. He popped it into his mouth: sweet, succulent, and juicy. He nodded. "This row, this entire row!" Sarkis said, instructing the men, including Dikran and Garbis, who immediately started cutting and placing the grapes into wooden baskets. The baskets were passed, hand-over-hand, as they wound their way from the field to the house. Takouhi passed to Lucine to Maritza to Anahid to Armen. He lifted the basket above his head and Hagop, lying on the clay roof, reached down and grabbed it. His shirt was open, the sweat pouring off his body. It was late morning, the sun was high, and it was hot. Souren helped him to carefully spread the grapes. The strong summer sun would do the rest and the grapes would slowly shrivel and wrinkle, concentrating their taste into chameechner, raisins.

Later, the grapes and their juice would be used for a variety of foods, influenced by regional tastes. While Lucine was from Kharpert, Takouhi was from Palou. As a result, during the first years of the marriage, there were some differences when it came time to make certain meals. One such ignominious occasion was the time Takouhi had to watch over a sick neighbor. She had left, instructing Lucine to serve the family kuftah for dinner and Lucine set about preparing the meal. Kuftah, at least for Takouhi, consisted of a mixture of ground lamb's meat and bulgur wheat, rolled into the shape of a small ball. In the center of this ball was a small amount of por, or filling, which was made with beef. After they were shaped, they would then be cooked in chicken or beef stock.

Takouhi returned from the neighbor's home as Lucine proudly brought out the steaming container. Everyone eagerly awaited the meal, which was accompanied by a most delicious smell. Lucine watched as Takouhi took a bite. Bedros bit into his kuftah and paused, a funny look on his face. Sarkis did the same. This was before Hagop and Anahid were born, and Lucine, alone amongst her new family, sank in her chair as she saw the reaction her meal had brought. Takouhi, Bedros, and Sarkis looked at one another and then, as if on cue, all three looked at Lucine, who sat, close to tears. Finally, Bedros broke the silence.

"She's put vosb in the middle!" he declared.

"Lentils?" Takouhi questioned.

"I... I don't understand," was all that Lucine could manage. Sarkis started to laugh and then Takouhi and Bedros joined him. Lucine sat, speechless.

"I always use lentils!" Lucine said, almost in tears.

"Oh! That's it!" Takouhi said. She patted her daughter-in-law's hand. Lucine looked up at her. "Don't worry! Here we put in beef!"

"Beef? Oh, I did not know..."

That was many years ago and Lucine developed one additional trick that provided no end of joy to Hagop and Anahid when they were young. As she rolled the kuftahs, she would place a tiny coin in the center of one of them: the lucky diner receiving an additional treat.

"Now come over here, boys," Takouhi commanded.

The boys followed as Takouhi walked over to a flat stone surface that sat in the shade of a large apricot tree. The boys crowded around her and she uncovered a cloth covering a thick sheet the color of apricots.

"Look at the bastegh!" Armen blurted. Bastegh was made by taking grape or apricot juice, thickening it with sugar, and drying it into thick, tasty sheets.

"I think you should try some and tell us how it is," Takouhi said, winking at Hagop and Souren. She gave pieces to each of them. Armen took his, rolled it up into a tube, and gobbled it down.

"It is good! Very good!" he said, eyeing the cloth. Takouhi laughed and gave him more.

CONSTANTINOPLE

A light rain fell as Ambassador Morgenthau walked briskly towards the American Embassy. He crossed to the right, past the Italian Embassy, and to the Petits Champs Gardens. He looked on as Wangenheim, seated at a small bootblack's stand, got up and gave the merchant a few coins.

"Ah! Mr. Ambassador! Good morning!" Wangenheim called out.

"Herr Ambassador," Morgenthau said.

"Dreadful weather, wouldn't you say?"

"I find it rather refreshing, to be honest," Morgenthau replied. "It's a rather nice departure from the stifling heat."

"I am told that more than fifty thousand enlisted in Britain in two days alone," Wangenheim said.

"Yes, at least that many. And many more in France." He looked at Wangenheim. "And the disposition of the Turks?" he asked.

"Warships, Mr. Ambassador," Wangenheim said, "Warships."

"Ah, I see," Moregenthau said. "The Goeben and the Breslau."

"Will be sold by Germany to Turkey," Wangenheim replied. "The Turks are desperate and Germany is more than happy to accommodate them."

THE DARDANELLES
10 August 1914

The mouth of the Dardanelles was enticingly near as the Goeben and the Breslau approached.

'At last!' Souchon thought. 'We have done it!'

In the daytime heat, Souchon, standing on deck, saw that a large steel net was draped across the entrance and armed Turkish soldiers lined the dock. Souchon was being prevented from entering! After coming all this way!

"What the hell do they think they are doing?" he fumed.

Almost three hours later, Ensign Zimmer entered, holding a document.

"Cipher from Berlin, Admiral."

"Read it."

"To: Souchon, Admiral, SS Goeben. Wait entrance Dardanelles until further orders received. Political situation Constantinople unresolved. Tirpitz, Admiral, Imperial Navy."

"Unresolved?" Souchon spat. "Then, I will go to Constantinople and resolve it for them! Ensign, get me transport!"

"Yes, Admiral! At once!" Zimmer said, scrambling out.

CONSTANTINOPLE

The palace of Grand Vizier Said Halim was a stately design boasting high columns and overlooked a large private courtyard. But while Halim represented Turkey as the solemn commander, all power and authority was held by the Committee of Union and Progress, namely, Enver, the Minister of War, and Talaat, the Minister of the Interior.

Halim was born an Egyptian royal. He had financed the Young Turks in their campaign and as his reward he was named Grand Vizier. His mustache, beard, and hair were grayer than black and his uniform consisted of an ornate gold-leafed tunic, decorated with heptagonal and octagonal gold stars with gold buttons rising from their center. His eyes were very deep set and his furrowed brow betrayed his constant worries and preoccupations.

Despite the overhead fan, he sweated profusely.

"The moment is here," Enver said, eyes riveted on Halim.

"But our neutrality will disappear," Halim said.

Enver slammed his fist down on the desk. Halim flinched.

"They have upheld their part of the bargain," Enver said. "They have delivered the ships."

Halim nervously rubbed his hands together. He watched as Enver withdrew his pistol from its holster and placed it on the desk.

"Are you really in a position to challenge this?" Enver asked.

Morgenthau sat, reading the reports forwarded to him by Taylor, the military attaché. The Admiralty had been informed at 2030 hours that the Goeben and the Breslau were at the Dardanelles, waiting to enter. Churchill had ordered the mobilization of a fleet to prevent them from exiting.

The sun glinted off the steel mesh as the Turkish soldiers lifted the nets from the entrance. On the docks, Turkish and German soldiers stood alongside curious onlookers. The Goeben let forth a huge billow of smoke and she and the Breslau steamed forward. A huge cry of cheer came up from the crowd as the ships entered the Dardanelles. As they did, several rifle shots went off from the fortresses on either side of the mouth, celebrating their entry.

Constantinople lay some one hundred fifty miles to the north of the Dardanelles and it was late afternoon when the Goeben and Breslau made their triumphant entry into the main harbor. Hundreds of people had gathered on the docks and cheers and rifle shots greeted the ships. Both Enver and Talaat watched from the dock and shook hands as the crews threw down the mooring ropes. Admiral Souchon walked briskly through the crowd. He had come to Constantinople to expedite the "unresolved political situation". But getting the ships to Constantinople would only be the beginning.

"Admiral on deck!" Zimmer yelled, as he and the other men snapped to attention.

"Stand at ease," Souchon commanded. He paused for a moment. "Very well, Ensign. Make the change."

"Yes, Admiral!" Zimmer replied.

As if on cue, the German flag on both the Goeben and the Breslau was taken down and replaced with the Turkish flag, eliciting a huge roar of approval from the onlookers and more rifle fire from both the Turkish and German soldiers.

"Now the men," Souchon commanded.

The order was passed and the crews of the Goeben and the Breslau stripped off their uniformed tunics. Again, the crowd cheered as they donned Turkish uniforms and fezzes. Talaat and Enver positively beamed. As the journalists fired off flashbulb after flashbulb, Souchon observed the scene with curious detachment. This was all part of the charade. There were spies everywhere. It was important that they see the transformation.

'Let Turkey have her fun now,' Souchon thought. 'They'll learn soon enough.'

Conspicuous in his absence, Wangenheim sat behind his desk and quietly attended to his daily activities. He had no need to watch the entry of the ships. It was what lay ahead that now demanded his complete attention.

Talaat got up slowly from his desk, interlocked his thumbs behind his back, and walked to the window. The other three men sat quietly and Talaat shifted his stance and looked out onto Constantinople. The city streets were bare of people and the gas lamps flickered as they illuminated the wet cobblestone streets.

Talaat turned to the men: Enver, and two of their most trusted colleagues, Dr. Baaeddin Sakir and Dr. Mehmed Nazim. Although they were trained medical doctors, they had long ago ceased to practice medicine. Enver, Nazim, and Sakir each held several sheets of paper.

"We must begin now so that when the time is right, we will be ready," Talaat said. "For our purposes, we will require men who are not identified as military personnel and who hold no rank in our military. We will slowly begin the stages for the introduction of a bill within the Congress to create this Special Organization."

Both Nazim and Sakir looked at one another. Talaat glanced at Enver who nodded for him to continue.

"It will be known as the Teskilati Mahsusa. As Turkey must prepare for war, we will need every man at our disposal."

"Do we anticipate any opposition?" Sakir asked.

Talaat walked behind his desk, sat down, and rested both hands on the armrests.

"There will be no opposition," Enver answered.

"That is right," Talaat added. "The bill will pass without question. But we must do this formally as a pretense of using the men for the war effort."

Enver looked directly at Nazim and Sakir. "If there are any questions, or if questions arise at a future time, this step will provide us with official explanation on behalf of our military interests."

Nazim waved the document he had been given. "The difficulty I see is that with no possibility of a commutation of their sentences, it will be difficult to obtain their participation."

"Men condemned to death have no reason to do anything but wait," Sakir added.

"All of this has been considered," Enver said.

"When the measure passes, there shall be a proviso for the commutation of their sentences," Talaat said. "They will participate for their freedom and for their necks. After they are informed of this proviso, they will beg for the chance to serve us."

Nazim and Sakir nodded, satisfied.

"Doctors, you are hereby in charge of this Special Organization," Talaat said. "Monies will be appropriated from our secret funds for their training and for equipment. You will begin these preparations at once. Passage of the bill will follow soon enough."

"See to it that they are trained well," Enver said. Talaat shifted his eyes from Enver and looked directly at Nazim and Sakir. He placed his palms flat onto the desk and rested the weight of his arms onto them. "When the time comes," he said, "choose the most violent: those who have been condemned to death. They will do as we wish."

PALOU

Hagop stood with Souren and Armen in the same field where Azniv's wedding celebration had been. The boys were dressed in their Sunday clothes, and were surrounded by the other villagers. It was the Feast of the Assumption, the Blessing of the Grapes.

And it was hot. Two deacons flanked Father DerArtinian and they, in turn, were flanked by two altar boys. They stood before baskets of newly picked grapes, figs, dates, and mulberries. Truth was, no one could be sure how long any of the ceremonies would last.

"Could be five minutes, could be two hours!" Bedros had said, laughing out loud.

Sometimes it could be immensely confusing. In fact, there seemed to be so many ceremonies, observations, commemorations, customs, and occasions that it became difficult to keep track. Once, Bedros was sitting with three other men drinking soorj, coffee, when the men tried to remember what outing was next.

"Ah, next Sunday there will be the baptism of Mourad's son, then the Sunday after we have the Blessing of the Water, then..."

"Mourad? Mourad has a son?" said the second man, interrupting.

"Ah, where have you been, you?" the third man chastised.

"How am I supposed to know?" the second man shot back, insulted. "That Mourad's wife is having a baby every week!"

There were also strict protocols to observe and these were ingrained at an early age. In small villages such as Palou, seats were unknown within the church interior. Everyone stood, sometimes for hours on end. In a larger church, there could be a small balcony, open only to the women. In Constantinople, there were pews in the church and the sheer flurry with which the priest there, Father DerGhazarian, delivered his sermons made even the elders confused. Often people had to look at one another to know whether to stand or sit.

Once Takouhi heard a slight clicking sound as they stood in the tiny church. She looked over and saw Hagop's jaw moving back and forth. He was chewing tzuit, gum, a concoction made with sugar and mint. Takouhi could not believe her eyes and, without warning, reached out her dainty black shoe and pressed it directly into his right foot. Hagop stopped chewing, caught his tongue, and looked at her. She said nothing, but repeatedly stabbed the open air with her finger pointed towards his mouth. Hagop got the message and, left with no alternative, swallowed hard.

Death was met with long term observation. After burial in the village's small cemetery, adorned with carved headstones and khachkars, stone crosses, there would then follow the karasoonk, or forty days, patterned after Christ's forty days of walking the earth prior to the ascension. During this time, there were continual visitors to the home of the departed. There would be no laughter, no music. After the person's karasoonk, there would be a feast of food and friendship as family, friends, and neighbors came to the family home and shared stories. Next, was the dareleetz, the year anniversary of the person's death. This would continue for each and every year that the family so desired, but the first year was mandatory.

Hagop would sometimes remark to his mother that he found it strange that there was a dareleetz for forty or fifty years for someone.

"Why do you find that so surprising?" Lucine asked.

"Because it is fifty years. That is a long time," he answered.

"Hagop, believe me," she answered, "when it is someone you love, no matter how many years have passed, it will be as if it was yesterday."

Lucine was, by nature, a quiet, reserved woman, and there were times when Hagop very much wanted to talk with her about things. But the time never seemed to be right.

Father DerArtinian raised his hand and made the sign of the cross. Hagop crossed himself and there was silence for a few moments.

"My friends: mothers, fathers, and children. Each year at this time we celebrate and observe the Feast of the Assumption of the Holy Mother of God, the blessing of the grapes." He gestured towards the many baskets. "We have had a bountiful harvest given to us by the grace of God and the sun is warm on our faces." He opened his worn Bible and began reading.

"I am the vine, you are the branches. If a man remains in me and I in him, he will bear much fruit. Apart from me you can do nothing. If anyone does not remain in me, he is like a branch that is thrown away and withers. Such branches are picked up, thrown into the fire, and burned. If you remain in me and my words remain in you, ask whatever you wish, and it will be given you. This is to my Father's glory, that you bear much fruit, showing yourselves to be my disciples."

He paused, then continued.

"As the Father has loved me, so have I loved you. My command is this: Love each other as I have loved you. This is my command: Love each other. In the name of the Father, The Son, and the Holy Spirit."

He made the sign of the cross and the congregation followed. Hagop, Souren, and Armen quickly moved to the baskets of grapes and began carrying them to where tables had been lined up. The celebration began amidst large casks of wine, raisins, rojig, bastegh, and many other delicacies.

Hours later, the celebration was still in full swing. Some of the casks were empty, and many of the men walked with a noticeable wobble. Hagop, Souren, and Armen sat in the shade as the afternoon sun waned.

"Have you had enough?" Souren asked.

"I am going to burst," Armen answered. "This time, I have eaten too much."

"What we do not understand," Hagop said, "is where it all goes. Your father is right to call you a rabbit. Running here and there, eating all the time, and yet you gain no weight."

"And you walk constantly," Souren added.

"Yes, where do you walk to when you take these walks?" Hagop asked.

"And what do you think about?" Souren piped in.

Armen paused, considering. His mother, Sabiné, had died when he was eight years old. His father Garbis had been so deeply in love with her that he would not remarry. But he had many friends in the village, and Armen was well looked after.

"Ah. I... I don't know. I just walk and think and ideas come to me."

"What kind of ideas?" Hagop asked.

"No. You will just make fun of me, you two," Armen said.

"No," Hagop said, seriously. "We want to know."

Armen paused, looked away, and then looked back to his friends. "Sometimes I am walking and I let my mind not think of anything. Just to let the thoughts come and go. And sometimes I think of these people grabbing at me. They are like people but they are not like people. There is no color to them. They are black and white, but no color. And their arms are like branches on trees that sway in the wind and grab you. And they hold me there. And then I break free and run out from this black and white forest into a field. And it is your field, Hagop, your father's field. And there are people everywhere, walking, walking, but they do not know me."

Hagop and Souren sat in silence. Finally, Souren spoke.

"Armen, your imagination, like your appetite, is too big for me! Next time I ask you what you are thinking, do not tell me!"

"Ah, I knew that you would make fun of me," Armen answered.

"Armen," Hagop said, looking seriously at his friend, "do not think too much. Just be happy you are here."

"Yes. Yes. Perhaps you are right."

"Come, let's go. It's time to clean up this mess. Grapes! They are everywhere!" Souren said, laughing.

CONSTANTINOPLE
28 August 1914

The late days of summer were unbearably warm and the heat stuck in the afternoon air. Talaat sat behind his desk and blotted his forehead with a handkerchief. Enver sat opposite him. To these Young Turks, Wangenheim was an enigma. But he represented Germany and Enver had long held a special affinity for his country.

"The situation is very grave, Herr Ambassador," Talaat said. "The British and the French are applying pressure to us. Even the Americans."

"Mr. Interior Minister. Mr. War Minister," Wangenheim said. "Several months ago, you thought it was impossible for Germany to deliver our warships to Turkey. We did so."

"The allies want Germany out of Turkey," Enver said. "But Turkey is not obligated to do anything. Germany is the aggressor. The obligation therefore remains with Germany."

Wangenheim shifted towards him. "And now Turkey trusts the allies?"

"Once Turkey embarks with Germany, our cause will be one with Germany," Enver said. "But have no illusions, it will be blood that stains us both."

"We lack the funds to adequately protect ourselves," Talaat said. "Therefore, we must be neighbor to all but partner to none. You understand."

Wangenheim leaned forward.

"Close them," he said. "Close them and we will ensure that the territories that rightfully belong to you are returned to you." Wangenheim stood, turned, and walked to the door. Talaat opened his mouth to speak but Enver shook his head.

Wangenheim opened the door.

"All is possible," he said. "After you close the Dardanelles."

ON THE MEDITERRANEAN SEA

A convoy of British battleships, battlecruisers, lightcruisers, and destroyers churned up the waters of the Mediterranean. Soon, the French ships would arrive. The British flagship, the Battleship Queen Elizabeth, maintained a pace of between twenty and twenty-two knots as she led the ships towards the Dardanelles. In her command stood Vice-Admiral Sackville Carden, installed after the Admiralty had removed Troubridge.

After having studied the objective, Carden requested fifty more ships as well as aerial support; it would take time, but he felt that the Dardanelles could be taken.

"Position, ensign."

"Currently eighteen miles from entrance to the Dardanelles, Admiral."

"Very well. Maintain speed. Cipher to Admiral Lapeyrere on the Bouvet. Give her our position and course."

"Aye-Aye, Admiral."

CONSTANTINOPLE
September, 1914

The ambassadors were gathered in the small back room that served as the American Embassy Club. Morgenthau sat, listening intently to Major Taylor. Bompard, the French Ambassador, drank his cognac and brushed back his white goatee.

Ambassador Mallet, officially Sir Louis Mallet, was not a force to be misjudged. He was a shrewd thinker with pristine credentials. A bachelor, he occasionally sported a monocle, and was always impeccably dressed.

"The ships will be there soon enough, Ambassador," Taylor concluded.

"Oui. The French are arriving as well. Under Lapeyrere," Bompard offered.

"Major," Morgenthau said. "Exactly what preparations have been made to circumvent the Dardanelles? Has an estimate been made as to how long the Russian stockpiles will last?"

"Unfortunately, we know very little," Taylor replied.

"And the British position, Ambassador?" Morgenthau inquired, turning to Mallet.

"Tomorrow, Britain will once again demand that the German presence in Turkey be removed," he said, shaking his head.

"And once again, the Turks will declare that they are just being good hosts," Bompard added. "I am told that the sale has been approved."

"Sale?" Mallet answered, smirking. "Ha! It's not a sale, it's a gift!"

"Turkey is insisting that the transaction is legal and above reproach," Morgenthau said. "Essentially, they're saying that it represents nothing more than an acquisition that was agreed upon prior to the declaration of hostilities. They are planning to turkify them completely."

"Oui. They have changed the ship names," Bompard said. "The Goeben is now the Javus Sultan Selim and the Breslau is now the Midilli."

"And yet, our intelligence indicates that their German crews have remained intact and on board," Taylor added. "Immediately upon arriving in Constantinople, the Germans and the Turks made an obvious public display of changing uniforms. Later that evening, our people received reports that the Turks left the ships and the Germans became German again."

"The Germans have just bought the whole country," Mallet said. "All they have to do is wait."

"What do you mean?" Bompard asked.

"Ambassador Mallet is correct," Morgenthau answered. "As long as Turkey remains uncommitted, neither to Germany nor to the Allies, there is a great deal of danger."

"I agree," Taylor said. "The Russians cannot make an attack on Constantinople because of an impasse at the Black Sea. Further, the Russians must keep forces in the Caucasus while England must strengthen her forces in Egypt and India."

"While at the Dardanelles, the British and French ships sit and watch," Morgenthau said.

"Correct," Taylor replied, "ships that are badly needed elsewhere."

"Christ, the Germans are playing the Turks like a violin and they're too bloody blind to see it," Mallet said.

BITLIS

Bitlis stood some one hundred sixty kilometers to the southeast of Palou and less than five kilometers from Lake Van to its northeast. When they were young, Sona's mother and father would take Sona and Azniv to play in the lake's cool, refreshing waters. They would sit, feet dangling in the water, Sona watching as the little tzemerougs, watermelons, bobbed up and down. Elise turned, watching as if in a trance, as Sona's fingers dipped under the surface.

"Nishan! Nishan!" she yelled, running toward the water. Sona had fallen in and was now gulping, flailing her arms. Azniv began to cry. Nishan jumped in, stretching out as far as he could. Sona began to go under, but Nishan grabbed her arm. She began to gurgle and spit. He lifted her above his head and Elise grabbed her. That had been thirteen years ago; she was barely two years old.

Afterwards, Elise kept a close eye on the girls whenever they went to the lake, relaxing only after Sona had reached her eighth year. Even so, Sona had maintained her distance from the water. Finally, Nishan picked her up and threw her in.

"Nish! Are you crazy? What are you doing?" Elise said, running to the water. Nishan held her back.

"Do not worry, she will swim now," he said.

"Papa, papa! Help me!" Sona said, struggling to remain on the surface.

"Swim!" her father demanded.

"Nishan!"

"Be quiet!"

"Mama!"

"Swim, Sona! You can do it!"

Sona struggled and sent great buckets of water flying into the air. As she reached the water's edge, Elise grabbed her arm.

"Are you all right?"

"Yes, mama, yes," Sona said, drops of water leaving her mouth. They looked at Nishan.

"Next Sunday, you swim again," he said, walking away.

That night, their daughters fast asleep, Elise lay down next to her husband. He had learned his trade from his father and began running the family business, Khatchaturian Tailor Shop, when he was eighteen. He was lean and even boned, and his face was particularly dark, the color of tanned hide; it contrasted greatly with Elise's clear white complexion. As a child, she had harbored an intense fear of dark and closed places. Her mother would simply light a candle and leave it burning until sleep came to her. Little did the young girl know that her mother was also methodically shortening the candles from day to day until her habit was broken!

"I know that I frightened you today," Nishan said. "But there comes a time when we all have to be thrown into the water, or into the fire, or however you would like to say it."

"Yes, I know, Nish," Elise said, using her sobriquet for him.

"I would not have let anything happen to her."

She laid there for some time that night, her children and her husband sleeping, their breaths comforting to her. She held up her hands and looked at them in the moon's light. They were lined now, certainly not like when she was a girl, and at times they ached. But they were as nimble as ever, and they could still craft some of the finest needlepoint the village had ever seen.

Her grandmother had been a seamstress, and as a little girl, Elise would spend hour after hour watching her create fine and delicate work from precious silk. Her grandmother, Almas, had lived well into her nineties, and would silently nod or shake her head while watching Elise sew. When it came time for an intricate loop or stitch, Almas would point with a bony, weathered finger to the large crystal vase and Elise would bring it near and use it as a very adequate magnifying glass. Looking over her shoulder, there would be Almas, opening her little tin snuffbox, inhaling the fine tobacco.

Her family was from Kighi, some one hundred twenty-five kilometers northwest of Bitlis. Almas's Aunt Hasmig lived in Bitlis and once, returning from a visit to Kighi, had brought some of Elise's handiwork with her. These she took and displayed for Nishan's father, Ardash, while Nishan silently worked in a corner. The needlework was deemed excellent and it was only a matter of time before Elise packed her small wool satchel with its wood and leather handles and took up residence in Hasmig's home, sewing fine needlepoint and embroidery.

Elise and Nishan were married after the traditional courtship. Nishan assumed more responsibility in the shop and Elise came to work there. After Azniv and Sona were born, Nahabedian, the village doctor, told Elise that she should not try again; it would be too dangerous for her.

"Sons, they just will not come, Nish," she said, wetting the white cotton string with her fingers.

"Ah, then, we will make do with these two!" he said, laughing.

"Yes, and if you keep throwing them into the cold water, they will become as strong as oxen," she said. They both laughed long and full and when it was over, Nishan looked at his wife and then turned back to the suit he was creating. Elise looked at him and drew the string through the eye of the needle.

Sona pulled back the string, tied it off, and cut it between her teeth. She turned over the blue and gray pants. Her father sat in silence, fitting a lapel onto the thick wool suit of Nahabedian's son, who was now the village doctor. Sona watched as her father worked; he was in his sixties now, and gray flecks dotted his hair. To the rear of the shop was the family home. Nishan examined the suit and, satisfied, put it down. It was late, and he was quite tired. Elise had offered to help, but Nishan waved off the idea.

Elise was fifty-three years old now and her fingers needed the rest. Sona was there each day after school and Azniv was already learning the basics of nursing in Nahabedian's storefront office.

"Come, Sona, your mother will be waiting for us."

"Yes, papa. I am just finishing now."

Nishan pulled the front door shut and locked it. They walked toward the back of the shop and entered the house. The aroma of the meal that Elise had prepared filled the air. Nishan said grace, and they ate, sharing their stories of the day.

PALOU

Hagop, Souren, Armen, and Anahid sat quietly in the small church anteroom. There were three long, narrow tables each accommodating five students. Normally the students would have sat along the corners of the room, on their doshags, cushions. That was until Sarkis and Dikran had crafted the tables and chairs, methodically cutting notches into the wood so that each piece fit snug and firm.

After several hours of instruction, and weather permitting, the students would go outside for twenty to thirty minutes. They would gobble down small snacks, raisins, walnuts, or mulberries that they had stuffed into their pockets. Or maybe some nice bread spread with jam and sesame seeds, ground into a rough paste.

A small gray slate board stood at the front of the room, and their teacher, Miss Zepure, wrote out a series of words in French separated by dots. Anahid walked to the front of the classroom. She took the chalk and quickly filled in the blank areas.

"Excellent Anahid," Miss Zepure said. "Tres, tres bien. Dimanche est une journee de repos. That is very good. Sunday is a day of rest."

Anahid nodded modestly. She was an excellent student and languages came easily to her. Lucine had great hopes for her, and it was her desire to send her to the College for Women in Constantinople, some seven hundred kilometers to the northwest of Palou. But it was the exception to send a child to university. Thus, schooling had to be as encompassing as possible: it could be the only education a child would ever receive. As a result, the literacy rate of villagers in Palou, Husenig, Kharpert, Moush, and Van was more than eighty-five percent.

Sarkis and Lucine had only recently given thought to the matter. While a good student, Hagop did not excel in his studies. But they came naturally for Anahid. She was just over five feet in height and had dark, black, curly hair. This she wore short, unlike most of the other girls. Her eyes were brown and had vanilla flecks in the corner. At thirteen, she had chores which she was expected to do each day.

CONSTANTINOPLE

The Seraskeriate, War Office, was a massive building overlooking a large public square and was marked by the tall Serasker's Tower. Its impressive façade bore tall, symmetrical, oval windows.

The office of Enver Pasha, Minister of War, was equally majestic. From the carved walnut desk with its gold edging to the display of photographs in their silver frames, Enver wore well the power he had amassed.

"This document was received this morning from the British Ambassador," Talaat said. "The British are demanding that the German military mission in Turkey be withdrawn."

"We must acknowledge their communication," Halim said. "We cannot be caught in the middle of two warring parties."

"The time for neutrality is over!" Enver exploded. "We will use the Germans until our objectives are met. Now the world will know that Turkey refuses to lose any more of its territories. And when this war ends, we will have Turkey to ourselves. I hereby order that the Dardanelles be closed."

THE DARDANELLES

The steel mesh net hit the water.

"Now! Into position," the German lieutenant commanded. A group of soldiers wheeled a black iron cannon into position. "That's it. Stop!" He looked up, checking the progress of the men who were constructing a dug-in encampment above them. The soldiers dropped the machine guns into position and set about cleaning them.

Carden stood on the deck of the Queen Elizabeth and lowered the binoculars from his eyes.

"Ciphered message to the Admiralty," he said. "Tell them what's going on. Fleet awaiting instructions."

"Aye, aye, Admiral."

PALOU
October, 1914

The nights had become colder now, and the leaves had long fallen from the trees. October in Palou brought with it more rain, stronger winds, and a rawness that cut through the villagers. Autumn was Hagop's favorite time of the year. After the heat of summer, the cool air breezed over his skin and brought long desired relief. But Anahid was the exact opposite and loved to bask in the summer sun. Winter brought with it more tutoom: squash, kednakhuntzor: potatoes, sokh: onions. They would be harvested and then it would be time to pickle and store them for the winter months.

Now they sat, brother and sister, opposite one another at the family table, their schoolbooks open before them. Hagop was engrossed, furiously writing on a piece of flimsy onion skin paper with a madid, pencil. Anahid closed her book and looked across the table.

"Let me ask you some questions. It will be good practice," she said.

Hagop looked up, reluctantly sighed, closed his book, and nodded.

"Good," Anahid began. "Now, in French," she said. "Comment t'appelles-tu?" What is your name?

Hagop took a deep breath. He really did know the language, but he seemed to get stuck in places and the words simply would not come. He always seemed to do better at home.

"Je m'appelle Hagop." My name is Hagop.

"Et tu viens d'ou?" And where are you from?

"Je viens de Palou." I am from Palou.

"Combien de freres as-tu?" How many brothers do you have?

"Je n'en ai pas. J'ai un soeur." I have none. I have one sister.

"Elle est jolie?" Is she pretty?

Anahid smiled. Hagop smiled back.

"Ma soeur est tres jolie." My sister is very pretty.

"Merci beaucoup, monsieur," she said, smiling. Thank you very much, sir.

"Pas du tout, mademoiselle." Not at all, miss.

"Tu aimes bien la soeur d'Aznivis?" Do you have a fondness for Azniv's sister?

Hagop sputtered, barely sure if he had heard correctly.

"Comment? Je ne comprends pas." What? I do not understand.

His sister smiled, and pointed at her brother's book. "Hagop, mon frere, tu parles mieux le francais que tu ne le penses." Hagop, my brother, you speak French better than you think.

"C'est vrai?" It's true?

She nodded.

"Alors, tu aimes Sona?" So, do you like Sona?

Hagop opened his mouth and then, thinking better of it, stopped himself.

"C'est un question pour la prochaine lecon, ma soeur cherie." That is a question for our next lesson, my dear sister.

Anahid smiled and they both began to laugh.

"Touché," she said.

CONSTANTINOPLE
9 October 1914

The busy street was alive with people who rushed about in the cool, gentle wind. Peddlers with their pushcarts offered apples and pears. Morgenthau crossed the street, walking quickly, eager to get to the Embassy. It would be a busy day. At 2200 hours the night before, King Albert had dispatched Davignon, the foreign secretary, with the surrender papers. Across Antwerp's horizon, fires flamed. The incessant pounding of the seventeen-inch German Howitzer cannons could no longer be endured.

PART TWO

PALOU

The village square bustled with activity amidst the sounds of people haggling. From end to end, it brimmed with peddlers from the surrounding regions. From the north, the carts were full of salted cheeses, dried and salted meats, and butter. From the south: dried fruits, olives, and currants. There were piles of wool and silk. There was leather, silver, and gold.

While it was chaotic, it was also serious business. Lucine and Takouhi strode through the square, looking at the wares arrayed from cart to cart. Anahid trailed along, carrying a woven basket for their goods. She watched as they touched the various items, examining them, poking them, and listened closely to their arguments and counter-arguments. Soon, she would have to do this herself.

Hagop, Sarkis, and Bedros stood next to the family's cart, which carried fresh and dried meat, both lamb and pork, and fresh and pickled eggs. On the ground were barrels of wool, raisins, figs, and walnuts. Sarkis and Bedros were busy bartering with several men.

Lucine, Takouhi, and Anahid stopped, and Lucine examined silk strands that were displayed in the back of a cart. The peddler, a man Takouhi's age, saw them and quickly approached.

"Ah, good morning, good morning!" he said, brushing back his beard.

"Good morning," Lucine said.

"The finest silk," began the peddler's prattle. Lucine ran her hand over some of the strands and shook her head as she looked at Takouhi.

"No, I think not," Lucine said, beginning to walk away, Takouhi and Anahid dutifully following.

"Oh! But wait! Wait!" he said, rushing to the front. "Look at these!"

Lucine, Takouhi, and Anahid stopped as if on cue. The peddler expected them to dismiss the first batch, prompting him to produce some higher quality goods.

"Ah, these are a bit better," Lucine said.

"Oh, no! These are the finest I have brought in many months, I assure you!"

"They are not the finest I have seen," Takouhi said, running a quick hand over them.

"Ah, but they are also not the most expensive either!" the peddler said, laughing.

"And how much for these?" Lucine said.

"Ah, you have an eye for excellent goods, dear lady. Those are fifteen liras."

"Fifteen liras!" Takouhi howled. She turned to Lucine. "You see, my daughter, I told you they were too expensive!" Again, they began to move away.

"Too expensive?" the peddler said his voice full of disbelief. "No, no! These are worth at least that much." He looked at Anahid. "But I see that you have a young mouth to feed. I tell you. Let me see. Yes, I think twelve liras. Twelve liras, that is my final price. I am sorry," he said, moving to take them away.

"Twelve liras! These are worth eight. Twelve! No, let me tell you, I have paid twelve liras and this is not silk that I would pay twelve liras for," Lucine shot back.

Takouhi was impassive. Anahid looked away. She saw Souren, carrying a crate full of salted cheese and dried meats from a peddler's cart. Dikran presented the peddler with a pair of new shoes, the new owner receiving them with a toothless grin. Armen assisted his father, who was busy showing some of the peddlers his iron works. Anahid looked to the right and saw Azniv and Vache bartering with a goldsmith, who was holding up several linked chains and some ornately etched crosses.

"Ten liras! That is my final offer!" the peddler said. He had tiny little sweat points on his forehead now. Lucine looked at Takouhi. Anahid looked at her mother. The peddler looked from one to the other. Lucine and Takouhi nodded and the peddler let out a breath. He wiped his forehead with a handkerchief as Lucine opened her small purse and counted out the coins. The peddler gathered the silk together and tied it with a rawhide strap.

"Thank you! Thank you!" he said.

"Good day," Takouhi said.

"Good day!" the peddler answered.

They walked on and Lucine handed the bundle to Anahid who placed it in her basket.

"And good riddance too!" the peddler muttered as he watched them go.

A cloud of dust was kicked up as yet another cart pulled into the square. The donkey hee-hawed and stopped as Nishan Khatchaturian put down the leather reins. He helped Elise down from the cart. Hagop looked up from his work and saw Sona. That last time he had seen her was at Azniv's wedding. Sona and Elise began arranging the garments they had brought, and Hagop watched as she delicately placed dresses, pants, and stockings side by side.

"Hagop! Let's go!" Sarkis commanded, bringing him back. "These men want more raisins."

"Yes, papa."

Sona looked up from her arranging and watched as Hagop placed a small barrel in front of Sarkis who dipped his hand into it and brought out a handful of raisins to show the men, who nodded approvingly.

Azniv saw her family and rushed over, leaving Vache to continue haggling with the goldsmith.

"Mama! Papa!" she said, hugging them both. "It is so good to see you! Sona!"

Sona came around and hugged her. Hagop watched for a moment, but he was surrounded by so many people that he could only catch glimpses of her. Nishan had come over and was busily looking at the wool, examining its quality and thickness.

"Good morning," Lucine said.

"Good morning to you," Elise said, beckoning them closer.

"Mama," Azniv said. "This is Mrs. Melkonian. Mrs. Melkonian, this is my mother."

"Very nice to meet you," Elise said, bowing her head slightly. "I am Elise Khatchaturian."

"I am Lucine. This is my mother, Takouhi and my daughter, Anahid."

"This is my daughter, Sona."

Sona smiled demurely, and nodded. Elise pointed toward the group surrounding Hagop. "There is my husband, Nishan."

"Ah. He is with my husband, Sarkis," Lucine said.

"And the young man?" Elise inquired.

"That is my son, Hagop." Lucine saw that Nishan was looking at their wool and then gestured toward the garments in the cart.

"Your husband is a tailor?"

"Yes. Yes. Please have a look," Elise said. Already, Lucine and Takouhi could tell that the work was excellent.

"The work is very good. My compliments," Lucine said.

"Thank you. It is very kind of you to say," Elise replied.

Azniv looked back towards her husband and saw that he was just about to conclude the deal.

"Mama. I left Vache with the goldsmith."

Elise looked at Lucine and winked. "Then hurry back, my daughter. That goldsmith is a thief!" Azniv hesitated for a moment, unsure as to whether her mother was serious or exaggerating, then rushed off. They all watched as Azniv returned to Vache and put her hand out to stop the transaction. The goldsmith looked as if he would be in need of a doctor at any moment.

"We have dresses, vests, suits, heavy stockings," Elise said.

Hagop looked towards them, but his attention was again called back by Sarkis who was busy showing Nishan the newly shorn wool. Lucine picked up a colorful blue and white dress.

"Anahid. Come here." Lucine held up the dress against her and judged its size. Takouhi nodded her approval. Sarkis shook hands with Nishan and Hagop picked up two bushels of wool. He followed Nishan to the cart and moved carefully past Sona as his eyes met hers. Both Lucine and Elise noticed, but neither said a word. He put the bushels into the cart.

"The quality of the wool is excellent," Nishan announced.

"Nishan," Elise began. "This is Lucine Melkonian, Takouhi, and Anahid."

"It is my pleasure, thank you," he said, tipping his black hat.

"And this is their son, Hagop." Nishan nodded once, and Hagop nodded back.

"Ah. My daughter, Sona," Nishan said.

"Hello," Hagop said.

Sona quickly nodded and looked away.

"Is there something else you find acceptable?" Elise asked Lucine.

"The dress is excellent," Lucine answered. She paused for a moment. "Hagop. Come here. You need a warm vest for the winter." Hagop stepped forward. Elise and Sona looked at him for a moment and Sona picked through the garments, finally choosing a thick vest, made of lamb's wool. She looked at Hagop and smiled slightly as she handed it to Elise who passed it to Lucine.

"That fits well," Takouhi said.

"A fair trade for the wool?" Lucine asked.

"Yes," Elise answered.

"Good day to you then."

"And to you."

As Lucine, Takouhi, and Anahid moved on, Hagop and Sona stood there, motionless.

"Ah," he began. "Have you sewn all these things?"

She quickly opened her mouth, startled that he was actually speaking to her.

"Yes. I work in my father's shop. With my mother, too."

Hagop nodded, and then motioned towards Azniv and Vache who were now looking at small bottles of spices.

"Azniv is your sister…"

"Yes. We will make our visit after, when there is time."

"Yes. I saw you at her wedding. In June."

She hesitated.

"Sona, help me with these people," Elise interrupted.

"Yes, mama." She looked at Hagop and dropped her voice slightly. "I, yes, I saw you there also." She moved to the back of the cart and grabbed some vests and dresses for her mother.

"Are you coming to Palou often to visit her?" Hagop asked.

"No. It is difficult to travel in the winter months."

"Sona, now," Elise prodded.

"Here I am, mama," she said, handing the clothes to her. Sarkis waved towards Hagop, beckoning him to return.

"Ah. That is my father. I must help him." He paused and held out his hand. "A safe journey home."

"Ah. Thank you," she said.

"Goodbye."

"Goodbye."

SEVASTOPOL
29 October 1914

At three o'clock in the morning on the Black Sea, the Goeben and the Breslau, now flying the Turkish flag and with their new names, the Javus Sultan Selim and the Midilli, sneaked into the Black Sea port of Odessa. It was Baivam, a religious holiday, and there were only a few Turks on duty. The rest of the crew was entirely German.

'Provocation of Russian forces required to stimulate neutrality of Turkey' read the cipher. Leave it to Souchon. It had to be done: Enver's procrastinating had to stop and this was the only way. Souchon ordered the ships to a safe distance and took one last look at the sleepy port town. The buildings were dark and the petrol tanks were large shadows against the night sky.

"Simultaneous order to the Breslau, Ensign. Fire at will."

In a flash, fire burst out of the Goeben's guns. The Breslau followed and the petrol tanks were pierced. The tanks exploded with a roar that shook the port. Flaming liquid gushed in all directions, setting the adjoining buildings on fire.

A military guard, most wearing only their uniform pants and carrying rifles, ran toward the port, but it was futile. Souchon waited. He had to make sure the Russians knew who was responsible and he ordered that the Turkish flags be flown on high. There would be no mistake. Turkey would have to answer now. Souchon watched as the soldiers pointed toward the flags and then he ordered his ships to deeper water.

CONSTANTINOPLE

The British Embassy was a three-storied rectangular stone and brick building, surrounded by an elaborate and immaculately manicured garden. A long stone pathway led up to its front steps and ornate Latin letters were carved into the façade:

AEDES.LEGATONIS.ANGLICANAE.AEDIFICATAE.
VICTORIA.REGNANTE.ANO.DOMINI.MDCCCXLIV

Construction had been completed in 1854 and despite the majestic inscription and its stately exterior, Ambassador Mallet's office resembled more an English sitting room; it was comfortable, boasted a twin fireplace, and was as close to England as Mallet could come without actually being there. He sat behind his desk, examining several official cables when the knock came.

"Come in," he said, not looking up.

Mallet's assistant, Mr. Parrish, entered, along with a Turkish emissary. Mallet stood to receive the agent, who handed him the envelope.

"Thank you," Mallet said. Parrish showed the man out, closing the door behind him.

The envelope had been sealed with wax and the official stamp of the Empire had been pressed into it. Mallet pulled the string and withdrew the document.

"Good God, they've gone mad," he said.

Almost at the same time, Ambassador Bompard read the document that had been delivered to him at the French Embassy.

Morgenthau was reading the official cables that had arrived from the State Department while Constantinople slept. His assistant, Mowbry, rushed in. Morgenthau looked up.

"Sorry, sir. Excuse me."

"Yes, Mr. Mowbry?"

"The Turks, sir."

Mowbry thrust the document forward and Morgenthau reached to grab it.

"They've declared war on the Entente Powers."

Absolute bedlam! Groups of men stood throughout the Ottoman Turkish Parliament, shouting and waving their fists in the direction of the cabinet members who were seated at the long table. They had been under siege since Souchon's escapades at Sevastopol. Now their position of avoiding a declaration of war was being viewed as an act of cowardice. Standing towards the back, quietly observing, were Enver and Talaat.

Bustany Effendi, the Minister of Commerce and Agriculture held his hands up, trying to quiet the crowd, but it only served to draw more screaming and yelling. He looked at the other cabinet ministers: Oskan Effendi, the Minister of Post and Telegraphs, Mahmoud Pasha, the Minister of Public Works, and Djavid Bey, Minister of Finance. Finally, in unison, they stood up and began walking out of the room. This drew even more howls, both of delight and contempt.

"Traitors! You are all traitors," a man in the group cried out.

"We resign!" Bustany answered back. "We do not agree with this action! We all resign!"

"You desert your mother country now?" called out another.

"We do not agree with this act!" Oskan said. "It is insanity!"

Enver turned his head and silently exchanged glances with Talaat. Their Committee of Union and Progress was now in full control of the Government.

RUSSIAN-TURKISH BORDER
2 November 1914

The soldiers marched through the cold night. The Lieutenant leading the patrol flipped up the protective steel cover of his watch and checked the time. He would later record that Russian forces had crossed into Turkey's eastern border at 0200 hours.

One nautical mile off the Dardanelles, Carden, aboard the Elizabeth, reported to his men that Turkey had declared war on the Entente Powers, Russia had declared war on Turkey, and he had been empowered by Kitchener and Churchill to commence against the Turkish fortresses.

PALOU

It was early afternoon and Hagop, Souren, Armen, and Anahid walked quickly from church.

"See you tomorrow," Anahid said, as they reached the square.

"Bye," Armen called out. He and Souren lived in the opposite direction and they left together.

The journal slipped off her grandfather's lap and Anahid stepped forward, catching it before it hit the floor. How many times had Bedros simply fallen asleep in this very way?

"Anahid, how was your day?" Lucine asked. She and Takouhi were preparing the evening meal.

"Good, mama." Anahid put down her schoolbooks, took off her coat, and hung it on the wooden peg. Hagop stepped inside, closing the door behind him.

"How is your French coming?" Takouhi said, turning to him.

"Trés bien. With Anahid's help," he replied.

"Hav yev pilaf?" Anahid asked. Chicken and rice.

"Ayo," Lucine answered.

"Mama, I am going to feed the animals," Hagop said.

He left the house through the side door and stepped into the shed. The chickens scurried about. He put on his pair of high boots and his thick leather and wool overcoat and went outside to the pen. He filled the water and feed troughs and the animals immediately crowded one another.

Shadows began to form, the clouds growing darker. Looking at the sky, he judged that harder rain was still several hours away.

"I think we will have rain all week," Sarkis said, walking up to the small fence.

"Hello, papa."

"Come, let's go inside."

"Yes, papa. I am just finishing."

THE DARDANELLES
3 November 1914

For months, the buildup at the Dardanelles had been under the supervision of General Otto Liman Von Sanders. He and his officers had begun training the Turkish troops in August. Von Sanders was almost always dressed in a twelve-button tunic, his Iron Cross in the center of the top row between the first and second buttons.

For Von Sanders, a widower, and a consummate soldier, the assignment was one he viewed as a necessary evil. Of its importance to Germany there was no doubt. But he loathed having to put his soldiers side-by-side with the Turks who he viewed as vastly inferior. Still, he had to admit that they had learned well. Morgenthau too, had taken notice, and remarked to Mallet that in only a few months the Turkish soldiers seemed to have been transformed.

Asian and Mediterranean traders seeking to enter Russia had made their way to the Aegean Sea, traveled past the narrow strips of land on either side of the body of water known as the Dardanelles, through the Sea of Marmora, and, finally, into the Black Sea. At points, however, the water's depth was shallow; a ship could easily run aground.

Facing the mouth of the Dardanelles and forming the outposts were the Sedd-Ul-Bahr and Kum Kalé fortresses. But these were only decoys: they consisted mainly of antiquated equipment and gunnery. Enver, Sanders, and the Turkish Commander-in-Chief at the Dardanelles, Djevad Pasha, knew that these two locations would be the first to be shelled. Still, Sanders had to admit these Turks were ingenious. He smirked as he looked at the long metal tubes that stuck out of the soft sand, pretending to be long-range artillery guns. At the moment an Allied bomb struck close, some hapless soldier would ignite a pile of black powder, releasing a cloud of thick smoke and creating the impression that a significant hit had been made.

The newer and more powerful artillery had been reserved for defending the Inner Straits. After the Allied fleet broke through the entrance, they would pass unobstructed for approximately five miles.

"This will develop their confidence," Enver had said.

But upon reaching that distance, they would be bombarded with artillery fire from four parallel German howitzer emplacements between the Intépé and Eren-Keui batteries. Should that fail to stop them, four miles further up, commencing at the Baikral emplacement, and continuing through to the Anadolu Hamidié battery, they placed more howitzers and laid a minefield which stretched almost seven miles long. Halfway through the minefield was the Dardanos battery. The fortress here consisted of five steel turrets each armed with fifteen centimeter guns roughly a decade in age, Krupp models of 1905. It was almost exclusively Turkish, with only a few German soldiers in evidence.

At Dardanos, Enver stood with Von Sanders, Djevad Pasha and General Merten, the German Technical Officer. All knew that once the attack commenced, it would be Dardanos that would take the brunt of the Allied fusillade. But if they manage to sink some ships mid-way through, it would cause a pile-up.

"Each moment of delay," Enver had said, "is to our favor. For once a fog lays into this area, it will take days to leave."

Toward the end of the minefield at the narrows that formed the entrance to the Inner Straits, lay the fortresses of Kilid-Ul-Bahr and Anadolu Hamidié. The location of the Anadolu Hamidié was ideal. It lay on the water's edge outside of Tchanak and consisted of a ten-gun turret. The French had built the parapets and winding traverses in 1837 and they stood the same, with little reinforcing iron or wood.

German officers and soldiers almost exclusively manned Anadolu Hamidié, in contrast to the Dardanos. Eighty-five percent of the men had come from the crews of the Goeben and the Breslau. Colonel Wehrle was the Commander-in-Charge.

If the ships made it through the minefields, past the Dardanos and the Hamidié, they would be without opposition for almost four miles. There, at the last narrowing of the Straits, they would encounter reinforced steel cables draped across land, and just past that awaited a barrage of anti-submarine artillery. But if all failed, and the ships did make it through this last defense, they would enter the Sea of Marmora. Within hours they would be at Constantinople with nothing to stop them.

Meanwhile, Carden, on The Elizabeth, had begun a ferocious bombardment that was sending shell after shell into both Sedd-Ul-Bahr and Kum Kalé. The bombs whistled through the sky and sent massive amounts of sand and sea into the air. In the fortresses, the Turkish soldiers could do little. They held their positions and lit the black powder when a shell came close.

Carden watched as the Irresistible and the Bouvet launched their shells and tore up the ground at the mouth.

"Cipher to the fleet. We enter at night."

"Aye, aye, Admiral!" Reynolds answered.

CONSTANTINOPLE
19 November 1914

Wangenheim sat at his desk, studying the cable. Morgenthau walked quickly down the corridor, carrying a folded copy of the Ikdam, one of the Turkish daily journals, and entered the office.

"Mr. Ambassador. A delightful surprise."

"You have gone too far, Wangenheim," Morgenthau said.

"What do you mean?"

"We strongly urge Mr. Wilson to stop supporting the British and French bombings that are killing innocent Turkish citizens," Morgenthau said, reading the headline. He looked at Wangenheim and threw the newspaper onto the desk.

"Mr. Ambassador. Newspapers are entitled to publish their opinions."

"These are not Turkey's opinions. Germany controls the press here," Morgenthau said.

"Come, come, Mister Ambassador. You're making much too much of this."

Morgenthau stepped to the edge of the desk and leaned towards Wangenheim. "Do you want me to tell the Turks exactly what you think of them?"

Wangenheim sat for a moment, considering. America was neutral and he needed Morgenthau as an ally. Besides, everyone knew that the daily journals were bought and paid for with German money.

"Very well, Mr. Ambassador. I will see if the editor is a reasonable man."

Morgenthau nodded, for the moment satisfied. Wangenheim stepped over to the small liquor cabinet.

"Will you share a drink with me?"

"Yes," Morgenthau said, sitting.

Wangenheim nodded. He opened the bottle of Armagnac brandy and poured the liquid into two glasses and added a dash of soda. They drank and a few moments passed.

"Lodz," Wangenheim said.

Morgenthau nodded, gravely. "I have heard. Madness."

Lodz, on the Eastern front between Germany and Russia, had been a show of horror between two hundred fifty thousand German soldiers against one hundred fifty thousand Russians. The Russians had been hastily armed with only shovels, picks, and machetes. The battle had waged through the night until the Germans were forced to call a retreat in the crippling weather.

Wangenheim shook his head, looking off. "A half million soldiers, freezing rain, snow. I tell you Mr. Ambassador, if we had dispatched with Paris quickly, the British would have been too late," Wangenheim said.

Morgenthau set his drink on the table. "Mr. Ambassador, America is neutral and I do not have a military background. But I do believe one thing: Germany will not win this war."

"Indeed, from war comes peace," Wangenheim said. "But peace must be made on Germany's terms. And as part of the peace process, we will divide the Ottoman Empire in two. Egypt will go to Britain and Mesopotamia will go to Germany."

Morgenthau nodded. "A route from Hamburg-to-Baghdad. A short campaign with large territorial gains."

"Yes, but short has turned into long," Wangenheim answered. "But, next time we will have enough supplies to support our troops for as long as it takes. Now, though, the winter will make things difficult."

Morgenthau had heard enough. He got up, excused himself, and thanked Wangenheim for the drink. He exited the office, looking back to see Wangenheim sitting, absorbed.

THE DARDANELLES
3 November 1914

The Dardanos Battery lay two-thirds of the way from the mouth of the Dardanelles and one-third from the Inner Straits. The bombardment had been massive. At the mouth, the fortress at Sedd-Ul-Bahr was in ruins. It would be torn up, bomb after bomb during the day, and at night the Turks would rebuild it with whatever they had. Soon it and

Kum Kale would fall, and the ships would begin their journey to the Inner Straits.

Further into the Narrows, Dardanos stood and here the ground shook as the fourteen-inch guns of The Elizabeth lobbed shell after shell past the mouth and at the base of Dardanos. Beyond these front lines, Enver sat with the combined Turkish-German command.

"The damage we are suffering here is not all that severe," Merten, the German Chief Technical Officer said. "We are rebuilding at night, but we are falling behind. If they get through Eren-Keui Bay…"

"This foundation is solid," Enver said, cutting him off. "The ships will not pass."

"Mr. Minister," Von Sanders said. "What makes you so sure?"

Enver looked at him. "They cannot hit the fortress and their bombs fall short of their target. Do you know why?" Von Sanders slowly shook his head.

"Then I shall tell you," Enver said. "During the daytime, the sun reaching Dardanos strikes first upon a ledge of rock. There it is reflected back to the water."

The men looked at one another.

"I defy anyone to tell me what the distance is from that ledge to the entrance," Enver said. "Dardanos is so distinct that it looks easy. But the whole thing is nothing more than an illusion. This is why it will not fall."

OTTOMAN TURKISH PARLIAMENT
25 November 1914

The suspended ceiling fans did little to alleviate the heat inside the Parliament meeting room. At the front, the Reader, a slight man in a white linen suit read the official proceedings. In the back of the room, Enver, Talaat, and Doctors Nazim and Sakir stood, silently observing the course of action they had set into place. Though the Committee of Union and Progress, CUP, controlled by both Enver and Talaat was truly in charge of the Ottoman Empire, official doctrines were handed down on a domestic basis and for international dissemination by the Parliament. Of course, since CUP had chosen and installed the new cabinet members after the wholesale resignation of the former members, parliamentary control was in its hands. Still, the official policy-making procedure would be done through Parliament, absolving CUP from any national or international retribution or condemnation.

The Reader flipped the thick docket to the next item requiring voting.

"Under special consideration, a bill authorizing the release of prisoners to assist in the war effort. What say your vote?"

The members raised paddle after paddle, signifying a unanimous vote. Turkey was at war and her forces had to be fortified by all necessary means. All able-bodied men would be put to use.

"Let the record show that the vote is unanimous, with all members present."

The gavel struck the worn piece of wood, signaling the bill's passage. The group of four looked at one another, silently acknowledging their success.

The Special Organization had been officially created.

PALOU

Late November brought with it winter squalls that threw soft, wet snow onto Palou. People rushed about, bundled against the harsh weather. Inside Hagop's home, the fire burned. Cold winters and torrid summers were normal for Palou; Hagop could tell by the length and curl of the coats of his lambs that this winter would be long and especially frigid.

There were two large and three smaller earthen crocks on the table. Sarkis stood, cutting thick cubes of freshly cooked lamb's meat. The steaming chunks gave off the most delectable aroma. Lucine was busily cutting green squash, onions, peppers, pumpkin, and carrots into small pieces while Takouhi and Anahid were peeling boiled eggs. The large cast iron pot hung over the fire, the fat from the lamb's meat burning off and turning into a cloudy, fragrant liquid.

Bedros stood to the side. He was the family 'chemist' as Sarkis liked to call him, and he was entrusted with mixing the katsakh choor, literally vinegar water, the brine used for the toorshee, the pickled vegetables. He sat over the bucket of water and vinegar and carefully dropped spices into it. The house became redolent with the aromas of cooked meat, onions and the mingling of spices. Dill, garlic, salt, mustard seed, gingerroot, cloves, cinnamon, turmeric, cumin, the amount and order, according to Bedros, were extremely important. And, he insisted that the brine never be boiled; it should be cold. All the others boiled their brine and then put in the vegetables. But Bedros could taste the difference. His tasted better.

"Now stir," he commanded. Anahid took the long wooden spoon and began stirring the mixture as Bedros watched over her. He dipped his finger into the liquid and licked it.

"Perfect!" he declared. "Hagop, this is ready."

Hagop picked up the bucket and brought it to the table. Lucine finished placing the cut vegetables into a crock and Anahid was now helping Takouhi put the boiled eggs into a second crock.

"These are ready," Lucine said. Hagop stepped over and filled the crock halfway with the brine. Lucine took a heavy earthenware plate and placed it on top of the vegetables.

"Now we cover them up," Takouhi said, and Anahid took the plate and carefully placed it on the eggs, pushing them into the liquid. Lucine took a large flat rock and put it on top of the plate, weighing everything down. Anahid did the same.

"All right, everyone," Lucine declared. "Now we move to the meat."

"This pile has cooled," Sarkis said, pushing forward the large plate of meat.

The women took the chunks of meat and placed them in the small pots.

"Hagop, bring the yiugh, the fat." Hagop wrapped a thick cloth around his hand, grabbed the handle of the pot, and brought it to the table.

"Now that we have the first layer," Takouhi said, instructing Anahid, "we cover it with the fat."

"Be careful, that is hot," Lucine warned. Hagop carefully tipped the pot until the liquid just covered the layer of meat. He moved on to the second and third pots.

"Good," Takouhi said, approvingly. "Now, we make another layer."

Layer after layer of meat was added and, finally, Hagop finished sealing in the meat.

"Now we put the top on," Takouhi said. She took the large flat top of the pot, slid it into place, and Lucine and Anahid helped her turn it upside down. The suction built up from within held the cover tightly in place. The fat would solidify and the pots would be stored like that, upside down. As the winter grew on, Lucine would dig her hand into the pot and break out several pieces of meat that would be warmed and eaten with thick slices of bread and soup. Along with the pickled vegetables, and some fresher potatoes and onions, this was to be the family's staple meal until spring arrived.

Then it was time to bake the lavash, flat bread. Lucine, Takouhi, and Anahid kneaded the dough while Hagop poured in the water. From the round oven that also provided all the heat in the home, Sarkis used a flat wooden paddle to slap the wet dough against the oven's side. It stuck there, cooking. In moments, he pulled out the bread that he then added to the growing stack.

They were all exhausted as Hagop and Anahid carried the last of the pots to the shed.

"That makes eighteen," Sarkis said, counting. "Last year, we had fifteen." He paused, then winked at Hagop and Anahid. "But the two of you are growing bigger!" he said, laughing.

CONSTANTINOPLE

Morgenthau walked, accompanied by Mallet and Bompard. After the official Turkish Documents of War had been delivered, both the British and French governments had immediately informed Turkey that they were recalling their ambassadors. Safe passage was to be given to all British and French citizens who wished to leave Turkey and the care of any remaining British or French citizens would be transferred to Morgenthau. It had been a grave meeting, and as they walked through the busy streets, they were silent.

As they drew near the American Embassy, Bompard suddenly stopped, tapping the brass end of his cane several times on the cobblestone surface.

"There. Look. All the French signs are being taken down," Bompard said, shaking his head.

"It will only be Turkish from now on, Louis," Mallet said.

The small cobbler shop stood in the Zeirek Kilissi district, directly facing the old bridge that crossed the Golden Horn, almost directly opposite the Pera district. Inside the shop, the slight tap-tap-tap of a small hammer filled the air as the cobbler worked on a pair of brown leather shoes. He wore a white robe and fez. His name was Veysel Kutan.

The door opened and two men entered. They were dressed in tan linen suits. Veysel stopped his work and rushed from around the table to greet them.

"Good day! Good day! May I help you? May I be of service on this glorious day?"

"You are the owner of this shop, citizen?" the taller one asked.

"Yes! Yes! I have owned this shop for twenty-seven years, my father before me. Is there something wrong?"

The shorter official flipped through a small note pad and ran his finger down the list of names.

"You are Kutan, Veysel?"

"Yes, yes. That is I."

"You have in your employ an Armenian and a Jew? Is this correct?" the shorter one said.

Veysel hesitated, watching the two officials.

"Yes, that is true. But, but they are just boys. For things I cannot do anymore. I am not as young as I used to be, you see," he said, attempting a slight laugh.

The taller one looked at him.

"A new law has been enacted by order of the Committee of Union and Progress. For each non-Ottoman citizen you employ you must pay a luxury tax."

"But I pay them very little, almost nothing," Veysel protested.

"That does not concern us," the shorter one said. "If you do not wish to incur such a tax, employ only Ottoman citizens."

They turned and left. Veysel stood there. The boys were hard workers, but he could not afford any additional taxes. He would just have to make do without them.

Morgenthau beckoned Mowbry into his office.

"Mr. Mowbry, you will be witness and record keeper."

"Yes, Mr. Ambassador."

"Mr. Ambassador, let the record show that on this day, the British Ambassador to Turkey, I, the Right Honorable Sir Louis du Pan Mallet do hereby transfer the care of all British citizens residing in Turkey to the American Ambassador, Henry S. Morgenthau."

"Mr. Ambassador, let the record show that I also, Louis Maurice Bompard, French Ambassador to Turkey, am compelled to transfer the French citizens in Turkey into your care."

"Let the record now show that I, Henry S. Morgenthau, American Ambassador to Turkey, upon the authority granted to me by President Woodrow Wilson, do hereby accept into my care all British and French citizens residing in Turkey."

A blast of black smoke filled the air as the train engine came to life. Mallet and Bompard climbed up the small steps. Mallet hesitated, then turned to face Morgenthau.

"Henry," Mallet said.

"Yes, Mr. Ambassador?"

"Don't stay here too long."

PALOU

December's cold. Vapor trails leaving the mouths and nostrils of the lambs as Hagop took them out for small amounts of time. Evenings spent with the family, going over things. Bedros and Sarkis talking about what they would plant come the spring, Lucine and Takouhi mending clothes.

There were many games that occupied the hours. Dikran and Armen would come over, and, two-at-a-time, they would take turns throwing the arshoog. This was a small bone that was cut away from the first joint of a lamb's back quarter. One side was grooved, the other, flat. On a human, it was akin to the knee. The game was simple and they lost hours playing it. The two players would choose a side, either flat or grooved, and flip the arshoog. If you chose the grooved side and it came up on that side, one point to you. If it landed on the flat side, no points, and the toss would be your opponent's. The first to win ten points won the game. And if one of the players had the lucky touch and got the arshoog to stand on end, the game was immediately won.

Mostly boys flipped the arshoog. Girls, instead, tossed walnuts. First, a walnut was placed at the end of a room, close to, but not touching a wall. Then, from a distance, each girl would roll a walnut down towards the wall. As the number of walnuts increased, the winner was the one who could hit the original walnut. The prize: all the walnuts.

Then there were the games of strategy: tavloo and skambil. Tavloo, backgammon, was a favorite, and almost every home had a tavloo board, most of which were intricately carved with designs. The one in Hagop's house had a hoviv, a shepherd, with a lamb at his side. Souren's had a khatchkar. Armen's had a dove.

Skambil, on the other hand, was a card game, and strategy was critical. The game could be played with either two or four people. First, the fours, fives, and sixes were thrown out. Then the cards were shuffled and dealt, each player getting three cards. A card was dealt face up, the trump. And then it would be a simple affair to avoid wasting trumps on cards that yielded little or no points. Jacks were worth two points; Queens three; Kings four. Then, the important cards: twos were worth ten points; Aces eleven; threes thirty.

You had to know what cards had been played. It was a tie if each player reached one hundred twenty points each. Otherwise, the highest points took the game. If it was a rout, and one player held less than eighty points, the winner won two hands. The game went to the first player to win ten hands.

Tavloo was Souren's specialty, Armen a close second. Bedros was almost unbeatable. Lucine and Takouhi were even when it came to skambil. They were good; Anahid was better. It seemed as if she could play the game for hours without tiring.

These were the good times. These were the times where the bonds were forged, the respect given and earned, the memories created.

Reading, by the light of the kerosene. Sewing, looking through glass to see better. Hearing all the wonderful stories. In the warmth of the fire, they would drink hot tea, served in tall glasses, sometimes a touch of dried, ground lemon or nutmeg floating on the top.

Hagop looked up from his book. Anahid was busy studying. Lucine was working on something for Maritza's baby. Sarkis sat, reading, while Bedros napped: his family.

BITLIS

Sona watched as the snow curled around the trees. It was quiet outside, peaceful even, and bundled against the wind and the cold, she couldn't help but appreciate how beautiful it was. She lowered the pail into the well and hurried home.

"Shood, shood," Nishan said, taking the pail from her.

"Come, here is hot tea," Elise said, pushing the tall glass toward Sona.

"Thank you, mama."

Sona sat, cupping the warm glass between her hands, her long fingers wrapping around it.

"Mmm. It is good," she said, sipping it.

Elise cut several thick pieces of katah, sweet bread, and set them onto a plate.

"Ah!" Nishan said, reaching for a piece. He took it and dipped it into his tea. Always with the katah he did that. He walked over to his chair and began reading his journal.

"Eat," Elise said, pushing the plate toward Sona. "You need some meat on you."

Sona reached for a piece and took a bite.

"Very tasty, mama."

Elise nodded; she was tired. Over the past weeks they had all worked doubly hard: Sona and Nishan at the shop, Elise at home, preparing the foodstuffs for winter and also for the trek to Palou. If the weather permitted traveling, they would spend Christmas with Azniv and Vache.

"I am going to bed," Elise said. She reached for the plates, but Sona put her hand out.

"I can do that, mama."

Elise nodded. "Everything is ready for the trip." She turned to Nishan. "Do you think we will be able to go?"

"I think so," Nishan said. "I think the weather will hold."

"Good," Elise said. She turned to Sona. "Not too late for you, Miss."

"Yes, mama."

"Sona, the fire will go through the night," Nishan said, getting up.

"Yes, papa."

Sona sat, finishing her tea. The house was warm and the fire flickered. It was quiet, save for the crackling and the occasional popping as the wood burned.

She worked hard and was a good student. Both her Mathematics and French were good; her penmanship was excellent. She was shy. She had a dark complexion, full round eyes, long black curly hair. Her face, particularly her smile, was beguiling. In time, Elise knew, she would be well sought after.

As with Azniv, Elise and Nishan had instilled in Sona a profound respect for God. She sang in the church choir. She was respectful of her elders, but moreover she had what to Elise was most important.

"She has a good heart, Nish."

"Yes, I know," he said. "That is because of you."

"Nish, you know that she and the Melkonian boy..."

"Ah," he said. "I thought there was something." He rubbed his chin. "Leave it to a woman to see it first."

"What do you know about his family? Anything?"

"You feel that strongly about this?"

"Yes, Nish." She held his eyes for a moment. "I do."

She would be sixteen years old soon. Hagop was only a month older. Her closest friend was Shushig Antounian. Shushig was sixteen, and had already been betrothed to a boy, Ara Bamian, in Moush. Shushig was a sweet, simple girl, and as with many of the arranged marriages, she had never even met the boy until the betrothal day.

"Weren't you scared?" Sona had asked.

Shushig hesitated, thinking.

"Well, yes. Yes, I was. After they told me, they said how do I feel about it?" Shushig said, continuing.

"And...?"

"And I thought about it for a moment and then I looked at my mother and I knew that they would not put me to something that would not be right."

"Just like that?" Sona asked.

"Yes," Shushig said, waving her hand. "Just like that."

Sona sat, listening. She had been sick when Azniv had been betrothed to Vache, and did not see the ceremony.

"And?"

"And I remember thinking the funniest thing. I almost started to laugh," Shushig said, smiling.

"Why?" Sona asked.

"I was thinking, he was nice looking, but shorter than me. And then what popped into my head? I tell you, I don't know where it came from."

"Yes, already, what?"

"I remember repeating to myself that his name was Ara. His name is Ara. Easy name to remember!"

Sona looked at her for a moment and blinked.

"That's what you were thinking?"

"I know!" Shushig laughed. She looked at Sona. "But, as scared as I thought I would be, I was not."

Sona slowly nodded her head.

"I am happy for you Shushig. I am so happy for you."

"Thank you."

"Sona," Shushig said, pausing. "Is there someone? I mean..."

Sona allowed herself a small smile.

"I'm sorry," Shushig said. "I don't mean to..."

"No, it is all right," Sona said. She could feel her face getting warmer. She was not one to offer much of her feelings to anyone. But this was Shushig. And if she didn't tell someone, she would practically burst.

"There is a boy..."

"There is?" Shushig said, excitedly.

"Yes," Sona said. "From Palou."

"Palou! Same as Azniv!"

"Yes."

"What is his name?"

"Hagop," Sona said. "His name is Hagop."

Now she sat, watching the fire. Why did she hold something for this boy who she had met only once? It was a strange feeling but she didn't dare ask her mother. Was it the way he looked at her? The way he had looked at her even when he was far away on the other side of the square? Why, just last year, she wouldn't have noticed.

"Do not think of such things," she tried to tell herself.

But each time she had tried to push the picture of him away, it just came back that much faster. She took out her needlework. It would be a nice gift. She hoped he would like it.

CONSTANTINOPLE
December, 1914

It was a moonless night and soft snow drifted down. In the dark, isolated office, there were five rows of long tables, and three men sat at each row. They pored over sheet after sheet, running their fingers down the hundreds of names that had been gathered. On the walls were various sized photographs of men, some dressed in business suits, others in clergy vestments, others in plain, everyday clothes. They ranged in age from 30 to 70.

The men worked without talking. Smoke from their wrinkled, hand-rolled cigarettes curled in the already stifled air.

Toward the far wall, the words 'Azatamart Newspaper' were written. Below the words were photographs of the newspaper's editors and journalists. The Azatamart was an Armenian publication, financed solely by the local Armenian population.

The men sorted through the lists name after name, photograph after photograph. The first man checked the list, the second man matched a photograph to the selected name, and the third man recorded the last known address.

TREBIZOND

Trebizond bordered the Black Sea. In the small, secluded area, a series of makeshift huts rose as if from nowhere. The men stood about, listening to the instructions being given to them by the Turkish officer. One by one they walked to the rickety table and each was issued a standard Turkish military uniform: pants, tunic, boots. Observing everything were Doctors Sakir, Nazim, and General Mahmud Kamil, Turkish Military.

"My compliments, General," Nazim said.

"Thank you, Doctor," Kamil replied "If any of the cabinet members becomes curious regarding the exact placement of the Special Organization, we will respond that it is a matter of security and cannot be divulged."

Sakir nodded. "When will they be given weapons?"

"We will outfit them with bayonets and rifles when they are dispatched to their locations."

Nazim gestured toward a group of prisoners. "You see that group there, General?"

"Yes, Doctor?"

"They are Kanli-Katil, the most violent. These were specially chosen."

"Yes, Doctor," Kamil said, nodding.

"See to it that you use them quickly," Sakir said.

"And efficiently," Talaat said. He kept his eyes on Sakir, who was seated before him. Talaat got up and walked to the window and looked down on Constantinople.

"When they are ready, deploy them from Trebizond to Ras-El-Ain and Chabur," he said. "This is close enough to Deir-El-Zor. There they will lay in wait for the caravans."

Sakir nodded. "I have spoken to Dr. Nazim. Everything is proceeding without delay."

"They must hurry," Talaat said. "The work to be done must be done now. After the war, it will be too late."

CONSTANTINOPLE

Enver and Talaat sat at the rectangular table in the brick building that served as the headquarters for the German Military command. It was late and seated opposite them were Marshall Colmar Von Der Goltz and Generals Von Bronssart and Von Sanders.

"Mr. War Minister. Mr. Interior Minister," Von Der Goltz began. "There are certain realities of this war which are going to be inevitable. The German High Command has devised a strategy to ensure our mutual success."

"And what is that, General?" Enver asked.

"Germany requires Turkey's assistance against the Russians," Von Bronssart said. "If Turkey concentrates her forces in Eastern Turkey, massing a native population against the Russians, our combined forces will bring them to their knees."

He looked over to Von Sanders who unfurled a map of the Eastern Turkish border.

"Move the Armenian population out of Eastern and Northern Turkey," Von Bronssart said, tracing the demarcations on the map. He moved the pointer down and to the right. "Relocate them to Mesopotamia."

Enver intently studied the movements. Von Der Goltz watched both Enver and Talaat. The pointer moved from central southern Turkey back to the eastern border.

"You are then free to move in the native population and defend the Caucasus," Von Bronssart continued. "The Russians are gathering strength now."

Enver paused. "General, in order to defend the Caucasus we must move troops away from Egypt," he said.

"Then do so," Von Bronssart replied. "After the war, you will be able to walk into Egypt."

"We will discuss what we must do," Enver said, looking at Talaat. The Germans looked at one another.

"Thank you, Mr. War Minister. Mr. Interior Minister," Von Der Goltz said. "Time is our enemy now, so please give this your utmost consideration. We await your answer."

The generals stood as Enver and Talaat turned and left. Von Sanders closed the door behind them.

"I would say that went quite well," Von Bronssart announced.

"Why do we have to go on with this charade?" Von Sanders spat. "The Turks would be nowhere without our presence here!"

Von Der Goltz calmly sat and clasped his hands together.

"Maybe so, General, but at least for now, Turkey is strategic."

"Yes," Von Bronssart said.

"If things go badly for Germany during the war, Turkey will be good bartering material."

"You realize that the Turks will use this as an opportunity to settle their Armenian Question?" Von Sanders said.

"That does not matter to us," Von Bronssart said. "The Armenians are like the Jew vermin. It does not concern us. Let them do what they will."

Harootiun Mugerditchian was an Armenian who had based his life on opportunity: seeing it and seizing it. All that mattered to him was that his personal situation improved. He had expensive tastes, and it was his ambition to rise above what he termed the rabble of Armenians crying for themselves in the streets.

Now he sat as shadows fell across the room, looking at the photographs laid out before him.

"This one, yes," he said, pushing the photo forward.

"This one. This one."

"No. He is nobody. No. No."

"This one. This one."

"Ah, I remember this one. Yes, him."

One by one, he pushed the photographs forward or to the side, separating the Armenian elite from the rabble. Talaat sat, watching him, collecting the photos one by one.

THE WESTERN FRONT
Christmas Day, 1914

The battles on the Western Front had been of unparalleled brutality. A precious meter of ground was won and then lost. Christmas Day 1914 was dark from smoke that hung in the air and had blackened the earth. Constant shelling, the stink of cordite, and the sickness of men dead and of men dying. Sickness of hearts and souls and of dreams that were being ripped out from each side.

Bombs will strike
And flesh will fly
And photographs of you and I
Will drift with smoke into the sky

But at noon, the two flags rose silently and slowly from their respective trenches.

"Look, there!" the British private said.

"I see it!"

The two flags were raised a bit higher.

"Careful! They may shoot," the German soldier warned.

"No, I think no."

The British soldier raised his head until it was just above the trench.

"I see him, now!" the German said.

"What is he doing?"

"He is looking at me. Holding his flag."

Both soldiers slowly got to their feet. On each side, helmets slowly rose over the surface. The two soldiers crossed from their trenches and looked at one another. It was the German who finally cracked a smile and as they met, they simultaneously extended their hands. They patted each other on the shoulders and exchanged flags. The soldiers emerged from their trenches, and they slowly walked towards one another.

"Christ, they're as young as we are," the young British private said.

"Don't blaspheme. Especially today, you heathen," came the reply.

One of the Germans produced a metal box, opened it, and offered cigarettes to the other side. A British soldier passed out some of the foul-smelling, two-inch long cigars that even his fellow soldiers hated to see him light up. It was just fine, they reasoned, that he was giving them to the Germans. Maybe the stink will kill them!

Late into the evening, the songs and liquor began to subside. And as the soldiers jumped back into their holes, the vacant stare began creeping back into their eyes.

LONDON
5 January 1915

The men watched as Prime Minister Asquith pointed to the locations on the map.

"If we can convince the Bulgarians to march on Constantinople, Greece and Romania most certainly would join them," he said. He circled the Dardanelles and drew the pointer up. "If we capture the Dardanelles it will take us to the Danube and position us for an attack on Austria-Hungary."

Churchill, Kitchener, and the other advisors nodded. The door opened and an orderly carried in a silver tray of glasses filled with brandy. Asquith nodded to the orderly who then offered a glass to each of the men. Asquith stepped closer to the map and began pointing out specific sections.

"Certain arrangements have been made," he said. He circled the area to the west of Russia and drew the pointer directly over to Constantinople. "Russia will receive Eastern Armenia and Constantinople."

He drew the pointer down and slightly to the west. "The Greeks will obtain Smyrna."

The pointer moved down and to the east. "The French will retain Syria and Lebanon."

He swung the pointer again, diagonally and to the northwest. "And if the Bulgarians enter, she will get her beloved Dedeagatch on the Aegean."

Asquith sat down and quietly sipped his drink.

"Does anyone care to add anything?" he said.

No one uttered a word.

PALOU

The sixth of January brought with it clear, crisp weather. In other parts of the world Christ's birth was celebrated on the twenty-fifth of December, but in Palou the sixth of January was Astavadz-a-haytnou-tiun, literally, the appearance of God.

It had been the practice of pagans to celebrate the birth of the sun on the twenty-fifth of December. Gradually, the observance of Christ's birthday shifted from January back to December, replacing the pagan custom. Yet for Armenians, who had adopted Christianity before the Romans, it had remained the sixth of January.

Early that morning with the moon still shining, the church bells had rung out, signifying the birth of Christ. True to form, Anahid had awoken like a shot: everyone else still fast asleep. Gradually, the ringing grew, calling the villagers.

"Wake up!"

"Yes, wake up, will you!" Souren said. He and Armen were standing in front of Hagop's bed.

"Oh, you two," Hagop said, squinting.

"You should hurry you know," Armen said.

"Yes, you are very fortunate today," Souren said, "In the night, God has sent you a present!"

"What do you mean?" Hagop said, brushing his hair from his face.

Souren and Armen looked at one another.

"This present has long dark hair," Armen answered, smiling.

They had all gotten up, dressed quickly, and made their way toward the small church. The veils covering the heads and faces of the women blew in the cold breeze. They crowded in, filling every space, the kerosene lanterns illuminating the church interior. Father DerArtinian delivered the Divine Liturgy, and they stood hands out, palms upraised, receiving the word of God.

"Krisdos dznav yev haydnetzav," Father DerArtinian said. Christ is born and manifested.

"Orhnyal eh haydnootiun uh Krisdosi," the congregation answered. Blessed be the birth of Christ.

They kissed one another while delivering the greeting and the response. As Hagop leaned over to kiss Anahid, he caught a glimpse of Souren and Armen. Hagop nodded and Armen turned, gesturing. Hagop looked to the right and blinked.

Sona.

She stood with her family and Azniv and Vache. She was wearing a long black veil.

Sona, Elise, and Nishan had arrived late the night before. The weather had held out, and the trip had gone without incident.

Father DerArtinian stepped before the baptismal font. In his left hand he held a beautiful ornate gold cross; in his right, a gold metallic dove. This was Jur-orhnek, the Blessing of the Waters. He passed the dove over the cross, pouring holy water onto it.

"This Blessing of the Water is a celebration not only of Christ's birth but of his baptism as well," he said, turning to the group. "As you celebrate this holy day, remember what you mean to one another and why you are here." He stopped, looking into their faces. The sun was well over the horizon, and rims of light illuminated the walls of the church.

"What you have learned in your time on earth, what you have taught your children, what you have passed on to them, is but a reflection of what God has given us: His only son," he said. "Live as good Christians, so that you may celebrate the birth, baptism, and the life of Jesus. Live as good Christians so that you may hold in wonder his resurrection and his ascension. Live as good Christians so that you may spread the word of Jesus and the word of God. Amen."

"Amen," they said.

"Aysor Don e Sourp Dzununtian, Avedis," he said. Today is the feast of holy birth, good tidings.

"Shnorhavor sourp Dzunount," they answered. I wish you a Christmas full of grace.

They slowly filed out of the church.

"Shnorhavor nor daree yev soorp dzuhnoont!" Hagop said, shaking Souren's hand. Happy New Year and Merry Christmas.

"Tsez yev mez medz Avedis!" Souren answered. For you and for us a great, good news.

They turned in unison, perfectly timed, and greeted Armen.

"Shnorhavor nor daree yev soorp dzuhnoont!"

"And tsez yev mez medz Avedis to you!" Armen said, grinning.

"Turn!" Souren said. He grabbed Hagop's arm, spinning him around. Azniv and Vache walked out of the church followed by Sona, Elise, and Nishan.

Sona looked at him and stopped. Hagop opened his mouth to greet her, but nothing came out.

'But, my God, she is beautiful!' he thought.

'He is very handsome,' she thought. 'What are you thinking, girl? Amot eh! Shame! You have just left church!'

Souren and Armen stood there, watching. Finally, Souren slapped Hagop hard on the back, propelling him towards Sona. She stepped back, startled. Hagop looked quickly to Souren and then turned to Sona.

"Sona," he hesitated. "Hello."

"Hello, Hagop."

"Let's go and bother Anahid," Souren said, pulling Armen's sleeve.

"I did not know that your family was coming," Hagop said.

"My father made the final decision only yesterday," Sona replied. "The weather..."

Hagop looked up. "No, it is going to be clear."

"Can you tell just by looking?"

"Ah," Hagop said, hesitating. They were less than an arm's length apart, but still she looked...

Wonderful.

"Yes, I can tell weather pretty well."

"Yes, but how?" she asked.

"I do not know!" he said, a small grin breaking out.

"But are you ever wrong?" she pressed.

Hagop put his hand to his chin and looked off, thinking.

"Not that I can remember!" he said, smiling.

Sona saw her mother talking with Azniv. Elise looked up, eyeing her.

"I must go," she said. "My mother…"

"Yes, yes, I am sorry to keep you."

"No, no. Not at all."

"Shnorhavor nor daree yev soorp dzuhnoont!" he called after her.

"Tsez yev mez medz Avedis!" she answered.

He watched as she joined her family.

"Nice of you to join us," Armen said, grinning, as Hagop approached.

"Yes, we did not want to disturb you," Souren added.

"You," Hagop said, looking at him. "Next time you push me like that it will be your last."

"Ah, I do not think so," Souren said, smiling.

As the families dispersed, Lucine looked across the way and saw that Elise was looking at her. They nodded, almost simultaneously, and in that instant, it was acknowledged. Now it would be up to Lucine. Inquiries would be made.

Late afternoon brought with it the beginning of what would be a brilliant sunset. Hagop's home was full of people. Even Hovan the beggar strolled from one home to the next, stuffing choregs, boormas, big thick pieces of bread, and boiled eggs into his baggy pants. When he got to Hagop's home, everyone instantly stopped eating. Lucine and Takouhi immediately set upon him, offering him a sack of foodstuffs. Anything to get him out as quickly as possible.

"It is the good Christian thing to do," Takouhi said, "but Hovan needs a bath!"

Anahid sat, showing Armen her new book. It had been wrapped with blue silk, which she could fashion into a kerchief. Hagop awoke to a small package wrapped in brown oilskin paper. Coiled inside was a leather belt. He stretched it out to reveal his initials, HBM, Hagop Bedros Melkonian, burned into the stiff brown leather.

Now Hagop and Souren sat, watching Armen. He had started with the choreg, moved to the rojig, over to the simit, and now had a handful of raisins and walnuts.

"You amaze me," Souren said, poking his index finger into Armen's stomach.

"Watch it!" Armen replied. "I am in a delicate condition!"

"No, my mother is in a delicate condition," Souren replied, gesturing to where Maritza sat, her stomach bulging.

"Watching you eat is good entertainment!" Hagop added, laughing.

Sarkis, Bedros, Dikran, and Garbis drank their coffee after which Sarkis got up and returned with a bottle of raki. This one was made from toot, mulberries. He filled four little glasses with the potent liquid and they drank in unison.

Lucine tied a small red ribbon to a basket filled with assorted sweets and a jar of toorshee.

"Hagop."

"Yes, mama?"

"Please take this basket to Azniv and Vache's house."

"Yes, mama," Hagop said, getting up.

"It is good luck to make a gift to newlyweds on their first Christmas," Takouhi said to Anahid, who nodded.

Hagop took his coat from the wooden peg and cradled the basket in his left arm.

"Are you coming?" he said to Souren and Armen.

"No, it is nice and warm in here!" Souren said. He gestured towards Armen. "And as for him, you can see he is too busy eating!"

Hagop shook his head.

The wind was still as Hagop walked toward the Samuelian home. Snow lined the dirt road, and the trees bore up against the weight of the white flakes. The house was about a half-kilometer away. He knocked on the door and a few moments passed before it opened. As it did, his eyes met Sona's. For an instant, small smiles broke out on both their faces. Before either of them could speak, Azniv came rushing up, an apron tied around her waist.

"Hagop! Don't stand there! Come in! Sona, take Hagop's coat."

"No, it is all right," Hagop said. "I just came to bring this basket."

The house was full of people. Azniv motioned to Nishan and Elise. "You remember my parents." She turned to her right. "And my sister, Sona."

"Yes, yes thank you, I remember her. I mean them," he said.

Hagop handed the basket to Azniv. "My mother sent this basket with our good wishes."

"Thank you," Azniv said, taking it. "Sit down. Have something to eat."

"Ah, I would like to, but my home is full of people," Hagop replied.

"Sona, bring the basket for Hagop's family," Azniv said, turning towards her.

Sona nodded. Hagop couldn't help but watch her go. Her hair was tied back with a small white ribbon and she had on a handmade blue dress that had white stitching along the sleeves. He looked around the room. As he did, his eyes rested on Elise, who was looking directly at him.

Sona returned, carrying a small basket, brimming with treats and small wrapped packages.

"Hagop, this basket is for your family," Berjouhi said.

Sona handed him the basket.

"Thank you," Hagop said.

"Paree keesher," Berjouhi said.

"Looys paree," Hagop replied.

"Sona, see Hagop out," Elise said, watching them.

Sona nodded and opened the door for him.

"Thank you," he said. He looked at her. With her hair clipped back, her face shone clear, her eyes bright. There was a small brown birthmark on the left side of her neck, and it was... it was...

Nice.

She felt his stare, and although she wanted to... had always been told to... turn away...

She could not.

"Thank you," Hagop said, turning to leave.

"Hagop," she said, his name coming off her lips quicker than she could think.

"Yes?"

She reached into her dress pocket and withdrew a small package wrapped with blue paper.

"This is for you," she said, handing it to him.

Hagop looked at the package for a moment and then into her eyes. She smiled slightly and while the room was full of people, and the air stirred with noise and commotion, they stood there, alone.

"But I," Hagop began.

Sona pushed the package into his right hand.

"I hope that you will like it," she said. "I made it myself."

"Ah. Thank you," he said. "It is very kind of you, but you did not have to…"

"It was nothing," she said.

"Ah, well. Good night again."

"Good night."

She closed the door behind him, stood for a moment, and then the sounds came rushing back to her ears as she turned and joined the others.

"Hagop! Back so quickly?" Bedros asked.

"Yes, grandpapa," Hagop said. He handed the basket to his mother. "This is from Azniv's family."

"Ah. Thank you." She picked out a small package and read the Armenian script. "Anahid, this is for you," she said.

"For me?" Anahid said, excitedly. She got up and took it, all eyes watching as she opened it.

"Mama! Look!" she said. She held up a delicate, blue bottle, filled with liquid.

"It is beautiful!"

"Make sure you thank Azniv," Lucine reminded.

"I will."

"What have you there?" Takouhi said, looking over at Hagop.

"Hagop! Open it!" Anahid said.

"No, I have many things to do," he answered. "I will open it later."

"Yes, open it!" Souren and Armen said in unison.

Lucine shot an imploring look his way and Hagop shrugged. He had seen that look before and it was pointless to argue. He sat down and looked at the neat precise script for a few moments.

"Come on! Are you waiting for it to talk to you?" Anahid said.

Hagop looked her. He opened the package and withdrew a thin white handkerchief. It was folded and on the front was an ornate letter H. He held it up for all to see.

"Ah! It is very delicate!" Takouhi said. "Let me see it closer."

Hagop handed it to her.

"Ah. Very fine silk," she said, turning and examining it. "And with your letter on it! It looks like Azniv is getting better."

Hagop shook his head. "No, Grandmama. This is a gift from Azniv's sister. Sona."

At what seemed to him at exactly the same moment, Lucine, Takouhi, Anahid, Souren, and Armen all looked at one another. Even Sarkis and Bedros looked up.

The house was quiet now, and Lucine silently watched the figure sitting before the fire. She stepped forward and put her hand on Hagop's shoulder.

"Do you see only her face in the fire, my son?"

He stared ahead. "Is it so clearly written, mother?"

She pulled forward a chair and sat next to him. "Only when it is meant to be. There are many things mothers can see before anyone else."

"What do you know of her?" he said. The words tumbled out and he could hardly believe he had spoken them.

"Not very much, though she has kept her honor and is of good stock."

"Mother!" he said, turning to her. "You speak of her as if she is one of my sheep!"

Lucine laughed hard and then caught herself.

"I am sorry! It is just a saying of an old woman!" She looked at him, running his finger over the letter on the handkerchief.

"Good night, my son."

"Good night, mama."

Bundled against a stiff wind, Elise, Nishan, and Sona stood, saying their farewells to Azniv, Vache, and his family.

"Stay well," Azniv said, hugging Sona.

"I will."

Nishan took the reins as the donkey snorted.

"We will see you soon!" Elise said.

"Safe journey!" Azniv said, waving.

Elise looked up as Hagop ran toward the clearing. Sona stood in the back of the cart.

"Mr. Khatchaturian, Mrs. Khatchaturian, Sona," Hagop said. "I am sorry to disturb you!"

"Hagop?" Elise said.

"My mother sends this jar of toorshee for you," he said.

"That is very kind," Elise said, taking it from him. "Please thank her for me."

"I will do it." He looked at Sona. "I hope you have a safe journey!"

"Thank you, Hagop," Elise said.

Hagop looked at Sona and raised his hand.

"Goodbye!"

"Goodbye, Hagop!" Sona said.

Nishan snapped the reins and the group waved them off. Souren and Armen walked up and Hagop threw his head back in resignation. Armen took a handkerchief from his pocket and draped it over his head as if it were a veil.

"Ah, don't you both have anything better to do?" Hagop said, shaking his head.

Souren smiled and Armen began blowing kisses in Hagop's direction.

"It would be better like this," Hagop said. He reached over, and pulled the handkerchief down until it covered Armen's face.

"There, now that flatters you!" he said, laughing.

CONSTANTINOPLE

Morgenthau sat, reading the reports. It was late. Josephine had beckoned him to bed almost two hours ago. He read on, fascinated, trying to think what six hundred bombs launched at the mouth of the Dardanelles could be like. Six hundred! They had churned up water and earth, but still there had been no breaking through.

LONDON
24 February 1915

"Gentlemen," Asquith said to those gathered in the War Council room. "We can talk all evening about the weather and the sea conditions, but, in the end, we must find ways to meet our objectives."

Churchill looked over to Fisher and then to Kitchener.

"Lord Kitchener?" Asquith said, sitting down.

"Thank you Prime Minister." Kitchener stood and walked over to a large map. "Five days ago I authorized the transfer of the twenty-ninth division to the Eastern Front; the Russians are falling to the Germans and are in desperate need of reinforcements. We acted quickly and it appears that it is succeeding. The Russians are now willing to march on Constantinople from the East and the Greeks will send us three divisions." He paused. "That is, if we begin the attack."

"Attack where?" Grey blurted, then caught himself.

"There are three points of contact," Kitchener said. He touched the tip of the Peninsula. "Here, at Cape Helles." The pointer moved up until it rested in the middle of the Peninsula, along the coast. "Here, we'll land troops at Gaba Tepe." The pointer moved up again, further north near the rocky outlines of a bay. "And here," Kitchener said, "at Sulva Bay."

"You're advocating a combined assault?" Grey asked, concerned.

"Mr. Secretary," Kitchener said, "If the Fleet cannot make its way through then the Army must."

"But where are the men going to come...?" Grey began.

"From here," Kitchener said, stabbing the small island. "Lemnos." The island lay some seventy kilometers to the southwest of the peninsula. "It provides excellent cover for moving large numbers of troops."

"We will have no problem whatsoever maneuvering them into place," Churchill said.

"Who are we trusting this to?" Asquith asked.

"General Hamilton," Kitchener replied. "He's the most senior who's not currently engaged."

"When is the earliest we can begin?" Asquith said.

"My best guess... Ten to fourteen days," Kitchener said.

Asquith paused, considering. "Well, if that's it, let's get Sir Ian confirmed and be on with it. In the meantime, batter the hell out of the forts. Throw everything you have at them."

At the Dardanelles, shell after shell careened into the hillsides while the combined Turkish and German forces hunkered in their bunkers. Their situation was dire: the ammunition was almost all gone.

PALOU
March, 1915

Siranoush Araxian, sixty-seven years old, was the village matchmaker. She stood taller than both Lucine and Takouhi, almost two meters in height, and her long black hair was streaked with red strands of henna. Anahid gave her a wide berth whenever she came near. Her nickname for her was 'clink'.

"She clinks," she had said to Maritza.

"What do you mean?"

"I mean that when she walks, you can hear her before you see her!"

"Oh!" Maritza replied, laughing. "You mean because of all her gold!"

Siranoush's gold bracelets, among the largest that anyone in the village had ever seen, along with her huge gold circle earrings, combined with her flowing, billowing, black dresses to give her the appearance of a whirling gitano, a Romani wanderer. Still, Takouhi had to admit she was good at what she did.

"If they're bad, I'll give you the sign," Takouhi said as they walked.

Lucine nodded. It was also known that Siranoush fancied her simit to be much better than they really were. Once, Nune Abdourian had broken two teeth on the terrible things. "Hard as rocks, I didn't know," she had announced when Adamnapuyz Akgulian, Akgulian the dentist, had pulled them out.

As they drew closer to the door, it suddenly flung open, and with the wind drawing back into the house, there stood Siranoush Araxian.

"Ah! Come in! Come in!" she said, waving her hands, the bracelets clinking together.

"Thank you, Degeen Araxian," Lucine said.

"Oh, Lucine, you can call me Siranoush."

"Thank you," Lucine began.

"Degeen Siranoush," Siranoush said.

"Degeen Siranoush," Lucine said, correcting herself.

Lucine gave Takouhi a quick look and Takouhi shook her head slightly.

"Hello, Siranoush," Takouhi said, eye-to-eye.

"Hello, Takouhi," Siranoush said, returning the stare.

They entered Siranoush's home, and she drew past them, clinking as she went. She didn't offer to take their coats and they didn't venture to take them off. Siranoush was known for keeping her home cold. She wasn't about to waste good money by burning it.

"Please! Please sit! I have just made the coffee."

Lucine and Takouhi sat. Siranoush poured thick brown soorj, coffee. She set the simit in the middle.

"Drink!" she commanded, loudly clapping her hands, the bracelets clinking.

Lucine and Takouhi took careful sips. Could be that it was too hot, could be that it was terrible. Either way, they couldn't let it show. Siranoush was the type who relished compliments.

"Very good, Siranoush," Takouhi announced.

"Yes, it is so good, Deegeen Siranoush," Lucine added.

"Oh, thank you Takouhi," Siranoush said, smugly.

"Thank you Lucine. I am glad you like it!"

"Simit! You must try it!" she said, pushing the dish forward.

Lucine and Takouhi each took one and Takouhi expertly sniffed hers. Lucine hesitated for a moment, waiting, as Siranoush finished her coffee. It was just the instant that Takouhi needed, and she nudged her right foot against Lucine's.

Don't eat.

"Eat! Eat!," Siranoush commanded. They both took small bites, careful to chew on their back teeth, the strong ones.

"Mmm!" they announced in unison.

"I am glad you like them!" Siranoush said, pleased. She crossed her arms. "Now. What service may I perform for you?"

Lucine slowly put the simit down, so as not to draw attention to it.

"Deegeen Siranoush," she said. "You of course remember my son, Hagop?"

"Yes, yes," Siranoush said, nodding up and down. "Hagop. Yes." Lucine paused for a moment.

"Come, my dear, how can Siranoush help you?"

"There is a girl."

Siranoush unfolded her arms and put her hands on the table, all business.

"Who is this girl?" she asked, leaning forward.

"She is from Bitlis," Lucine began. You know Azniv Khatchaturian. No, her name is Samuelian now."

"Yes, yes," Siranoush said, impatiently.

"She is Azniv's sister," Lucine said. "Sona."

Siranoush leaned back in her chair and once again folded her arms."Aha!" she said. "I see that Hagop has learned well!" She looked from Takouhi to Lucine. "He has inherited his good sense from his mother!"

"What do you know of her?" Takouhi said.

"Father is a tailor. Mother is a seamstress," Siranoush declared. She looked at them. "Of course, the girl is herself honorable and chaste."

"You know all this?" Lucine said.

Siranoush shook her head and laughed. She tapped her right temple with her index finger. "It is all in here."

Lucine looked at Takouhi who nodded.

"My family would like to make an offering of our intentions," Lucine said.

Siranoush nodded, gravely.

"I will undertake it immediately and leave tomorrow," she said. She looked at them both. "For my trouble, you will provide me with one bag of bulgur and two chickens. If it is to progress, we will discuss further compensation."

Lucine nodded.

"Good," Siranoush said. She stood up. "Now I must prepare. There is much to do."

It had been a long day and Souren's father, Dikran, had only to punch the leather and affix the eyelet through which the laces would be strung. Then he would be done.

The door opened.

"Ah, Souren, you are a little early today," he said, not looking up.

The two kevasses, policemen, stepped forward.

"Jamgochian, Dikran?"

Dikran looked up, alarmed. "Yes?" he said, rising to his feet. "May I help you?"

"You are Jamgochian?"

"Yes, I am Jamgochian."

The second policeman said nothing, keeping his eyes on Dikran. The other stepped forward.

"You will supply fifteen pairs of shoes each week and perform all repair services without charge for all Turkish military persons."

"I do not understand," Dikran said, blinking rapidly. It was an affectation that would return, especially in moments of great stress.

"You will do as you are told, Jamgochian, or face the consequences of your insolence."

"But I have done nothing wrong," he stammered.

The silent policeman stepped forward and with blinding speed slapped Dikran across the face, hard, drawing red. The breath left Dikran's lungs and he crumbled to the floor. He put his hand to his mouth and looked at the blood.

"Many good Turkish soldiers die each day so that you may live here making your shoes," the second policeman said.

"Fifteen shoes, " the first policeman said.

"Yes, yes! Fifteen shoes!" Dikran said. "Anything."

The two policemen turned and left.

"Papa! Papa! Are you all right?" Souren said, rushing in. He grabbed a cloth from the table and pressed it against his father's face.

"I am fine. It is nothing."

"Come, let me see!" Souren implored. "I saw them leaving. What did they want?" Dikran put his hand over Souren's and drew it away from his face. He looked into his eyes.

"Souren. Say nothing to your mother about this."

"But papa..."

"Listen to your father. It is better left forgotten."

Siranoush had summoned them early.

"Thank you for bringing my provisions," she announced, tapping the basket beside her. Lucine and Takouhi had provided the meal that she would eat on her journey. Takouhi and Lucine looked at one another. As if they had been given a choice.

"A safe journey, Deegeen Siranoush," Lucine said.

"Good luck," Takouhi added.

"Fear not!" Siranoush said. "I will return in a few days time."

She looked ahead and yelled.

"Yertank!"

She pulled down hard on the reins and the donkey started moving.

"Pretty spry for an old woman," Lucine said.

"I'll give the old bat that," Takouhi said, laughing.

If Siranoush met with success, the men would go next.

BITLIS

Though Bitlis lay some one hundred sixty kilometers to the southeast of Palou, Siranoush Araxian, full of fire in her esh-drawn buggy, traveled the distance in three-quarters of the time that it usually took. Lucine and Takouhi had roasted a chicken and Siranoush sat, cleaning the bird to the bone, throwing the scraps into the dense woods. It was late evening when she pulled into the village square. The esh snorted and fell instantly into a semi-trance, eager to rest.

"Getsir!" Wait, she commanded.

She walked across the small square, looking at the houses that were arrayed, three by three.

"Excuse me!"

"Yes?" the man answered.

"I am looking for the home of Khatchaturian," Siranoush asked. The man looked at his wife and turned back to Siranoush.

"Khatchaturian who is the tailor or Khatchaturian who is the black-smith?"

"The tailor!"

"Go to the right, pass five houses, cross the street to his shop. He lives in the back."

"Thank you. Good night," she said, rushing off.

Siranoush crossed the street and walked up to the glass window of the Khatchaturian Tailor Shop.

She peered inside. It looked very neat, very in order. She made a mental note and walked to the back of the dwelling, checking the metal plate that was affixed to the jamb.

"Khatchaturian."

"Hmm," she said, stepping closer and tapping the metal. "Brass."

Another mental note.

She knocked, loudly, three times. Within moments, Elise was at the door, needlepoint in her left hand.

"Yes?"

"Mrs. Khatchaturian?" Siranoush inquired.

"Yes, it is I," Elise replied, slightly confused. It was odd to receive visitors at this hour. But that was just as Siranoush had planned.

"Better to get them late after their day is done," her mother, Soor-pouhi, also a matchmaker, had said. "That way you see them at their worst and find what they are really like!"

Siranoush stepped forward and reached out her hand.

"I am pleased to meet you. I am Siranoush Araxian from Palou."

"Hello," Elise said, shaking her hand. "How may I help you?"

"No, it is I who am here to help you," Siranoush replied. Several mental notes had already been saved: good work ethic; sews at night; good appearance; good manners.

First impressions were important; the daughter would be like the mother. If the mother didn't sweep after the meal, the daughter wouldn't sweep after the meal. If the mother cut short the amount of maleb she put in the choereg, so would the daughter. These weren't idle musings or conjecture. They were based on observation and her study of human nature.

"I am sorry for the late hour," Siranoush said, continuing. "I have been asked to come on behalf of the Melkonian family."

Elise paused. "Please come in," she said.

The house was warm, and as Siranoush passed by the fire, she took mental snapshots of the room. Makur: clean. Nishan sat, reading his journal, and as Elise pushed the door closed, he stood.

"Let me take your coat," Elise offered.

Siranoush nodded, removed her thick, heavy coat, and handed it to her.

"This is my husband, Nishan," Elise said. "Nishan, this is Siranoush Araxian."

"Pleased to meet you," Nishan said.

"It is my pleasure," she said, nodding.

"Please have a seat," Elise said, "You must be tired from your journey."

"Yes, thank you," Siranoush said. She sat and Nishan took his seat at the head of the table.

Elise moved quickly and methodically and within minutes there were cups of coffee, just made with the jezveh. Siranoush looked around; everything was in excellent order. She leaned slightly to the right and through the bedroom door, she caught a glimpse of Sona reading a book.

'Lovely girl,' she thought to herself.

Again, more mental notes. Reads. Studies. Idle hands are the devil's workshop, but not in this house.

Elise laid out plates of choereg, boereg, and slices of basturma. Siranoush took a deep whiff of the food. It smelled delicious.

"Please help yourself, Mrs. Araxian," Elise said.

"Please call me Siranoush."

Another mental note. Minds her elders. Good girl. So, too, will the daughter.Elise reached for the jezveh and filled Siranoush's cup. The jezveh, a brass cup with a long wooden handle, was filled with water, freshly ground coffee, and sugar. Invariably some of the grounds poured out with the liquid. After the soorj had been consumed, the cup would be swirled around, casting the grounds this way and that. They would then be read, the holder's future decided by the size and the lie of the precious remains.

"The coffee is very good," Siranoush said.

"Thank you," Elise replied. "Please have something to eat. You must be hungry."

Siranoush reached for the choereg and took a bite. It was excellent. Just the right amount of maleb, grindings from cherry pits, gave the choereg a sweet taste.

"Very tasty," she said.

Elise nodded. "Thank you. My grandmother's recipe."

Siranoush smiled and let a few moments pass. When she had finished her coffee, she began.

"As I said earlier, I have been asked by the Melkonian family to bring you good tidings and wishes." She paused for a moment and looked at them. "You are aware that there is a son? Hagop?"

Elise nodded. "Yes. We have met him."

"Then you are aware that there is interest in Sona?"

Elise and Nishan exchanged glances.

"Yes," Elise said, with a small margin of a smile. "Both looked as if lightning had struck."

Siranoush threw her head back, her wild hair blowing about, and burst into laughter, long, hearty, and deep. It was just the right moment, too, for it broke the tension.

"Yes, yes!" she said. "Well, that is good news! At least we have something to work with!"

Elise and Nishan sat, amazed at the spiritedness of their guest. Siranoush leaned forward and looked at them.

"But it is now my function to find if there is interest on the part of your family." She looked from Nishan to Elise, waiting for a response. Elise looked at Nishan, who nodded.

"There is interest," Nishan said. "Provided that we can be assured that Sona will be properly matched."

"Naturally," Siranoush replied. "You should expect nothing less."

Siranoush finished her coffee and looked at the grounds: nothing objectionable.

"Good, then," she said. "Now we may begin. First, tell me about Sona's schooling and activities."

Siranoush lay on the small mattress, made from thick warm blankets, snoring loudly. From the moment that Sona got up to the moment she went to bed, Siranoush wanted to know everything. School, housework, church activities, friends, accomplishments. She had to be thorough. She had to create a proper report. Behavior could be faked for a few moments, a few days, but the zebra could not change his stripes. It was what it was. And Siranoush knew how to spot a fake. That was, after all, her gift.

Nishan was fast asleep and Elise was moments away from retiring. As she slowly opened the door, Sona turned to her, wide-awake.

"Sona? Can you not sleep?"

"No, mama," she said, slowly shaking her head.

Elise nodded and stepped forward. She walked toward the small mattress and sat on the edge. She stroked Sona's long hair.

"Sona," she began. "A woman has come from Palou…"

"Yes, I know, mama."

Elise stopped for a moment and looked at her. Their eyes met and Elise resumed stroking her hair.

"You remember I used to do cun cush mazuht when you were small?"

"Yes, I remember," Sona said, smiling slightly. "It put me to sleep every time."

"Sona, this woman…"

"Yes, mama," Sona said, looking up.

Elise rested her hands on her lap. Their eyes met.

"I must know what are your feelings, my daughter."

Sona looked at her for a moment then dropped her eyes.

"You know these things, mama."

Elise bent over and kissed Sona's cheek.

"Sleep well, my girl. Everything will be fine."

"Yes, mama. I know it will be."

The days passed quickly and Siranoush saw much. Always from a distance, but close enough to observe fully. Sona hard at work in Nishan's shop; singing in the church choir; walking with the other girls. Standing out from them. Radiant.

Once a week, the women and the girls would go to the communal bath. In Bitlis, this was usually done on Shapat Or, Saturday. Even in the baths, Siranoush watched, taking note of Sona's figure. She did so discreetly, but being thorough meant being complete. Sona's figure was full: her breasts were ample, her hips wide enough to bear enough children. Her skin was clear, dark tan, the color of good coffee, and without any blemish that Siranoush could distinguish. Her legs were long and firm. Not muscular, but firm. All in all, the only fault she could find was that the feet were a bit on the large size.

Big feet, she noted. After all, she had to show that she had been thorough.

PALOU

Lucine, Sarkis, Takouhi, and Bedros sat, watching incredulously as Siranoush gobbled down bite after bite of everything that Lucine put out before her.

'My God! She eats like a horse!' Takouhi thought.

Siranoush finished the rest of her coffee, swirled around the grounds, and sat for a moment, studying them. Both Hagop and Anahid had been sent to Souren's house.

Siranoush made a clucking sound with her tongue, glanced one last time into the cup, and then put it aside. Takouhi shook her head but said nothing.

"A good catch, of that I have no doubt," Siranoush said. "The girl is a fine seamstress. Not an expert, mind you, but in that she shows great possibilities." She looked at Takouhi and then to Lucine. "She has a beautiful voice and knows without consultation to the song books all of the church hymnal songs." She threw back her scarf. "She is also of fine figure. Her form will bear many children." Lucine looked from Sarkis to Takouhi.

"And of the family? There is interest?"

"Oh, yes!" Siranoush said, emphatically. "Of that you can be sure! Previous meetings between the boy and the girl did not go unnoticed by the mother."

Sarkis looked from Bedros, who nodded, and then to Takouhi, who also nodded, and then finally to Lucine. She looked at him for a moment and then slowly nodded.

"Very well, then," he said. "There is interest on both sides. We proceed."

Siranoush nodded. "Good. Then, as is tradition, I will return with the men. When you have decided on the compensation for the girl's family, send for me and we will make the journey to Bitlis."

PART THREE

THE DARDANELLES

The fortress at Anadolu Hamidie stood on the Right Bank, exactly opposite the Kilid-Ul-Bahr fortress, at the entrance of the Inner Straits. For the Entente to reach the Marmora, they would first have to pass through the mouth. They would then travel past Sedd-Ul-Bahr and Kum Kale, which the Entente was now battering mercilessly. Next came the Outer Dardanelles and Eren-Keui Bay, where opposing artillery and gunnery stations would attempt to sink them, the waters becoming gradually more shallow.

Once they had cleared Eren-Keui, approximately eight miles from the mouth, they would then encounter the minefield. The landmasses would constrict again, quickly become narrower, and artillery and howitzers from the Dardanos Battery would hammer the ships. As they reached the end of the minefield, they would come into contact with the parallel forts of Kilid-Ul-Bahr and Anadolu Hamidie. Again, they would encounter heavy artillery.

But, if they were able to pass through this gauntlet, they would be totally unencumbered. The Inner Straits lay just beyond, then the Sea of Marmora, and then it would be on to Constantinople. It was a daunting task. But the reward was the jewel: Constantinople.

Both Enver and Von Sanders knew that they could delay passage of the ships. But without heavy artillery, the key lay in the ability to cause a large traffic jam. They had to disable enough ships further up, in the Outer Dardanelles, before they had even entered the minefield.

CONSTANTINOPLE

Talaat, Nazim, and Sakir sat, listening intently.

"This telegram will be sent via cipher to the outlying regions," Enver said. He looked at each of them. "I expect absolute secrecy and accordance." He looked at Nazim. "Dr. Nazim, you will transcribe."

Nazim nodded and began writing as Enver dictated.

"Deport any Armenian over five years of age. Separate Armenians who serve in our army. Take them to desolate areas and shoot them."

Talaat said nothing. He kept his eyes on Nazim and Sakir.

Morgenthau was eager for the latest news. Ever since Mallet and Bompard had left, he looked forward to meeting with Taylor.

"Well, the word from London is not good," Taylor said. "Carden's at the Dardanelles and is shelling the outer fortresses." He looked at Morgenthau. "Word is that Churchill is champing at the bit to get the German ships."

"It's too late, Major," Morgenthau said. "Passage is too difficult. It's too narrow, too shallow."

Taylor nodded. "But who knows what the War Council will do?"

Morgenthau nodded. "My God, I can't believe it's going to come this close."

THE DARDANELLES
18 March 1915

Eighteen ships were ready now. The first line was ferocious: Agamemnon, Lord Nelson, Inflexible, and the Elizabeth. The French ships were in the second line.

The gears were being turned now, and the gun turrets rose, taking position.

The blasts came in a stagger progression of four seconds. Bang! Bang! Bang! Bang! One after another, the six-inch guns joined with the fourteen-inch guns. On and on it went, the copper shells piling up so quickly that the men could scarcely keep up with the pace. Steaming hot, the shells were ejected, clanging against the metal deck.

"More! Send up more!"

"Aye, aye sir!"

And at the end of the third hour, the forts had been blasted into nothing more than piles of sand and wood, the bodies of the soldiers buried deep beneath. The initial defense positions, Sedd-Ul-Bahr, Kum Kale, and Intépé Battery were all silent.

The minesweepers were deployed and they made short work of the thin line of mines and steel mesh netting across the entrance to the mouth.

Ashore, those who were stationed at Kilid-Ul-Bahr and Anadolu Hamidie could only wait. The ships were still out of range. The guns at Dardanos were capable of reaching the warships as they entered Eren-Keui Bay, but their fifteen-centimeter diameter meant that they would have to be extremely fortunate to inflict any serious damage.

Two of the French vessels, the Bouvet and the Gaulois, maneuvered into position, followed by those from the British contingent: the Irresistible, Ocean, and Inflexible. To the rear, more than a dozen ships waited, their lookouts peering through binoculars. Merten and Von Sanders could only wait. Enver had already returned to Constantinople.

When it came, it happened so suddenly that the soldiers at Dardanos were not sure if their guns had hit their mark or whether there had been an explosion in the munitions store onboard the ship. But as the Gaulois drew forward, a tremendous explosion hit from below the water. The invisible line of twenty mines that Enver secretly ordered laid had been breached.

"Mines!"

"We swept them!"

"They're not supposed to be there!"

The Gaulois stalled, and then, trying to reverse, the gears screeched as the salt water rushed in, scalding the hot iron.

At Dardanos, a huge cheer went up as the men watched the Gaulois beach herself on a small strip of land. As the Bouvet turned starboard, the ship was torn apart, large metal chunks flying in all directions. A huge cloud of black and blue smoke went up, and the men scattered, vainly trying to get on deck. The water rushed into the massive hole, pushing them back. Suddenly, the munition stores were ignited, touching off an enormous explosion.

Less than one minute after she first hit the mine, the Bouvet disappeared underwater, taking the lives of six hundred and twenty men with her.

"Huzzah! Huzzah!" cheered the soldiers on land.

"It is working! The Infidels!"

And now it was the Inflexible that hit a mine and immediately lost most of her main steering. She was able to turn slightly and began steaming out of the Straits. Then the Irresistible met her fate. She was within moments of blasting the façade of the Dardanos into oblivion when the cap of the mine was triggered. She wobbled and faltered as the soldiers in the fortresses watched with glee.

Steam, spray, and black clouds of smoke were making it difficult to see through the already chaotic scene. And now it was the Ocean that ground to a halt, unable to move. So much had gone so badly in so little time. And as the combined forces of the Entente fleet retreated, the fortress commanders could not believe what they were seeing. By nightfall, the ships on the sea were silent, their crews still unable to grasp how calamitous it had been.

In the forts, the men sat smoking, and the sound of an oud and a soldier's singing drifted from one fort to the next, the words of Chanakkale Ichinde, In the Dardanelles, filling the air.

And beneath the folds of Eren-Keui Bay, the crew of the Bouvet slept in their watery grave.

CONSTANTINOPLE
23 March 1915

Five days had passed since the disaster, and while the Fleet was still under orders to batter the fortresses, they held a line just past the shelling distances the fortresses could muster.

"Ten ships were lost," Morgenthau said, consulting the papers spread out on the table.

"What happened?" Josephine asked.

"The report says that a defensive line of mines went undetected." He looked up from the papers and sighed deeply.

"They'll have to go by land now, won't they?" Josephine asked.

"Yes," Morgenthau said, nodding slowly. "Taylor says to mount something of that scope will take at least a month." He looked at her. "This is just the beginning."

PALOU

The dry wood crackled in the fire. Hagop and Anahid sat studying as Lucine, Takouhi, and Maritza finished their coffee. Maritza found moving about particularly difficult.

"There must be two or three in there," Armen had joked.

"It is time for me to go," Maritza said, pushing up from the chair. She took a few steps and suddenly her legs seemed to go one way while her belly went another.

"Maritza!" Lucine shouted, jumping up. Hagop was on his feet in an instant and put his hands under her arms, easing her into a chair.

"I think the baby is ready now," Maritza said, managing a slight smile.

"Hagop!" Lucine commanded. "Go and get Mrs. Avakian! Quick! Anahid! Go to Maritza's house and tell them to come!"

Hagop and Anahid put on their coats and rushed out. Both Sarkis and Bedros were down at the market and had not yet returned.

"I think it is better if I lie down," Maritza managed.

"Not just yet," Takouhi said gently.

"You have to wait a little more," Lucine said.

Maritza nodded, and took a deep breath.

"That's a good girl," Takouhi encouraged. "Breathe a little."

"Do not worry," Lucine said, "this baby is waiting."

Hagop knocked rapidly on the door. He waited a few moments and then knocked again. He wasn't sure who he should bring if she wasn't home. He couldn't remember anyone else other than Old Lady Avakian.

Perouz Avakian was the village midwife, and she had delivered practically everyone in Palou. She must have been at least eighty-five years old; she never said. Midwives were treated with great respect, not only because they often represented the only medical care available but also because their place in history had been cast in biblical terms. Perouz's mother had explained it:

"In Genesis, it is written that midwives deliver the newborn. In Exodus, the midwives would not kill the male babies. They suffered the wrath of the King of Egypt."

The door opened with such force that it knocked Hagop back a step. He looked up and saw her standing in the doorway, her hot white hair billowing around her, anger on her dark lined face:

Perouz Avakian.

For a moment, he wondered how such an old woman could be so quick and so strong.

"Hagop!"

"Mrs. Avakian! I am sorry to disturb you! Please come! It is Mrs. Jamgochian. She is having her baby!"

"Ah!" she said. "What is the fuss? No baby is born in this village without Perouz Avakian!" she said defiantly. She drew her hair back and tied it into a bun atop her head.

"Now you will take me, my boy."

Now Perouz sat, alone, amidst the revelers. The house was full and Sarkis was busy congratulating Dikran and his new son. Maritza sat quietly on a mattress of several heavy blankets, holding her new baby boy, Vahe, named in honor of Dikran's father.

"Togh gyanket yergaree!" Sarkis said, raising the glass. Let your life be long.

" Genatsuht!" echoed the wellwishers.

"Thank you, thank you!" Dikran said, raising his glass.

Anahid sat next to Maritza, admiring Vahe. Maritza was pale, but the birth had gone well. Perouz had done it quickly. Just at the right moment, she had pressed her left hand and poked with her right and suddenly there was the baby.

Lucine and Takouhi were busy cooking eggs for the group. Hagop and Souren each grabbed a havgit-hahts, literally egg-bread, and took a bite. Armen was already ahead of them. The men laughed loudly at something Garbis said and the glasses clinked together. Perouz, calm and collected, sipped coffee from a small cup.

"How many babies do you think Old Lady Avakian has delivered?" Armen asked.

Souren nudged him. "Do not call her that."

"Why? She is an old lady."

"That may be true, but it is no way to talk about the woman who helped your mother deliver you!"

"Me?" Armen said, chewing.

"Yes, you," Hagop said. "And Souren, and me, too!"

"And most of the people in this village," added Souren.

The boys looked over towards Perouz. She reached inside a small leather pouch and pulled out a small tin. They watched as she reached in her thumb and forefinger and pulled out a pinch of snuff and snorted it. The boys turned back to their circle.

"You know," Armen said, "ever since I was small, I can never remember seeing her husband. What happened to him?"

Hagop started to chuckle. "Oh him," he said. "He died!" Souren and Armen looked at one another.

"That is not very funny," Souren whispered. "Old Lady, I mean, Mrs. Avakian is right over there."

"And she can probably hear every word we are saying!" Armen added.

Hagop leaned in slightly as did the others. "The story goes," he said, "that when she got married, her husband had already been married four times and had outlived every one of his wives."

"And?" Armen said.

"So, on the wedding day, before the priest begins, Old Lady Avakian digs her shoe deep into his foot, leans over, and says, with the sweetest, kindest voice, 'You may have buried four women but I am going to bury you!' And she did!"

Souren and Armen looked at Hagop. Then, in unison, the turned their heads toward Perouz. She slowly looked back at them as if she had heard everything that they had said. The boys quickly looked away.

The next morning, Sarkis and Bedros sat, flanking Siranoush in the family carriage. Tradition held that if there were interest on both sides, the men from the boy's family would travel to the girl's home to carry out the negotiations. Siranoush would act as the go-between. As Sarkis took the reins, Lucine, Takouhi, Hagop, and Anahid stood by. It was bitterly cold, and they were wrapped well against the weather. Hagop looked on somehow detached from it all.

"Travel safely," Lucine called out.

Sarkis looked at her and smiled, hoping that it would reassure her.

"We will return in two days, if the weather is clear," he said.

"Oh! Do not worry!" Siranoush said, waving her right hand with a flourish. "Siranoush never fails!"

Sarkis looked at Hagop and nodded. He snapped down the reins, and with a "Hahh!" spirited the esh into movement.

The family turned and began walking back toward the house. Hagop looked at the back of the carriage, growing smaller and smaller.

"Come," Anahid said, tugging at his arm. "It is too cold to stay out here."

BITLIS

It was almost midnight when they pulled into Bitlis.

"This way. Follow me," Siranoush commanded.

Sarkis reached into the back of the carriage and slung a sack over his shoulder.

"Unbelievable," Sarkis said. "Look at her."

"Yes, I know," Bedros said. "It looks as if she just got up after a night of rest."

"This is the father's shop," she said, pointing.

Sarkis and Bedros peered inside; it looked impressive.

"Do not worry," Siranoush said. "I told you it was very busy. The home is in the back."

Elise opened the door to greet them.

"Welcome," she said, "please come in from the cold!"

"Thank you!" Siranoush said as she swept in.

"Please," Elise said, beckoning Sarkis and Bedros enter.

"Thank you," Sarkis said.

"Madam," Bedros added.

As they entered, the warmth of the fire was an instant relief. Siranoush removed her coat.

"Let me take that," Nishan said, stepping forward.

"Thank you," she said, thrusting her coat and gloves into his hands. Nishan's brother, Hrant, stood by.

"Let me take your coats," Elise said to Sarkis and Bedros.

"First I will make the introductions," Siranoush said." She gestured toward Sarkis. "This is the boy's father, Sarkis. And the boy's grandfather, Bedros."

Nishan and Hrant stepped forward and shook their hands.

"I am Nishan Khatchaturian, and this is my brother Hrant."

Elise had laid out the blankets and pillows by the yertik, and as the hour was late and they were all tired, Siranoush declared that negotiations would begin in the morning.

"There will be nothing done in haste," Siranoush declared. And then she fell into a deep sleep, snoring loudly and heavily.

As the sun came up, the table was laid with plates and foodstuffs of all kinds. Siranoush reached for a thick slice of bread and looked at the preserve jar.

"That one is apricot," Elise said, handing her a knife.

"Ah!" Siranoush said, "just what I need. Apricots go through you when you are blocked."

Elise looked at Nishan and Bedros looked at Sarkis. Siranoush merrily spread a generous portion of jam onto the thick piece of bread. They sat for a few moments, each side wondering how to begin. That would be left to Siranoush. Finally, she looked up from her plate.

"Very good then," Siranoush said.

"How was your journey?" Nishan asked.

"It went very fast," Sarkis replied. "The cakes are very good," he offered.

"Yes, very tasty," Bedros added.

"Thank you," Nishan replied. "They were made by my daughter."

"Ah, that reminds me," Sarkis said, reaching for his sack. He opened it, pulling out a heavy crock container.

"This is lamb," he said, looking at Elise. "Packed in fat." He looked at Nishan. "My son's lambs."

Nishan raised his eyebrows slightly and accepted the container as Sarkis pushed it forward.

"Thank you. That is very kind." Nishan looked at Sarkis, eyeing him directly. "My daughter is a good girl and has been raised correctly."

"Yes. That is very clear," Sarkis replied, eye-to-eye.

Nishan nodded and eased slightly. Elise said nothing. She had the right to be present, but she did not have the right to interfere. This was between the fathers.

"Mrs. Araxian tells me that your son is an excellent shepherd, respectful of his elders," Nishan said.

Sarkis nodded. Both Bedros and Hrant sat silent. They would say nothing unless they felt their guidance was necessary.

"My son is also a gardener," Sarkis said. "He can make anything grow."

Nishan nodded.

"I would like to say something," Nishan said, looking at Siranoush.

"Of course," she replied.

"Well, then," Nishan began. "We have spoken of this, my wife and my brother that is, and we feel that the children will have no problem with this arrangement." He looked at Sarkis. "You and I have both seen this with our own eyes."

"Yes," Sarkis replied. "My wife and I have seen them."

"Good, then," Nishan said. He paused. "There is the matter of the dowry..."

Sarkis looked from Bedros to Siranoush. She nodded.

"Yes," Sarkis replied. "My family will contribute the bridal bed covering, handmade in silk." He looked from Nishan to Elise. "My wife's work, of course."

Nishan nodded, approving. "My daughter will bring with her silver candle holders."

"Very good," Sarkis said. "There is a small family khatchkar. It has been in the family for five generations." He looked at Bedros, who nodded his consent. "With my father's permission, this will be willed to my son and to his new wife."

"Very good," Nishan said. He turned to Bedros. "I am sure it is a beautiful object and it will be a considerable addition to their household."

Elise opened her mouth to speak, caught herself, and looked at Siranoush, who nodded her assent.

"My daughter will carry our family Bible," she said. "It will be wrapped in her grandmother's silk cover."

"Of course, there is the matter of the actual wedding day," Nishan said.

"My family will undertake the obligation of the food and the services of the priest," Sarkis declared.

"And my family will sew the bridal gown and the garments for the members of the wedding party," Nishan said.

"The materials will be made of the finest silk," Elise said. She looked at Siranoush. "Pearl buttons, gold trim."

Siranoush nodded, pleased.

Sarkis looked at Bedros, who nodded.

"I am duly impressed, Mr. Khatchaturian," Sarkis said.

"As am I, Mr. Melkonian," Nishan said.

They looked at one another and then to Siranoush. She nodded, solemnly. She stood and looked from Nishan to Sarkis. "Then we accept each other's position?"

Sarkis nodded to Bedros and stood.

"Mer khoskuh goodank," he said, eyeing Nishan. "We give you our word."

Nishan looked at Elise and Hrant. They both nodded to him and he stood.

"Menk tsezee guh havadank," he said, looking at Sarkis. "We receive and accept your word."

"Then it is done!" Siranoush said, loudly clapping her hands together, and grinning broadly. She reached down into her satchel, produced a bottle of raki, and set it on the table.

"Now we will drink to this agreement!"

Elise stood and quickly returned with a tray of small glasses. Siranoush filled them.

"To your daughter," Sarkis said, raising his glass toward Nishan.

"And to your son," Nishan answered.

"Genatsuht!" Siranoush said, tilting her head back and emptying the glass. They looked at her for a moment and then drank from their glasses.

"Congratulations to you all!" Siranoush said.

The door swung open and Sona entered, carrying several folded garments. They looked up, staring at her. She stopped, frozen. Sarkis and Bedros looked at one another and Sona's eyes went to her mother.

Elise took a step forward and Sona rushed to her. Elise looked into her daughter's eyes and kissed her forehead. Sona said nothing, her face all at once complex and full of so many questions. "And now to my beautiful daughter," Nishan said. He drank and banged the empty glass onto the table.

PALOU

More raki was poured into the empty glasses and Sarkis drank. The house was full of family and neighbors. Souren and Armen were busy shaking Hagop, who stood, appearing to be dazed by it all. Was it really happening?

"Of that you can be sure!" Souren said, laughing.

"You are very lucky," Armen said. "She is very beautiful!" He looked at Souren. "And that is good news for you, Souren," he said.

"What do you mean?" Souren said, turning to him.

"Well," Armen said, grinning. "If someone who looks like Hagop can capture such a beauty, think what a face like yours could get!"

And so it had gone, through the evening and into the early hours. Too much food and too much drink. Tomorrow they would pay the price.

Ah, but that was tomorrow.

LONDON

Hamilton sat with his three senior commanders, Lt. General Birdwood, Sir Aylmar Hunter-Weston, and Maj. General Paris. Hamilton still felt the Fleet could push through the Straits, but the weather was not cooperating; the preparations for a full-scale landing at Gallipoli continued. Birdwood commanded the ANZACS, the Australian and New Zealand Army Corp, Hunter-Weston the Twenty-Ninth Division.

Churchill sat in his study, thinking. Fisher had resigned five days earlier. At the Dardanelles, the weather had become the enemy and there were no prospects for it to brighten. On land, at Dardanos, Kilid-Ul-Bahr, Gaba Tepe, and Anadolu Hamidie, the German commanders kept driving the Turks. Under cover of night, they changed the gun emplacements, strung the beaches with barbed wire, and continued mining. Von Sanders was now in command at Gallipoli; he had assumed command of the Turkish Fifth Army.

Kitchener, meanwhile, knew a landing on the Peninsula would be delayed. This meant the third week of April before everything could be ready. Hospitals had been set up both at Malta and Egypt, but the troops would need constant supplies of water, food, and ammunition.

VAN
11 April 1915

The city of Van stood, almost two thousand meters above sea level, eighty kilometers to the east of Bitlis, bordering Lake Van. To the northeast, stood Mt. Ararat. The Armenians called Ararat Massis, and the smaller peak next to her, pokrig Massis, little Massis. Regardless of the time of year, there would always be a white covering of snow atop the peaks.

There were two parts of Van, the ancient walled city and the gardens. The fortress of Van had been built by the Urartians in the early ninth century, before Christ, and had, by the seventeenth century after Christ, been invaded by the Seljuks, Kurds, Mongols, Persians, and, finally, the Turks.

Surrounded by the lakes and mountains, the Vanetzis were almost entirely self-sufficient. The region was naturally fertile, and the men were skilled in ironwork, carpentry, and gold work. Education and literacy were held in high regard, and more than one hundred schools had been built. Within a three square kilometer area, thirty thousand Van Armenians lived in relative prosperity.

The Vanetzis had a saying.

"In Heaven, Faith. On Earth, Van."

The previous Vali of Van had maintained good relations with the Vanetzis. But all that was in the past now. Enver had installed his brother-in-law, Djevdet Bey, as the new Vali, and he had wasted no time in carrying out Enver's wishes. The group of Armenians gathered around, looking carefully at the posted edict that hung on the church wall.

"By order of Djevdet Bey, Vali of Van. Four thousand men of Armenian heritage are required to fill the ranks of the Ottoman Army."

Aram Manoukian turned from the edict. He was born in Zangezur, in the lower Caucasus amidst rugged mountains and dense forests. He was thirty-six years old, and was already a respected political leader.

There would be a meeting later that night, and he wanted to think about what alternatives they had.

"We are not obligated to furnish four thousand men. We have an option," Aram said.

"What do you mean?" Arshag asked. "The edict says we must provide them for military service."

Arshag Vramian had been born in Constantinople forty-four years earlier, and, like Aram, was a member of the Dashknaksutuin, Dashknak, political party. He served in Van as deputy to the Armenian political committee.

"No," Armenak said. "It is written law that we may furnish a portion of the men. Is that not correct, Aram?"

Armenak Yekarian, of the four men in the room, was the only Vanetsi. He was forty-six years old, with a clear complexion and a neatly trimmed black mustache. He commanded great respect from the other Vanetzis, and even though it had happened almost twenty years earlier, occasionally there would still be those who pointed at him, uttering the word 'Bashkale.'

Armenak paid no attention. It had been horror enough. He had been a fierce fighter, providing resistance to Abdul Hamid's regime during the atrocities. He was arrested, and was thrown into the prison at Bashkale, eighty kilometers southeast of Van. He had survived the tortures and, before the end of 1896, had been released. Upon his return to Van, he was given a hero's welcome.

"Yes," Aram, said, answering him. "We could provide, say, five hundred men, and pay an exemption for the remainder. We can still do this and abide by the law." He stroked his long, black handlebar mustache, thinking.

"That is all fine," Ishkhan said, "but it still does not solve the problem."

Aram, Arshag, and Armenak looked at him.

Ishkhan was born Nikoghazos Poghosian, in Karabagh, northeast of Van, and was the same age as Aram. Ishkhan, his nickname, meant prince. Like Arshag, he too, was a Dashknak, and had distinguished himself in seeking out Kurds who had massacred Armenians in 1896. He sported a neatly trimmed full beard and a thick shock of black hair.

"No, it solves nothing," Ishkhan continued. He stood up, shaking his head. "We will still be in the position of fighting against our brothers on the Russian side. And," he said, looking at the others, "in the last few weeks, things have begun to go upside down."

"There are reports that the Valis are demanding men from every village," Arshag said.

"But these men do not always reach their destination, do they?" Armenak added. "Many of these men have disappeared. To where?"

The other men sat, considering.

"There have been reports from the villages that the men are being rounded up, marched to the outskirts, and from there they are never heard from again," Ishkhan said.

"Under the pretext of military service, the inshaat taburu," Armenak added. "The construction regiments."

"We have to protect ourselves," Arshag said, looking at the others.

"The Vali will want something," Aram replied. "We furnish him with either men or money."

"There is another possibility," Ishkhan said. "We can resist."

The men looked at him. He was not a man who spoke rashly.

"It would be difficult," Armenak said, finally. "Not impossible, but very difficult. The problem is the arms; we have very little."

"Then we should begin planning, now," Ishkhan said. "We may not be given a choice."

Djevdet Bey, the Vali of Van, prided himself on results. Constantinople and Enver were counting on him to bring order to the eastern region. These Vanetzis were different from the rest, Djevdet knew; they would not just submit, as had the others. They were made of something else. But it was his job to break them; he resolved to do so quickly and efficiently.

"As long as the Dashknak leaders are among them, the Armenians here feel secure," an assistant said.

The man sitting next to him placed three photographs on the tufa stone table.

"The three Dashknak leaders are Arshak Vramian, Aram Manoukian, and their leader, known as Ishkhan. Manoukian is their political leader. He has organized them into a political council and has been active in a military nature." The man pushed forward another photograph.

"This is Vramian. He was involved at the Ottoman Bank."

Djevdet picked up the photograph and studied it. In 1896, a group of Armenians had attempted to stop business at the Ottoman National Bank in protest of unfair treatment, taxes, and violence against Armenians.

"This man is a terrorist," the aide said. "He has a long history of gunrunning, bomb making, and has written anti-Turkish propaganda while he was in America."

"This man was in America?" Djevdet asked, glancing at his assistant.

"Yes."

"Does he have ties there, now? Any powerful friends that may cause us problems?"

"Not that we know," the aide answered. "He has been here since sometime in 1908, possibly 1907."

Djevdet paused for a few moments, considering. He nodded for him to continue.

"This is Ishkhan." The photograph was fuzzy, but sufficient.

"So this is Ishkhan," Djevdet said, picking it up.

"Yes, Vali Bey. He is their fedayee. Their freedom fighter."

Djevdet nodded slowly. "And Ekarian?" he asked.

"We do not have a photograph of him," the aide said. "But we know that he is their military leader. He, alone, was born here, in Van. He knows the land better than any of them."

"Talk to me of their strength," Djevdet said.

"They do not have much," the first assistant said. "There are between twenty-five or thirty-thousand of them, but less than two thousand of them are capable of fighting."

"And weapons?" Djevdet asked.

"Nothing to speak of. Old rifles, some pistols, axes."

"Assume that they will refuse to give us the four thousand men," Djevdet said. "What is your estimate on how long it will take to put them down?"

The aides looked at one another. Finally, the third one spoke.

"If heavy artillery is brought to bear," he said, "it would be a matter of days, perhaps hours."

Djevdet studied Ishkhan's photograph. The aides watched him, but said nothing.

"I want you to get word to this Ishkhan," he said. "Tell him I want to set a meeting to enlist his aid in quelling some disturbances. We will pick a location where he will feel comfortable, say in Shatakh, or Hashir, or Moks. He will come with others, so the location must be close enough so that he will feel comfortable, but far enough that he will not be able to bring many men."

Djevdet paused, running the plan through his mind.

"Tell him there are some uprisings in other villages. Make him believe that if he comes to our assistance, we can arrive at some agreement regarding the enlistment of their men. After we are done with him, we will take care of his deputy, Vramian. Manoukian is a political type; he will seek a bargain. And as for Ekarian, without the other two, he will not be able to mass any resistance whatsoever." He nodded slowly, convinced.

"Cut off the head," he said. "Everything else dies."

The church anteroom was small and cramped, and Ishkhan, Arshag, Aram, and Armenak sat. Through the walls came the muffled sounds from the crowd gathered in the church. It was almost eleven o'clock at night.

"Today, the Vali sent his representatives," Aram said. "He has rejected our attempt to buy exemption even though it is written law." He looked at the others. "Khalil, the tall one, said that there are uprisings all around Moks and Hashir, and Shatakh." He looked at Ishkhan. "Khalil says that if Ishkhan goes to Shatakh and helps to stop the problems, Vali Bey will take a reduced number of men."

"It is a trap!" Arshag said.

"You do not know that," Ishkhan said, looking at him. "Besides, there is no alternative. If I do not go, then they will send their soldiers and take our men."

"But," Arshag began.

"You know that it is the only way," Ishkhan said. He looked at Armenak, whom he respected immensely. "What do you think?"

Armenak paused for a moment. "It is dangerous. Naturally, we will not let you go alone."

"I will go with you," Arshag began.

"No," Armenak said. He looked from Arshag to Aram. "None of us can go with him."

"He is right," Ishkhan said. "I will take three other men. If something happens to me, they will need you to lead them."

Armenak nodded.

"When will you leave?" Aram asked.

"In five days," Ishkhan said. "On the sixteenth."

The church was full and heads turned toward the four men as they entered.

"As you have heard, the attempt to buy exemption for our men has been rejected," Aram said. "Vali Bey is requesting our services in the mediation of a disturbance in Shatakh."

They looked at him, faces both eager and worried.

"I will go to Shatakh," Ishkhan said. "Aram, Arshag, and Armenak will remain here." He looked at the faces before him. "I shall leave in five days, but I must ask for three to go with me."

Man after man, young and old, raised his hand. Ishkhan looked at them, and slowly picked the three.

BITLIS

The period of betrothal usually lasted an entire year. Tradition held that it was the boy's family that traveled to the girl's home. At the head of the table, Sona stood, apart from everyone. Her dress was long, and covered her from neck to ankle, the material blue silk with green and red patterns in the shape of flowers: the dress cut by Nishan and stitched by Sona; the flowers by Elise. Her face was shrouded, covered in a delicate white veil.

She waited, opposite Father DerArtinian and her family's priest, Father DerSimonian. Behind them Hagop stood his view of Sona hidden by the two priests.

On the left side of the table stood Nishan, Elise, Hrant, Azniv, and Vache. On the right side: Lucine, Sarkis, Takouhi, Bedros, and Anahid. Through the open door, straining to get a look, stood Dikran, Souren,

Armen, and Garbis. They had all come, save for Maritza who remained in Palou with baby Vahe.

"Can you see anything?" Armen asked, nudging Souren.

"Yes," Souren said. "She is at the far end."

"Let me see," Armen said, pushing to the front.

"But she is beautiful," he said.

"Yes. Yes, she is," Souren agreed.

Father DerArtinian looked at Father DerSimonian who nodded. "Now that we are all present, we shall begin," Father DerArtinian said.

He nodded at Sona, who walked slowly toward Takouhi, the oldest female. Hagop leaned to his right, saw the blue of her dress and then finally all of her. As she drew near, Takouhi outstretched her hands and Sona took them in hers and kissed them both. Takouhi nodded, and gently pulled them away.

Sona walked backwards, retracing her steps. Her mother, Elise, was the next oldest, older than Lucine by one year. Elise held out her hands and Sona took them. She could feel her mother squeeze and it helped calm her. She could swear that her heart was beating so fast that it would burst through. She kissed her mother's hands for a long moment and then Elise slowly drew them away from her.

"What's happening?" Armen said. "I can't see anything!"

Sona made her way toward Lucine. Then it was to Azniv, and then to Anahid, the youngest. She looked down, waiting. There were so many eyes on her. She could feel them.

Father DerSimonian nodded at Lucine. She stepped slowly toward Sona. Friends and neighbors moved in slightly, looking in from the open door.

"Hagop's mother is going to her," Souren reported to Armen.

Lucine pushed back her left dress sleeve, revealing several gold bracelets, varying in size and shape. Each held particular significance in her life. This one at birth: lengthened now. That one at her betrothal, this one at the wedding. Since diamonds were scarce, it was gold that adorned the necks, ankles, hands, and fingers of Armenian women. If they owned it, they wore it.

Lucine looked at Takouhi for a moment and then removed one of the chains. It had been her betrothal bracelet, given to her by Takouhi.

The bracelet consisted of three sections of small oval links of gold. As Lucine removed it, tiny indentations were left on her skin.

She reached out for Sona's left hand and drew the bracelet around her wrist and closed the clasp. It fit well, although a bit snug. Lucine looked up, nodded slightly to Sona, and stepped back next to Sarkis. Outside the home, Armen, Souren, and the others struggled to get a view.

Sona stood, watching as Hagop slowly walked toward her. He stopped inches from her, followed by Father DerArtinian, with Hrant to the rear. Hagop could see her eyes through the veil, their deep chestnut brown staring back at him. He kissed her once, through the veil, directly on the forehead. She, in turn, took his hands and kissed them. There was a moment of silence and then they both turned, facing Father DerArtinian. He motioned for Hrant to hold the small gold cross above their heads.

"This day, we witness the declarations of two individuals and two families," he began. "The word has been tied and the word has been accepted."

He paused for a moment, clearing his throat.

"Hagop Melkonian. Sona Khatchaturian," he said, looking at them. "The period of this betrothal will last one year. During this time, you will both be virtuous. Though you will be separated by distance, you will spiritually grow together before you exist together. Remember that nothing will be denied to he who believeth in Christ, and nothing is more sacred than the bond of man and woman, husband and wife, mother and father. In this, you make your first commitment. May this one year pass brightly and quickly, and with prosperity."

He took one step forward and raised his cross.

"In the name of the Father, the Son, and the Holy Spirit, Amen."

"Amen," came the reply from the onlookers.

Father DerArtinian took their hands and turned them. Cheers erupted and Souren and Armen rushed in. The celebration began and continued for hours.

CONSTANTINOPLE
15 April 1915

Talaat put the pen down and waved the document to dry the fresh ink. There was a knock on the door and Enver, followed by Dr. Nazim, entered.

"I have just finished it," Talaat said. He cleared his throat. "To all Governors and Town Authorities. Russian and English governments have united to wage war against us. The Committee of Union and Progress has determined that our Armenian question be decided once and for all. We must exterminate this element and deport all Armenians to the deserts of Arabia."

He looked at Enver and Nazim. "At the sunrise of April twenty-fourth this order will be implemented. Anyone who protects Armenians shall be branded an enemy of the country."

He looked up from the document. Enver and Dr. Nazim nodded. Talaat signed his name, followed by Enver and Nazim.

"Now we are set," Talaat said. "The twenty-fourth of April."

PALOU

The days of Easter were solemn and devotional. During the Lenten period, the families would fast, eschewing all forms of meat. The ladies improvised, and the kuftah was made with wheat and walnuts or lentils instead of lamb. As Thursday evening approached, it was a day of total fasting, with only liquids taken. Throughout Friday and Saturday, Father DerArtinian saw to it that there were services three times a day.

On Saturday morning, Lucine and Takouhi were up early. Lucine was busy stirring a pot of boiling water and the smell of newly peeled onions filled the room. Anahid rested a basket of fresh eggs on the table next to the mound of onions and skins.

"Anahid, I will stir, and you put in the skins," Lucine said. She took the wooden spoon and began stirring as Anahid dropped the skins into the water.

Armen sat at a small bench in the back of his home. From a small sack he produced a piece of wood, a wooden mallet, chisels and files of various sizes. He pulled out a small jar that contained a white liquid. Then, he got to work.

Lucine stood, stirring the bubbling liquid.

"This batch is ready," she announced. She handed the wooden spoon to Anahid. "Anahid, take them out and put them in this dish."

"Yes, mama," Anahid said. She dipped the spoon into the liquid and carefully withdrew an egg.

"Perfect!" Takouhi announced. "Nice and brown."

Anahid brought the spoon to the surface with another perfectly brown egg.

"This one is better!" she announced.

Already, the wedge of wood was beginning to take shape. Woodwork came naturally to Armen. He stretched his fingers and continued to carve. Within the half-hour, he brushed the file back and forth over the wood, its surface growing smoother. He dipped the tip of the brush into the white liquid and held the wooden egg carefully.

Takouhi, Lucine, and Anahid sat at the table, surrounded by a mass of brown, yellow, red, and orange eggs.

"I think this is one of the best batches yet," Anahid said, satisfied.

Lucine smiled but said nothing. There was a church service only two hours from now and there was still much work to do.

Armen squinted, concentrating. He put the brush down, and carefully propped up the egg. He leaned back and smiled. Soon the wet egg was covered in the rays of the sun, where it would dry.

EASTER SUNDAY
4 April 1915

"And Jesus looked upon Mary and said, Touch me not, for I am not ascended to my Father, but go to my brethren, and say unto them, I ascend unto my Father, and your Father, and to my God, and to your God. Go forth to Galilee. There they will see me."

Father DerArtinian paused for a moment, letting the words hang there. Hagop stood next to Souren and Armen, their families beside them.

"And when the eleven disciples saw Him there, they worshipped Him. But some doubted. Then Jesus came to them and said, All authority on Heaven and on Earth has been given to me. Go and make disciples of all nations, baptizing them in the name of the Father, and of the Son, and of the Holy Spirit."

He closed his Bible and scanned their faces.

"And surely I am with you always, to the very end of the age."

He made the sign of the cross and they followed him.

"Krisdos haryav ee merelotz," he said. Christ has risen from the dead. "Orhnyal eh harutiunuh Krisdosi." Blessed is the resurrection of Christ.

The congregation turned to one another and echoed the greeting.

"Krisdos haryav ee merelotz," Hagop said, turning to Souren.

"Orhnyal eh harutiunuh Krisdosi," Souren answered.

They kissed each other on both cheeks and Hagop turned to Armen.

"Krisdos haryav ee merelotz."

"Orhnyal eh harutiunuh Krisdosi!"

It was early afternoon by the time they sat, surrounded by pots and pans brimming with delicacies of all kind, the basketful of colorful eggs in the middle of the table.

"Hagop, you will give our thanks this year," Sarkis said.

Hagop nodded. They bowed their heads and raised their palms upward.

"Dear Lord," he began. "Today you show us that there is nothing that cannot be done. Today you show us that belief is all that matters."

Sarkis looked in Lucine's direction. Neither had ever heard Hagop speak so... so...clearly.

"Today you show us that you have given to us your only son and that he died for all our sins. And that he lives today not only with you in your kingdom but with us in our hearts."

Anahid slowly inched her head up until she could see him. Was this really her brother?

He paused again. "For the food we are about to receive, for our good fortune, for our prosperity. All of this is in your hands. We are grateful and humble before you. Amen."

"Amen," everyone echoed.

"Abris!" Bedros said, turning to Hagop. "Now we eat!"

Lucine reached for the pilaf and passed it along. There was sempoog yev misovhorovatz, baked eggplant with lamb; vosbov abour, lentil soup; derev pattoug, stuffed grape leaves, and more.

Later, neighbors and the adults sat, socializing. Bedros had immediately fallen into a slumber, followed by Sarkis not fifteen minutes later. They had dozed off for at least an hour, oblivious to all, until they both awoke within seconds of one another.

"Ah! Welcome back!" Takouhi said.

Bedros looked at her and nodded, his eyes mischievously dancing.

"Ah! But where did you go?" he shot back.

Anahid gently cupped her right hand around the egg she had chosen, a yellow one, flecked with spots of brown. She closed her eyes, bracing herself.

"Crack!"

Hagop, Souren, and Armen leaned in slightly to see whose egg had cracked. Anahid opened her eyes and was relieved to see that it wasn't hers. Maritza looked at her egg and then turned it so the others could see the big dent.

"Oh!" Anahid exclaimed. "I have the champion egg! I have the champion egg!" She opened her hand, and held it up for everyone to see.

Souren took the challenge. "We will see about that," he said, sitting down opposite her. He looked at the basketful of eggs and pointed his right index finger at one, then another, trying to make a choice.

"Oh, just pick one!" Armen said.

"No, I take my time," Souren said. He picked up two eggs, one in each hand, judging their weight.

Finally, after much deliberation, he chose one.

"I am ready!" he declared.

He curled his fingers around the egg and outstretched his arm. Anahid hit his egg with hers.

"Crack!"

Souren looked at Anahid and then down at his egg, which was badly splintered.

Anahid smiled and then turned her egg for all to see: no cracks.

"Now. Who is next?" she said, turning to the others.

"I think that leaves me," Armen said, sitting.

"Very well, then," Anahid said.

"Pick an egg," Hagop offered.

Armen looked over the eggs in the basket, moving them back and forth, examining them.

"No, I do not like any of these," Armen said, shaking his head.

Hagop, Souren, and Anahid looked at him.

"I prefer this basket," Armen said.

He started rummaging in the basket that he and Garbis had brought earlier.

"It does not matter which one you pick anyway," Anahid said.

"Maybe," Armen said, poking his fingers all the way to the bottom of the basket. "But my fingers can tell a champion egg."

"Oh, is that so?" Anahid said.

"And this is it!" he said, holding the egg he had chosen.

He held the egg and nodded. Anahid, grinning slightly, tapped her egg against his. There was a slight crack and Anahid drew her egg away, confident. Hagop and Souren leaned forward slightly, and as she looked down at her egg, the grin on Anahid's face slowly disappeared.

Her egg was cracked.

Armen simply sat there, saying nothing. He motioned for her to try the other end. She turned her egg over.

"Crack!"

She pulled it back.

Shattered.

She looked at Armen.

"All right! All right!" she said. "Just do not sit there, smiling like that!"

Outside, the square was empty. Everyone was inside, celebrating. The car pulled up and four policemen got out. They paired up, one carrying a tin can, the other consulting his list. They stepped through the village, and began pointing at the homes. The first pair moved closer, and the one with the tin can withdrew a paintbrush.

The table was strewn with eggshells. After Anahid's disastrous loss, Armen had gone on to defeat Souren twice, Anahid again, Takouhi, Lucine, Sarkis, and Garbis. Only Bedros had chosen not to play and, as he declined, he winked slyly at Armen. This had momentarily given Armen a start, but he quickly regained his composure.

"So," Armen said. "Who is next? Who will challenge me now?"

"I guess it is my turn then," Hagop said, stepping forward.

Armen positioned his egg over Hagop's and was just about to bring it down when Hagop drew his egg away.

"What are you doing?" Armen asked.

"I am sorry," Hagop said. He looked quickly at Souren and Anahid and then over at Bedros, who said nothing, but who was clearly following the action.

"I have just remembered," Hagop said. "You do know that it is customary for the winner to trade his egg to the last loser when there is only one egg left."

Anahid looked at Souren.

"It is?" Armen said, alarmed. "No, I did not know that."

"Oh, yes," Hagop said. "It is tradition that the last winner and last loser exchange eggs." He paused, drawing out the moment as Souren and Anahid drew a bit closer. "Come, now," he said. "Give it to me."

Hagop held out his hand. Armen knew it was futile, and with a shrug, handed over the egg.

"Oh! This is very heavy!" Hagop said.

The others, especially Anahid leaned in.

"This must have come from a very big hen!"

Armen looked from Souren who simply smiled to Anahid who sat there, tapping her fingers on the table.

"This will be very good to eat," Hagop said, drawing out the moment. "And I am so hungry." He looked at Anahid and handed the egg to her. "Here, sister, you do it."

"Yes, time to crack it open," she said, taking it. The others watched as she made a grand gesture of holding the egg at arm's length, high above the table. Armen looked on, a slight smile curling on his lips. She paused for a moment, and then let the egg drop. They watched it as it came down, hitting the table with a thud.

"Hmm," Hagop said, looking at Armen. He picked up the egg and then tapped it several times on the table. Each time little white patches of paint were left.

"All right, all right!" Armen said, raising his hands. "You have found me out!"

The adults laughed and as Armen brought down his hands, Anahid and Souren looked at each other and nodded. From behind their backs, they produced handfuls of eggshells and launched them at him.

It was late now, and Hagop dropped the garbage into the wooden bin near the side shed. Armen looked up and as he turned toward Hagop, he saw that both Hagop and Souren were already staring at it. The newly painted cross dripped little beads. They looked at one another but no one said a word.

They turned, and as they walked past home after home, white crosses marked each one.

"My house too," Souren said.

"Mine, too," Armen said.

"All of them," Hagop said, looking at his two friends.

"Every one that has an Armenian in it."

AKANTZ
15 April 1915

The men, numbering just over five hundred, stood against the golden rays of the sunset.

"You are required for the war effort," they had been told.

"You will be trained and serve on behalf of the Empire. This is your duty."

Now, the Armenian men stood, side by side, tied at the wrists in groups of four.

"Why are they tying us?"

"I do not know."

"Be quiet! Better to do as they say and we will be treated better."

"Yes, you are right."

"What are we waiting for?"

"We will leave when the trucks come."

The glare of the sun made them squint. Behind them, the Turkish soldiers raised their rifles. And in less than three minutes, five hundred men lay dying.

KIGHI

Kighi lay some one hundred twenty-five kilometers to the northwest of Lake Van. Chemeshgezak was only a few kilometers away, then Kharpert, and then Palou, which lay just sixty kilometers to the south. As the sun disappeared over the horizon, the shadows cast by the hanging men, faded, then disappeared into the night.

ERZEROUM

Seventy kilometers to the northeast of Kighi, Erzeroum sat, quiet now. They had gone back to their homes as they had been told.

"It will be fine," the mothers said, consoling the children.

"Yes, they will be back tomorrow."

"Come, tsakus, come."

The Armenian men of Erzeroum were told to kneel. The younger ones sat, wondering what to do; the older ones prayed. The soldiers waited for them to finish. And then the shots rang out, bloodying the ground.

MOUSH

Moush lay one hundred kilometers directly to the east of Palou and less than half that distance from Bitlis, which lay to her southeast. The peddler had been riding all day and now walked alongside the esh, allowing the animal to rest. He reached an open clearing and his eyes widened. He saw the piles of men. Though it was dark, he could see the deep, dark stains through their torn clothes.

CONSTANTINOPLE

The group of men stood in Wangenheim's main office. The delegation had been hastily assembled, and their worry showed plainly on their faces. The men shuffled nervously back and forth as Wangenheim's assistant, Leitner, sat behind his desk.

"Why is he making us wait?" Father DerGhazarian asked.

"Because he can," the businessman answered.

They stood there: clergy, businessmen, local political leaders, and a few journalists. They had met the night before and had discussed approaching Wangenheim.

"We have to do something!"

"But why go to Wangenheim? We should go to Morgenthau!"

"Morgenthau cannot intercede."

"I do not understand. Why can he not?"

"Because we are not French and we are not British."

"What does that matter? I have heard that he also protects the Belgians and the Serbs."

"Yes, but they have treaties with Britain and France."

"The difficulty is not with Morgenthau," the Azatamart journalist said. "We are technically only guests here. Guests who can be forcefully ejected."

"And who have overstayed their welcome?" Father DerGhazarian asked, drawing their stares. "Morgenthau's hands are tied," he said. "We must ask to be placed under the protection of the German Ambassador." He paused for a moment. "If he does not help us, then we will know what kind of man he is."

"The Ambassador will see you now," Leitner said, leading them to the door.

"Good day, Gentlemen," Wangenheim said, rising from his desk.

Carnig Zakarian, who owned the prosperous Voskee jewelry shop on Saint Sophia Square, had been asked to speak for the group.

"Thank you for seeing us today, Herr Ambassador," Zakarian began.

"Not at all," Wangenheim replied.

"Herr Ambassador, we are in a difficult moment now and require your assistance. We do not take this step easily."

"Yes, continue please," Wangenheim said.

"There have been several incidents against Armenian merchants in the last few weeks."

"What type of incidents?" Wangenheim asked.

Father DerGhazarian took one step forward and rested his weight on the wooden cane.

"Herr Ambassador," he said. "Yesterday there were two dreadful beatings. The men had done nothing. They were sitting, drinking their afternoon coffee. Two policemen entered and accused the men of stealing. They began beating them. Herr Ambassador, I know these men. They are above reproach. They are not thieves."

"Father, I sympathize with your situation but..."

"Herr Ambassador, there have been many changes since the Committee of Union and Progress has come into power," Zakarian said. "Our businesses are ransacked, the taxes have increased. We can barely pay them now."

"Yes, I understand the taxes can be officious."

Father DerGhazarian lifted his hand. "Herr Ambassador. On behalf of the Armenians here in Constantinople, and for Armenians throughout the Empire who are under German consuls in the outlying regions, please, I ask you for formal German protection."

"Yes, it is the only way," Zakarian said.

Wangenheim clasped his hands in front of him. "During these trying times of war and conflict, unfortunate actions sometimes occur. However, please understand the position of the German Government which I represent." The men looked at one another. "We are guests at the pleasure of the Turkish Government. For me to intercede, or to begin making official inquiries would go beyond my official capacities." Father DerGhazarian looked away from him. "I am unable to take any action in this matter. I cannot interfere. I am sorry."

OUTSKIRTS OF VAN

Shatakh lay some eighty kilometers directly south and slightly to the west of Van.

"Send word of your arrival when you are able," Arshag said.

Ishkhan nodded. He held out his hand and Arshag took it. They kissed one another on both cheeks.

"Take no chances," Aram said. "If anything goes wrong, get out quickly."

They kissed one another and the four men left. Each had a knife, but among them, they had but one rifle and one pistol.

PALOU

The Turkish soldiers stood and the Lieutenant stepped forward. From his tunic he pulled a sheet of paper. Hagop, Souren, and Armen looked at one another. The notice had been posted for all men from ages fifteen to thirty to appear exactly at noon.

"They need men to dig the roads," Bedros had said to Sarkis.

"Yes, I know," Sarkis had replied, "but just the same, I hope that they do not pick him."

The Lieutenant calmly unfolded the paper and started to call out names.

"Abdalian."

"Avedisian."

"Baronian."

Hagop watched as the three men stepped forward. A soldier handed each man piece of paper.

"Dadourian."

"Garabedian."

"Hagopian."

"Jamgochian."

Hagop and Armen turned to Souren, who looked back at them for a moment, and then stepped forward. The soldier came over and handed him a sheet.

"Kalustian."

"Khatchoian."

"Mardirossian."

"Melkonian."

Hagop looked from Armen to Souren and then stepped forward; he took the paper from the soldier.

"Nigoghosian."

"Rustigian."

"Sarkisian."

"Shakarian."

"Takvorian."

"Varadian."

"Yeremian."

"Zaroogian."

The Lieutenant went on for another forty names and then carefully folded the document.

"As loyal citizens, you have been called to serve in the defense of the Ottoman Empire. You will be expected to depart in one week's time."

The men watched as the soldiers piled back into the three vehicles. The trucks roared off, kicking up sand and rocks.

"Why was I not chosen?" Armen said, as the three boys walked from the square.

Hagop shook his head once, and Armen did not press the matter.

"One week!" Souren exclaimed. "Where do you think they will send us?"

"To Ctesiphon," Hagop said, calmly. "It is written here," he said, waving the document.

"Where is Ctesiphon?" Armen asked.

"To the southeast. On the Tigris," Hagop answered.

"I think it must be five hundred kilometers," Souren offered.

"Five hundred kilometers!" Armen exclaimed.

"Yes, at least," Souren replied. He turned to Hagop. "Our families need us to work," Souren said. "We can buy our…"

Hagop stopped and turned. He looked directly at Souren and Armen saw that his friend's face had suddenly changed.

"Listen to me. Both of you," Hagop said. "Souren, you are right. It is true that any Christian may buy exemption from military service, but it is a cost too high to ask our families to bear."

Souren paused, considering. "You are right," he said. "Yes. You are right. We must go."

Hagop nodded. They turned and walked in silence, making their way back to their homes. Hagop said goodbye and walked alone along the dirt road. He looked up at the sky.

"Rain coming."

NEARING SHATAKH

The plan had been to arrive at night. Ishkhan wanted to quietly slip into the village. If there were disturbances, he wanted to know why and that meant meeting with the village leaders.

"People do not do things to cause more trouble for the sake of causing trouble," he explained to Berge, the youngest of the men in his party. "No," he said. "There is something more."

They walked in single file and Ishkhan looked around. He motioned to the others to remain silent, but there was nothing. They were now in a clearing. Just ahead stood the makings of what would be a healthy crop of wheat and corn.

Suddenly, to the right, Ishkhan heard a small crackle. He turned, but it was too late. From the right, coming at them with blazing speed, were a group of men.

Ishkhan opened his mouth to tell his men to run. The men raised their pistols and fired.

"No!" one of the men cried. He watched as Ishkhan began to stagger.

The other men stepped forward, rifles high, and fired. Ishkhan fell to the ground. He looked up and saw Berge struggling with one of the assassins. The man brought his rifle butt down, cracking skull. Berge fell, his body convulsing.

The leader of the group drew his pistol and aimed it at Ishkhan. Another turned him over. He was dead, eyes still open.

"The Vali will be pleased," the man said. "We will inform him at once."

PALOU

The house was quiet now, and Lucine sat at the center table with Sarkis. She was tired and it showed heavily on her face. Hagop sat by the fire, staring at it, seeing things that only he could see. Lucine looked at Sarkis and then to Hagop.

"I must go to bed," she said, finally.

"Goodnight, Hagop."

"Goodnight, mama."

Lucine again looked at Sarkis and slowly walked into the small room. Sarkis watched her go and drew the paper toward him, turning it over and over. Hagop looked at the fire; it moved back and forth, flickering and darting. Sona drifted in and out, looking at him, turning. Laughing, smiling, holding his hand, kissing him on the cheek, kissing him on the lips. Ah! Why did he feel this way now? God, he would be leaving soon. And there would be hard work ahead.

Hagop looked up from the fire and saw his father holding the letter. He got up and sat opposite him. They sat for many minutes. Finally, Hagop reached his hand out and gently took the letter from his father's hands. The rain had come, just as Hagop had thought, and it beat down on the roof.

"Ah. I had hoped this would not happen," Sarkis said, gesturing to the piece of paper.

"The war made it so, papa. There is nothing to worry about," Hagop said, hoping to reassure him. "They are sending us to Ctesiphon. What is in Ctesiphon? Nothing is there. Ctesiphon is so far from where they are fighting we will never even see battle."

"Hagop. Listen to me," Sarkis said. "My father has never left Palou. His father never left Palou. And I have never left Palou."

"Papa…"

"No. Let me finish," Sarkis said, raising his hand slightly. "Listen to me. I am not an educated man. But I know things. And I am a full man. I have been blessed with a good family, a good wife, and good children."

"Papa, you act as if…"

"Listen to what I tell you my son," Sarkis said, leaning closer. "In this world, there are masters and there are those who are mastered."

"No one masters a man who believes in himself, papa," Hagop said. "You told me that."

Sarkis smiled slightly. "Yes. I remember. But I have asked myself many times. What can my son build here? To stay here and be at the mercy of those who take everything and give nothing in return?"

Hagop looked at his father. And slowly, they both nodded. A father. A son. Two men.

"No matter what you do here, you will never be allowed to enjoy it for what it is. This is the reason why when you return, I want you and Sona to go to Paris."

"To Paris!" Hagop said, his eyes widening.

"Yes, to Paris and then to America."

"But to leave," Hagop said, "and it will cost much money."

"Do not worry about that. We will manage it."

"Yes, but you, mama..."

Sarkis put his hand up, cutting him off. "There are many Armenians in both places and you will find work," he said. He looked at Hagop. "There you will find a future."

"Papa. We will talk about it when I return."

"Yes. But put this thing in your head now," he said, touching a finger to his son's temple. "Now, before you leave."

"Yes, yes... If that is what you want, papa."

Sarkis nodded. "Be careful. Tell Souren to watch out for you and you watch out for him. Do you understand me?"

"Yes, papa."

A few moments of silence passed between them.

"And the crosses?" Hagop asked.

The painted crosses now dotted each of their homes and a public decree had been made that they were to remain throughout the duration of the war.

"I do not think it will come to anything," Sarkis said. "It is just another tactic to remind us that we are the millet. They will devise and administer some new tax. Then all will return to normal. The Vali needs more money for himself and we bear the cost. Nothing changes."

"Still..."

"It will be fine," Sarkis said. He reached out his hand and touched his son's cheek. It was an old Armenian custom, whether from the old to the young or the young to the old.

VAN

It was mid-afternoon and Aram and Arshag were becoming nervous. They had not heard from Ishkhan, though it was still early. If it were to come to pass, Armenak had spent the last days working out their plan of defense. He hoped that it would not be necessary; they could only hold out so long. Sooner or later, they would be overrun.

Arshag touched Aram's arm as the kevass, the Turkish policeman, stepped forward.

"Arshak Vramian? Aram Manoukian?" he said, looking at the men. "I bring good word from Vali Bey."

Aram and Arshag looked at one another and nodded slightly.

"I have been dispatched by Vali Bey to inform you that he has received word that your party has been of good service at Shatakh. Vali Bey requests a meeting to discuss favorable terms."

"Tell Vali Bey that we will come shortly," Arshag said.

"Very well," the kevass said. "You are to come to his home. You will be received." He turned and left.

"Ishkhan sent no word," Arshag said.

"He could have been delayed," Aram replied. "Or he may not yet be able. Even so..."

"We must hear what the Vali has to say," Arshag said.

"I agree," Aram replied. "We should not wait long to take advantage of a positive situation."

"Plus, many people have seen the kevass come here," Arshag said. "It would be stupid for the Vali to try anything."

"I will meet you here in a few moments and then we will go," Aram said.

"Where are you going?"

"I must get something first," Aram replied. "It will be only minutes."

Aram rushed into his home. He pushed back the canvas that covered the small barrels holding the family's stores of cracked wheat, rice, and barley. He reached his hand inside one and withdrew the bundle of cloth that covered the pistol. He tucked it behind his back and pulled his shirt down over it.

He quickly made his way back to the village square but Arshag was nowhere to be found. A young boy walked by, carefully carrying a pair of clean, just-shined black shoes.

"Young Zaven!" Aram called out.

"Baron Aram," the boy said, stopping.

"Have you seen Baron Arshag?"

"Yes," Zaven said.

"Where is he then?"

"He came into my father's store, but he told my father that you took too long to come back."

"Too long!" Aram began, then stopped short. "Do you know where he went?"

"To the Vali's home," Zaven answered.

"Thank you, Zaven," Aram said. He turned and quickly began walking. "I was gone only minutes," he said aloud. "Ah, it is just like him. Always impatient."

The Vali's home was about a half-kilometer from the square. Just ahead, a horse drawn cart was fast approaching. It looked like Levon Adamian was steering. The cart swiftly went past, the driver's face a study of concentration.

Aram continued walking and then stopped, listening. He turned and quickly jumped to the side of the rutted road. The cart had turned and was now hurtling back towards him. Aram reached back, resting his hand on the pistol.

"Baron Aram!" the driver called out, bringing the horse to an abrupt halt.

"Levon! What is the matter?" Aram asked.

"They have arrested Arshag!"

"What?"

"Yes! I saw it myself!" Levon blurted. "He was only steps away from the Vali's compound and two kevasses came and took him away!"

"What do you mean, away?" Aram said. "Took him where?"

"Inside!" Levon answered.

Aram looked at him, his mind racing. One part of him screamed to go quickly. But another voice told him to stop and think. He looked at Levon.

"Take me back," he said.

"Yes, Baron Aram! Right away!"

"He is being held in Djevdet's compound," Aram said. "There are three people who saw him enter; no one has seen him leave."

"All attempts at approaching the entrance have been turned back," Armenak said. "I sent two men there only one hour ago. They were told that there was no such man there."

The group of men sat in the church anteroom, considering.

"There are police and soldiers at the entrance," Varouj said.

"How many rifles do we have?" Aram asked. The men turned to him, and the seriousness in his voice dug deep.

"We have less than three hundred," Armenak said. "They are old, but they function."

"But we have limited ammunition," Varouj offered.

"That will not matter," Armenak said. "We can manufacture ammunition."

"Are you sure we should move so quickly?" Varouj asked.

"They have killed Ishkhan," Aram said. "We all know it, don't we?" He looked around the room, face by face. "And now they have Arshag. If they have not killed him, they soon will."

"Yes," Armenak said. "Yes, I am afraid you are right. They will want to know how many arms we have, how much ammunition there is."

"Arshag will not tell them," Aram said.

"What should we do about the demands for our men?" Varouj asked.

"I will continue to negotiate with Djevdet's men," Aram said. "Delay them. These men will never see war."

"What do you mean?" Ovhannes, another deputy, asked.

"Now we know what before we only surmised," Armenak said. "Ishkhan was a leader and leaders are dangerous. Capture them or kill them. Leaders, doctors, priests."

"That is right," Aram said. "If you cannot be led, if your wounded cannot be healed, and if your people cannot be led in prayer, there is not much else."

"But why?" Ovhannes asked.

"It is simple," Aram said, looking at him. "They want to be done with us now."

Even the strongest man would eventually break when he was subjected to the bastinado. First, he was stripped to the waist, left barefoot. Then his hands were tied behind his back and a rope strung around his ankles. The rope would be slung over a wooden or stone beam and the man would be hoisted upside down.

At first, they would just let him hang there, swinging, turning, sweat and salt pouring off his body, into his eyes, stinging them. Then they would come in. Usually there were three of them. Two would ask the questions. The third would use the cane.

It was made of hard wood, usually oak, the raised knuckles of the timber rough and jagged.

"Talk, Christian!"

"You are a conspirator with the Russian Army!"

Arshag twisted as the faces of the men twirled around the room. He said nothing.

The third man drew the cane back. WHACK! Right on the soles of Arshag's feet.

"Ah!" Arshag grunted.

"Admit the truth and this will end."

"I... I..." Arshag managed, stinging from the blow.

WOOMF!

The cane came down hard.

"Ahh!" the air rushed out of Arshag's lungs. He had been hit only twice and already the skin had broken and was bleeding.

To someone who had never seen it, never experienced it, it was impossible to understand the excruciating pain. In time, the feet would bloat, then burst. Then they would move on to the fingers and the hands. Once the hands were broken, the man would be left to hang overnight. If he was lucky, he would pass out, but they were careful never to take it that far. Suffering. They had to suffer or they would not talk. They were all alike. Besides, these Christians enjoyed their suffering.

"I... am...not...a...conspirator..." Arshag managed.

"How many rifles are they hiding?"

"How many bullets do they have?"

"Nothing...nothing...we...have...nothing..."

The cane swung out, hitting the fingers of his left hand. There was a sickening snapping sound and a deep red gash opened.

"Ahhhh!" Arshag moaned. His eyes fluttered. The men swung around and around.

"Talk!"

"I...have...done...nothing."

The two men nodded.

SNAP!

The cane came down, and split his feet open.

"Talk or die, infidel dog!"

"The choice is yours to make."

"Please...do...not...do...this..."

"How many weapons do they hide, Christian!"

"None...there...are...none..."

WHACK!

"Ohhhhh...." Arshag groaned.

A long red line opened on his back.

"Talk and this stops now!"

"We...gave...everything...we...had..."

"Djevdet's edict stands," Aram said, looking from face to face. The proposal for offering five hundred men was rejected."

"He never intended to accept it," Varouj added. "All of this was to lay a trap for Ishkhan."

"They want four thousand men," Aram said, looking at the Vanetzis gathered in the church. "These men will be worked like dogs and then murdered. We must fight. There is no alternative."

"If we begin this, we must end it," a man shouted out. "Otherwise, they will kill all of us."

"Boghos is right!"

"They plan to kill us no matter what we do," Aram answered.

"This is the only way," Armenak said. "Djevdet sent for Arshag and Aram. If the Vali wanted to achieve our cooperation, he would produce Arshag, but he does not."

"We must vote," Aram said.

"We will need every hand," Armenak added. "Without that, we will not have a chance."

Aram looked out at the villagers. "Those who agree, must raise their hands."

One by one, the Vanetzis all raised their hands.

Djevdet set the porcelain cup onto the polished oak desk.

"Has he given us the information we require?"

"No, Vali Djevdet," the aide said. "He insists that they have no weapons."

"He lies," Djevdet said, looking at him. "So, these Armenians think that they can deny us these men for our army?"

No one answered him.

"Issue a command on my order," he said. "Begin digging a trench around the Armenian sector. We will see how quickly they change their position."

"They are digging!" the lookout said.

"There are about thirty men. It is going to be a wide trench."

"This is how it begins," Armenak said. "First, they isolate us. If they cannot starve us out, they will try to burn us out. First, we organize a group of men who can dig." He laid out a piece of rough brown paper and drew shapes representing homes.

"We dig a trench after the first line of homes. If we cannot get out, then they will not be able to get in." He drew another row of homes behind the first. "The first positions will fall, especially if they use mortars." The men looked at him. "We must plan for the worst," he said. "We dig another trench behind the next row of homes, and behind that row, we dig another trench. We fight as long as the positions hold, then retreat and fight from the next trench."

The men nodded. It could work.

"We put dead branches, tree trunks, rubbish and sharpened sticks in front of the trenches. This will slow them down.

"We begin tonight," Aram said. "Go to every home and assemble the men. Establish the sentries. We do everything at night."

He was the Vali of Van. He was Djevdet. But he was also known as the Horse-shoer of Van. Men brought into the torture chamber in the root cellar of his compound were seldom brought out alive. If they did live, they were maimed in grotesque ways. Many were nailed to wooden crosses. Others had horseshoes nailed to their feet. Usually, the men died of shock.

"Talk, Christian!"

"I... have...told...you..."

WHACK!

Arshag's head drooped as he swung back and forth.

They would start with him in the morning, and leave him there through the afternoon. Then they would come back in the evening, cut him down, and throw him into the damp cell. There was a small mat, green and brown with mold and dried blood. He would lie there, drifting in and out, the screams of other men echoing back and forth.

"This is a tough one."

"Look at him. He will not last long."

The Armenian women had been warned by their men to walk together, never alone, and to always wear their veils down, covering their faces. While the trench digging continued, the women hurried from store to store, buying flour and sugar. Over the last days, the ridicule and harassment had risen, but they had been careful not to respond.

The four women walked hurriedly, and as they did, a group of Turks stood, watching them go. The women entered the store and made their purchases. They exited, carrying their goods in burlap sacks. One of the men reached out and grabbed a woman by the arm. She screamed, and as she did, three of the Turks rushed forward.

Two women stomped their feet, managing to break the grips, and ran off. The men laughed, but made no attempt to run after them. The other two women struggled, screaming.

"No! Good Pasha!"

"Please!"

Two Armenian men rushed forward, and began wresting the women away from the men. Two soldiers lifted their rifles and butted the men, dropping them. One of the women screamed as blood from the man's forehead splattered on her. The men released them and the women ran away. A group of Armenian men rushed forward, and as they did, a soldier aimed his rifle. One of the men was hit in the chest, killing him instantly.

Within seconds, the fighting had broken out. Within the hour, torches were being catapulted and the homes began erupting in flames.

Despite the bedlam, both Aram and Armenak maintained their calm. Aram stood behind the third row of homes, while Armenak was near the front, issuing orders.

"Instruct the sentries to take up their positions. Gather all our shovels, hoes, and axes. We will need them," Aram ordered.

"It will be done immediately," Varouj said.

"Varouj," Aram said. "Tell the men to use their ammunition only if they must."

Though the homes were now surrounded by the trench that Djevdet had ordered dug, when the Turkish soldiers came forward, past the first row of homes, they would find an equally long and deep trench dug by the Vanetzis. Armenak stood, supervising the men, pointing at holes and breaches, ordering them filled.

"They think they can come against us?" Djevdet said, his voice rising. "I will show them who they are dealing with here!"

"They are digging trenches at night and have put up armed sentries," the aide reported.

Djevdet looked at the men standing before him. "Tomorrow you will arrest this Manoukian and this Yekarian on charges of conspiring with the Russians!" He slammed his fist on the solid desk and glared at them. "And then you will bring me my four thousand men!"

"Yes, Vali Djevdet!"

It was dark, and as the side doors joining the Armenian homes were opened, the men carried kerosene lanterns to light their path. They moved silently from home to home, carrying rifles, pistols, shovels, picks, and axes. They walked toward the first trench and took up their positions. Armenak issued orders to the sentries and checked on their readiness. Outside the perimeter, the Turkish troops waited. Soon, the order would be given. The torches would be lobbed forward and then they would advance.

CONSTANTINOPLE
23 April 1915

Friday night and the twenty-third of April would become the twenty-fourth in less than one hour. It was quiet. Homes were dark, their inhabitants fast asleep. The photographs had been studied and the lists had been meticulously prepared. Mugerditchian had separated the vital from the unimportant.

They represented the Armenian leadership.

They were the politicians, the businessmen, and the clergy. They were the journalists, the doctors, and the writers. Professors. Lawyers. Architects. Composers. Musicians. Teachers.

Without them, the Armenian population would be leaderless. They would not resist and they would have no one to whom they could turn.

The military trucks pulled up outside the different districts. The men had their lists and photographs. They looked at their watches, waiting for midnight. The first group that would be taken was the staff of the Azatamart journal. The editors, reporters, and photographers could not be left to get words or pictures out to the rest of the world. Everything depended upon that.

Now the groups of men fanned out over the Armenian quarter. At Father DerGhazarian's home, the men were respectful, but insistent. He had but minutes to dress quickly, grabbing his Bible and crucifix. Carnig Zakarian, the jeweler, resisted. They dragged him from his home while his wife, Araxi, pleaded.

The greatest resistance was put forward by the journalists. Some of the men were struck with a quick crack of a pistol across the back of the head. After they were removed, the men tipped over the tin cans of ink and solvent. In seconds, fire consumed everything.

"What are you doing? Where are you taking us?" the journalists demanded.

"I must know where you are taking me," Father DerGhazarian said.

"I have done nothing! Why are you arresting me?" Carnig Zakarian shouted.

Home after home, the groups moved forward, checking their lists, taking the men. Children cried. Wives and mothers could only look on in disoriented shock.

Group after group. Name after name. Picture after picture. The men were rounded up and sent to their temporary holding cells in the city jail. They were packed together, fifty, a hundred, two hundred.

"Where are you taking my husband?" the woman screamed.

"They have done nothing wrong!"

"They are being moved away from war zones. They will not be harmed. When the threat is over, they will be returned."

More than six hundred of the elite were taken. Later, another four to five thousand from the general Armenian population. No one could be sure.

In time, the Armenians in Constantinople would be sent to join the other deportees as they walked toward Deir-El-Zor. Some would be slaughtered in their homes, some in the streets. What had begun as an invisible massacre, began to take on shocking, visible truth.

VAN

The rifle and pistol flashes punctuated the night sky with puffs of white smoke. Flickering torches seemed to be everywhere; ahead of them, the first row of homes lay burning. Behind them, Armenak stood, pistol in hand. They had only three hundred rifles, but they would have to do. They had taken hoes and sharpened the blades. With a powerful blow, they could sever a spine.

Armenak had run the plan through his mind time and again. The first row would fall. He could not prevent that. But as the soldiers rushed forward, they would fall into the trap. They would not be able to overrun the trench the Vanetzis had dug. Then he would order his men to shoot. And he could use fire. The kerosene bombs were thin glass bottles filled with kerosene, a rag stuffed into the top as the wick. They had only seven mortars, but they were rapidly making more.

"They are coming!" the sentry cried.

Armenak crouched down and kept his men waiting. In moments, they could see Djevdet's troops, some carrying torches, all carrying rifles. Armenak put their number at five to six hundred. The troops reached the first row of homes and as they did, they saw the jagged line that had been dug before them.

"Trench!"

"Fire!"

Djevdet's men began shooting into the dense row of brush and dead trees that stood before the trench line.

"Wait until they are closer!" Armenak said. "Let them use their ammunition!"

The soldiers drew forward.

"Now!" Armenak shouted.

The Vanetzis started firing. The bullets found their targets and a group of soldiers were hit. Others moved up and took their places. They returned fire and two of the Vanetzis were struck. Behind the riflemen were the bomb crews.

"Now!"

They stepped forward and threw bottle after bottle into the standing mass of soldiers. They exploded upon impact, throwing burning kerosene everywhere.

"Aghhh!" a soldier screamed. Some fell to the ground, trying to extinguish the flames. Others panicked and ran. They collapsed in a heap, the stench of burning flesh wafting up.

Now a second row of soldiers appeared, and they kept their distance. They would have to change their attack. The trench was deep, well guarded, and the frontal debris would have to be cleared.

In the dark, wet cell, Arshag lay on the thin mat. His feet and legs were grossly bloated a sickly gray and black. His hands no longer worked and he could not feel his fingers. His eyes were shut, welt upon welt.

But he could hear.

And the sounds of the rebellion that the Vanetzis had begun reached him and spoke to him. He listened and drifted off, smiling.

In moments he was gone. His fight ended.

CONSTANTINOPLE

"Mr. Ambassador! Mr. Ambassador!" the people called out, knocking at the thick doors of Morgenthau's residence. It was just past seven o'clock in the morning. Morgenthau heard the ruckus and, dressed in his bathrobe, shaving soap still on his face, walked to the door. They poured in and around him, each one of them talking at once. He tried to calm them: it was impossible to understand what they were saying.

"They have…"

"They are being held…"

"They came last night…"

Josephine appeared and the women immediately seized upon her. Morgenthau held up his hands.

"Quiet! Quiet," he yelled.

Like a wave, the shouting and protesting eased and then stopped.

"Now what is this all about?" he asked.

Morgenthau walked quickly. The Italian, French, Austrian, and Russian embassies were cloistered together, in the Pera district, and he lived only minutes away from the American Embassy. Bedri, the Prefect of Police, kept a small office close by. Bedri sat, stirring spoonfuls of sugar into the thick, dark coffee.

"Ah! Mr. Ambassador," Bedri said. "Good morning!"

"Prefect," Morgenthau answered, stepping inside.

Bedri drank the coffee down in one gulp.

"Would you like to join me?" Bedri asked.

"No, thank you," Morgenthau replied. "Perhaps you can tell me what is going on."

"What do you mean, Mr. Ambassador?" Bedri said, a blank look on his face.

"Early this morning, many Armenian families came to my home, telling me that their husbands were taken away last night. What has happened?"

"Oh, that!" Bedri said, nonchalantly. "It is nothing to worry about! It is for security reasons."

"What do you mean?" Morgenthau asked. "What security reasons? Where are these men being taken?"

"Ah, you should ask Talaat exactly that question!" Bedri replied.

"I plan to do precisely that!" Morgenthau said, turning to leave.

VAN

"I order this rebellion crushed! At once!" Djevdet said, slapping the desk.

"We may have misjudged their capabilities," his assistant said.

Djevdet glared at him. "Is it your intention to tell me that these untrained, uneducated, Christian dogs are superior to our trained armies?"

"No, Djevdet Bey," the man stammered.

"Send a ciphered telegram to Constantinople," Djevdet said. The aide began writing. "We possess evidence of Armenian conspiracy with Russian forces," Djevdet said, dictating. "They have refused to provide Armenian men to join our military forces. We have attempted peaceful negotiations. The Armenians have armed themselves and we have suffered hundreds of Turkish casualties. The Armenians are killing any non-Armenian persons. They have declared a holy war."

The men looked at one another, but no one said a word.

"Dispatch it immediately," Djevdet said.

"Yes, Djevdet Bey! Immediately!"

CONSTANTINOPLE

Morgenthau crossed the street, paused, and looked up towards Talaat's window.

"Mr. Ambassador! So good to see you!" Talaat said, motioning for Morgenthau to take a seat.

"Mr. Minister. Good day."

"And what can I do for the American Ambassador today?"

"Mr. Minister. Many Armenian families have come to me during the last hours."

"Oh, these Armenians are always with their hands out for something."

"That may be, Mr. Minister, but Mrs. Morgenthau and I were awoken early this morning by several families."

Talaat shifted his weight, the beneficent smile transforming into his infamous glare.

"They were in a distraught state," Morgenthau continued. "Surely you are aware that many of the leaders of the Armenian community were awakened last night and taken away. I would like to know why."

"But it should not concern you, Mr. Ambassador. It is entirely an internal matter," Talaat replied. "But if you insist, the men who were taken away have all been identified as security risks." Talaat reached for a folder and waved it back and forth. "We have gathered intelligence reports which show without a doubt that many of these men have been providing sensitive details to the Russians."

"May I see that?" Morgenthau said.

"No, I am sorry, Mr. Ambassador. It is not permitted."

"Then perhaps you can tell me where they are being taken," Morgenthau said. "At the very least, I can inform the families..."

"Certainly," Talaat replied. "They will be taken to Angora, to the Interior, away from the war zones."

"And when will they be returned?" Morgenthau said.

"That is simple," Talaat answered. "When the combined military command determines that the threat they pose is over."

Morgenthau opened his mouth to speak, but merely sighed in frustration.

"Do not worry, Mr. Ambassador," he said. "They will be safe."

Morgenthau paused for a moment. "Mr. Minister," he began. "I would be grateful if you would intercede on my behalf."

"I do not understand," Talaat replied.

Morgenthau reached into his suit jacket and produced a folded sheet of paper.

"Some of the men are in questionable health," he said, handing the paper to Talaat. "Many of these men have families in Paris and in Italy."

"And so?" Talaat asked.

"They can go there and Turkey can be rid of them."

"Oh, Mr. Ambassador," Talaat said. "Why do you insist on helping them? You waste your time!"

"It is the humanitarian in me I am afraid," Morgenthau said.

"Ah, but, good relations with America are always important," Talaat said. He put his hand atop the list. "I tell you what. I will help you if I am able."

Morgenthau nodded. Talaat leaned back in his chair. "Now tell me, when can you make some more nice publicity for Turkey in America?" Morgenthau stood and began walking to the door.

"Why, as soon as I hear of the successful movement of these men," he said.

"Ah! Ah! Mr. Ambassador," Talaat said, wagging his finger. "Again you are always getting things from me!"

"Good day, Mr. Minister," Morgenthau said, closing the door behind him.

"Henry, come to bed. You look tired," Josephine said. Morgenthau looked up from the desk.

"I am tired. Very tired."

She leaned against the door jam, dressed in her night robe. It was almost midnight.

She was born Josephine Sykes in Stuttgart, Germany. Morgenthau's junior by seven years, she was a remarkably intelligent and compassionate woman, fluent in English, French, and German. They had first met as members of the Emerson Club as the small group read the sonnets of Shakespeare. Thirty years later, she was with him in Constantinople.

"I went to see Talaat today about the Armenians."

"What did he say?"

Morgenthau sat back. "He said that they were moved because they posed a security risk, probably in light of the rebellion at Van."

"Do you believe him?"

"No. I can't believe him," Morgenthau said, shaking his head. "Oh, it's easy to believe on the surface, but the facts are otherwise."

"What do you mean?"

"Because for months, the Turks have been preparing lists of the leading Armenians in Constantinople."

"How do you know that?" she said, alarmed.

"Intercepted ciphers, consul reports, informants."

"Can they be trusted?" Josephine asked. "I mean, can they be verified?"

Morgenthau nodded. "The Consuls have no motive for exaggeration or falsification. And even if the informants are questionable, one fact cannot be challenged."

"What's that?" Josephine asked. Morgenthau handed her a document that was torn and soiled.

She looked at the list of names.

"Because if it is true that these Armenians were removed because of a security risk or because of the rebellion at Van, why were the lists distributed prior to the rebellion?" he asked.

"Before?" she said, looking down at the list.

"Yes," Morgenthau nodded. "There is no question. This act is a premeditated one."

"Can you do anything?"

Morgenthau lifted his eyebrows and sighed. "I can only do so much. Talaat agreed to divert some of the men to Europe."

"What will they do with the others?"

"That is the problem," Morgenthau said. "They are not my charges. I have no right to interfere. Technically, it is an internal matter that does not concern the United States."

"I don't understand," Josephine said.

"Imprisoning them is one thing. Deporting them to parts uncertain is entirely different. I can make suggestions and official protests, but these people do not exist here."

"I am confused, Henry, really, I don't…"

"You see it is like this," Morgenthau said. "I have care for the British, the French, Belgians, the Serbs. These are recognized peoples. They have governments, policies, and some have treaties. In short, they exist."

Josephine nodded.

"But anyone absent a government, absent a representative, or absent a guardian…" He paused, considering the gravity of it all. "They are only guests. They must adhere to the rules and laws of the Empire."

Josephine unfolded her arms and let them fall to her side.

"Of course, now we know that their rules and laws are meaningless," he said. She looked at him for a few seconds.

"Henry…" she said.

"I will do everything I can," he said, looking into her eyes.

It was remarkable that he had even come to Constantinople. He was born Heinrich Morgenthau, a German-Jew, in 1856 in Mannheim, Germany, at the nexus of the Rhine and Neckar Rivers. His father Lazarus eventually moved the family to New York.

He mastered English, worked as an errand boy in various law offices, and entered Columbia Law School. He took a night job teaching people from all walks of life: plumbers, blacksmiths, and laborers.

By 1905, the Henry Morgenthau Company was buying and selling real estate all over New York. He loathed the dirty nature of politics, but when he heard Governor Woodrow Wilson speak, he was captivated by the man's genuineness. At age fifty-five, Morgenthau became Chairman of the 1912 Democratic Finance Committee.

Wilson campaigned brilliantly, besting Theodore Roosevelt, the Progressive candidate, and William Taft, the Republican candidate, to become President.

Morgenthau finally relented to Wilson's desire to have him as his ambassador in Turkey. On the twenty-seventh of November his train arrived in Constantinople. A thousand different scents instantly came to him. The freshly cooked lamb's meat being grilled on the streets. Figs hanging and drying in the air. The smell of bitter, dark coffee. The finjans sitting about, reading the coffee grounds for a few coins.

Constantinople. The Jewel.

"Mr. Ambassador! I am Phillip Hoffman, the Conseiller," he said, holding out his hand.

"Ah, Mr. Hoffman," Morgenthau said.

"Welcome to Constantinople."

"Thank you."

The train station was, as usual, a flurry of activity. They quickly passed through the official reception office reserved for foreign diplomats and exited the station.

"Bring him here! Bring him here!" the man said.

Morgenthau and Hoffman looked to the right and watched as a young boy who was very dark in complexion, was being dragged by two policemen toward their Prefect, Bedri Bey.

"We should continue on our way," Hoffman said.

"No. Not just yet," Morgenthau replied.

The kevasses dragged the boy and deposited him at Bedri's feet.

"Do you think you can take something and not pay for it?" Bedri demanded. The boy looked up, fear on his face.

"But I took nothing! I swear I have done nothing!"

"Silence!" Bedri said. He brought down the thin bamboo rod onto the boy's back. It landed with a thwack.

"Ahhhhh!" the boy said, the air rushing out of his lungs. Morgenthau grimaced, feeling the strike. He turned to Hoffman, who shrugged.

"Do not tempt me further," Bedri said. "It would not serve you well."

"Yes, yes!" the boy said.

"Good," Bedri said. "Now, tell me that you have stolen from the merchant and it will be easier for you."

"Good Prefect," the boy said. "I have not taken any…"

"Whack!" The rod came down again.

"Ahhhh!" the boy uttered. A thin red line appeared beneath his cloth shirt. Morgenthau turned to Hoffman.

"I'm going to see what this is all about."

"Mr. Ambassador!" Hoffman said, astonished. "That is not something I would suggest…" But it was too late. Morgenthau broke from him and crossed the street. The kevasses turned towards him, but Bedri shook his head.

"Ah, Mr. Ambassador Henry Morgenthau," Bedri said. "I have heard you were coming today."

"How do you know my name?" Morgenthau asked.

"I have been provided with your photograph," Bedri replied "Welcome to Constantinople. I am Bedri. Prefect of Police."

"Thank you," Morgenthau said. "Now, about this…" he said, gesturing to the boy who sat still, saying nothing.

"Oh, this is nothing," Bedri replied.

"It certainly does not look that way to me," Morgenthau replied.

"Oh, it is just a matter of truth versus fact. But as a gift to celebrate your arrival, today I will let this Armenian go." He looked down at the boy. "Be gone!" he commanded. The boy looked up, disbelieving. He glanced quickly at Morgenthau and scurried away.

"But I will be watching you!" Bedri said, calling after him. He turned. "Mr. Ambassador," he said, lowering his voice. "You are new here. In time, you will learn that this was nothing."

Bedri nodded and the door was opened for him. He walked down the stone and iron staircase and wrinkled his nose slightly. The stink down here always did that to him. The smell of fetid water, the wet stone walls, and the feces and urine combined for a hellish discharge.

He passed the isolation cells and saw wrinkled, dirty fingers sticking out of the small slats. He approached the large cell that held more than three hundred men. Two policemen stood, oblivious to the protests. Most of the men who had earlier visited Wangenheim were here: Father DerGhazarian, Zakarian the jeweler. Hovag, the Azatamart journalist, was missing: no one had seen him. Father DerGhazarian stood silent and from time to time whispered with the priest next to him.

'God, why must he be here too?' Father DerGhazarian thought. 'Me, I am no one. But why him?'

Upon seeing Bedri, the prisoners quieted. Bedri approached, carrying a sheet of paper.

"The following men will come forward."

The men began to protest. Father DerGhazarian looked at them.

"Fear nothing!" he commanded.

"That is right, Father," Bedri said. "Calm the men. I bear good tidings." Father DerGhazarian looked at Bedri for a moment.

"Aharonian, Ohan"

The jailed men parted as the man came forward.

"Donabedian, Vartan"

Again, slowly, a man stepped forward.

"Me!"

"No, choose me!"

Father DerGhazarian looked at Bedri one last time and slowly shuffled back, withdrawing into the center of the mass of men and next to the other priest.

"Etmekjian, Garo"

"Komidas, Vartabed"

The other priest looked at Father DerGhazarian. For a moment they just stood there. Finally, Father DerGhazarian touched Komidas on the cheek. The two priests embraced, kissing one another.

"Komidas, Vartabed!" Bedri shouted. "I will not say it again!"

The priest stepped forward. He was forty-six years old now, and the garments he wore had been issued to him at Etchmiadzin. Their crisp black color had faded to a worn, dull gray, and the hood hung at his back.

He had been born Soghomon Soghomonian. Barely twelve years old, he had left for Etchmiadzin, where his voice, strong and clear, sang the Armenian hymns and prayers. He began to write poem after poem, hymn after hymn. He was ordained a priest and given his name in tribute to Komidas I of Aghtzik.

He had come to Constantinople in order to continue his teachings and to assist in the organization of a formal choir. When the police had come, he was rounded up along with the others. He commanded such respect that Father DerGhazarian would have gladly given his life in exchange.

"Shishmanian, Mushegh," continued Bedri.

Zakarian, the jeweler, wiped his forehead. God! Was it hot in here!

"Zartarian, Aramast"

Bedri looked up from the list and into a sea of eager eyes. He neatly folded the sheet of paper amidst their waning hope and put it back into his pocket.

"Is that all?" Zakarian asked.

"What will you do with them?"

"What are you going to do to us?"

Bedri did not answer them. Instead, he turned to the two kevasses.

"You are to secure and transport these men. Await my orders."

"Yes, Prefect!"

Bedri looked at the six men who had been called. "You have a generous benefactor who watches over you. Good for you, too bad for me!" he said. He turned and left. The stink had finally gotten to him.

The men were transported to a holding area and then placed on a barge on her way to the port of Marseilles. All, that is, save for Komidas. Separated after his vestments came under scrutiny, he stood silent as he was led to the hangman's noose. And, miraculously, for that was the only way he could later describe it, he was rescued by, of all people, a German official. The German's son had been one of his students.

"I have been plucked from death," he would repeat. "The serpent was at me."

Unable to understand why he had been saved, he sunk deeper and deeper into madness. The doctors in the Paris hospital were unable to help him.

"The serpent bit and I was plucked from him."

"The serpent bit and I was plucked from him."

"The serpent bit and I was plucked from him."

He died in 1935, little knowing what his contributions would be. Yet, through the years, his two most famous works, "Soorp, Soorp" and "Hayr Mer", became the most important hymns ever sung under an Armenian cross.

TOWARDS ANGORA
24 April 1915

Before it was known as Ankara, its name was Angora. It stood, some two hundred kilometers to the southeast of Constantinople. The men had been put into groups, and truckload after truckload had been sent away towards this place. They had been told that they were being sent to the interior to wait out the war.

"You are extremists, despite what you say," they were told. "On direct orders from the Sublime Porte, you are to be held here until the threat of war in the west has passed."

The Armenians looked at one another, but no one dared argue. Some had black and blue marks about the face and hands. It made no sense to them. What had they not considered? Would the French and the English move forward? The Bulgarians? The Greeks?

It was early evening, and within the hour the sun would be down. The trucks stopped at Ayash, more than one hundred seventy-five kilometers east of Constantinople and at Chankiri, some one hundred twenty kilometers northeast of Ankara. The Armenians waited inside. A captain stepped forward.

"You will be arriving at Angora in a few hours," he said. "Take this time to stretch your legs."

"Everyone out!" a soldier commanded. "We stop for only a few minutes!"

The Armenians looked at one another. Their legs were stiff from sitting and they shook them out. As they did, the canvases were pulled back. The Turkish soldiers began firing from the dual German machine guns, the rapid-fire bullets finding man after man. The Armenians ran, stumbled, and fell over. Three of the men jumped down a ravine. One was a priest. He would eventually make his way to Paris and record the episode.

VAN

The night sky was aflame; every home in the first row was burning. The Turks had wheeled in the catapults and the torches had found their mark. But the first trench line had held. The Turks had made attempts at rushing them, but were cut down each time.

In the rear, Aram supervised Varouj and the other men. They had enough food but the ammunition stores were low. The women fed the men and bandaged the wounded. Children gathered bottles, rags, lanterns, nails, hammers, and sticks. The older men, especially those experienced in metalwork, concentrated on the creation of casings, ammunition, and shields.

Still, both Armenak and Aram knew that the worse was yet to come. Armenak knew that soldiers feared coming into close quarters, where every corner offered a sniper an easy target. That meant prolonged, protracted fighting. Unless heavy artillery was used, the conflict could easily last months.

Soon they would have to fall back to the second trench. And Djevdet would not wait long. Every day they resisted was one more day that he had to explain to Constantinople that Van was still not under control; soon he would call for cannons.

"How long for them to break through the second row?" Aram asked.

"One, two days," Armenak said. "Then we go to the last trench."

"How are the men?"

"With all they have been through, I can think of no finer men to command," Armenak replied. They sat for a moment, thinking.

"We need help," Aram said.

"Yes," Armenak replied.

"Do you think we could get a message to Antranik?" Aram asked.

Armenak looked up, pondering the question. "We are most vulnerable to the east," he said. "To the west, and southwest, no. But if they come up from the southeast, we will not be able to protect our flank."

Aram nodded. "That is Bashkale."

"Yes," Armenak said. "My old friend, Bashkale," he said, thinking. "Yes," he said, finally. "We should try to get word to him."

"Pick two men," Aram said. "They leave tonight."

The two volunteers stood. Aram and Armenak watched as the cloth message was sewn into the first man's robe.

"Take no chances," Aram said. "That message must get there."

The men nodded and set off. Armenak had arranged for two Kurds to be their guides. They would take the men to the northeast, toward the Zola River. It was on good information that Antranik and his army would be there. They had to hurry.

PART FOUR

AEGEAN SEA
25 April 1915

The Gulf of Saros lay to the north of Suvla Bay and formed the point of confluence for the Entente Fleet. The outlines of more than 200 vessels were barely visible in the moonlight.

Two hundred!

As the lead ships pulled within ten miles of the Gulf, the Fleet began to disperse, heading to their pre-arranged points. The twenty-ninth division was bound for Cape Helles, at the tip of the Peninsula, near Sedd-Ul-Bahr; the Anzacs at Gaba Tepe. Aboard the ships, the men were ready, young and hopeful. The Australians and the New Zealanders were particularly optimistic; it was time to show the stuffy British that they were worthy of upholding the honor of their home-lands.

In the dark of night
Out upon the sea
Watching for the Turk
Wherever he may be
Anzacs! Anzacs!
All for Liberty!
Anzacs! Anzacs!
Fight for you and me!

The soldier flipped back the metal hinged cover and checked his watch. Just past one o'clock in the morning, the twenty-fifty of April.

He braced himself, and then stepped into the water. All along the beach at Ari Burnu, the soldiers came ashore. On land, Von Sanders stirred in his bed. There was a loud knock and he awoke.

"Yes?"

"General! They are landing!"

Von Sanders got up, reached for his tunic and buttoned it as he strode out of the makeshift barracks. As he reached the ridge high above the Gulf, he raised the binoculars to his eyes.

"Give the orders!" he called out. "Ring it down! Now!" The men scurried, calling to the outposts along the Peninsula.

The tranquility ceased just after four o'clock. The warships began their barrage, careening shell after shell against the Peninsula. This would form the cover under which the troops would land.

"Now! Now!" the men said, as the troops rushed into the water. The Anzacs were supposed to have landed at Gaba Tepe, but at the last moment, the plans had been changed; now they disembarked at Ari Burnu, south of Sulva Bay. Hamilton and his staff had agreed that the landings would be made simultaneously and as the Anzacs came ashore, so did the twenty-ninth at Cape Helles. They were joined by troops landing just to the west, at Tekke Burnu, and those landing at Sedd-Ul-Bahr and Kum Kale, and to the south of Kum Kale, at Besika Bay.

As the Fleet approached the Peninsula, the twenty-ninth was swung out to the tip at Cape Helles while the Anzacs were ferried north, past Imbros for the landing at Ari Burnu. Meanwhile, the French warships departed Lemnos and proceeded directly east, curved around the small island of Tenedos, and landed men at Besika and Kum Kale.

At Helles, the Turks rained down shell after shell, the machine fire cutting into the men as they stumbled ashore. At Ari Burnu, the landings proceeded more smoothly. But as they came ashore, these young Australians and New Zealanders were struck by the obvious: behind them was the water, in front of them was the enemy, and there they sat, on a long stretch of narrow sand.

Waiting.

CONSTANTINOPLE

Robert College had been established more than fifty years earlier by Christopher Rhinelander Robert, a wealthy importer from New York. It was situated approximately ten kilometers up the Bosphorus on the heights of Rumeli Hissar. Now comprised of almost a dozen buildings, it was inarguably Turkey's finest educational institution.

Morgenthau walked up the steps of the main building, crossed the central lobby, and stepped into the office of its President, Dr. Caleb Frank Gates. He had been appointed to the college in 1903 and, at fifty-eight was one year younger than Morgenthau. Gates had begun as a missionary and was fluent in Turkish.

"Mr. Ambassador. Good afternoon," he said.

"Thank you for seeing me at such short notice," Morgenthau replied.

"Not at all. I've had our history department gather and prepare some documents that chronicle their history. Please, have a seat."

"Thank you," Morgenthau said. He sat down at a long table. On it were arrayed a variety of folders, photographs, and several oversized books. Gates took a seat next to him. Morgenthau adjusted his pince-nez glasses and nodded.

"Very well then," Gates replied. He motioned for Morgenthau to open the book; the first image an amalgam of several mapped areas.

"It is a civilization more than two millenia old," Gates began. "They are an Indo-European race, a mix of Urartians, Assyrians, Chaldeans, and Armens." Morgenthau flipped the page.

"By 4 BC, Armenia was a part of the Persian Empire but remained relatively autonomous, denying conquest even by Alexander. By 95 BC, Tigranes the Great consolidated Greater Armenia to the East and Lesser Armenia to the West. He conquers Cilicia, Mesopotamia, Palestine, and Syria."

"Very impressive, especially given the distance and conditions," Morgenthau said.

"Quite," Gates replied. "And, as you can imagine, this did not set all that well with Rome." He nodded for Morgenthau to turn the page.

"An alliance is formed between Rome and Partha, and Lucullus and Pompey the Great convince Tigranes' son to betray him. Tigranes is left no choice and surrenders. Two-and-a-half centuries later, Armenia was ruled by King Tiridates the Third and Armenians practiced paganism."

Morgenthau flipped the page. On either side were two figures.

"Christ's disciples, Bartholomew and Thaddeus," Gates said. "After the resurrection, they bring forth Christianity to Armenia but it must continue underground for two-and-a-half centuries."

Morgenthau turned the page. On the left was a picture of a man in some type of dark cage.

"Gregory the Illuminator," Gates said. "He begins preaching Christianity and succeeds in converting the King's daughter. Incensed, Tiridates has him tortured and imprisons him for thirteen years in a pit below ground."

Morgenthau looked at Gates, who raised his eyebrows slightly. Morgenthau turned the page to reveal King Tiridates lying on a bed. On the right side was a rendering of an ornate cross.

"Later, a sick and infirm Tiridates calls for Gregory who summarily forgives him his sins and cures him of his infirmity. In 301 AD, Armenia converts to Christianity, becoming the first Christian nation, well before Rome." Gates paused for a moment, resting.

Morgenthau turned the page and looked at a magnificent snow peaked mountain and to its right, a smaller one.

"Mr. Ambassador, I assume you are familiar with Mt. Ararat?"

"Yes, in the East, the resting place of Noah's Ark."

"Indeed, according to the bible the Ark came to rest there and the Armenian Apostolics hold that Christ descended and appeared to mark the spot where the first Christian Church of Armenia was to be built." Gates nodded and Morgenthau flipped the page, revealing a simple stone church in cylindrical style.

"The church Etchmiadzin is built at the base of Mt. Ararat." Morgenthau flipped the page and the intricate Armenian script filled the page.

"By the fourth century, the Catholicos, the Armenian spiritual leader, under King Vramshapuh, instructs the priest Mesrob Mashtots to compose a unique alphabet, consisting of thirty-six letters."

"Ensuring their identity," Morgenthau said, looking at the script. "Once you have an alphabet and a language, it becomes very difficult to be assimilated."

"Precisely, Mr. Ambassador," Gates said. "With their conversion to Christianity, an alphabet, and their unique language, they begin their culture. Until 1048, a period of growth ensued. Freedom, economic prosperity, and the building of hundreds of churches with Ani as the Armenian capitol." Morgenthau turned the page.

"In that year," Gates continued, "the Seljuk Turks draw across the kingdom north of Lake Van. Ani is destroyed." Morgenthau looked at the drawings of Ani in ruins and a mass of men on horseback.

"Everywhere the villages are in shambles, the populace massacred or enslaved. For the next twenty-five years, there are unprecedented invasions: the Mongols, Genghis Khan, Tamerlane, Turkomen, and the Turanians. These were decisive and crippling campaigns." Morgenthau nodded. "By the eleventh century, Armenians settled here, where we sit, in Constantinople. And, five hundred years later, they spoke their language, tended their land, opened businesses, and prayed to Christ."

He looked at Morgenthau. "Would you like to stop for a moment?"

"No, thank you," Morgenthau said. "I would like to continue."

"Fine, then, book number two," Gates said. Morgenthau drew it near and opened it.

"By the sixteenth century, the Ottoman Turks ruled Armenia, imposing work taxes, religious taxes, and so forth. Even though Christians were barred from military service, they had to pay a tax for this exemption. But in point of fact, until the mid-1800's, relative prosperity endured though there was occasional mistreatment. Dispersing themselves, the Armenian intelligentsia concentrated here in Constantinople, and eventually began to settle in Europe, mainly France and Italy."

Gates turned to Morgenthau. "Of course you are familiar with the Treaty of Paris."

"Yes, of course," he said, turning to face Gates. "By the mid-1800's Turkey was tired and corrupt, prompting Czar Alexander's regard of Turkey as a very sick man," Morgenthau offered. "Of course, any child can see its importance. Here we sit in a country resting on two continents, with important trade routes, access to the Mediterranean, Asia, India, to the Caucasus." He looked directly at Gates. "The Treaty of Paris in 1856 puts Turkey on notice: answer to a European Council and face political and social reforms because your house is not in order. Of course, as we now know, it was an empty treaty."

"Indeed," Gates said. "The Russians declare war on Turkey in 1877 over the Balkans and the Treaty of San Stefano is signed in 1878. Turkey loses a portion of Armenia to Russia and almost all of its European territories. Czar Alexander intervenes once again and demands that reforms be afforded the Armenians. Of course, it is not an altruistic gesture: the Czar merely intends to increase his land holdings."

"And I am sure that did not sit well with the Sultan," Morgenthau added. Gates nodded, and turned the page for Morgenthau, revealing a portrait of Sultan Abdul Hamid.

"Precisely. And, I'm afraid, tragically," Gates said. Morgenthau looked at dots on a drawn map and aged drawings of men and women in peril. "For two years," continued Gates, "beginning in 1894, a series of massacres was organized and carried out. In Bitlis, Erzurum, Diyarbakir, Sassoon, Palou, Kharpert, Van, Sivas, and Aleppo. Village after village. Over two thousand villages."

Morgenthau was silent for a moment.

"How many?" he said, finally.

Gates paused for a moment, recalling the figures. "Eight thousand at Aleppo, ten thousand at Van, Sixteen-hundred in Palou, thousands in Kharpert."

"No," Morgenthau said, softly. "How many?"

Gates paused. He cleared his throat. "Mr. Ambassador. Official numbers are, as you would imagine in such circumstances, difficult, but even conservative numbers based on official consul reports place the number at more than two hundred thousand."

Morgenthau slowly pushed himself away from the table and stood up. Gates watched as he walked to the window and looked out.

"And all this because of their religion?" Morgenthau said, turning.

"No, Mr. Ambassador," Gates replied. He paused for a moment. "Mr. Ambassador. I am not a theologian, but a basic tenet of the faith of Islam is religious tolerance. This could not have been for religious reasons."

Morgenthau nodded.

"Again, I must stress that relations between Muslims and Christian Armenians were quite fraternal. They shared business interests. They were neighbors. They were even buried in the same cemeteries. No, any exploitation of religious differences was exploited by the Administration." His voice became quieter now. "The devastation," he said, "was severe: a culture without a country."

"A soul without a body," Morgenthau replied. "Only nineteen years ago."

Gates cocked his head and blinked.

"Six years."

"I beg your pardon?" Morgenthau said, turning.

"Six years. Six years ago, Mr. Ambassador," Gates said. He turned to the book and quickly flipped through the pages.

"Here," Gates said. "1909, in Cilicia and Adana. Eight days after they had been disarmed, the Armenian inhabitants in Adana were massacred by soldiers and brigands." Morgenthau looked at the photographs and scanned an eyewitness report signed and sealed with an official British stamp.

"The villages are burned down, the inhabitants are struck down, and..." Gates paused. Morgenthau looked at him, imploring him to continue. "And to ensure that no aid would be possible, the hands of doctors and nurses are hacked off."

Morgenthau closed his eyes for a moment and shook his head. He looked at Gates.

"Behold I send you forth as sheep in the midst of wolves. Be ye therefore wise as serpents and harmless as doves," he said.

Gates nodded. "Matthew."

It was late afternoon, and the sun was quickly receding. Morgenthau stepped into the street and buttoned his thick coat. A light rain was falling and would soon freeze over.

It was the twenty-sixth of April 1915.

His birthday.

He was fifty-nine years old.

NEAR BASHKALE

Bashkale, eighty kilometers southeast of Van, was in sight. Khalil Pasha's troops were exhausted, and the Turkish commander had no choice but to let them rest. His orders had been clear: take Bashkale, then sweep up and crush the Van Armenians in a vise. They would be pulverized between his forces and Djevdet's. Soon he would take Bashkale, and once it was secure the area to the rear of his forces would be protected as he marched his men toward Van.

ON THE ZOLA RIVER
28 April 1915

General Antranik sat, thinking. He was part of the combined Russian forces and he was bound to take orders from his Russian counterparts. Only eleven days earlier, Khalil's forces at Shaitakht had soundly defeated the Russians. They were on a path toward Bashkale, and with Bitlis lost, and with the fighting at Van, he was faced with a decision. To Bashkale and block Khali's army, or to the west, to Van and on to Bitlis?

He was born Antranik Ozanian on the twenty-fifth day of February 1865 at Shabin Karahissar in Sivas. He commanded some five thousand men now, all volunteers, almost all members of the Armenian Revolutionary Federation. He had participated in countless insurgencies against both Turkish and Kurdish forces, and was one of the most feared fedayees, freedom fighters.

Now he had to think. He had enough men to send toward Bashkale and attempt to secure it from Khalil. Or he could send them east, toward Van and Bitlis.

But he could not do both.

PALOU

Sarkis stood and raised his glass. The meal was finished; Lucine and Maritza put plate after plate of chicken and pilaf in front of the boys. Sarkis cleared his throat.

"We hope for you both a safe journey."

Hagop nodded. "Thank you, papa."

"Then let us drink this toast," Sarkis said. "To my son and to the son of my friend Dikran. May they represent us courageously and by the good grace of God return to us safely."

"And soon," Dikran said, raising his glass.

"And soon," came the collective reply.

"I would like to say something," Bedros said.

Sarkis and the others turned to him. Throughout the evening, he had been particularly quiet.

"Boys," he began. "If the weather turns bad, do not wait for the storm to come to you."

Sarkis, Dikran, and Garbis, who was standing next to Bedros, looked at one another.

"Do you understand?" Bedros said. His eyes met Hagop's.

"Yes, grandfather," Hagop said.

VAN

The shadows of the trees moving outside waved back and forth in the church interior. The young girl reached the aisle, knelt, and crossed herself. She moved forward, grabbed the two brass candlestick holders, and put them into a canvas sack.

Inside the home, candles flickered. Three men worked in silence, the scraping of metal punctuating their work. One man removed the brass tip from a cane and tossed it into the pile of shiny metal. The other men worked on candlestick holders and lanterns.

The special knock came on the side door, three followed by a pause followed by two, and one of the men opened it. The young girl walked into the room, struggling with the heavy sack. The man helped her and with a thump it plopped onto the table.

"Abris!" he said, patting the girl's head.

The men were arranged in an assembly line. The metal was thrown into a bucket and walked over to the kiln. A man dipped the cup into the bucket of molten metal and began filling the molds for the casings. The next man examined the bullets. He was looking for tiny cracks. They had to be strong. Otherwise they would burst. A man could lose his hand or his eyesight.

The measuring room held the different ingredients: saltpeter, sulfur, and carbon. But the amount of each was critical: long combustion cycles meant less power, but more range. Short combustion cycles meant ferocious power, but less range.

Once the casings were filled with powder, the next man placed the lead into the small holder and, turning the crank, squeezed tightly until the lead snapped into place. He lifted the crank, pulled out the bullet, and examined it. Now they could make more than two thousand cartridges a day.

TOWARDS VAN

The Armenian volunteer unit rested. They had been marching for nearly eight straight hours, but still there was no sign of the Russian forces they were supposed to meet. The distance from their initial point on the Zola to Van was approximately one hundred kilometers. To Bashkale, it was approximately fifty kilometers. Below Van stood Edremit, then Mengene Dag. Below it was Gurpinar and then, finally, Bashkale. The plan was simple: the unit would go from the Zola, travel northwest to Van and at Gurpinar, which was only ten kilometers to the southeast of Van, they would link up with the Russians. If they could keep up their rate of travel, Andranik's unit would get to Gurpinar in twenty hours.

PALOU

"See you tomorrow," Armen said.

"Early!" Hagop called out after him.

"Yes, yes, I know!"

Hagop and Souren watched him go.

"He is a good friend," Souren said. His words came out slightly slurred.

"Yes, he is," Hagop said. He paused for a moment and then looked at his friend.

"Souren?"

"Yes?"

"Are you drunk?"

"Me?"

"Yes, you. You smell like old potatoes!"

"Ah!" Souren said, wavering slightly. "I may have had a bit much!"

"I think that makes two of us!" Hagop said, laughing.

"Hagop, I have to move some boxes for my father. Can you help me?"

"Yes. Yes, sure. At what time in the morning?"

"No. I mean tonight!" Souren said.

Hagop looked at him.

"Tonight? You are serious? Tonight?"

Souren nodded. "Yes, come on... We have only to nail the boxes shut. We can move them in the morning."

Hagop nodded. "If we have to do it tonight, then, let's go."

"Good," Souren said.

Less than five minutes later, both staggering slightly as they walked, they entered the small shed adjoining Souren's home.

"I will be right in," Souren said. "I look first on my parents."

"Be quick," Hagop said. "I do not want to do everything myself!"

"Ah, do not worry," Souren said, grinning. "Would I do that to you?"

"Yes, you would!" Hagop said, calling after him.

Souren closed the shed door and Hagop walked over to a row of crates. He reached for the wooden mallet and a handful of nails. He lined a cover atop one of boxes and began nailing it shut.

"Ah, it is just like him," he said to himself. "To leave me like this alone..."

"Not alone..." the voice called out to him.

"Who is there?" he said, turning around.

From behind the crates a figure was formed from the shadows.

"It is I."

"Sona!" Hagop exclaimed.

"Yes!" she said, running towards him.

Hagop reached his arms out and as she came toward him, he took her hands in his. They kissed one another on both cheeks and he pulled her away from him, looking at her.

"But, how...?"

She smiled.

"Oh, I see," he said. "Souren."

"He thought we should see each other before you left."

"Hmm," Hagop said.

"He is a good soul," Sona said, squeezing his hands.

Hagop looked at her. Her face was beautiful to see. Her eyes danced. Her face smiled. It had been so long. He held her hands tightly and felt the bracelet that Lucine had given her. It had made slight oval indentations in her skin. "Ah. This bracelet is too tight. It should be loosened."

"No, no. It is fine."

Several moments passed, and their full brown eyes looked at each other, his face shimmering with life. She felt warmth around her, covering her, enveloping her. She looked away.

"What is it?" he said, turning her toward him.

"We are not supposed to be together without the eyes of our parents," she said.

Hagop smiled, catching Sona off guard.

"Yes, I know," he said, laughing. "Another custom. Sometimes, I think we have too many of them!"

"Yes, that may be," she said, taking his right hand in hers.

"When did you arrive?" he asked.

She looked at him, her eyes watching him, wavering. A tear dripped down her face. She turned away. He put his hands on her shoulders. He could feel her trembling. Slowly, he turned her around to him. Her eyes were red, and her cheeks were wet.

"What is wrong?"

She looked at him. It had been months since they had seen one another.

"I have missed you so," she said, as tears fell from her eyes.

Hagop reached his hands up and wiped away the wetness.

"Ah...Why do you cry? I will not be gone long."

Sona nodded slightly and Hagop cupped her face in his hands.

"I... I... I do not know," she said. "I am happy. I am sad. I..."

"Ah, do not think of anything," Hagop said.

"Souren says you are to go to Ctespihon."

"Yes, that is right."

"I did not even know where it was," Sona said. "My father had to show me on a map."

"Ah, well, it is nothing," Hagop said. "We will go, dig the roads, lay the track for the trains, and then they will let us return."

"Yes, but it is so far away..."

"Before you know, I will be back and we will be together."

She looked at him, and managed a slight smile. And then the tears came again.

"Ah, but you should not cry," he said. "I do not want to remember your face like this…"

"I cannot help it," she said. "They are not tears of pain, though…"

"Yes, but you look as if you are in pain," he said, attempting to make her laugh.

She smiled.

"Hagop."

"Yes?"

She looked into his eyes so deeply that her gaze caused him to blink.

"I want you to know something," she said. "I want you to know that this is the first time that I know, in my heart, that there is someone who loves me as you do."

"Yes, it is true," he answered. "I have thought of you every day, wondering what you would be doing at this hour, at that hour."

"Hagop," she said, dropping her hands. "Promise me that you will take care of yourself. Souren, too."

He nodded. "Do not worry about that. I will take care of both of us."

"Is there anything you need?"

"No, everything is in order."

"Something to be sewn… it will be hot in Ctespihon."

"No, no," he said, gently shaking his head. "It is all right."

She closed her eyes and the tears flowed once again from beneath the lids.

"Sona…" he whispered. "Sona."

"Yes…"

"Do not cry. We will be together soon enough." He put his arms around her and hugged her tightly for several moments. "And then, never apart," he said, pushing her slightly away from him. "This is my promise to you."

She nodded and managed a slight smile. He drew closer and kissed her gently on the forehead. He moved his left hand to the small of her back and she arched slightly. She looked up at him and he drew downward. They kissed, their lips touching.

It was the first time they had done so. It felt... It felt...
Wonderful.

And he would remember it for the rest of his life.

VAN

The heavy black cannons rolled by, followed by trucks of soldiers.
Djevdet motioned to his assistants.

"They are to take up positions immediately," he said. "Based on
authorities granted to me directly from Constantinople, I order you to
level the village."

Pandemonium! The heavy cannon fire ripped into the front row of
homes. Fires erupted. Large, powerful trees were splintered and shattered. Had they been in the first trench, the men surely would have
been decapitated. The front row of homes would not last long. They
had been burning for days now, and the cannon fire would demolish
them. Then the second row of homes would fall under attack. The earth
shook. The noise was deafening.

ERZEROUM

Erzeroum lay, one hundred thirty kilometers to the northeast of
Palou. General Mahmud Kamil stood, surrounded by a group of Turkish soldiers and Gendarmes. Occasionally they glanced at the group of
Armenians who had brought forth their shovels, hoes, axes, and rakes
and threw them onto the shallow pile.

Kamil nodded at the chief gendarme who stepped forward.

"Good," he said. "You have pleased the Vali."

He looked at Kamil, who nodded.

"You are dismissed," the gendarme said. "You may go back to your
homes."

Kamil watched them go. Then he nodded to two soldiers. They
walked forward, dragging a burlap sack. They emptied its contents
onto the pile of tools.

Old rifles, pistols, and sabers tumbled out and the soldiers kicked
the items left and right, scattering them among the farm instruments.

Kamil nodded to the chief gendarme holding the large camera. Kamil motioned to one of the officers who rushed over.

"Send the photographs to Constantinople along with this official report," he said.

The officer nodded his readiness and Kamil dictated.

"We have located a large store of weapons and have disarmed the Armenians who continue to remain uncooperative. Enclosed find photographic evidence. Kamil."

"Yes, General," the officer said. "Immediately!"

VAN

Aram, Armenak, and Varouj sat in the church anteroom. The ancient walls of the church shook and shuddered with each cannon blast. Outside, fires raged.

"We cannot withstand much longer," Varouj said. "Rifles against cannons do not last long."

"We will fight to the last man," Armenak said, looking at him.

"And then what?" Varouj asked. "We cannot get out." He turned to Aram. "And we have heard nothing from Antranik's forces. Are they even coming?"

"It does not matter," Aram said. "We will be killed anyway." He looked from man to man. "You know what will happen to our women and to our daughters."

A few of the men nodded, but no one spoke.

"No male child will be allowed to live lest he grow to seek revenge," Aram said, his voice rising. "No Armenian woman will be allowed to live lest they have Armenian children." He looked from man to man. "Do you all understand?"

"Everyone understands, Aram," Armenak said.

The men nodded in silence and then, quietly, went back to work.

ACHI BABA
8 May 1915

The men sat, caked in mud, the signs of the constant fighting etched on their faces. They were dug in now, and the trenches snaked from side to side, shorn up with inadequate supplies of timber. From their lines behind Krithia, Hamilton had been ordered by Kitchener to make a run on Achi Baba; it lay on the Gallipoli Penninsula, some four thousand yards from the Allied front lines.

They rose to their feet, crouched down just beneath the trench line. Adrenaline pumped through their young veins. They waited until they heard the whistle; then it would be time.

The fighting along the Peninsula had become brutal. To the North, at Anzac Cove, the Anzacs were fighting heroically but in a six day period more than eight thousand men were lost; the Turks had suffered almost doubly. Further south, at Cape Helles, the Twenty-ninth had already lost ten thousand men, either dead or injured, and the French had lost more than half of her twenty-two thousand men. At Malta, the hospital was overrun and the dead lay in the sun, their bodies bloating grotesquely.

The commander looked at his troops, bayonets fixed, rifles ready. He inhaled and brought the whistle to his lips.

"Hurrah! Hurrah!" they shouted as they came over the top.

Magnificent: the finest boys from Australia, New Zealand, Britain, and Ireland. They ran forward, undaunted, valiant. And they fell. The Turkish machine guns cut through them, cut through their flesh, the live rounds setting their clothes afire. The ground, already bone-dry in early May, absorbed the dark red blood.

Hamilton had been deeply disturbed at the enormity of the losses and had called Birdwood, instructing him to draw up a withdrawal plan. Birdwood had argued: the losses were not excessive. They had to win Achi Baba yard by yard. Finally, Hamilton agreed. The men would stay.

And many, many more would die.

VAN

The bombardment continued and now the men valiantly fought from the third trench.

"Rifles up!" Armenak commanded.

The Turkish soldiers moved forward and the Vanetzis fired. Suddenly, the Turks faltered slightly. To the right, shots rang out, but they were from larger caliber guns; Armenak's ears could tell the difference. He looked quickly to the right and saw puffs of white smoke coming from the brush.

"Fire!" Armenak shouted. "Fire! Fire!"

Caught in the crossfire, the Turks went down. They began to retreat, scrambling backwards. Armenak looked up as Aram rushed to his side.

"What has happened?" Aram asked.

Before Armenak could answer, from the brush two flags were raised. One was red, blue, and orange, Armenian, the other, Russian. The flags bobbed up and down as the combined forces appeared. Armenak and Aram looked at one another. Behind them, cheers went up from the Vanetzis. Within minutes, Aram, Armenak, and Varouj were talking to their counterparts, congratulating and thanking them. That evening, the Vanetzis flew the Armenian flag within their compound. As they did, Djevdet, beyond rage, informed Constantinople that the Russians were conspiring with the Armenians and the eastern region was in danger of being lost. Reinforcements were necessary. Quickly.

It had been more than six weeks since Djevdet's edict calling for the men. But, as both Aram and Armenak had known from the beginning, they could not stay.

The Vanetzis, who had lived here since before Christ, now gathered what belongings they could carry and began their journey across the Caucasus. More than one hundred fifty thousand of them marched out across rough, rocky terrain. Many of them would not survive. Disease, dehydration, and starvation consumed thousands. But those who did make it to the eastern side, to their Russian-Armenian countrymen, would have better chances of survival.

Armenak would make his way to Cairo. But Aram, made frail and weak by typhus, succumbed in the winter of 1918. They fought, and the Vanetzis never forgot them.

KHARPERT
27 May 1915

Turmoil!

The Armenian homes stood, marked with chalk-white crosses, while Turkish soldiers, policemen, and gendarmes stood around, most on foot, some on horseback. The Kharpertzis ran back and forth, careful to avoid contact. On every wall official documents were posted, and an

Armenian man adjusted his glasses as he read the words above the gold seal stamp.

"Official Edict of Deportation," he read. "All persons suspected of treason or espionage will be deported to areas to ensure that they will pose no threat to the Empire."

"But this is our home," the woman standing next to him said. "We have done nothing."

"They want us out," the man replied.

"Yes, but..."

Suddenly, a group of eighteen men, tied together two-by-two, were led through the square by a group of gendarmes. They were gaunt, and from the wounds on their faces and arms, it was obvious that they had been beaten.

"Where are you taking them?" a woman asked. "What have they done?"

"They are being deported on suspicion of espionage," the gendarme answered. "Do not interfere. They will return after the war ends."

In less than one day, the Kharpertzis had been driven out, and were making their way toward the desert.

BITLIS

Sona sat at the table, drawing the needle through the delicate silk. Elise was seated opposite her, and occasionally she would look up at her daughter. Nishan sat, reading the day's journal. He had been married to Elise for seventeen years. While the girls were still small, he and Elise had discussed sending them to Paris. This had not come to pass, for Azniv had met Vache and Sona had met Hagop. But Nishan still secretly clung to the idea that they both belonged far away from Bitlis.

The knock on the door was swift and heavy. It startled Sona. It was late.

"Khatchaturian!"

Nishan looked at Elise as he picked up the kerosene lamp and walked to the door.

"Khatchaturian, Nishan!" the voice called out, again accompanied by a loud rap.

"Please, one moment. I am coming," Nishan said, stalling.

"Sona, go into the bedroom," he said. "Close the door."

Sona looked from him to Elise. "No, Papa," she said. "I will stay here with you and mama."

Nishan reached the door and looked at Elise.

"Khatchaturian, Nishan!"

"Sona, do as I tell you to do," he said. He motioned to Elise who nodded.

"Khatchaturian! Open the door!"

"Go, I will stay with your father," Elise said. Sona looked at them and walked toward the back bedroom and closed the door.

Nishan moved to the door and opened it. Elise saw the two policemen standing in the doorway and gasped. Nishan took a step backward.

"You are Khatchaturian?" the first policeman asked.

"Yes," Nishan replied.

"We have come to your home because your name arose during questioning of a confirmed Russian conspirator," the second policeman said.

Nishan looked back at Elise and saw that she was terrified.

"No, no. That is not possible. I am just a tailor," he said.

The first policeman stepped inside. "We know your shop," he said, looking around the home's interior. "We know that you are a businessman."

"And businessmen come into contact with many types of people," the second policeman offered.

"Many different people come into my shop, it is true," Nishan said. "But I have no..."

"Khatchaturian," the second policeman said, cutting him off. He took a step forward. Elise opened her mouth, but Nishan shook his head.

Sona leaned her head against the door and tried to listen. The second policeman looked at Nishan, his eyes moving over his clothes. "We know that you have no political connections," he said.

"Let us say that perhaps this Russian pig informer is lying," said the first.

"We could be persuaded to allow you to continue your business," added the second.

"What must I do?" Nishan asked.

"You are a good craftsman," the first policeman said. "Officers and soldiers need uniforms. You will need more help. Your wife and daughter will no longer work at your shop. We will bring you Turkish citizens."

Sona struggled to hear, but everything was muffled.

"You will train and supervise them," the second policeman said.

"But I don't need..."

"Khatchaturian," the first policeman said. "There will be much change here. We are offering you something that you should take. Be a loyal citizen to the Empire and you and your family will live out this war with few problems."

Nishan and Elise exchanged glances. He closed his eyes and nodded.

"Yes. Yes. I will do as you ask."

"Very good, Khatchaturian," the first policeman said. "We will return tomorrow with your new workers."

Nishan nodded.

"There is one other thing, Khatchaturian," the second policeman said, stepping closer.

"Yes?"

"As a good Ottoman citizen, you will no longer need this," he said, reaching his hand out and flicking the cross which hung from Nishan's neck.

Elise and Nishan exchanged glances.

"I do not understand," Nishan said.

"Khachaturian," the first policeman said, looking directly into his eyes. "The Armenians are being moved out because they are traitors. For you to live here in Turkey, you will observe our principles. Conversion is mandatory."

Elise stood, motionless. From beneath the door jamb, Sona saw forms moving across the floor.

"I will do as you say. Everything you ask I can do," Nishan said.

"Good, then, we are finished with this discussion," the first policeman said.

"But I will not forsake my beliefs..."

The first policeman stopped and turned. He looked at his colleague and for a moment, there was nothing. When Elise thought about it weeks later, she remembered that it was as if everything had stopped and they were all just there.

Slowed down. Suspended.

And then, in one continuous blinding motion, the second policeman reached up and struck Nishan with the side of his pistol. He went down, and the base of the kerosene lamp hit the floor with a loud clink.

"Nishan!" Elise screamed. She moved to go to him. Sona got up and reached for the metal latch. She fumbled with it and finally it lifted. She rushed out into the main room and saw her father, slumped to the floor, his face rapidly covering with blood from the gash in his forehead.

"Papa!"

"No, no!" Elise said, holding her back.

"You see, I told you that he would be so," the second policeman said.

"Please, stop! Please, stop!" Elise said.

The first policeman looked in her direction. The second looked past her, directly at Sona. Elise moved in front of her.

"No words from you, woman!" the first policeman said.

Nishan braced himself against the wall, brushing back the blood. "No, no. Please leave them alone," he said. The policemen turned to him. "I will do everything you ask of me but not this," Nishan said. "I was born a Christian and I will die a Christian."

"Then I will take you to your God now!" the first policeman said. They grabbed him, lifting him from the floor.

"Nishan!"

"Papa!"

The second policeman looked back at Elise and Sona.

"Stay in this house. If you attempt to stop us, I will have you both shot."

Sona took a half-step forward, but Elise held her back.

"Papa!"

"Stay in the house!" Nishan managed. He looked at Elise, the fear paralyzing her. "Stay in the house."

The door slammed behind them, and Elise and Sona stood there, holding each other.

The policemen dragged him through the darkness of the night, his feet and legs brushing against coarse gravel and dirt. His heart pounded; it felt as if it was bursting! But he would return to his family. They would bring strangers to work in his shop. Fine then, if that was what he had to do.

But, gradually, he would make preparations to move Elise, Sona, and Hrant to Paris. It could be done. His family would protest. He would insist. If Hagop wanted Sona, and Vache wanted Azniv, they would both have to leave Palou. It was Nishan's decision; he would set the conditions.

The blood from the cut dripped into his mouth. He spat onto the ground. He was having trouble seeing clearly, the blood was clouding his vision. Trees. They quickened their pace. The flickering light of hanging kerosene lamps painted strange moving images. As they stood him up, Nishan's eyes widened. He saw the makeshift structure, and knew that he would never see them again.

They dragged him to the wooden gallows, designed to hang several people at once. The nooses swung slowly in the nighttime breeze and the swinging of the kerosene lamps gave Nishan a feeling of vertigo. From the right, three Turkish soldiers and two other policemen brought forward five Armenian prisoners. Their legs and hands were tied; some had bruises that had grown into deep welts. The nooses went around their necks.

He could not believe it was happening.

Nishan felt the noose go around his neck, its rough stringy edges digging into his skin. A short cord of rope went around his hands. There were no hoods, no blindfolds. He looked to his right at the other men. Three were close to his age but the other two were no more than twenty. They were terrified. One of the older ones had soiled himself and the widening stain showed on the front of his pants.

The policemen and soldiers stood. The nooses hung from the same central pole that was supported by two cross braces. With a soldier positioned at both ends of this cross brace, lifting it would raise the center beam and lift the men off their feet. Normally, they would be suspended and dropped, the floor falling away from them, but there hadn't been time to construct that. Not yet at least.

One of the younger men whimpered. The two soldiers walked to either end of the cross brace. Nishan looked at them and he began to shiver. Automatically, for he did not know how it was happening, he relaxed. His lips began to move.

"From this Belief no one can move us, neither angels nor men; neither fire nor sword, nor water, nor any other horrid tortures..."

The two younger men raised their heads. They turned to their left and saw Nishan. He kept looking straight ahead, and the words came to him now, quicker.

"...All our goods and possessions are in your hands, our bodies are before you; dispose of them as you will."

The older men turned to Nishan. The two policemen looked at one another. The two soldiers stood, awaiting the order. Nishan stopped for a moment and when he again opened his mouth, he was joined by the voice of one of the younger men.

"Tortures from you, submission from us; the sword is yours, here are our necks..."

The words had been learned and memorized by all the men as part of their church teachings. They had first been spoken some fifteen hundred years earlier. In 499 A.D., the Persian King Yazdegert had pronounced to the Armenians an ultimatum: that they should accept Mazdeism, the perfect religion, or face their assured destruction. These were the words that Yazdegert had received from his Armenian populace.

"We should die as mortals, that He may accept our death as that of immortals."

Nishan closed his eyes and when he opened them, he saw flashes of white light. Elise, Azniv, Sona, Hrant. The sounds of the zourna, and the dhol. The procession. Hagop. Elise, smiling. White. Flashes. Azniv. Babies. The Eiffel Tower. Sona. Dancing. Walking toward him. Elise holding out her hand.

The soldiers looked at the corporal who nodded. They lifted the cross brace. The ropes went stiff and the men were lifted off their feet. The wood strained and creaked under the weight but held strong. Their bodies kicked up in protest and blood and spit worked together as the gagging sound rose and then began to subside. Nishan blinked faster and faster. And now the images coming to him were different.

Sona. Walking. Elise. Crying. Tears. Walking. Walking. Walking. His eyes fluttered and lost their muscular control. His body went slack and he hung there, still.

PALOU

Sarkis stood with Dikran, Garbis, Armen, and Vache in the square with boys and men ranging from thirteen to sixty. The official edicts had been pasted to the walls of their homes and the church. Lucine, Bedros, Takouhi, and Maritza stood together, while Anahid was home, watching over Vahe. Lucine saw Azniv standing alone and called to her. When she came over, Lucine noticed that she was shivering. In this heat.

To the right, the Turkish soldiers and gendarmes stood together. The chief gendarme waited until there was silence.

"To guard against any possible collaboration with opposing military forces, and by order of the Ottoman Empire, able-bodied men of Palou are temporarily being moved to the interior of the country."

Murmurs rose from the crowd. Sarkis looked at Lucine who was already staring at him. The gendarme put his hands up, quieting them.

"I assure you," he said. "There is no reason for concern. These men will return as soon as the danger to our eastern border passes. Good subjects of the Empire, you will report here tomorrow at sunrise. Now you may go."

"I do not understand why they have to move you," Lucine said. "I do not understand it."

Sarkis put his hand on her shoulder, quieting her. They all sat around the table, including Vache and Azniv.

"There is nothing to understand," Sarkis said. "They do it to avoid any risk."

"What risk is there?" Maritza said. "You are not soldiers."

"They move them because they fear them," Bedros said.

All eyes turned to him, and he paused for a moment.

"What do you mean?" Takouhi asked.

"They fear us because they fear that we will aid our Armenian brothers in Russia," Bedros said.

"But we are so far from the border," Lucine said.

"It does not matter," Sarkis said. "This is a time of war."

"And men do not think clearly during such times," Bedros added.

"For me I do not care," Garbis said. He motioned to Armen. "But my son is a young man."

"Do not worry about me, papa," Armen said.

"They have decided and we do not have a choice," Sarkis said. "We must go. If we do not, they will take us anyway." He looked from Anahid to Lucine. "And then they will make our families suffer for our stubbornness."

"But, we have been loyal and they know this," Dikran said.

"Yes, and the Vali benefits nicely from our labors," Bedros added.

Takouhi looked at him and nodded. She glanced at Lucine. "When the cow is giving you milk, you do not put the cow out in the cold weather to starve."

Bedros chuckled. "She is right," he said.

There was some nervous laughter, and it helped alleviate the tension.

"Even so," Sarkis said, looking at them. "After we leave tomorrow, stay close to one another and travel in pairs."

The women nodded silently. Beneath the table, Lucine squeezed Sarkis' hand so tightly it hurt.

Sarkis had slept soundly. But for Lucine, sleep would not come. Thoughts had come into her head, and she had pushed out the bad ones. It hadn't helped that there had been no word from Hagop and Souren.

Damn war!

Now Sarkis walked through the small home, looking at the stores of wheat and rice. He counted the jars of preserves, meats, jams, and toorshee. There was no telling when he would be back and with both him and Hagop gone, and with spring turning into summer, there would be so much to do. Bedros could not manage it, and Anahid would have to do more.

Damn war! What threat are we to them? They have swords and pistols and rifles and we have farm tools! It is crazy! He sat down. He thought of Hagop and Souren. It would be the same for Dikran. Vakh, poor Dikran! 'What kind of a thing is that?' he thought. 'He has to leave his baby before he is even baptized. Shame on it!'

He watched as the sun crept over the horizon. His small bag, packed, sat in the corner. Within the half-hour, the room was fully illuminated, and he could tell that it was going to be a warm day.

"You should eat more," Lucine said. She sat opposite him, pushing the plate toward him. They were the only ones awake, but he had promised Anahid that he would not leave without saying goodbye. Sarkis finished the cup of coffee and put it down.

"Ah, it is enough," he said. He sat for a moment, his plate empty, her plate full.

"You should eat instead of worrying about me," he said. He smiled slightly, hoping that it would relax her, but she sat, her eyes filling up with water.

"Do not worry," he said.

"You will send word?" she said, trying to smile.

"Yes. As soon as possible." He reached his hands over the table and put them on hers. "I will be thinking of you always, and I will return as soon as I can."

"You promise me?"

He nodded. They walked quietly to Anahid's small room, and peering in, watched her sleeping soundly.

"Look at this one," he said.

"Dead to the world," Lucine said.

"Yes, I hate to wake her."

"If you do not, she will never let you forget it."

"Yes, I know," he said, smiling. "She has a memory like yours."

He walked over, knelt down, and gently shook her.

"Papa," she said, groggily.

"Stay in bed," he said. "Rest. Your father is leaving."

"I… A safe journey, papa. Come back quickly."

"Before you know I am gone," he said. He bent down and kissed her on the forehead.

In the square, the men stood some still half-asleep. Dikran, Garbis, Armen, and Vache stood together. Watching over them were several mounted gendarmes. Other gendarmes on foot milled about.

"Now it is time," Sarkis said.

She nodded, and Sarkis drew her close to him. After all these years, she still felt good to him. Maybe a little more plump on the top and on the bottom, but, all in all, a nice package.

"Mi muhdahokveer," he said. Do not worry.

"Inchoo bidee muhdahokveem?" she answered. What am I going to worry about?

They hugged one another tightly and he kissed her full on the lips.

She watched him go, and when she could no longer see him, she closed the door, sat at the table, and wept.

Sarkis turned the corner leading into the square. Armen saw him first, ran to him, and brought him over to the others.

"Did you get up late?" Dikran said. "Too much raki last night?"

"Ah, I was up before you!" Sarkis replied.

The sparring helped raise the mood a bit, and some of the tension, especially on Vache's face, subsided. Azniv: he could think only of her. His father, Ashod, stood off to the side and occasionally glanced over.

The chief gendarme nodded to another who stepped forward and read off the names from his list.

"They are all present," he said, folding the paper.

"Very good," the chief gendarme answered. He turned to the men. "You will march in an orderly fashion."

"Where do we go?" called a voice from the crowd.

The gendarme turned towards the men.

"You go toward Mezre," he said.

Mezre!

The men looked at one another. Mezre was near Kharpert, at least fifty kilometers away, Armen calculated, and even if they walked arak-arak, fast fast, it would take at least ten hours to get there.

"Just outside of Mezre, trucks will take you to the interior where you will stay until the threat of war on the eastern front is over," the gendarme said. "Now, we go!" He turned his horse and the men began marching towards the outskirts of Palou.

Four hours later, with one stop made for the men to relieve themselves, the chief gendarme drew up his horse. He looked back at the line of men, some straggling far behind.

"You march like women."

Sarkis and Dikran glanced at one another.

"Papa, are you all right?" Armen said to Garbis.

"Yes," he said, resting a hand on Armen's shoulder. "I am thirsty. How are you?"

"Good. Thirsty."

As Sarkis had thought, the day had proven to be warm, and they had not been given any water. Maybe at the next stop.

"We must get to our meeting point at the time that I have been given," the gendarme said. "Therefore, you must march faster. Each man will be tied to another."

Sarkis, Dikran, Garbis, Vache, and Armen looked at one another. The other men, some of whom were sitting, seemed confused. Four gendarmes moved from man to man, tying their wrists together.

"Why must we be tied?" one man asked.

"Your line extends too far back," the gendarme answered, annoyed. He pulled the rope strap tight, linking both men together. "This will make you march in step."

Now, twenty groups of two men each were tied together. Sarkis to Dikran. Garbis to Armen. Vache to Nerseh Bagdoyan, a neighbor.

"That will help you women move faster," the chief gendarme said.

He turned and the men slowly followed. At first it was difficult, but the steps between each man began to even out. Surprisingly, it seemed to be working. Garbis tugged on the strap and Armen looked at him. He pressed something into Armen's hand and, without looking, Armen knew it was Garbis's small carving knife: the one that he used to whittle wood.

Armen looked at his father.

"Baranuh guhdreh," he whispered, turning his head slightly toward Armen. Cut the rope.

Armen hesitated for a moment, then nodded. He cupped the knife in his left hand. It was small but it was sharp; Garbis kept it that way. As they walked, Armen slowly worked the knife against the rope.

ERZEROUM

Deportation!

The Armenians were gathered in the village square, their belongings piled atop eshes, carts, and on their backs. The men had been gone for days; all that remained were women, children, and old men. The Vali's official stepped forward and unraveled the proclamation. He looked at the group, noting that they had taken as many possessions as they could possibly carry.

That was good. Very good. They had argued about that.

"No. I tell you, if we prevent them from taking their possessions, they will hide what we really want. They will hide the gold, the jewelry, the coins."

"Why does that matter? We will find it. We will have all the time in the world to find it."

"Sometimes I think you do not think before you open your mouth."

"What do you mean?"

"By allowing them to take anything they wish, we are assured that they will take their valuables. Now do you see?"

"Ah. Yes. Yes."

"They will leave with what we really want. We will only have to search them for it."

"By order of Tahsin Pasa, Vali of Erzeroum," the official said. "Your safety here cannot be ensured. You will be relocated for the duration of the war." He looked at the crowd. "I see that many of you have brought some of your belongings. Valuable possessions may be kept for safekeeping in Erzeroum bank. Your homes will be sealed and it will be forbidden for anyone to enter."

NEAR MEZRE

It was late afternoon now, and the caravan of men continued. The sun was bright: the core of it seemed to burn like hot moving liquid. Armen had managed to cut through almost half of the rope. As they walked, they did not notice that the four mounted gendarmes had slowly begun to draw back and away from them.

Now they were to the rear.

The gendarmes on foot slowed their pace slightly as the shackled men passed by. The chief gendarme nodded at the others. They reached back for their rifles and began shooting.

"Run! Run!"

The shots rang out, and for a brief moment, Sarkis looked at Dikran. The men tried to scatter, but in their panic, they had forgotten their bindings. One went left the other right, and the bullets found their mark.

"Run, get away!" Garbis said. He tugged at the rope, trying to snap it.

"No, Papa! Come on, come on!" Armen said.

Sarkis and Dikran turned and ran. The gendarme raised his pistol and fired. Dikran brought his right hand up to his neck, the blood so deep and thick that he fell over instantly, pulling Sarkis down with him.

"Dikran! Dikran!" Sarkis screamed.

One of the bullets had taken down Nerseh Bagdoyan and Vache managed to pull the rope free from the dead man. He started to run. A bullet struck him in the back.

Armen pulled the rope fast and short and it snapped. He looked at his father.

"Papa!"

"Go! Go!" Garbis said. "Go now!"

"No!"

Garbis looked up. A shot rang out, ripping open his chest.

"Papa! Papa!" Armen cried, shaking him. He looked from the wound to his father's eyes. His body twitched and then went still.

Sarkis crouched. He raised his head. As he did, the gendarme fired, hitting him in the back. For a moment, it felt like fire: like putting your hand too close and then pulling it away too late. That was the thought that hammered into his head as he sailed down, the sky falling away from him. His face hit the ground. The shhhhhhhhh of air and wind came into his ears. His vision fogged and clouded and blurred all at once.

"My God," he said, gurgling blood. "My holy God."

And then he was gone.

The rhythm of the shots was broken now, and Armen lay still for a moment, his heart pounding his temples so hard it felt like he was going to explode. He could hear laughing now, and the smell of cordite and gray smoke hung over the dead men who were scattered every which way.

Sarkis. Dikran. Vache. His father.

He would have one chance. He looked at the row of trees to the left. The gendarmes stood in a row, posing, their rifles held aloft. One of them aimed the camera and took the photograph.

It was customary.

And as the flash powder subsided, the men cleared their visions. None of them would notice the slight movement among the branches as Armen made his escape.

PART FIVE

CONSTANTINOPLE

Mowbry collected the previous evening's telexes and climbed the stairs to the office.

"Excuse me, Mr. Ambassador."

"Yes, Mr. Mowbry?"

"The overnight telexes. Top one from Secretary Bryan."

"Thank you," Morgenthau said. He began reading the Bryan telex and as he did so, Mowbry stood for a moment, watching him. Finally, he turned, closing the door behind him.

To: Henry S. Morgenthau, United States Ambassador, Constantinople

From: William Jennings Bryan, United States Secretary of State

Regarding: Armenian Situation

Mr. Ambassador,

Situation in Turkey unacceptable. I urge you to continue strong official American protest to the Ottoman Government on behalf of the Armenians. Details of various humanitarian aid programs follow under separate communication. My regards to you and Josephine.

WJB

Morgenthau looked up from the telex and closed his eyes. Whatever assistance he could provide would be of his own doing. There would be nothing from the State Department.

Well at least now he knew.

BITLIS

They sat in silence, and occasionally Sona looked up from her work to check on her mother. Elise reached for the small blanket.

"This will do," she said. She wore a black mourning veil and it shrouded much of her face. Beneath it, her cheeks were wet, had been for two days. After they had taken Nishan, Elise had grappled with Sona, who tore at her hands, trying to go after him.

"No! You must not!" Elise had said.

"I have to, mama! I have to!"

"Listen to me. Listen to me!"

"Papa! Papa!"

"If you go there, you will be shot! You did not see the look in their eyes!"

"Let me go!"

"No! Your father wants it this way…"

"He wants it this way…" Elise repeated, more a moan than anything else. In the end, Sona had relented. She was scared, trembling. And her mother had been right. If she had gone, she, too, would be dead.

Old man Dobalian found the bodies the next day, twisting in the wind, grotesque figures dancing on strings, the thick lines around their necks black, red, and dark blue. He picked up some stones and threw them at the wild dogs that had come to lick up the blood and tear at the feet and legs. When he drew closer and saw what they had done, it had made him sick enough to vomit.

Hrant had gone to the Vali to protest. Elise had begged, pleaded with him not to, and he had disappeared. She would never know what had happened to him. Nishan and the others were quickly buried, and as Elise and Sona stepped forward to throw in their palm full of sand, Sona had broken down; Elise drew her close and whispered to her.

"You cry all you want in your home, but here, you will not let anyone else see."

Sona nodded, wiped the tears from her eyes, and tightened her resolve.

Now she carefully folded the fine silk clothes and placed them in the saddlebag. Elise took the blanket and turned it lengthwise. She opened the small white sack and poured the contents onto the table.

Coins. Money.

Sona looked up as the coins toppled onto the table.

"Sona, come here," Elise said. "See what I do now."

"Yes, mama."

Elise divided the coins into two piles. She placed some alongside one end of the blanket.

"Hold this for me," she said.

"Yes, mama."

Elise carefully folded the blanket over, creating a hem to hold in the coins. She looked at the beautiful silk material. Nishan could always pick the best. She pushed back the tears and began sewing the coins into the material.

"You take the other pile and sew it into the rug," she said.

"Yes, mama. I will do it now."

"Double stitch, Sona," she said. "Double stitch."

"Yes, mama."

When she was done, Sona brought the rug over for Elise to inspect. She took it, turned it over, and tried to pull apart the stitches.

"Good."

Sona nodded.

"Now sit down."

Elise put a leather pouch on the table. She untied the short string and spread the leather flat, revealing several glistening pieces of gold: two bracelets, one ring, and a small family Bible.

"The money in the blanket and in the rug we use in case of any emergencies on the way," she said. Sona nodded. "The bracelets we are wearing we use next."

"But mama, I do not understand," Sona said. "We are coming back…"

Elise looked at her for a moment, reached her hands up, and gently pulled off her veil.

"We do not know how long we will be gone," she said, "and we have to plan."

"Yes, mama."

"Now, these things here. You take these two bracelets and this ring. Wear the bracelets on your ankles. They will fit." Sona nodded. "Put

the ring on your necklace and wear it inside your shabeeg. The Bible is
small, we'll need it with us."

"Yes, mama."

Hot.

The eshes strained under the weight of possessions. The old men,
women, and children of Bitlis stood in the square while the gendarmes
stood watch.

Sona followed Elise out of the house and gently closed the door
behind her. Elise looked into the empty shop and could still see Nishan
there, working at his table, measuring, figuring.

"Let us go," she said.

They walked together in silence, both carrying bundles, and
stopped when they saw the throng of people.

"So this is what they do to us, after all these years?" a woman said.

"Koghut var kasheh," Elise said. Pull down your veil. Sona did,
and they made their way through the crowd, taking note of the gendarmes, and settled into a small area.

"Elise! Sona!" the woman said, running toward them.

The woman pushed her way through the crowd and Elise could see
that it was Yilmaz, their neighbor. Yilmaz was a Turk from Konya who
had been brought to Bitlis by a Turkish man. She, Elise, and Nishan had
spent hours talking Turkish and drinking coffee.

"Yilmaz!" Elise said.

Yilmaz drew closer and Elise could see the tears on her face.

"What is wrong?" Elise said.

Yilmaz drew forth and hugged Elise and Sona.

"I had to come to see you," she said, stammering. She looked at the
gendarmes. "They told us not to."

Elise nodded and glanced quickly at Sona.

"I am glad you came," Elise said.

"I brought you some food," Yilmaz said, thrusting the brown package into Elise's hands. "Basturma. Your favorite."

"Thank you Yilmaz, my friend."

Sona looked down and could see that the old woman's right hand
was twitching.

"What they did to Nishan was wrong," Yilmaz said. "Wrong, wrong, wrong."

Elise looked at her.

"I know, Yilmaz, I know."

"I am so sorry! They are sending you all away." She looked at Elise. "But you have done nothing." She looked around at the other deportees. "None of you have done anything! Damn war!"

Elise closed her eyes for a moment. A shiver passed through her. She put her hands on the old woman's shoulders and looked into her eyes.

"Yilmaz. It is not the war."

The woman looked at her, but her face was confused.

"Remember to any American who comes here," Elise said. "It is not the war. It was never the war."

Sona looked from Yilmaz to her mother.

"We have the wrong name," Elise said.

"I do not understand," the woman said. "What do you mean? What is wrong with your name?"

Elise drew Sona closer and they embraced the old woman, hugging her tightly.

"God be with you," Yilmaz said. "God be with you."

OUTSIDE MEZRE

It was quiet now, had been for hours. Armen rolled up off his stomach and sat in the brush. His head hurt and there was a small cut on his forehead. At the flash, he had slid down a small hill, away from them. He crouched as low as he could and ran until he could no longer hear their laughing, knowing that they were stepping through the bodies, picking them clean of their belongings.

Now the sun was on the other side of the ground. Armen stood. There was nothing nearby that he could see: no homes, no fields. First, water. He had to find some water. Then he could think about what to do.

BITLIS

Sona and Elise watched as the Turkish policemen went home by home, laying wooden boards against the doorways, nailing the entrances shut.

"Look," an older woman said. "They are closing up the homes."

"Good," the older man answered.

"Mama, oor gertank?" a small boy, tugging at his mother's dress said. Where are we going?

"Chem kider," the mother answered. I don't know.

The chief gendarme nodded at the other mounted gendarmes.

"By order of Vali Mustafa Halil, I am instructed to escort you to Diyarbekir," he said. "From there, you will be transported to the interior, away from the conflict on our eastern borders." Talaat, his brother-in-law, had installed Halil in Bitlis.

Sona and Elise exchanged glances. Low murmuring came from the group.

"I know that you are wondering why you must go to Diyarbekir, but there is no alternative. Once you arrive there, you will be taken by truck to Malatia and then to Sivas. There you will stay until it has been determined that you may return."

The deportees turned to one another. Sivas! It lay almost directly in the middle of Turkey and easily three hundred kilometers northwest of Bitlis. Elise looked at Sona and cocked her head slightly.

"Khent eh," Elise whispered. "It is crazy. Why go down to go up?"

It was true. First they would travel south to Diyarbekir, only to swing wide and curve up to Sivas?

It made no sense. Why not travel directly to Sivas? They could go from Bitlis, through Palou, past Kharpert, Arabkir, and then on to Sivas.

Throughout the last few months, almost all of the men aged fifteen to fifty had been ordered to report for either direct military duty or to support the effort building roads or laying track. Even Father DerSimonian was gone. One day the Vali sent word that he had received a communiqué from the Vali at Moush. There were religious disturbances; would he come and help quell them?

"Because of the distance, we will stop to let you rest," the chief gendarme continued. "But we must be at Diyarbekir according to the schedule that I have been given."

"Have you been, mama?" Sona asked. "To Diyarbekir?"

"Yes," Elise replied. "A long time ago, when I was small."

"Is it far?"

"Yes," Elise said. "It is."

Diyarbekir lay some one hundred twenty-five kilometers south of Bitlis. Watermelons. There were big succulent watermelons there. But you had to be careful: the scorpions loved to curl among the patches.

"Now we go," the gendarme said. "Pay attention and we will get to our first stop on time."

The mounted gendarmes turned their horses and began leading the way. The deportees looked at one another and, some riding donkeys, most walking with their belongings on their shoulders or on their heads, followed. Elise and Sona walked side by side and within minutes their view of Bitlis receded.

PALOU

The Turkish official looked upon the assembly. Lucine, Bedros, Takouhi, Maritza, Azniv, and Anahid stood, surrounded by their neighbors. It was strange, Anahid thought. There are only old people and children left. The official cleared his throat.

"Due to dangers posed by nearing Russian and Entente military forces and by order of the Vali, be it noted that all Armenians of Palou will be temporarily relocated to areas of the Interior."

Lucine looked from Takouhi to Bedros.

"You are to collect all essential belongings and report for relocation tomorrow morning. Your homes will be sealed and protected. You will return as soon as the danger has passed."

There was murmuring from the crowd as the old men and women looked at one another. Vahe slept as Maritza rocked from side to side. The official folded the document.

"You need not be concerned," he said. "When our eastern borders are secure, you will be returned to your homes. If you require items to be put into safekeeping, they will be sent to the State Bank at Erzeroum and you will be given a receipt. You will then be able to reclaim these items upon your return."

"Yes, but where are you taking us?" a man yelled out.

"For security reasons, I am not allowed to disclose that information," the official said. "When the security risk has lessened, your final destination will be known."

The voices grew louder now, and Anahid drew closer to Lucine, who put her hand on her shoulder. The official knew that he could not leave it this way; he had to make them as comfortable as possible. That was critical.

"I am, however, at liberty to tell you that already there have been evacuations at Bitlis, Moush, Kharpert, and Chemeshgezak," he said, looking at the group. "These citizens have been moved because our military has determined that there is a possibility of loss of life on our eastern border. We will do what is necessary to protect our loyal subjects."

People in the crowd looked at one another. Takouhi opened her mouth to say something, but Bedros shook his head. He had heard enough.

"Due to the length of the journey, furniture and the like will be prohibited. Because of the size of the caravan and the speed we must make, families with working farm animals may bring one, and only one, animal with them."

Again there was murmuring from the crowd.

"Our men will be occupied with the securing of this territory. Therefore, the State will be unable to care for these animals. You must therefore make arrangements with those remaining in the territory to receive your livestock. At noon, we depart."

"But, why? Why?" Lucine asked. "What have we done?"

"Nothing," Takouhi answered. "We have done nothing."

They sat, along with Anahid, Maritza, and Vahe. Bedros tapped his spoon on the table.

"They want us away from here," he said. "They do not want us to be tempted when the Russians come."

"Fine, then," Lucine said. "I can understand why they do not want us here."

"An Armenian will never fight another Armenian," Takouhi said.

"That is not true," Bedros replied. "Our men fight alongside the Turks every day. And our Armenian brothers on the other side are fighting alongside the Russians."

"Then what do we do?" Takouhi said.

Bedros shrugged his shoulders, thinking. "If we resist, they will drag us away," he said. "That is pointless. And no way will we leave any valuables with them…"

"To be put in the bank at Erzeroum! Ha!" Takouhi exclaimed.

"We would never see the money again," Lucine said.

"They will conveniently lose the papers," Bedros added. Maritza nodded in agreement.

The animals would have to be sold. Everyone knew that they would not bring their full value.

"Robbery!" he spat under his breath. He could still remember the story of the farmer in Adana who during the 1909 massacres had slit the throats of every last one of his lambs, chickens, and pigs rather than sell them for a fraction of their price. The ground had been sticky with the thick blood for months.

"Will they send us where they sent Papa?" Anahid asked, looking at them. They all stopped, and for a moment there was silence.

"I do not know, tsakus," Lucine said. "Maybe so."

Now they worked, trying to decide what to take and what to leave. Anahid carefully rolled several small rugs inside one another while Takouhi tied them with brown string.

"Good," Takouhi said.

Anahid would wear what she could. It would be hot and she could pack only a few items. She folded the dress that had been bartered from Sona's family, and put it in the saddlebag.

"Mama, I am going outside to feed the animals."

"Good," Lucine replied. "Extra water."

"Yes, mama."

Lucine, Takouhi, and Bedros sat at the table. Before them was a small pile of gold coins.

"That is it," Bedros said.

"Including the animals?" Takouhi asked.

"Yes, including the animals," Bedros said softly. He had sold them at a pittance.

Lucine counted out the coins and then divided them into four piles: one to each of them, and the fourth she pushed to the side.

"We hide the three piles," Bedros said. "From the fourth, we each draw an equal amount to use along the way."

Anahid draped the rugs and the saddlebag over the esh's back, securing each with a length of cord. She opened the pen and the animals moved aside. She began filling the troughs.

Lucine sewed a crisscross line and then doubled back parallel to it. No one was going to break that stitch. But if you pulled at just the right place, a single coin could be slid out between thumb and forefinger. She held it up for Takouhi and Bedros to see; they nodded. She drew up the hem of her dress, placed the cloth under it, and began sewing it into place. Bedros sewed the coins inside his brown leather vest. Takouhi was almost done, working quickly and quietly.

"Mama, the rugs are tied and I put extra feed and water just as you said," Anahid said, entering.

Lucine did not look up from her work, but motioned with a nod of her head.

"That is good. Come here with us."

"No. No. It is fine," Anahid said. "I have more to do."

CTESIPHON
July, 1915

Ctesiphon sat on the Tigris River, not far from Baghdad. The men were mostly Armenian, although there were Greeks and Jews as well, supervised by the contingent of Turkish and German soldiers. The ground would be leveled and the wood and track would be carefully laid out and aligned. The Baghdad-to-Berlin route was critical.

Hagop and Souren had been here almost three months. God! Was it hot! They had left early the next morning and Souren had spirited Sona out the moment that she and Hagop had said goodbye. Their families had waved the boys off, Sarkis and Dikran saying nothing.

Hagop leaned the shovel against his leg. He wiped his forehead with the handkerchief that Sona had given him.

"Bahbam," he said, "Dak eh." It is hot.

"Ayo," Souren said, nodding. The sweat beaded up on his arms and chest and all he could think of was a tall, cool glass of tahn, yogurt, cucumbers, and mint. All in all, they had been treated well. They worked bare-chest, and already the few months had done wonders for Souren's physique, while Hagop's took on a harder sheen.

"After we finish this line, do you think they will give us soldier uniforms?" Souren asked.

"I don't know," Hagop said, folding the handkerchief and putting it back in his pocket.

"Do you think they can win the war?" Souren said.

"The Germans are fine and disciplined," Hagop said. "Look at them."

Souren looked over at the Germans who stood off to the side.

"Very fit," he said. He glanced down at their black boots, polished highly. "Good boots, too. Better than the Turks."

"Smart, too," Hagop added. "Yes, maybe they can win."

"Do you think of her?" Souren asked.

Hagop looked at him for a moment. "Yes," he said, finally. "I think of her all the time."

Souren smiled slightly.

"Good! She is right for you," he said, slapping his friend on the back.

"Is that so?" Hagop asked. "Since when did you become such a philosopher, my friend?"

"Ah. I can tell these things."

"Oh. I see."

"Now," Souren said, digging his shovel into the ground. "When will they give us rifles to fight?"

Hagop leaned on his shovel and looked at his friend.

"Soon," he said, hiding the suspicion he held. "Perhaps soon."

PALOU

Lucine thrust a small shovel into the grass in the adjoining pen. She carefully drew it beneath the sod until the piece was free. She looked around, making sure no one was watching, and they began scooping out the soil. It did not take long.

"That is enough," she whispered.

Anahid nodded and handed her the piece of rough leather. Lucine laid it down and Anahid handed her the items: the family Bible, two candlesticks. Sarkis' watch. She had wondered what to do with the baptismal certificates, but decided to take them. She tied the bundle and placed it in the hole. Anahid looked at her.

"We have to do it," Lucine said. "We cannot carry everything."

They worked in silence, replacing the dirt and the top grass, tamping it down.

The sun came up early, and the July day would grow to be very hot. The remaining Armenians in Palou took one last look at what had been their home for generations and began walking. Lucine, Takouhi, and Bedros, who every now and then would steady himself with his cane, were only steps behind Anahid, who led the esh. Maritza carried Vahe. Ahead, Lucine could see Perouz Avakian and, to her right, Azniv walked, almost as if in a daze. The Samuelian women, her mother-in-law Berjouhi, her mother Agavni, and her two sisters-in-law, older Margarite and younger Ani tried to keep up her spirits.

Vache. It was all she could think about. Vache.

Bedros turned his head to see a group of Turkish policemen move in past them, carrying boards. The caravan stopped, and the gendarmes let them watch as the homes were boarded up. The chief gendarme clicked his spurs into the horse and the caravan moved on.

ERZEROUM

The Turkish official unfolded the document. The boarded up Armenian houses were empty and the inhabitants of the village, only Turks and the occasional Kurd waited for him to speak.

"Loyal citizens of the Empire. As you can see, the Armenians have been removed for security purposes. We are in a time of war and no chances of collaboration with the enemy can be tolerated. These homes will be entered by our police force and searched for weapons. You will then inhabit these homes."

Some people in the group looked at one another, but no one uttered a word.

"You will not be indebted to nor will you assume the taxes that the Christians were responsible for." He looked up and saw eagerness in their faces. "But let me be clear," he said. He held up the document and turned it toward the crowd. It had elegant script and an official gold seal.

"By order of General Mahmud Kamil. Anyone harboring an Armenian will be hanged."

The crowd murmured slightly and then grew silent. Within two hours, the police squads had entered every one of the Armenian homes, ransacking them. By nightfall, the homes had all been claimed and the village silently changed the hand of ownership.

TREBIZOND

The shimmering waters of the Black Sea glistened and danced. The prisoners were now dressed in uniforms, though they bore no official nametags or identification. They had relished their freedom, and they had trained well. Soon they would be dispatched from Trebizond to Ras-El-Ain and Chabur. From these locations, lying north of the desert, they could lie in wait for the deportees headed for Deir-El-Zor. Every man's freedom depended on doing the job and doing it without remorse.

Besides, the Armenians were dogs. No one would miss them. The men of the Special Organization, SO, had gone through the tiny Armenian hamlets, rounding up the males from age fifteen to seventy.

"There is no reason to be alarmed," they had been told. "You will be taken to Rize. You are needed to stave off possible attack by the Russians."

Rize lay on the Black Sea some one hundred twenty-five kilometers to the northeast of Trebizond. There had been little protest; in a twisted logical way it made sense. If their countrymen on the Turkish side were close to the border, the Armenians serving on the Russian side might think twice before advancing. They had been obedient and now they stood in groups of eighteen men, and watched as the boats were brought in.

"Board the boats!"

They stepped into the wooden rowboats. In each, two SO soldiers sat behind the men. The boats began to drift off, the oars dipping into the cold water. The SO commander hurried away: it was important for him to report to Doctor Sakir and General Kamil.

The men had their orders. After the boats had gone ten kilometers, the SO soldiers sitting aft would shoot them. Then they would step forward and throw the dead and the dying overboard. The cold water would finish the rest.

TOWARD DIYARBEKIR

The caravan of deportees moved along and as the sun began to recede, the deserted landscape somewhere between Palou and Diyarbekir turned cold.

"We stop here for the night," the gendarmes said.

The deportees looked around, searching for shelter, but the entire area was open, treeless. They began settling down, laying blankets. They had been walking for the better part of three days.

"Anahid, bring the blankets," Lucine said. "We will lay them down here."

"Yes, mama."

Bedros labored and he leaned heavily on his cane. Takouhi helped him to sit.

"Oof!" he said. "I am not in shape for this."

"Ah, you will be fine," Takouhi said. He wiped the sweat from his forehead.

"Maritza, come and sit," Lucine said.

Vahe stirred and Maritza held him carefully as she eased down next to Takouhi. Lucine draped one of the blankets around Bedros and Takouhi and draped another over Maritza's shoulders.

"Thank you," she said, drawing the blanket closer around Vahe. She had filled a small, flat flask with water and had fashioned a string around its neck. She pulled it up from underneath her shabeeg, and tugged gently on the cork. She wet her fingers slightly, holding them up to Vahe's lips for him to lick.

Anahid took the rugs and the saddlebag from the esh and laid them down near Maritza.

"Anahid, give me those reins," Lucine said.

"Yes, mama."

"Go sit down and rest next to Maritza."

"Yes, mama."

Maritza held the blanket up and Anahid draped it over her shoulders. Lucine brought the esh around and stood in front of the animal.

"Now you listen to me, esh," she said, looking into the animal's eyes. "Tonight you lie down and keep us warm."

She slowly brought the reins down and placed her right thumb directly on the center of the animal's head. Sarkis had once shown her how to do it and she had never forgotten. The animal went down without protest.

Lucine draped a blanket over her shoulders. She sat, thinking, and was still awake as the others, exhausted, drifted quickly to sleep. As she watched them, thoughts came to her. Sarkis. Hagop. She could feel the tears coming but she ground them out. This was not the time and she would not do it. They could get through this. She knew that they could.

CONSTANTINOPLE

Enver sat at his desk. It was sweltering outside, the mid-July heat showing no sign of abating.

Wangenheim knew that Enver would not easily bend. But time and history were on his side. Trade, military exchange, and monetary compensation were not to be taken lightly.

"Mr. Minister," he said. "The time is short. This show of support and friendship is good for Turkey. You have studied war. We both know that the key to this war lies in the decision of Bulgaria."

"Yes, of course," Enver said.

"Then you also must freely admit that to protect Constantinople, Turkey needs Bulgaria. Turkey and Germany can drive a wedge through the Entente powers."

Enver nodded. "Yes, this makes military sense. The Entente needs Bulgaria on its side. But we could prevent that." Enver looked at Wangenheim. "But you ask Turkey to give up territory for which many thousands have died."

"Mr. Minister," Wangenheim began. "What Germany asks is that Turkey shows Bulgaria that she has a profound friend. The Entente Powers will never interfere with Serbia and will never give Bulgaria what she really wants."

"Macedonia," Enver said, thinking.

Macedonia had come under Bulgarian rule by the middle of the ninth century. But by the end of the fourteenth century, Macedonia,

Bulgaria, Serbia, and Bosnia had all succumbed to the Ottoman Empire. On the eighth of October 1912, as the first Balkan War erupted, Bulgaria, Greece, Montenegro, and Serbia attacked. Less than a year later, in Bucharest, Macedonia was divided amongst the victors. The land had been traded back and forth for hundreds of centuries and was one of the most fought after territories in the world.

"Precisely," Wangenheim said. "If we make this offer to Bulgaria, they will come to our side. It will cause absolute havoc."

Enver paused and both men sat, studying one another.

"Yes," Enver said, stroking his chin. "Yes, it would cause such a storm for the Entente if Bulgaria threw her forces to the west and to the east. Adrianople, Karagatch, Demotica."

"These are not of central interest to Turkey," Wangenheim continued.

"I will give you my answer tomorrow," Enver said, thinking.

"I know that you will make the logical choice," Wangenheim said. Almost six weeks would pass before he would know the outcome of the meeting. Enver, keen to delay, knew that the longer he could keep Wangenheim waiting would be to his advantage. In the interim, he could receive emissaries from the Entente Powers. Turkey's options would be left open and she would be able to make a deal from a position of strength. As July became August, Wangenheim's visits became more frequent.

Morgenthau took off his pince-nez glasses and rubbed his eyes. He had slept little the night before and had come to the office early. He replaced his glasses and looked at the reports on his desk from the American consuls all over the Eastern and Southern portions of Turkey. And there were the letters: from Paris, from Italy, from England, from America.

'To: His Honorable Ambassador Henry S. Morgenthau... ...Implore you to investigate the situation and please support them in any way you possibly can...'

'Dear Mr. Ambassador ...I fear that I will not be able to hear from my family which is still in the village of...'

'To Honorable Henry S. Morgantheu... ...I have in my possession eyewitness accounts of atrocities taking place in Angora in Turkey on the twenty-sixth day of April, 1915. One of the escapees is now in our care.'

Morgenthau turned over the small piece of thin, tanned leather and held it carefully in his hands. On it were tiny scrawls of Armenian script. It had been rolled up, and came to him from a German missionary in Diyarbekir. As he bent down to give a woman a taste of water, she had blessed him profusely, and had then placed the leather in his palm. The words had been translated from Armenian into English. Morgenthau had read them, again and again, the hopelessness and the agony of them ringing back and forth in his head.

'We walk to our death turks and kurds come kill us cetes here help us Ankine Abassian, kharpert written in my blood here diyarbekir june 1915.'

"Written. In her blood," Morgenthau said, softly, to himself.

"Pardon me, sir," Mowbry said. "Last night's cables."

"Thank you, Mr. Mowbry," Morgenthau said, stirred from his thoughts. "Please get your pad. I have a cable to send."

"Yes, sir." He left and returned with his writing tablet.

"Honorable William Jennings Bryan, Secretary of State," Morgenthau began.

Mowbry nodded, writing. Another cable to Bryan.

"Dear Mr. Secretary, it is my deep regret that I must report the continued tragedy befalling the Armenian population of Turkey. I have received numerous reports from our consuls of widespread massacres throughout the Empire."

Morgenthau paused, thinking. Mowbry waited, his pencil poised. All correspondence, no matter how trivial, was considered vital and had to be precise. But Mowbry, despite his office efficiencies had found himself being affected by these cables. Knowing that these things were happening. Out there.

"Mr. Mowbry?"

"Yes? Oh, sorry sir. I am ready."

"Entire village populations have been moved out and now march into barren desert terrain. The horror and pitiful condition of the Armenians begs for a solution. Yours with all courtesy... Finish it off will you?"

"Yes, sir," Mowbry said. When he looked back at the paper as he prepared the official cable, he would see strange little pencil marks and not know what they were. His shaking hand had made them.

TOWARD DIYARBEKIR

Lucine's eyelids had finally wavered, and she fell into a restless sleep. Bedros breathed heavily and despite the coolness, had night sweats. Takouhi saw to him, wiping his forehead.

"Sweat it out of you," she said.

But if it lasted much longer, it would be bad. His skin had taken on a slightly yellow tinge and for a few minutes that afternoon they had fallen behind. The gendarmes had immediately ridden up and commanded them to move. Bedros leaned his weight on Takouhi and they had rejoined the caravan.

The refugees slept, spread out among the barren landscape. Anahid's eyelids fluttered as she dreamed. Their faces were already dark brown from the incessant sun, and their lips were dry and cracked. And, already, the money was running out.

The water, save for the tiny bottle that Maritza carried for Vahe, had lasted the better part of five days, but as hard as Lucine had tried to ration it, they had to drink. Through the narrow passages, there were nomads, Turks as well as Kurds from the hills. They had bread, figs, and water that they sold for five, sometimes ten times their value. And there was Bedros. Lucine had seen a gendarme stab one of the deportees who had failed to keep up the pace.

She stirred awake. Her eyes burned, stung by the constant dust and blowing sand. She looked out among the deportees. Cries from babies mixed with moans from adults. In time, the cries would turn to wailing. And then to absolute, utter grief. Anahid slept close to Maritza and Vahe.

A woman's profile stood out from the rest. Was it Perouz? Lucine could not tell. She had looked for Siranoush, the matchmaker, but she had not seen her; maybe she was in another village. But now Lucine was sure it was Perouz, because the figure reached up and let down her long flowing hair. Yes, it had to be her. The woman turned her head in Lucine's direction, seemed to look at her for a moment, and then quickly turned away as if she had heard something.

In an instant, the old woman was up. Lucine sat up, looking around. The gendarmes were gone. Perouz Avakian, for it was Perouz, turned slightly and Lucine followed her eye line.

Kurds!

They had swept down from the hills and now rode on horseback into the mass of people. Lucine could see one of the riders reaching behind him. The moonlight caught a sliver of the metal blade and the Kurd brought the saber down, cutting into one of the old men. The screaming had begun and it took on an eerie echo.

The Kurds rode through and Lucine watched as two riders snatched up two girls, pulling them over the backs of their horses. The girls screamed. An old man yelled for them to stop. A Kurd took out his pistol and shot him directly in the chest. The man took one step and then fell, dead.

Lucine's family stirred, disoriented.

"Mama?" Anahid said, getting to her feet.

"No!" Lucine said. She grabbed her and pushed her to the ground.

"Stay down," she said. "All of you, stay down."

The riders continued coming in, making off with bundles of goods and rolled rugs. The screams grew thicker now, and Lucine watched as Perouz stood while the others around her cowered to the ground. She looked directly into the eyes of a Kurd who brought his horse directly in front of her. She stood there, her long flowing white hair blowing gently in the wind. The Kurd looked at her, his small scimitar held low in his right hand.

Lucine reached her right hand out and pushed Anahid's head down low.

"Mi nyeer," she said. Do not look.

Perouz stood there, dressed all in white, rail thin, those brown bony fingers. She would never cower. The Kurd smiled, revealing two dark spaces. He lowered the blade, kicked his heels into the horse, and rode off.

Perouz turned and watched them go. It was not long before the gendarmes returned. Soon the sun would be up, and it would all begin again. Lucine closed her eyes, shaking her head back and forth.

BITLIS

The boards were ripped away, clearing access to the homes that had been sealed. The men walked forward, their black iron crowbars swinging by their sides. They reached Nishan's shop. The door was pried open, and the stores of silk, cloth, and leather were looted.

On and on it went, through the day and into the night. In less than three days, the houses would be filled and the signs would be changed. Other than the churches, which would eventually be turned into mosques, there would be no trace that Armenians had ever lived here.

DIYARBEKIR

Diyarbekir lay some one hundred twenty-five kilometers to the southeast of Bitlis on the Tigris. The Romans had called it Amida. To the Armenians it was Dikranagerd. Two things came to mind when one traveled through Diyarbekir: the succulent watermelons and the constant clicking of the yellow scorpions as they scurried along. Those were to be respected, for, unlike their red or black cousins, they were lethal.

To the direct south, two hundred kilometers away, was the desert wasteland of Deir-El-Zor. From Moush, Palou, Kharpert, Mezre, Kighi, and Erzeroum; all would make their way through to Diyarbekir. Those arriving from Erzeroum, one hundred fifty kilometers to the northeast, were the worst off. Their skin was black with sun poisoning and hung loosely on their bones. Their feet were bloated. Many had few, if any, clothes left. First they had traded their possessions, then their gold, and then their clothing for whatever they could eat or drink.

They were grouped together: hundreds, thousands. The man in the uniform walked through them, and as he did the dry earth cracked beneath his boots. What little vegetation grew was plucked and women held the precious little tufts of grass for their children to eat. The man looked down at them. Their faces were dark; the teeth almost bleached white. He had a German flag on the right shoulder of his uniform and a small Red Cross button affixed above his left breast pocket. His name patch read Lepsius.

He smiled at them. They thrust forward their young. Children. Babies.

"Take this child, so that he may live," they had begged him. Makeshift orphanages were being constructed: some only straw mats on hard stone floors, but they were safe. Lepsius and the other missionaries took the children. As many as they could.

He was fifty-seven years old, a German Protestant pastor, theologian, and President of the Protestant German Missions in the Orient. They dispensed what assistance they could. The Armenians looked like shafts of wheat, slowly swaying in the wind as they parted to let the missionaries through. He peered into the camera and framed several shots, preserving the images.

OUTSIDE DIYARBEKIR

God!

It was so hot.

The caravan of deportees walked, and the toll showed heavily. They were bent over, careful to walk between the stones and rocks. Their leather shoe bottoms were long ago worn away and their feet were bloated a sickly blue and black color.

Lucine brushed the sand from her eyes. Almost all the coins were used now. There were still a few secreted away, but they would soon be gone. They had sold the esh for a few coins. Along the way, they had seen a horse, dead from the heat, and it had made Anahid sick when she saw the old Armenian women yelling to the fleeing vultures and then stepping forward, pulling the rotted meat and eating it raw. The blankets had been sold for water. The rugs had been sold for food.

After the first attack, there had been others since; Lucine had taken Anahid aside.

"With short hair, they will think you are a boy," Lucine explained. "Do you understand?"

"Yes, mama," Anahid said. "For when the men come."

"Yes, tsakus."

She did not complain once, especially when the rough jagged glass seemed to pull with every stroke. When they were finished, Maritza cut Lucine's hair.

Two days later, as they drew closer to Diyarbekir, Lucine sold the long braids for small pieces of bread and a drink of water for each of them. The man was an Arab and Takouhi, who knew a little of the language, had greeted him. It had made the difference. His eyes had lightened, and he had allowed them to drink as much as they could. It had tasted so wonderful, so soothing going down.

Lucine handed the bucket back to the Arab and bowed deeply.

"May peace be with you," Takouhi said.

The man nodded. 'There is death here,' he thought. 'Too much death.'

"Agh!" Bedros screamed. Words came quickly from his mouth, but his speech seemed strangely garbled. Takouhi and Lucine went to him but he didn't seem to recognize them.

"What is it?" Takouhi said, trying to calm him. She looked at Lucine. Finally, it had passed and he had fallen into a light sleep. Soon the gendarmes would be moving them.

'Why couldn't they see it?' Bedros wondered. 'What is wrong with them?' The water was there, waiting for them.

There. Below the sand. They could dive into it. Do not worry about the sand in your mouth, below it is water. Cool. Fresh. Water. Open your mouths. Come with me. 'All of you, come with me,' he thought, as he slept, his eyelids fluttering.

Anahid sat close to Maritza, who let her hold Vahe. Three or four days ago she had seen two young mothers beg her to take their children; they were starving.

"Gat chooneem. Gat chooneem," they said, thrusting their babies toward her. I do not have milk. I do not have milk.

She could only smile slightly and nod. She too was barren. She would hoard what little food Lucine could procure and gently push a morsel of bread or fig into Vahe's mouth. But his crying had become more insistent, and Lucine would occasionally shoot her a scolding look.

The baby must be quiet. The gendarmes did not like the squealing. They hated the sound. They had seen babies on the road, some no more than three months old, insides gutted.

Soon they would be in Diyarbekir. Occasionally Lucine would look back, checking on the others, but she could not let her true feelings betray her. Once, it had been several hours during that first day, she had let her mind wander and it had rested on Sarkis and Hagop. But it had been too painful. If she kept it there it would break her. Instead, she thought of her needlepoint. She imagined the intricate designs, and as they walked, she could see the designs in the sand, line after line, crossing over, end meeting end. She kept her mind occupied with these thoughts. They would see her through this. They would see all of them through.

Still, every moment, she had to think. Bedros had steadily grown worse. It was difficult for him to keep up with the rest, and his legs and feet had swollen terribly. But, soon, the money would all be gone, and then their gold. And then they would have only themselves. There had been attacks; some of the girls had been taken, raped. Some, Lucine knew, would become the wives or the servants of the hill Kurds. They would turn Kurd or turn Turk, and every trace of their Armenian past would be wiped from their memory.

There were screams through the night. They had heard that one woman had smothered her own daughter as she slept. A gendarme had been looking at her for days: soon the woman knew that he would come for her. The next morning as her daughter lay there, never to wake again, the woman had spat in the gendarme's face. He removed his sword from its scabbard, looked at her, and then ran it straight into her stomach and twisted.

'To her own daughter,' Lucine thought, walking. She shook her head and tried to get it out of her mind.

The road was more treacherous now, and the rocks felt like daggers to their swollen, black feet. Suddenly, Bedros stumbled, and his cane flung out from under him. He fell to the side, his weight bringing Takouhi down with him. Lucine and Anahid rushed to them.

"Keep walking," Lucine said to Maritza. She nodded, pressing Vahe close to her chest.

"Bedros! Bedros!" Takouhi said, shaking him.

"Ah," he said, grimacing. "Eem bijeghus." My ankle.

Takouhi looked at Lucine who gently touched his right ankle.

"Agh!" he winced, pulling away from her.

"We have to splint it," Lucine said. "We have to do it right away."

Anahid looked away just as sand and dust kicked up and the mounted gendarme brought his horse close to them.

"Why do you stop? You must continue with the others!" he said.

"He is hurt," Lucine said, looking up at him.

"Then you must leave him! Go! Go and join the others!"

Lucine looked at Takouhi, her mind racing. She turned to Anahid.

"Go," she said. "Run now. Run to Maritza." She looked into Anahid's eyes. "Right to Maritza."

"Yes, mama," Anahid said. She ran off.

"You move now," the gendarme said.

"Go on," Takouhi said. "I will stay here."

"No, no. Leave me," Bedros grunted.

Lucine looked at her and then to Bedros. She grabbed his cane and
thrust it into Takouhi's hands.

"Ahseegah bedk eh kordzadzes," she said, imploring Takouhi. You
must use this.

"Ayo," Takouhi said, taking it.

"Yergoo guhdor bedk eh sheenes," she said, quickly. The gendarme reared the horse backward a little, kicking up sand. You must
make two parts.

"Ayo, kidem, kidem," Takouhi said, nodding. Yes, I know, I know.

Lucine nodded. Takouhi could make the splint and fasten it around
his ankle. It would work. It would be painful, but it would work.

"Now!" the gendarme commanded. "March! Infidel dogs! Move
now!"

"Go, tsakus," Takouhi said. "Go. We will rest a few moments and
join you."

"March! I tell you one last time!" the gendarme said, reaching back
for his rifle.

Lucine bent down and hugged Bedros, kissing him on his cheeks
and forehead. He seemed not to know what was happening. She and
Takouhi kissed and hugged one another. Takouhi gently pushed her
away and their eyes met. Lucine's eyes filled with water and Takouhi
shot her a stern look.

"Mi uhner!" she said. "Mi uhner!" Do not do it.

Lucine nodded and drew away from her, shaking slightly. She
stood up and looked at the gendarme.

"March, you dog!" he commanded.

She began walking, slowly at first, and then increased her pace,
joining Maritza and Anahid. The gendarme looked down at Bedros and
Takouhi and then turned his horse and rode back to the caravan.

"But what about...?" Anahid began.

"Do not worry," Lucine said, taking her hand. "They will rest for awhile."

Anahid turned to look back, but Lucine tugged her arm.

"No. Look straight."

They were paces away from the other deportees, and as they reached them, the same gendarme quickly rode past. Lucine saw him go and closed her eyes. She bit deep into her lower lip, the slightest taste of blood warm on her tongue. Anahid turned.

"No!" Lucine said. "Keep your back and head straight and move."

"Yes, mama."

Lucine walked, and now the tears streamed down her face. The gendarme drew his horse up to Bedros and Takouhi. Lucine walked, trying to concentrate on Anahid.

'Anahid. Now for Anahid. Strong.' The words went flash-flash-flash in her brain.

Behind them, two rifle shots rang out echoing faintly through the tiny mountain pass. It sent a cold hard shiver through Lucine's bones, startling her. And she knew that they were gone.

OUTSIDE PALOU

He was exhausted. His clothes were shredded, cut by the branches. He was covered with dirt and mud. But he had to see for himself and, now Armen stood, propping himself against a tree. Just ahead lay Palou. He had traveled only at night, and had gotten lost twice. He drew closer, careful to stay in the shadows.

Where were they?

The homes were silent. He passed Sam the Barber's. The windows had been smashed; ransacked. Walking slowly in the direction of his house, a light burned inside. He could hear muffled voices. He was paces away from the door. He blinked, the color draining from his face. But he was sure.

Turkish. They are speaking Turkish.

He carefully backed away from the house, knowing it would be the same at Hagop's and Souren's. He glanced to his right, toward the church, and could see that the front door had been pried open. This would have been one of the first places to be looted. They would have taken everything.

He walked, trying to think of what to do.

God! He was so tired now. Wait!

Many Armenian churches had secret hiding places: fake walls, tunnels. These had been built as a precaution against marauders, had been since the time of Tamerlane, to protect valuable and irreplaceable Bibles and artifacts. But Armen did not know where the compartment was or how to reveal it. Still, he could not go on. Better to stay and then leave the next night. Besides, if he could find the opening, there could be others who were hiding. Armen looked around, making sure that he would not be seen. Slowly he slipped into the cold, dark church.

CONSTANTINOPLE

The reading room was bathed in a soft, gentle light and Morgenthau reached for the stack of yellow pages, studying the figures. They were the official consul reports: they outlined the manner of the deportations, the number and condition of the exiles, the aggregate numbers of the dead, and the entrance lists into the orphanages. Josephine looked up from her book, watching him.

His face showed signs of immense strain and, ever since receiving Bryan's response, he seemed to have changed. He was taking on more responsibilities, walking the fine line of not officially interfering but bartering.

This time, bartering for lives.

He positioned, exchanged, swapped, cajoled, coaxed, and played on the strengths of America to get Enver and Talaat to grant him favors. Sometimes it had worked, other times it had not. God! He was an Ambassador and here he was, scheming to save lives. He reached for the next page and as he did, Josephine gently touched his arm.

"Henry, is there anything I can do?"

He put down the document, and looked at her. He nodded, grateful for the interruption.

"No. Even I can only do so much. But this is beyond me. They keep coming in. Ezerum, Bitlis, Moush, Kharpert. Endless."

She sat for a moment and took a deep breath. "It's barbaric, Henry. I cannot understand the reason behind any of this."

"Yes, I know," Morgenthau said. He placed his right hand over hers. "They are deporting them, but it is just a disguise. They plan to exterminate all of them."

"Henry, I do not know how much longer I can stay here."

"And I do not want you to stay," he replied. "I want you to leave in September."

"But, Henry…"

"I will make the arrangements through the Consulate. It is better this way."

Even at night, the heat of mid-July bore through as Enver walked into the German Military Headquarters. He walked up the stairs, turned right, and entered the office. The smell of a fine cigar filled the air. Major Fritz Bronsart von Schellendorf looked up.

"Good evening, Herr General."

"Good evening, Mr. War Minister," Von Schellendorf said. "Please sit down." Although Von Schellendorf was technically just a guest in Turkey, his position of authority was equal to Enver's. And he, like Wangenheim, held no great respect for Enver.

"I have it just here," Von Schellendorf said, gesturing to the document that lay before him. "We are agreed then?"

Enver nodded. "Yes, may I see it?"

"Certainly."

To each man, it was clearly a clever situation. Enver could always lay the blame on the occupying Germans while Germany could proclaim innocence and say that the Turks had merely used the war as an opportunity to settle their internal ethnic matters. Fingers would be pointed in opposite directions, and as time passed, the entire matter would be forgotten. In the meantime, it would be done. The territories would be redrawn and no answers would be found.

'To All Local Commanders:

From: Enver, Turkish Minister of War and Von Schellendorf, German Chief of Staff at Ottoman General Headquarters. All commanders should immediately take severe action against Armenians in labor battalions.'

There were a few more oblique passages and two blank lines at the bottom for each of their signatures. The words had been carefully chosen, for although the document would remain within the cavernous archives of German Military Headquarters in Berlin, Von Schellendorf had been well trained: never use specific language. Local commanders

knew what 'severe action' meant: within the military structure there
would be no ambiguity regarding what was to be done.

"Good," Enver said.

"Then it is decided," Von Schellendorf said. "We will co-issue the
joint directive via secret cipher." Again, Enver nodded. They signed
their names. Von Schellendorf looked up and saw that Enver seemed
particularly troubled.

"What is it, Mr. War Minister?"

Enver looked directly at him. "The work must be done quickly. We
cannot wait forever."

Von Schellendorf looked at Enver and then slowly nodded. "We
must wait until the rail work is done," he said.

"Then let us dispatch these orders and pursue our objectives,"
Enver said, standing. "Good evening, Herr General."

"Good evening, Mr. War Minister."

DIYARBEKIR

Only a few paces ahead lay Diyarbekir.

Diyarbekir! The Tigris!

Lucine breathed heavily. She looked ahead and could see people
milling about. Bedouins, traders. They could get something to eat.
Something. Anything. All the money was gone. All their jewelry. Sold
for scraps of food, tastes of water.

Maritza held Vahe. He was badly dehydrated. The small bottle that
hung from Maritza's neck was empty. Anahid's lips and face were
dark. She had complained about a tingling along her right leg. Something had awoken her nights before, but she was too groggy to remember. Lucine thought it must have been a spider's bite, but what she
feared was scorpions. For two days Anahid had been in intense pain,
then nothing. But now Anahid said that her fingers and toes felt numb.
When her speech began to slur, Lucine knew that time was running
out.

The last two days had grown more perilous: deportees who were
too exhausted fell away. Moments later, there were sounds of pistols
and rifles. The stench of dysentery filled the air. The smells. The yellowness. The pus growing and oozing out of sick infected eyes. And at
night the gendarmes and the brigands would come for the women.

Especially the young girls. This had come to the Samuelians. First they had come for Margarite, Vache's older sister. During the night she had disappeared. So distraught was her mother Berjouhi that she had been unable to continue. Only a day earlier, Agavni, her mother, had fallen, dead of a heart which could no longer go on. By the morning, Azniv and Ani were gone. Taken by the Kurds. Taken for brides.

All, save for Perouz Avakian, seemed as if they were nothing more than walking corpses, waiting for death to come and take them. Some prayed, some wailed. But not Perouz. Lucine had gone over to her.

'What must it be like for her?' Lucine thought. 'That she has brought so many of these people into this world only to watch them die this way?'

Perouz seemed capable of subsisting on nothing. Occasionally she would spy small clumps of grass or weeds, would gather them into little tufts, and from a small wooden container would pour something onto them. When Lucine asked what it was, Perouz reached her hand into a pocket and held the container for Lucine to see.

"Agh."

Salt.

As Lucine turned to leave, Perouz reached out her bony fingers and took her arm. It was a surprisingly strong grip. Lucine turned and Perouz leaned into her. Lucine could smell the strong odor of tobacco on her breath and Perouz looked carefully at her for a few moments.

"Yeteh Diyarbekir ga desnenk, ait aghchiga hone bedk eh tuhnes."

Lucine drew back as if she had been slapped. She looked at Perouz, who stood there, eyes boring into her.

"If we see Diyarbekir, you must leave that girl there."

That girl. Anahid. My flesh and my blood. Lucine stared at Perouz and knew that the old woman had meant every word.

No!

No! No! No!

Now she walked, with Anahid, Maritza, and Vahe into Diyarbekir. In their caravan, there were only women and children left. The men were all gone. The chief gendarme got down off his horse.

"You rest here," he said.

The deportees staggered to the ground. Their condition was grave. Their skin hung loosely from their bones. Where once had been the finest clothes, now only strips of cloth remained. Some of the girls were bare-chest, and they crossed their arms in front of them, trying desperately to hide from view.

The chief gendarme walked up to three of the girls. They ranged in age from fourteen to eighteen. They dropped their heads, and in one swift motion the gendarme reached out and ripped the remaining shreds of clothing from them. Murmurs arose from the men in the crowd. Lucine brought Anahid close to her and looked quickly at Maritza. The men in the crowd stepped forward to get a better look. The three girls cowered. Suddenly, the men started calling out numbers.

They were auctioning them off.

Lucine looked around for some water. Maritza turned away from the crowd and brought Vahe close to her. Some of the men drew closer to the girls, inspecting them. These three were fine. They would make good servants.

Lucine looked back. Perouz caught her eyes, but her face showed nothing.

The bidding grew furious now, higher and higher, and, finally, one man won. Lucine looked about, still holding Anahid. Her eyes desperately scanned the faces of the onlookers. A mumbling grew from the crowd. Anahid was trembling. Whatever it was, she was getting worse. How long could she last like this? A few days? Hours? Slowly the crowd began to step aside, and as they parted, Lucine looked at the man who stepped through.

He was dressed in a spotless white caftan and was surrounded by four women. To his right stood a large, wide man, a bodyguard. His name was Ahmet Salim, and he had amassed a large fortune in the buying and selling of every conceivable article: spices, silks, and especially fine horses. Lucine looked at his dark face, his elegantly trimmed beard.

The chief gendarme walked back and forth, scanning the crowd and his eyes stopped on Maritza, Lucine, and Anahid. Lucine looked back at him. His eyes shifted from her to Anahid. He stepped forward and quickly reached out, grabbing Anahid's left arm. She screamed. It came out slow and heavy. Without thinking, Lucine pulled hard, snatching her away from him. And she knew that this was the moment that the decision had to be made.

Perouz had been right.

Lucine moved quickly through the crowd of people and drew to an abrupt halt. She looked up and Ahmet Salim, easily an arm's length taller than she, looked down at both of them. Salim's bodyguard stepped forward, but Salim casually put his hand out, stopping him. Two gendarmes quickly moved in and grabbed Lucine and Anahid.

"Leave them!" Salim commanded.

The gendarmes looked at him and turned to the chief gendarme, who nodded. He did not know who this man was, but he was not about to anger him. Better to let the Christian dogs go. There were others, many others, and he would make good money today. The gendarmes moved away. Lucine looked up at Salim.

"Good Pasha," she said. From a distance, Maritza stood, watching. Vahe started crying, and she began to gently rock him.

"Yes, good woman?" Salim said.

Lucine blinked, disbelieving his words. For a moment, she could not speak.

"Yes?" he repeated.

Lucine took a deep breath and drew Anahid forward. She hesitated for a moment, drawing up her strength. She looked him directly in the eyes. "My daughter will make a good servant, Pasha. She is an obedient girl."

Anahid turned her head, stunned. She opened her mouth, but her lower lip fluttered. She was weak. Salim looked from Lucine to Anahid, but said nothing. Lucine pulled Anahid close to her.

"Anahid. Indzee luhseh. Pan me asehm. Miayn ays tsevov guhrnas abreel." Anahid. Listen to me. Do not say a word. In only this way can you live.

Anahid nodded. She trembled and tears streamed down her face.

"Good pasha," Lucine said. "She is accomplished at sewing and languages. She has been raised with good morals."

Salim looked at Lucine and then at Anahid, considering.

"Is she ill?" he asked.

"The sun, good Pasha, that is all," Lucine said, hoping. A few moments passed. She looked at him, her eyes unwavering.

"I am looking for a language teacher for my children," Salim said. "What languages does she speak?"

Lucine's eyes brightened. "Yes! Yes, Pasha," she exclaimed. "She excels in French. There is also her Armenian, Turkish, and some English."

Salim turned to Anahid.

"C'est bien la vèritè, jeune fille?" Is this the truth, young girl?

Anahid stood, saying nothing. Everything seemed muffled, muted. Salim looked from Anahid to Lucine. Anahid stood, unable to respond. Her mouth hung open. Lucine looked directly into her eyes and squeezed her hand. Hard. The tears streamed down Anahid's face.

"Oui, brave Effendi," Anahid said. It was as if something inside was working automatically. She could barely understand the words. "J'ai ensiegné le franVais a mon ecole." Yes, kind Effendi. I have taught French in my school.

Lucine closed her eyes, relieved. When she opened them, Salim was looking directly at her, considering.

"Very well, then," he said. "If this is your desire, I shall bring her into my home."

Lucine nodded. 'I must. I must,' she thought.

"She will be well cared for, woman," Salim said, reassuringly.

Anahid opened her mouth to protest, but Lucine shot her a glance.

"Thank you, kind Pasha," Lucine said "Thank you." She looked at him. His eyes met hers and in that moment both knew that Anahid had been saved. Salim turned to Anahid.

"Comment t'appelles-tu, jeune fille?" What is your name, young girl?

Anahid stumbled, the tears streaming down. She looked at Lucine, who nodded, imploring her to answer him.

"Je m'appelle Anahid," she said. My name is Anahid.

Salim drew up his caftan. "We must leave now," he said. "Come."

"Mama! Mama!" Anahid said, clinging to Lucine. "No! I will stay with you!"

Lucine took Anahid in her arms and hugged her tightly. She was hot. So hot! The fever was eating her alive. Lucine drew her gently away and reached her hands behind her neck. Salim watched but said nothing. If this was what the woman wanted, he could make use of the girl. It would be better than what lay ahead. Lucine flipped open the clasp and took the gold chain and cross from her neck. She looked at it for a moment, then took Anahid's right hand, placing it in her palm. She closed her fingers over it.

"Anahid, my sweet daughter," she said looking into her wet eyes. "Never forget who you are and what happened to us here."

Anahid nodded. It was happening so fast, but everything around them had stopped. Lucine squeezed her hand and Anahid could feel the shape and the warmth of the cross.

"Do not forget this," Lucine said. She kissed Anahid on the lips.

"Mama! Mama!" Anahid cried.

And in that instant, Lucine quickly turned from her. The rest of the caravan had begun to move, and some of them, seeing how Salim had acted, rushed towards him. Salim's bodyguard stepped forward. Salim would take only one.

"Now we must go, child," he said. Anahid looked at him, weeping. "This is what your mother desires," he said. "And so I must now make you my obligation."

He nodded to one of his wives and she stepped forward, taking Anahid's hand. Soon the fever would overtake her. In moments she would go limp, and they would carry her to his home.

Lucine rejoined Maritza and Vahe. Perouz slowly turned to her left and looked at Lucine. She nodded, not a crack of emotion written on her face, and continued walking. Maritza said nothing. She had become withdrawn, and long stretches of time would pass before she uttered a single word. Mostly they had communicated in silent nods and glances. Inside, Lucine knew that Vahe was keeping her alive. God knew what thoughts were passing through her head about Dikran. For Lucine, she had put Sarkis on a tall hill, gathering apricots, a broad smile on his face. That had kept her. And it would keep her still.

The chief gendarme rode past, and as he did, he glanced backwards. Lucine stared defiantly at him. No matter what happened now, Anahid was safe. She had been rescued from him. The gendarme rode off. Remembering her face.

PALOU

The flat stone floor of the chamber felt cool against Armen's skin. He finally located the small latch at the base of the altar. He pulled it and then slid the small right side of the altar away. Below it were narrow steps leading into the dark chamber.

"Hello?" he whispered. "Anyone there?"

Nothing.

"Yes hye-em. Eem anoones Armen eh. Armen Khatisian," he said. I am Armenian. My name is Armen. Armen Khatisian.

He carefully pushed the move-away piece back into place, sealing out the light and concealing him. He could smell the mustiness. He stretched his hands out. Things tumbled away from the wall. A shelf. He felt the small, waxy candles and, reaching blindly, some matches. He struck one against the rough stone and lit a candle.

The space was small and narrow. Around him were jars of toorshee, a stack of Bibles, and a small wooden chest. He grabbed one of the jars of pickled vegetables. He pulled on the lid and it came off with a loud POP! The acid smell of the vinegar filled his nostrils. Never had it smelled so good. He dug his fingers inside and ate.

'Why hadn't anyone else come here?' he thought. 'There must not have been time.'

Holding the candle, he leaned over the small wooden chest and opened it. Laid out flat were Father DerArtinian's vestments. Even against the dim candlelight, they shimmered, flecked with real gold thread. He pushed the vestments aside, revealing Father DerArtinian's Bible, the cover of which was a thin sheet of pure gold, the cross on the cover dotted at each of the three points with small red rubies.

'This is the Bible I used to kiss,' he thought.

He sat against the stone wall and began to read. In time, the candle would burn out and he would sleep.

TOWARD MOSUL, MESOPOTAMIA

When they left Bitlis, they had been told that they were going to Diyarbekir, then by truck to Malatia, and then to Sivas. They could not go directly through Palou, Kharpert, and Arabkir. But what none of them knew, what none of them would know until Deir-El-Zor, was that they were all walking.

All of them.

Here, in the deadly heat of August, across the Ottoman Empire, more than five hundred thousand Armenians were walking. And dying as they went.

Elise and Sona had used the coins, traded the blankets and rugs. Their skin was dark and the flesh hung loosely from their bones. Liver spots, once dormant, raged from the constant sun, and dotted Elise's face, arms and hands.

Water. You could go weeks without food. But in this heat, more than two days without water, three at the most, meant you would burn up inside. Water.

The gendarmes had turned the caravan around several times, and both Elise and Sona could no longer judge how far they had gone or where they were going.

"Is this the way to Diyarbekir?" a woman asked.

"Chem kider," Elise replied. I do not know.

But they would never see Diyarbekir. Instead, the gendarmes were heading decidedly southeast. Toward Mosul.

Elise kept Sona close, but Sona would not relent to having her hair cut. It was braided, tucked tightly in a bun. Once soft and thick, the hairs were now dry and coarse. There were streaks where the sun had bleached deep black hair blonde.

The first attack had happened four days ago. The caravan had been winding through a narrow pass. The gendarmes had ridden away. For a few moments, the deportees stood confused. Were they leaving them? Suddenly they heard the clang-clang-clang of wooden sticks against tin pans and pots.

The din took on strange echoes, ricocheting off the rock surfaces. And as the pitch grew, Elise and Sona turned in horror as two groups, men carrying swords and scythes, and women carrying wooden clubs with sharp nails sticking out from them, rushed forward.

"Run!"

Some of the deportees froze like frightened rabbits. They were the first to go down. The sound of sharp objects cutting into dense but fragile flesh was gruesome and was overshadowed by the most abominable screams. Elise grabbed Sona and pushed her over a small ledge and fell on top of her. The killing went on as the hill people cut down anyone who stood in their way. The jihad had been declared.

"Kill the Christian infidels. On to greater glory for those who do!"

When it was over, the decimation was severe. Bodies lay about, denuded, their clothes taken. Valuables that had been in families for generations were plundered. The animals would come, and they would tear the flesh into pieces.

The gendarmes had returned as the attackers had withdrawn, and they whipped the exiles back into their line.

"Keep them walking," they had been told. "Wear them down. But do not let any outsider see. And no photographs. Confiscate any cameras you see and arrest such persons on the spot where they stand."

Two-and-a-half days after the attack they reached the outskirts of Hassan, bordering the Tigris. Hassan was almost two-thirds of the way diagonally from Diyarbekir to Mosul. But from Bitlis it was directly south. Though it grew steadily warmer the further south they went, nights were cold. Sona and Elise drew close to each other for warmth. Elise made a mental count of what they had: two rings, two bracelets, two anklets. Sona had been sure to conceal her betrothal bracelet with the sleeve of her shabeeg. If she had to, it would be the last item to give up.

As they walked, Sona saw an old woman sitting on the ground.

"Are you all right?" she asked.

"Ayo," the woman said.

"Here, I will help you."

Sona put her hands underneath the woman's arms. She leaned back and gently began to lift. Suddenly, a gendarme rode up, drew his pistol, and fired once into the woman's chest. It had happened so quickly. Sona looked down at the woman, the red circle in the middle of her chest spreading out. The gendarme waved his pistol back and forth, commanding her to join the line.

"March!" he said. "Or you are next!"

Sona stumbled away from the woman. Her arms were still outstretched, almost frozen into position. She could feel the gendarme watching her. She reached Elise and sat down. Elise saw the tears streaming down her face, took her in her arms, and rocked her until she slept.

ADANA

Adana stood beneath the Taurus Mountains in Cilicia. The journey would be two hundred kilometers, past Alexandretta, Dort, and Yol. Past Aintab, Harifan, and then to Aleppo in Syria. Blazing sun and extraordinary swelter threw off waves as the landscape moved and shifted through the heat vapors. Hundreds of Armenian deportees stood; almost all were women and children. The train cars were French forty-eights, made to hold forty men or eight horses. Now, commanded by the Turkish and German soldiers, hundreds of Armenians filed into them.

"Where are you from?" the old woman said.

"I am from Zeitun," a woman answered.

The woman bent down toward a young girl. "Tsakus. Vor deghatzi?" Where are you from?

"Marashen em," the girl replied, her voice high. I am from Marash.

"Koniaen," another woman said.

"Malatiaen," yet another answered.

The soldiers nodded and the doors were slid shut. Almost immediately, the Armenians drew forward, pressing their faces against the sides of the cars, trying to get air. Outside, through the narrow slits, their faces streamed by in one continuous blur.

ALEPPO, SYRIA

And now the Armenians descended from the open cars, the stench of feces and urine wafting out with them. Here and there, elderly men and women were carried out, some dead; others dehydrated until they could no longer move on their own.

"You two," one of the Turkish gendarmes said, pointing to the women. They stopped, frightened. He pointed to the lifeless bodies.

"Take them and put them there," he said, motioning to the back of a small half-truck. The women struggled with the body and dropped it into the truck. As they turned, they could see many bodies being pulled from the open cars behind them.

"Put all of them in there," the gendarme ordered.

"Where will we go?" a woman asked.

The chief gendarme looked up, and then returned to the document he was holding.

"You will go to Mesken," he said. "Your people are there."

MESKEN, SYRIA

The makeshift encampment was surrounded by hundreds of raised mounds of earth. These hastily dug graves served as the welcoming sight for the arriving exiles. They descended the train cars to find that their internment consisted of sand, some ragged and flimsy tents, and thousands of others. Five thousand was the estimate that the German missionaries had made, but no one could really be sure. There, in the blazing sun and the shivering cold of night, they could only wait.

It was madness! Sheer, utter horror!

These were the thoughts and words that came to Wegner's mind as he and the other missionaries walked through the deportees. They were pitiful. Dressed in rags. Skin. Bones. These were people once. No. These are still people. Despite how they look. They are people for God's sake!

Armin Theophil Wegner was a second lieutenant in the German-Ottoman sanitation medical mission. He would spend more than a year in Turkey, Syria, and Mesopotamia. He stopped, occasionally seeing to those who were particularly in need.

"Thank you. Thank you."

"God bless you, child," they would say.

It was a futile task. There were so many of them. Wegner reached into his canvas satchel, withdrew the camera, and clicked the button. The photographs would prove that it had happened.

SYRIA

The desert wasteland of Deir-El-Zor stood some one hundred twenty kilometers to the southeast of Rakka, on the Euphrates. From Palou, one could almost draw a straight line and hit Deir-El-Zor, a staggering two hundred kilometers to the south. This was the distance that the Palouzis had traveled.

Lucine slept. Occasionally her right hand fluttered uncontrollably. They needed water. Woeful cries, whimpers, and grief meshed together into a horrible sound. They had passed through Dikranagerd, where more refugees had joined the caravan, and then the line had snaked east to Nisibin and then to Ras-Ul-Ain. As new deportees joined the caravan, Lucine had asked them where they were from.

Chemeshgezak. Moush. Mezre. Severeg.

"Do you have news of Palou?" she asked.

Nothing.

"Bitlis?"

"No, I do not know. I do not know! Leave me! They will see us talking! They will come!"

They had nothing left to trade. Lucine and Maritza could only beg.

But all that changed at Ras-Ul-Ain.

As they had walked through, the sand blowing and causing them to bend over, the caravan had to stop. They could not see. And as the wind and the blowing sands subsided, Lucine and the others looked up to see a wall of men, many on horses, more on foot.

The Special Organization.

The men drew forth, carrying machetes.

In an instant, there were screams everywhere and the Armenians fled, searching for escape. Three, perhaps four people seemed to hit Lucine all at once and she toppled over, crashing into Maritza, knocking her down. Maritza managed to hold Vahe out from her and avoided crushing him.

"Stay still," Lucine whispered.

The SO rushed forward, swinging and hacking. Someone fell on top of Lucine, knocking the air from her lungs. She looked at a lifeless face that was a mass of blood. There were screams everywhere.

"Mi sharjehr," Lucine said. "Yeteh Vahen goolah, tzerkuht eer peraneen varah." Do not move, if Vahe cries put your hand over his mouth.

Maritza nodded. Finally, the SO retreated and the gendarmes returned. Again they walked. As they passed body after body, Lucine closed her eyes and bit down hard.

They had finally silenced Perouz Avakian.

Deir-El-Zor was bare and lying amongst thousands of others, Lucine slept, but no dreams came. Once, now it seemed like years ago, she saw Anahid's face, but she could remember nothing more.

"Will you help me? Will you help me?"

Lucine stirred, and the picture of Anahid shimmered and dissolved into the heat of dawn. She opened her eyes and winced as the bright sun worked its way above the horizon.

"Lucine... Will you help me?"

It was Maritza. In her outstretched arms, she held Vahe, thrusting him toward her. Lucine opened her mouth to speak and then looked from Maritza to Vahe.

The baby was dead.

Lucine took him in her arms.

"Ayo. Anoushig Vahe," she said. Yes, sweet Vahe.

Lucine looked at Maritza. She wrung her hands inside one another and looked back and forth from Vahe to Lucine. Some of the gendarmes began to gather on the outskirts of the makeshift camp. They slept away from the caravan, far from the stink and the disease. Lucine could see them lighting their hand-rolled cigarettes, the small plumes of smoke rising into the morning air.

Lucine held the baby. His skin was already becoming hard and stiff. She looked at Maritza.

"Mgrdootuin," Maritza said, over and over. "Mgrdootuin. Mgrdootuin." Baptism.

Lucine nodded, and they slowly walked away from the groups of people who were scattered about. The gendarmes watched them go, but paid them little interest. They knelt down and Lucine gently rested Vahe on the sand, his small blanket covering his face. She looked at Maritza and they both began digging with their hands. Within minutes, they had dug a small, shallow grave.

"Avelee khoroong," Lucine said. Deeper.

Along the way, she had been sickened at the sight of wild dogs pulling limbs from beneath such shallow graves. Soon the hole was as deep as the length of Lucine's arm.

Maritza's lips curled up and she started to tremble. Lucine reached her hand out, trying to calm her. In the distance, the refugees stirred. Lucine couldn't remember everything that was supposed to be done, or the exact words, but if this was what Maritza wanted she would do her best.

God!

She looked at the hem of Maritza's dress and leaned over. She tore off a strip of the dirty white cloth. Then she reached down to her own dress, and tore off a piece of cloth that had been stained red with blood; she couldn't remember when or how. Working in silence, Lucine braided them together. Maritza watched, fascinated. They crossed themselves and Lucine gently pulled the blanket from Vahe's face. He looked alive; he could have been sleeping. Maritza looked at him. Lucine gently drew the twisted red and white cloth under and around his neck, resting the strands on his chest.

White was for sacrifice and purity, red for the blood and water that had flowed from Christ's side. Lucine looked at Maritza, who nodded.

"It is Christ's will that we must be born of the water and the spirit," Lucine began. She paused for a moment, trying to remember the words; it would have to do.

"Fill thy servants with heavenly gifts," she continued. "And grant him the joy of being named a Christian." She reached out her right hand and touched the baby's forehead. "And make him worthy of baptism."

She gently picked up the baby. Maritza drew her hands toward her chest, palms facing upward.

"For this child do you renounce Satan?" Lucine said.

"Yes," Maritza replied. Her hands were shaking.

"For this child do you renounce evil?"

"Yes."

"For this child do you surrender and obey Christ and his teachings?"

"Yes," Maritza said, crying.

"And do you accept Christ as King and Lord?"

"Yes. Yes, to all these things. Yes."

Lucine slowly turned and laid the baby down onto the sand and she and Maritza knelt beside him.

When she was small, her mother had told her that the muron, the holy oil, had come directly from the mother church in Etchmiadzin.

"The muron is called the oil of gladness," her mother had said, "and this oil is blessed only by the Catholicos. No one else."

"It smells sweet," Lucine had said.

"It is made of olive oil, my child. Olive oil and forty kinds of flowers."

But they had neither oil, nor water. Lucine wet her right thumb with her tongue and drew it down and across the baby's forehead.

"Ays manooguh eench guh papakee?" she said. What does this child request?

"Havadk," Maritza said. Faith.

Lucine drew her thumb down and across the baby's chest.

"Hooys," Maritza said. Hope.

Lucine crossed the baby's left palm.

"Ser." Love

Lucine crossed the baby's right palm.

"Mgrdootuin," Maritza said, her palms upraised. Baptism.

They stood there for a few moments, not knowing what to do next.

"May God bless this child," Lucine said, finally.

Maritza, crying, nodded, and crossed herself. Lucine draped the blanket over Vahe's face. She looked at Maritza, but the woman could not bring herself to do it. Lucine nodded, and gently laid the baby in the shallow hole. They scraped the sand over and over until he was covered. Maritza stood up and watched as Lucine broke a twig into two pieces and laid them in the shape of a cross atop the tiny mound of earth.

PART SIX

CHUNUK BAIR
10 August 1915

The Gallipoli Peninsula. Sweltering heat and scorching sunlight.

Cramping and dysentery wreaked havoc among the men. They became hosts to hordes of lice, fleas, and flies, 'big green bastards' the Anzacs called them. These were the conditions all along Gallipoli during July and August. And yet, their progress, measured in precious yards taken and lost, was dismal.

Roughly two kilometers from their landing point at Anzac Cove lay Lone Pine, Battleship Hill, Chunuk Bair, Hill Q, and Koja Chemen Tepe. These points were mere yards from one another in a dense and hilly landscape. But the maps were old. Flats became hills. Distances were wrong.

When the fighting began, it was hellish and brutal. Just before the sun came up, the Brits and the Anzacs stared bleary-eyed as the forms of what seemed to be thousands of Turks marched toward them.

"Fire! Fire!"

"Fix bayonets!"

Neither side would give in; neither would turn and run. Even the most seasoned commanders had trouble facing the carnage. Many got sick at the sight of the blood and the hacked off limbs, the hacked off hands. God! In only a few hours, over a thousand had dripped their blood into the earth.

CONSTANTINOPLE
11 August 1915

Enver sat, thinking. He was particularly perturbed. Just a few hours ago, Lepsius, the German missionary, had come requesting assistance for the Armenians. Enver had looked him straight in the eyes and had made it clear that the subject was closed. Still, Enver was bothered. He had heard that Lepsius had obtained access to files from the Wilhelmstrasse, the Whitehall of Berlin, but what information was contained in those files he did not know.

In his office, Wangenheim withdrew a green folder from the stack on his desk. Drawing it near, his hand seemed to tremble slightly. This had happened just one week before, but Wangenheim had thought nothing of it; probably nerves.

The consul reports, from Kighi, Akantz, Moush and other areas amounted to thousands of Armenian casualties. That would not do. Within the hour, he would provide his contacts in the national and international press with information that would reduce the Armenian casualties by one-half and increase the Turkish casualties by two times.

He was suddenly very tired, but he had much work to do. Within hours, the editors of the morning papers: the Ikdam, the Tasviri Efkyar, and the Tanine had followed Wangenheim's instructions to the detail and the wires were sent to the international press.

TOWARD DIYARBEKIR

As Armen walked, his thoughts turned back to his father Garbis, Sarkis, and Dikran. Each time he pushed the images out of his head. He had to get to Ctesiphon: to Hagop and Souren. They would be all right. But how? He had never been, and knew only that it was to the southeast of Palou. Hagop had showed it to him on a map, and now Armen struggled to view how the lines had been.

"Near Baghdad," he remembered. "Diyarbekir to Baghdad."

He looked up and saw the moonlight working its way through the clouds, hitting the branches of almond and fig trees. God! It had been so beautiful! The most direct way to Ctesiphon was directly south, first to Diyarbekir, then further southeast to Mosul, through Tekrit, and then to Baghdad. Ctesiphon would be only ten or so kilometers from there. If he could only keep up his pace, it was possible that he could get to Diyarbekir in seven or eight hours.

CTESIPHON

The rail line was almost completed. Hagop and Souren had made quick friends with Setrak Ahydenian. He was from Kharpert and was particularly adept at measuring and laying the track.

"We are almost done," Hagop said, leaning on his shovel.

"I think in only a few days," Souren said. He took a deep breath and rested. Hagop glanced at the disinterested soldiers, turned. He shuffled over towards Souren and whispered.

"Souren. If anything happens, stay close to me."

"What do you mean?" Souren said.

Hagop picked up his shovel and began moving dirt. "Keep shoveling," he said. Souren nodded. "Listen to me," Hagop whispered.

"Yes?"

"All we have done is dig and lay tracks for this rail line," Hagop said. "But there has been no other training for us."

"What do you mean?"

"In all this time, did you see any extra rifles for us?" Hagop asked.

"No."

"And no extra uniforms, either," Hagop added. "Even in the storerooms there are only uniforms for the Germans and the Turks."

The Turkish commander finished reading the document. He buttoned his tunic and walked out of the temporary barracks. He crossed the line of working men and knocked on the door of the German barracks.

"Come in."

"Herr Commandant," he said, handing the note to him. "This cipher has been received from Constantinople."

The German commander took the document and read it.

"Upon completion of track work, all foreign workers who bear the name of an Armenian are to be destroyed."

He looked up at the Turk. "When will we be ready?" he asked.

"I should estimate two, three days."

"Inform Constantinople that they will be done in three days," he said, standing. "We will carry out orders at that time."

SYRIA

It was early afternoon when the caravan reached the outer perimeter of the main camp at Deir-El-Zor. The effects of the constant heat, sunstroke, dehydration, and dysentery shone on the faces of the skeletons that walked, head-bowed, faces blank.

Lucine and Maritza walked in silence. Lucine occasionally glanced at the thin, stiff bodies along the wayside. God! There were so many!

"I want to stop and rest," Maritza said.

Lucine looked at her. "We can stop only for a few moments," she said. "Then the gendarmes will be on us."

"I know," Maritza said. "You go on. Just a little while."

"No. I will stay with you and then we will start again," Lucine said. They sat on the soft sand. Around them, the other deportees drifted by. Ahead and behind, the mounted gendarmes stood watch. Martiza looked at Lucine for a moment and her eyes seem to glaze over. She said nothing and then began looking left, then right. She stood, frantic, and turned in short circles.

"Vahe! Vahe!" she screamed. "Lucine! Where is Vahe? I gave him to you!"

Lucine stood and looked at her. She reached her hand out and touched her shoulder. "Mari…"

"You whore!" Maritza, said, batting Lucine's hand away. "What have you done with my baby?"

Ahead, two gendarmes noticed the commotion. Lucine saw them, stepped forward, and put her hands firmly on Maritza's shoulders.

"Keep quiet!" she said, shaking her. "The gendarmes will come."

Maritza twisted away from her. "Did you sell my baby as you sold your daughter?" she screamed.

Lucine looked at Maritza and slapped her across the face.

"Maritza. Vahe is dead. Your baby is dead."

Maritza stood, stunned. The two gendarmes nodded and one of them clicked his spurs into the horse's side.

"You lie!" Maritza screamed. She pointed a finger at Lucine and took a step backward. "Blood is on your hands, you whore! You lie!"

"Maritza! Maritza!" Lucine said, trying to quiet her. She saw the gendarme riding toward them.

"You left him back there. Didn't you?" Maritza accused. "Didn't you?"

Lucine shook her head. "Maritza..."

"No!" Maritza screamed. She turned and ran.

"Maritza!"

Lucine started to run but her right foot caught the tip of a small rocky ledge and she fell. The gendarme rode past, and the animal's hooves threw up clouds of sand that blew into Lucine's eyes. She tried to clear them. She could see Maritza running.

"Maritza! Stop! Maritza!"

The gendarme rode on, drawing the horse close to her.

"Vahe! Vahe!" Maritza screamed, frantically. "Oor es? Maman hos eh!" Where are you? Mama is here!

"Maritza!" Lucine called out.

The gendarme drew back his saber and Lucine watched as he slashed it down. Maritza took a half step and then fell. Lucine covered her eyes with her hands and lowered her head into the sand.

CONSTANTINOPLE

Morgenthau sat, studying the consul reports. His desk was scattered with them now, had been for weeks and the descriptions of suffering leapt off the page as if the turmoil and misery were right there, with him, in this room.

He had been holding his suit jacket and was reaching to hang it in the closet. He found himself staring at the intricately woven pattern, but the checks and the cross weaves looked different. They seemed to be moving, to have come to life. In moments the varying patterns of cloth, thread, and color became a mass of people walking, endlessly, through the desert.

He shook his head, shaking out the vision. As he rose in his bed, Josephine had stirred.

"Henry? Are you all right?"

"Yes. Yes," came the groggy reply.

"Another nightmare?"

"Yes, he said, shaking his head.

Josephine looked at him. She would be leaving in four days.

SOFIA, BULGARIA
6 September, 1915

Inside the ornate headquarters, the long table was arrayed with sixteen chairs; these men represented the Central Powers. Baron Konstantin von Neurath, the Conseiller at the German Embassy in Constantinople, had been feverishly working out the details since the moment that Enver had given Wangenheim his answer.

Wangenheim had the last word. He made it clear to Enver that the Bulgarians were planning on massing more than three hundred thousand men who would besiege Constantinople.

"I do not believe it," Enver protested.

"Why?" Wangenheim replied. "Bulgaria knows that the Greeks and the Serbs will never voluntarily surrender Macedonia. And the Entente will never dare take Macedonia from them."

"Ah, I understand," Enver said. "Serbia."

"Exactly," Wangenheim replied. "Serbia makes a separate peace with the Central Powers and as a show of good faith, she provides her portion of Macedonia."

"And in return she asks for Bosnia and Herzegovina."

"Correct. And this Bulgaria cannot allow," Wangenheim said.

"It would constantly threaten her and inhibit peace in the Balkans," Enver said. Within the hour, Enver had given Wangenheim his answer. "Yes."

Von Neurath stood and raised his glass of brandy.

"Tonight, Turkey offers friendship and assurance. We are grateful to Germany for their assistance. May success be ours!" he said. They drank from their glasses.

Bulgaria had yearned for this stretch of land and now Turkey had given it to her. And, as soon as she could occupy her, Bulgaria would have Macedonia.

CONSTANTINOPLE

The night sky was clear. Morgenthau and Josephine stood surrounded by a bustle of activity. She was dressed elegantly in a gray shantung dress she had brought with her from New York.

It was difficult for her to leave him. Morgenthau saw that Bedri, the Prefect of Police, was off in the distance engaged in some form of histrionics with several policemen.

"He never changes, does he?" she asked.

"I am now firmly of the mind that nothing ever changes here," Morgenthau replied.

They turned to face one another. She reached out for his hands.

"Take care of yourself, Henry."

"I shall."

The last of the passengers were boarding now, and the shrill of the whistle caused her to start.

"Henry. Are you sure you want to stay here? There's only so much that any one person can do." She looked at him. Never before had her husband looked so tired, so... so... worn.

"I can save some of them and I can send my damned reports," he said, waving his right hand back and forth. "Words that move over wires from one world to another."

"Henry..."

"My God," he said, looking directly in her eyes. "I... It's going to be too late."

She squeezed his hands. Her eyes began to glisten, and then fill.

"Henry, if you save only one..."

He stood there, motionless.

"Yes. Yes, I know," he said. "And the longer I stay here the more the world will know."

Josephine caught herself, holding back the tears.

"February."

"February," he replied. He drew her close to him, and they stood, hugging one another. He kissed her and she touched his cheek. He followed her through the windows as she sat. She managed a slight smile. The whistle blew one final time and he watched as the train pulled away, her face receding from him.

But she was a determined woman. As the train drew away her mind became firmly set. Through diplomatic intermediaries, she had received word that Queen Eleonore of Bulgaria would meet with her.

Eleonore, born into royalty as German Princess Eleonore Von Reuss-Kostritz, was King Ferdinand's second wife. Determined and resolute, she had been put in charge of a Red Cross train in Manchuria during the Russo-Japanese War of 1904.

Now she sat, listening as Josephine related the plight of the Armenians. She became terribly angry; her own country was cooperating with Turkey and Germany.

"What you say is most unbelievable! It is dreadful!" she exclaimed.

"The papers in America are printing reports from eyewitnesses and from missionaries," Josephine said. "In the meanwhile, all America can do is to send and promote relief efforts. Some orphanages are being established. My husband has supervised some of the paperwork. But the atrocities are continuing day and night." She looked at Eleonore for a moment.

"One night, my husband could not bring himself to eat. He took his satchel into his office and closed the door."

"Yes…?" Eleonore asked.

"It must have been three or four o'clock when he came to bed. When I awoke, he was still sleeping and as I walked through the house, the door to his office was open."

Eleonore leaned forward.

"I walked into the room and on the desk were pictures taken by the American, German, Canadian, and French missionaries. And what I saw in those pictures will haunt me to my very last days on earth. For I saw death come to all ages of women and children, eaten away, nothing left."

Eleonore pushed forward a glass of water. Josephine cleared her throat and drank.

"And now we become their allies," Eleonore said.

"Yes," Josephine said, softly. "That is why I came here. To ask you to help."

Nearly two days had passed before Eleonore was able to discuss the matter with the King. The Bulgarian Minister to Turkey was summarily instructed to make a protest of the atrocities. But, despite her efforts, they were to no avail. The protest was a hollow one. It changed nothing. And Queen Eleonore could only watch as her country joined forces with those of the Central Powers.

CTESIPHON

The men leaned on their shovels and picks and watched as the last spike was hammered into place. The Turkish commander stepped forward.

"You men are to be congratulated for the work that you have done," he said. Hagop and Souren looked at one another. "Now that this job is completed, your military training will finally begin."

Souren nudged him, but Hagop said nothing. The commander turned the paper over.

"You will be separated into groups so that you can be taught in your own languages and in German. There can be no misunderstanding during war. If a command is given, you must understand it completely." He folded the document and looked at the men. "Because you have worked hard, you will be given two days of rest in Baghdad."

Souren looked at Hagop and opened his mouth to speak, but Hagop shook his head. The commander turned and glanced in the direction of his German counterpart, who nodded.

"You will gather here at precisely nineteen hundred hours. There have been reports of enemy planes patrolling the perimeters and we will not tempt them during the day. Therefore you will leave at night. Any man not on these trucks will be left here to work."

"Hagop!" Souren said, jostling him. "We are going to Baghdad!"

Hagop looked at him and then broke into a hearty laugh. "You are too young to go to Baghdad!" he said.

"Ah, what do you know?" Souren replied. "And after we come back, we begin our training."

Hagop looked at him and nodded slowly.

"What is in Baghdad?" Souren asked.

DIYARBEKIR

Through the trees, the view of Diyarbekir lay just ahead. Dusk would come soon. He could forage for food among the scraps, find a place to sleep for a few hours, and then move on under the darkness of night. He was tired, but the journey had been without incident.

Twenty-five kilometers outside of Diyarbekir, he had heard the marching of soldiers. He hadn't been able to get a look at them, but they were speaking Turkish.

Now he sat, waiting for the light to wane. His stomach rumbled. He was used to it now, and he had learned to ignore it. How he had enjoyed eating, he thought. Now, after what he had seen, he had no appetite. Still, he knew he had to eat. He would eat and he would survive. He put the idea in his head and kept it there.

They will never get me,' he thought. 'Never.'

CTESIPHON

The railway workers were gathered, eagerly awaiting transport to Baghdad. The Jews and the Greeks stood to the left, while the Armenians stood to the right. Hagop, Souren, and Setrak stood together. There were six trucks, two for the soldiers, the others for the men.

"Your leave begins now," the Turkish lieutenant said. "You will return here in forty-eight hours." He looked at the group of Jews and Greeks. "Group number one, board trucks one and two. He looked at the Armenians. "Group number two, trucks three and four."

"Come on," Souren said. "It will be hot. We can sit near the back."

DIYARBEKIR

It was a very large home with a small wall surrounding it and Armen could hear what sounded like trickling water from a fountain. There was a wooden box where the refuse was deposited. The sun was just on the cusp of disappearing. It was amazing what people would throw away. He had even once found almost an entire roasted chicken. He waited, his stomach growling and turning.

TOWARD BAGHDAD

The trucks continued, moving in a single line. They were almost parallel to the Tigris River and as they drew closer, the two middle trucks, carrying the Jews and the Greeks, veered off to the right.

"Do you smell that?" Hagop asked.

"Yes," Souren said, "what is it?"

"Smells like the river," Setrak said.

Hagop pulled up the flap. To the left, the Tigris moved swiftly past.

DIYARBEKIR

The creak of the wooden gate stirred Armen from his thoughts. The veiled figure walked slowly, carrying the basketful of trash. She stopped, as if sensing that someone was there, and Armen pressed his back against the wall. She dumped the trash and closed the lid. As she turned, a small gust of wind drew up, pushing back the veil.

"My God," Armen said, his eyes widening. "My God..."

He watched as the figure walked back to the house. He strained to see her profile through the veil. But it was too dark now. It did not make sense. She disappeared into the house.

'Could it be?' he thought. 'Anahid?'

He would wait a while longer and then see if there was food. He stood, thinking. He could stay and hope to catch another glimpse of her... if it was she. But what if it wasn't? Would she deliver him to the soldiers?

'No,' he thought. 'Impossible.'

He would eat, sleep for a few hours, and then leave. He could not take the risk.

OUTSIDE BAGHDAD

"We are slowing down," Hagop said.

Souren and Setrak nodded, and they looked at the other men sitting with them. The truck finally ground to a stop.

"We are having problems with this vehicle," a soldier said, pulling back the flap. "You men use this time to stretch your legs."

The men got down, reaching their arms above their heads, stretching. The soldiers from the lead truck shuffled around nonchalantly. Some of the men sat down on the sand, others lit cigarettes.

"Ah, every minute we wait here when we could be in Baghdad!" Souren said. Hagop saw that the two soldiers who had been driving their truck had the hood open and were peering inside.

"Maybe I should go and see if I can help them fix it," Setrak said. "I know some things about..."

Hagop reached his hand out, stopping him. "No, you stay here," he said.

Setrak opened his mouth, but Hagop shook his head.

"Jamgotch," he said, using Souren's childhood name. The Jamgochians were often called Jamgotches: it meant those who call people into the church. "Come here."

"Why?" Souren asked, coming closer.

"Keep quiet," Hagop whispered. "Listen to me. You too, Setrak." He looked quickly at the soldiers, who were still milling about, uninterested.

"It is a trap."

"What?" Souren began.

"I tell you, I know," Hagop said. "One of them was making hand signals to the other." He looked from Souren to Setrak.

"Hand signals for what?" Souren said.

"They know we understand Turkish," Setrak said.

Hagop nodded. "Setrak, you tell the other men, the group behind you. We will tell the men over here." Setrak nodded. "Jump into the river," Hagop said. "It is a fast current, you can make it."

Setrak lifted his arms above his head, pretending to stretch. He walked casually over to the group of men.

"Jamgotch," Hagop said. "Eem kovus getzeed." Stay close to me.

"Ayo," Souren replied.

They walked toward the second group of men. Hagop caught a quick flash of movement from the corner of his eye. He glanced quickly to the left and the green canvas was lifted. The machine gun began to turn bolts of fire shooting out from the revolving turret.

"Run!" Hagop said, pushing Souren. "Into the river!"

The men started to scream and ran in all directions. A bullet whizzed by Hagop's head. Souren bent down and ran towards the water. Setrak turned, trying to find his way. A bullet caught him, ripping open his throat. Man after man went down.

Hagop shook his head. A flash of powder had caught his eyes and everything was going from gray to white to vivid blue.

"Hagop!" Souren yelled.

"Run!" Hagop shouted. He could see him now. The machine gun turned, eating up the strand of bullets. Hagop drew closer to Souren.

"Jump!" he said.

Souren bent down. The bullet rang close and the sound of it passing seemed to stop. Hagop looked to his left and saw Souren as he was going down.

"NO!" Hagop screamed.

Souren looked at him, the red stain spreading quickly.

The rifles joined the machine gun and more men went down. Hagop turned and a bullet caught him square in his left thigh. The pain shot through him so quickly it felt as if it would rip his head off.

"Hagop…" Souren said.

Hagop fell to the ground, and pulled Souren closer to him. "Go," he said, softly. "You must…"

Hagop looked at him, but he was gone. He pushed himself up onto his knees and started to run. The bullets whizzed by and he could hear the sickening thud as they found their mark. Screams filled his ears.

He reached the ridge of the river and slid down the side. In moments, he was in the rushing water, clinging to a tree branch. Two soldiers rushed to the edge, but he ducked his head into the water. It was cool and soon it would help stop the bleeding. But he would have to get out of there quickly. Too long and the water would turn on him. He had to hide. He had to think.

CONSTANTINOPLE

A light rain fell and mixed with the coolness of the October day. Morgenthau crossed the public square until he was parallel to the entrance of the Seraskeriate, the War Office. He had been waiting for this meeting for weeks; Enver had finally consented. Morgenthau knew that the delay was due to the subject matter.

"Mr. Ambassador!" Enver said, rising to meet him. "Please sit down."

"Thank you for seeing me, Mr. Minister."

"I will discuss this matter with you because you represent the United States of America."

"I appreciate that," Morgenthau said.

"Then we can begin," Enver said. "The Armenians are enemy collaborators. They have assisted the Russians. You know what they did in Van."

"Yes, Mr. Minister, I am aware of Van," Morgenthau said, "but young women and children are being driven..."

"We are fighting and dying and sacrificing men all over this country!" Enver said. "When our own citizens ally themselves with our enemies, as they did in the Van district, they will have to be destroyed."

"But why punish the innocent?" Morgenthau replied. "Is an entire race worth the alleged crimes of individuals?"

"We cannot distinguish the difference," Enver said. "We must deliberately scatter them. Separated and divided, they can do us no harm."

"But they are defenseless!" Morgenthau said, his voice rising. "Old women, children. Without food, starving..."

"It is their own fault!" Enver said, exploding. He leaned forward and pointed a finger at Morgenthau. "You are responsible! Give them no hope and they will come to their senses. I know that you are shocked at what I am saying, but it is only because you are not from here. You prolong their hardships."

Morgenthau sat, incredulous. There were untold thousands of helpless persons who sat dying in exile. He walked slowly back to the American Embassy, trying to think what more he could do.

OUTSIDE BAGHDAD

Hagop grabbed for the branches that dangled into the water and pulled himself out. The rushing current of the Tigris had swept him for what seemed like hours, but was, in reality, only twenty minutes or so. He rolled onto the grass, exhausted. He had to get out of the wet clothes and into some kind of shelter. He reached his left hand down and felt his thigh. It stung, but the real pain would come when the muting of the cold water was gone. He looked around; there was a small group of homes in the distance.

He stood, and gently put his left foot down. A shot of pain ran up and into his lower back. He drew his foot up slightly, bending at the knee. He limped toward some fallen branches. He grabbed a long one and leaned onto it.

One home was set slightly apart from the others and adjoining it was a small barn. He stayed to the shadows and reached the barn's door. He pressed an ear to it, but there was nothing. He gently pushed the door open. It was dark, but he could make out the outlines of a hay stall. It smelled like cows and chickens. He stepped inside and closed the door behind him. Some of the chickens flitted away. He reached the pile of hay and sat. He grabbed some burlap sacks, took off his shirt, and draped two of the sacks around his chest and shoulders. He covered himself with the hay for warmth and put his head down. Within moments, he was fast asleep.

Outside, the man who had seen him enter his property stood, slowly turned, and went inside his home.

In his dream, Hagop was sitting at the table. Lucine and Takouhi had outdone themselves. Every few minutes they would bring out delicacy after delicacy. They were all there, together.

He stirred, the straw brushing against his face. He had slept for almost thirteen hours, and as he lay there, eyes still closed, he wrinkled his nose. Strange, he could almost smell the food on the table.

He opened his eyes and sat up, shocked.

"Hello," the man said.

Hagop looked at the man who sat, cross-legged, directly opposite him. He tried to stand, but the wound had stiffened during the night and the pain shot up. The hay beneath him was stained red with blood.

"You should not try to stand," the man said. On his lap sat a metal plate of cheese and bread.

"Who are...?" Hagop stammered.

"My name is Salleh Ahmet. This is my property."

Hagop looked at the man. He was lean, short, and sported a goatee. His skin was the color of dark chestnut.

"You have slept well," Ahmet said.

"You are Arabic?" Hagop asked.

"Yes," Ahmet said. "And you are Armenian?"

Hagop looked at him, but did not answer.

"Come. Do not be afraid. If I had wanted to alert the authorities I could have done so by now."

Hagop looked at him, trying to think.

"You must eat if you hope to heal that," Ahmet said. He put the plate down on the ground and pushed it toward Hagop.

"I am sure you are hungry. Please eat it."

Hagop nodded, pulled the plate toward him, and gobbled down a piece of bread and cheese. Ahmet held out a pewter pitcher.

"Only water," Ahmet said.

Hagop brought it to his lips and took a long pull.

"Thank you, Salleh Ahmet," Hagop said, tentatively.

"You are welcome...?"

"My name is Hagop."

"And your family name?" Ahmet asked.

"Melkonian," Hagop said. "My family name is Melkonian."

"Then welcome to my home, Hagop Melkonian."

"Thank you."

They sat there for a few moments, neither saying anything.

"Trader?" Hagop asked.

"Yes, I trade everything!" Salleh said, laughing.

Hagop managed a slight smile, but it quickly turned into a wince. The leg was paining him.

"I will send my daughter, Iman, to tend to your leg," Salleh said. "Mind me. If you are not careful, it will become infected."

"I cannot stay here long," Hagop said. He looked at Salleh. "I must return to my home."

Salleh nodded, his face taking on a serious tone. "From which village do you come?"

"I am from Palou. Do you know it?"

"Yes," Salleh said. "Yes, certainly. When I was a boy, my father would make many journeys throughout that region."

Hagop put down the plate. "Salleh Ahmet, what has happened?"

Salleh paused. "From where have you come?"

"We were enlisted into the Turkish Army. We have been building railroad lines in Ctesiphon."

Salleh nodded slightly. "Ah. I understand now. So you know nothing."

"No," Hagop said. "I know something has happened. We were never given uniforms or rifles. They shot everyone."

"Then you must know this, Hagop Melkonian," Salleh said. "They are driving out all the Armenians. It does not matter from where."

Hagop shook his head and blinked. "But why? What have we done?"

"I think it is less what you have done and more who you are," Salleh answered.

Hagop sat for a moment, thinking. "Do you have any news from Palou?"

Salleh shook his head. "I know nothing of it. But Mosul is near. And I have heard that there are caravans of Armenians that have passed through."

"Then I must get to Mosul!" Hagop exclaimed. He attempted to stand, but it was useless.

"Yes. Yes, if you must," Salleh said, rushing to his side. "But you cannot go like this." He gently eased him back to the ground. "Strengthen yourself and then you will be able to journey there." He looked at him and hardened his voice. "Remember what I have told you. If you do not, you will lose your leg."

Hagop nodded. "Where are they sending them?"

Salleh's face was grave. "All of your people are being deported. They travel to Deir-El-Zor."

The horror spread across Hagop's face. "Deir-Zor! But there is nothing there! Only desert! But why?"

"I do not know the reason," Salleh said.

"They are going to kill us," Hagop said, realizing the magnitude of it. He looked at Salleh. "They are going to kill all of us."

Salleh drew forth and spoke softly. "Listen to me. Turkish and German soldiers pass through here. You must be very careful."

"Why are you helping me?" Hagop said. "It will be dangerous for you to help me! They will..."

Salleh nodded and then looked Hagop directly in the eyes. "I am only a man. I am not a soldier. I am given what I have and I will return to the earth when it is my time. You are a Christian. I am a Moslem." He held his hands up, and then let them fall slowly to his lap. "I have read Turkish newspapers calling for a Jihad against Christians, but only Armenian Christians."

Hagop listened, shocked.

"But it is a lie," Salleh said. "It is all lies. Because there are German Christians, French Christians, there are the Americans. And yet they call for this against only the Armenians. Why?"

Hagop opened his mouth to speak, but Salleh waved his hand, cutting him off. "My Prophet and my God would not have me stand by. Would yours?"

Hagop said nothing. They sat for a few moments.

"Rest now," Salleh said. "I will send Iman to change your bandages. She will be frightened of you at first but she is a good daughter. Do not be alarmed."

Hagop nodded and Salleh left, pulling the door shut behind him. Hagop looked at the plate of food, but could not stomach it. His mind raced and the thoughts shot back and forth.

BERLIN

After his disastrous meeting with Enver, Lepsius had returned to Berlin.

"My name is Dr. Johannes Lepsius," he began, looking into the mass of people gathered in the square. "I am a member of the German Mission providing relief assistance for Armenians currently in exile in the Ottoman Empire. Fellow Germans, the plight of the Armenians is great. Many thousands have been driven from their homeland and forced to walk into desolate, barren areas with nothing to eat or drink."

Some of the women in the crowd looked at one another. A journalist from the Berliner Tageblatt took notes.

"We have buried hundreds and have dispensed supplies to those who survive," Lepsius continued. "We have seen starving women eat from the carcasses of horses which lay dead from the brutal heat. New mothers beg us to take their children." He looked out into the faces. "Good Christians of Germany: please do not close your eyes to the tragedy that is befalling the Armenians."

He would return to the desert. They would grab at him and thrust their hands out, and into them he would put a portion of bread. When the food had run out, the missionaries would place into their hands the prayer cards, printed in Armenian, showing Mary with the baby Jesus. Some cried, some wailed. And then they stopped. Went silent. The power to heal, the power to believe, the power of hope. Concentrated in one small slip of paper given to them by these uniformed strangers who came not to kill them but to care for them.

Lepsius never abandoned their cause. Before the deportations and the massacres became manifest, he had already been granted access to

the Wilhelmstrasse, and through its archives, uncovered documenta-
tion that detailed the mode and methods by which the Armenians
would be deported. By 1920, he had seen half of their entire worldwide
population decimated. But, still, they were not made extinct. And he
was forever to be remembered.

CONSTANTINOPLE
11 October 1915

Morgenthau crossed the busy street and walked up the stairs to the
American Embassy. Mowbry was there to meet him and handed off the
previous night's cables.

"Just what we feared, Ambassador," Mowbry said.

"Bulgaria?" Morgenthau said, taking the stack of documents.

"Yes, sir," Mowbry nodded. "She invaded Macedonia at 0700
hours."

"Well, I can't say I'm surprised to hear it."

"London removed the Bulgarian Foreign Minister and is treating
her as a hostile enemy. The British and the French are on their way to
the Greek-Serbian front."

"Thank you, Mr. Mowbry," Morgenthau said.

Morgenthau read one of Taylor's reports. At Anzac, they had tra-
versed less than half a kilometer of territory to battle valiantly at Lone
Pine. Half a kilometer! Even at the widest point of their insertion, to the
north and parallel with Sulva Bay, they penetrated a mere four kilometers to reach Scimitar Hill. And, soon, the vicious winter would be upon
them.

OUTSIDE BAGHDAD

Hagop gingerly stepped about. Each day that passed was torture,
and his thoughts, no matter how hard he had tried to keep them at bay,
brought him back to his family. To Armen, Souren, and to Sona. He
could see her face, clear, alive, laughing.

The door opened and Salleh entered, followed by another man.
Hagop saw him and took a few steps backward, startled.

"Do not be concerned," Salleh said. "He is a friend."

Hagop nodded, and the two men drew near.

"This is Ali Al-Fulani."

The man held his hand out and Hagop took it.

"You are doing well," Salleh said. "You will be able to walk soon without problems."

Salleh and Al-Fulani sat down opposite Hagop.

"Ali and I trade together," Salleh said. He looked at Hagop. "Hagop. He brings news."

Hagop nodded. He looked at Al-Fulani, waiting for him to speak.

"The war worsens," Al-Fulani began. "The British will come to Baghdad by the first of the next year."

"The Armenians?" Hagop asked.

Al-Fulani paused and then looked directly into Hagop's eyes. He shook his head decisively.

"No," he said. "There are many fires. Trees and fields are burning. I saw no men. Anyone who is left is deported. Women and young children. All walk. All walk."

"Do you know anything of Palou or Bitlis?" Hagop asked.

Al-Fulani shook his head several times. "I do not know. The Turks march all to Deir-Zor. Many long lines that disappear into the heat. There are Cetes."

Salleh took a breath.

"Cetes?" Hagop asked, looking from Al-Fulani to Salleh. "What does it mean?"

Salleh and Al-Fulani looked at one another.

"Hagop," Salleh said. "The Cetes are brigands. Murderers who are released from prison to attack the Armenians." Hagop looked at him, disbelieving. "I have heard this myself," Salleh said. "But I did not know until now that it is true."

"Mosul?" Hagop said, looking at Al-Fulani.

"I have come through Mosul," Al-Fulani replied. "There are many Armenians who lie there. All are dead or close to death."

Hagop slowly shook his head back and forth. "It is a madness," he said. "They are mad."

Al-Fulani looked at Salleh and then turned to Hagop. He reached his hand out and touched Hagop's shoulder. "I am sorry for you," he said. "I am sorry for you."

Hagop looked at him and nodded. "Thank you," he said. "Thank you for telling me."

Al-Fulani nodded. They got up and Salleh followed him out. As they reached the door, Al-Fulani said something to Salleh who nodded, but Hagop could not make it out. He turned, thinking.

"Murderers who are released from prison to attack the Armenians."

He stepped heavier onto his left foot. He had to get better. He had to see.

DEIR-EL-ZOR DESERT

Had Jesus walked among them, there, in a place so barren, with the thousands of beings lying about, perishing in a place that was never meant to sustain life, he surely would have wept.

Lucine could have sworn to God himself that his only son had been there.

She had seen Him. It was He.

He was moving through the ragged mass of deportees, and as He reached those for whom death was mere moments away, He would gently touch them. She had watched in awe as their faces seemed to lighten, and a strange light seemed to circle them. And then, most incredible of all, they seemed to fall lightly to the ground, but there was no sound, they just drifted down, as if they no longer had weight. One after another, they were touched, always on the forehead, always with the right index and middle finger held together. Lucine watched and she looked around her to see if the others were watching. But only she could see what was happening. Only she bore witness.

And then it was gone. A dream.

And as she awoke, she began her routine for yet another day. She had been here less than one week, but deportees arrived constantly. Disease, hunger, dehydration, exposure; everything took its toll. The stink of the place smelled like rotting meat.

Lucine moved from one group to another, attempting to comfort those who were in the worst condition. From time to time, visions of her family tore in; Sarkis, Hagop, but it was always Anahid's face that was the last she remembered. Anahid would have the best chance, she knew. Hagop would be a soldier by now; if careful, he and Souren would be fine. No. It would be Sarkis who would encounter the most problems. Especially since she now knew that the Armenian men were being systematically removed.

She reached an old woman and a young boy and girl.

"My name is Lucine," she said, bending down. "I am from Palou."

The woman looked up, her face weary. "I am Makrouhi," the woman said. "I am from Kharpert."

Lucine nodded. She looked at the young boy and girl, but they were afraid of her. They clung tightly to Makrouhi's dress.

"These children, they are from Diyarbekir," Makrouhi said. "This is Mihran and Zabel, his sister. They have lost their mother."

Lucine nodded. "Is there anything I can do for you?" she asked.

"Dear child, I am fine," Makrouhi said. "My husband died during the march."

"Without water, we will not last long," Lucine said. By her counting, it had been three days and then it had been but a sip.

"We have been bribing some of the gendarmes," Makrouhi said. "They take our gold pieces and give us a little water."

Lucine looked at her. "I have nothing left."

"If you wish, you can stay with us," Makrouhi said. "The children will like you."

Lucine managed a slight smile. "Thank you. I will see to some others and come back."

"God be with you, child."

"And with you."

CONSTANTINOPLE

Papers littered the dining room table of Wangenheim's comfortable home. His wife, Baroness Joanna von Spitzenberg, had already gone to bed.

The consul reports relating the atrocities that had been witnessed had grown in their frequency. Wangenheim's lock on the press had been almost four months ago, but the deportations and the mass of walking dead had drawn too much attention. The missionaries had come, and despite the Turkish military checkpoints designed to limit them only to areas where the exiles were still living, many had made it into other areas. Places where it was obvious what was happening.

As the bodies mounted, as the rivers ran red, and as the missionaries and journalists drew near, orders from Constantinople to the Valis commanded that the hundreds of decaying bodies that lined the roads be buried. For a time, this had worked. But the ground had turned hard, and now the orders were to gather and burn them. Put them in a pile and pour kerosene on them and burn them. Burn them now! Throw what sand you can onto the ashes. Do not hesitate! Do it now!

He had tried to protect Germany. Had tried to distance her from what he knew was the true motivation of the Young Turks.

"Turkey for the Turks," Talaat had said to him.

"That is their war," Wangenheim had reasoned. "All that matters is that we win. Germany is not responsible."

The missionary reports grew. Eyewitness accounts were printed in the world's press. And Berlin wanted to know why Wangenheim was not in command of the information coming out of Turkey.

He got up slowly, bracing himself. It seemed more difficult now, and he put it all down to fatigue and stress. He got to his feet. His face slowly drained of color and beads of water appeared all over his face. He took a step back, then forward, and his hands left the table. He fell forward. His vision seemed to fog and the sound rushing around his ears seemed muffled. Within moments his breathing stopped and his eyes, though they lost their focus, remained open.

DEIR-EL-ZOR DESERT

The night sky was clear and full of stars. The heat of the day had given way to the cold night air and the deportees huddled, trying to keep warm. Most of the older gendarmes slept while the night watch duties fell to the younger ones. Over the last few days, the gendarmes who had been at Deir-El-Zor over a long period had left, replaced by young men who seemed no older than Hagop and Souren. Lucine made a note of one in particular. He was much too young to be here in such madness.

But she would have to be careful. If she was wrong, it could mean her death.

She looked up from Makrouhi and the children. Their situation was desperate. They needed water; there was no money, no jewelry. Lucine looked at the young gendarme; his back was to her. He looked up, studying the star pattern. She stood, slowly and wobbly.

She took a few steps forward. The sand between her toes was cool now, and it felt good. Stepping slowly, she reached the perimeter and stopped several paces from him. She moved and, sensing her, he suddenly turned, raising his rifle.

"Get back!" he commanded. He pointed the rifle at her. "Get back now!"

Lucine held her breath. "I mean no harm to you," she said. She looked down at the rifle and saw his finger touching the trigger.

"Move back now or I will shoot!"

Lucine slowly raised and held out her open hands. "Please. Here are my hands, I can do nothing to you." She looked at him, her eyes pleading. "Here, you see, they hardly work anymore."

The gendarme looked at her and Lucine could see his shoulders ease slightly. She managed a breath.

"What do you want?" he said.

"I saw that you were looking at the stars. Do you know them?"

The young gendarme looked at her. He was told not to fraternize with these people. These Armenians.

"I am not supposed to talk to you," he said.

"What harm can it do now," Lucine said. "You see what's to become of us…"

He looked at her, but said nothing. They stood each considering the other.

"Yes. I learned of them in school," he said. "The stars."

Lucine nodded.

He lowered his rifle and then slung the weapon over his shoulder. "Before I was made a soldier, I attended University."

"What did you study there?" Lucine asked.

He looked at her, thinking. "I studied Cartography. To be a map maker."

"Then you have traveled far?"

"No, I have been only to Constantinople and to here. They are two worlds apart from one another."

Lucine nodded. "Yes. I have a son. He is in the Turkish Army now. He builds rail lines. He is in Ctesiphon. My daughter…"

The transformation was sudden and explosive. He turned on her, stepping forward. "What do you want?" he said angrily.

Her fright almost overtook her, but she had to see it through. She looked at him. "We must have some water. Not for me, but for the old ones, the children." She glanced quickly to his right. "You have a canteen there…"

"No!" he said. He put his hand on the revolver that hung from his right hip. "It is forbidden to give any of the deportees anything. You are enemy collaborators."

Lucine looked at him. "I am just a mother," she said. She held back her tears, knowing that they would only serve to make him angry. "Just a mother," she said. "Nothing more."

He looked at her, but said nothing.

"How many are deported?" she asked.

The gendarme eased. Suddenly, he was again the student studying to be a mapmaker. "I do not know," he said. "The caravans are constant now." He looked at her and shook his head. "We were only supposed to move you! To remove you from the war zones!" He looked around at the thousands of forms that lay on the cold sand. "And now…"

Lucine took a deep breath. "My name is Lucine," she said. "I can bring you no harm. I know that I will not be here much longer. No one can see that we are talking." She looked at him. "Please," she said. "The water…"

"Turn around!" he said, motioning with his rifle.

Lucine looked at him.

"Turn around now!" he commanded.

She slowly turned her back to him and tried to remain as still as possible. He took a few steps closer to her and she could feel her shoulders tense. The tiny fine hairs on her arms rose up. He moved closer still, and Lucine could now feel him near could feel and smell his breath on her. She stood, trying to remain calm; not knowing what he would do to her. The moments passed, hanging in the air. She started to feel her hands tremble and she struggled to keep them still.

'The water. The water.' She kept repeating the words to herself.

Suddenly, the gendarme's warm breath was gone. She waited and then turned; he was standing off in the distance, his back to her. She looked down and saw the canteen on the ground.

NEARING MOSUL

They had traveled almost three hundred kilometers. They were almost entirely women and children, though here and there Elise could count two, maybe three old men, their heads down, shadows of themselves. Mosul rested directly on the Euphrates, but it was futile to attempt to drink from it. The water was putrid with death.

Now she slept, Sona curled up against her. They had come this far; they had survived. They were surviving. Elise had planned and had rationed well what food she could obtain. But soon the money would run out. Above them, illuminated by a brilliant moon, a line of men on horseback appeared.

"Wake up! Wake up!" a young girl screamed. "They are coming! The Kurds are coming!"

Sona and Elise awoke, startled. Sona clung to Elise and they tried to make themselves invisible, tried to disappear. The horsemen drew down.

"Where are the gendarmes?" they heard a woman cry. "They have all left!"

The wails began again, and the women tried their best to keep their children down and out of sight. The Kurds rode through and shot off their rifles as they entered the encampment. Sona screamed as a woman was slashed down not five paces in front of her. There were screams everywhere.

Another man was dragging a young girl who was trying desperately to dig her heels into the soft sand. Sona broke away from Elise, ran to the girl, and grabbed her arm. Elise looked on, but before she could react, the Kurd lifted his rifle. Elise opened her mouth as the rifle butt came down, striking Sona. She went down, and the Kurd scooped up the girl.

"Sona! Sona!" Elise said, running to her. Sona struggled to sit and Elise helped her.

"I am all right, mama," she said. The butt had struck hard, but glancing. Elise pushed aside the cloth covering Sona's shoulder. The skin was broken but it was not serious.

"Sona...don't..."

"I know, mama," Sona said, looking into her eyes. "I know."

DEIR-EL-ZOR

Lucine walked slowly, clutching the canteen that she hid beneath her shawl. She reached Makrouhi and the children. The children slept, but Makrouhi stirred.

"Ah, dear," she said. "What do you have there?"

Lucine drew the cloth away, revealing the canteen. Makrouhi's eyes widened, but Lucine pressed her finger to her mouth.

"Wake the children," she said.

Lucine bent over and uncorked the canteen. She filled a small tin cup halfway and handed it to Makrouhi.

"God bless you," Makrouhi said. She took a sip and then handed the cup to Mihran. He drank and handed the cup to his sister, Zabel. "Now you must drink some," Makrouhi said.

Lucine drew the cup to her lips. She tasted the coolness of it. Life. Now she would have to choose who would get a taste of the life in that canteen. She would have to return it to the gendarme before the light came up. She would leave the canteen in the same spot. When the morning came, it would have been as if it had never happened.

LONDON
November 1915

The summer months had brought thousands of casualties and the British public wavered. By the end of August, Hamilton had lost more than forty thousand men. On Gallipoli, the men fought tirelessly, but their maneuvers along Plugge's Plateau, Shrapnel Valley, and Baby 700 had brought nothing but heartache.

Churchill was gone now, replaced by Balfour. Finally, Asquith could take no more. Hamilton, his reputation forever sullied left Imbros. General Sir Charles Monro replaced him and on the last day of October, he sent the cipher recommending evacuation.

On the second of November, Asquith took the podium in the House of Common and admitted that the campaign had failed.

CONSTANTINOPLE

Morgenthau sat, examining the Consul reports from Trebizond, Aleppo, Kharpert, Erzeroum, and beyond. The words came to Morgenthau in almost clinical terms: numbers, dates, genders. Four thousand. Six thousand. Forty-three thousand. The most compelling had come to him on the last day of June from Leslie A. Davis, the American Consul, stationed in Kharpert. In it, Davis wrote that Armenians from all six Armenian provinces had been deported. Men were being imprisoned and tortured until death.

And there were others. Consul Heizer, Dr. Heinrich Bergfeld, and the Austrian Consul-General Ernst von Kwiatkowski in Trebizond. Their heart-wrenching descriptions leapt from the pages.

There was a knock on the door.

"Come in," Morgenthau said.

"Ambassador Wangenheim..." Mowbry said, the words rushing from his mouth.

"Yes?"

"He died last evening."

"What?"

"An attack of apoplexy."

Morgenthau sat for a moment, thinking. "Have they named a successor?"

"No word yet from the Embassy," Mowbry replied.

"Funeral arrangements?"

"Should be forthcoming this afternoon."

"Very well, Mr. Mowbry. Thank you. We will set our agenda when we receive word."

Within two days, rumors would begin, emanating first from Rome and sent via dispatch to London and New York. The authorities were considering Wangenheim's death shrouded in mystery, with foul play suspected.

DEIR-EL-ZOR

Lucine sat, applying the bandage to the old woman's hand.

"Thank you, tsakus."

"It is nothing."

A cry went up from the left side of the encampment. A group of four Armenian girls, no more than fifteen years old, ran screaming, chased by two mounted gendarmes.

Lucine watched, but could do nothing. The girls fled down a winding ridge, towards the rushing Euphrates. They looked at one another and the oldest nodded. They had all agreed that this was better than being taken by the men. The gendarmes rode ahead; they had to swing around to reach them.

The girls stepped forward, moving in unison toward the rushing river. The gendarmes turned their horses and kicked them to move faster. The girls ripped shreds of cloth from their dresses and tied left hand to right until they were bound together. They looked at one another and moved toward the river's edge. The gendarmes were almost upon them now. The girls stepped into the water, and together they made the sign of the cross each time as they repeated the words.

"Der Voghormia, Der Voghormia, Der Voghormia." Lord have mercy. Lord have mercy. Lord have mercy.

They walked into the rushing river and as the gendarmes reached them, they saw the current taking the girls swiftly to their maker.

Now four mounted gendarmes stayed in a semi-circle as they guided their horses through the deportees. Half a dozen gendarmes walked on foot, picking them out.

"You," one of them said. "Over there."

"You," another said. "And you. Move to that group."

Lucine noticed that they were picking only women and young boys. The young girls were ignored.

She exchanged glances with Makrouhi. The gendarmes used their bayonets to prod anyone who refused to join the others. A second group of gendarmes began organizing the group into twos.

"You," the gendarme said, pointing at Lucine.

"You," he pointed at Makrouhi. "And the boy."

Lucine looked from Makrouhi to Mihran. His sister, Zabel, opened her mouth, but Makrouhi tugged gently on her hand, stilling her.

"Now!" the gendarme ordered. "On your feet!"

"Please, effendi," Lucine said. "Where must we go?" She did her best to hide the cracking in her voice, but it was to no avail. It was all too much.

The gendarme looked at her. "There are minerals which you will help dig," he said. "You will be given special provisions."

"Yes, yes, effendi," Lucine said, stealing a glance at Makrouhi. "Where are the shovels?"

The gendarme traded looks with another and laughed. "Shovels?" he said. "There are no shovels! You will dig with your hands, Christian! Like the dog you are!"

"Zabel," Lucine said, bending down. "We must go and work. You must stay here."

"But I can help you!" the girl protested.

"Yes, I know you can," Lucine said. "But it is not allowed."

"When will you come back?"

"I think toward the end of the day, after we have finished our work," Lucine lied.

"I will stay right here. I will not move," Zabel said resolutely.

"Good," Lucine said, putting her hand on the girl's shoulder.

Mihran looked at Zabel. "Do not worry," he said. "I will be back."

The group consisted of about sixty persons, and the gendarmes led them away from the main encampment. Some of the other deportees watched them go, wondering why they had not been chosen. The group turned around a mountain corner and disappeared from sight.

Lying directly in front of them was a small opening in the mountainside, a cave. Lucine reached her hand out, stopping Makrouhi and Mihran.

"It is a trick," she said. She looked from Makrouhi to Mihran. "Do not go inside." She knelt down in front of Mihran and put her hands on his shoulders. "Tsakus, when I tell you, run behind the mountain as fast as you can. Keep running. No matter what you hear, keep running. Do you understand?"

Mihran stood there, trembling. She shook him.

"Do you understand?"

"Yes," he said slowly. "But Zabel..."

Lucine looked into the boy's eyes. "Do not go back to the camp." He looked at her, not knowing what to do.

"There will be someone to come and take care of Zabel," Makrouhi said, glancing at Lucine. "She will be all right. You will see her again."

"Do you promise me?" Mihran said.

The gendarmes looked in their direction and one of them began walking towards them. Ahead, the group was being assembled outside the cave. Makrouhi looked at Lucine.

"Do you promise me!" the boy said.

"Yes, tsakus," Lucine said. "We both promise."

They began walking, and as they did, the gendarme eased his pace. Lucine looked to Makrouhi.

"There is nothing left to do," Makrouhi said. She grabbed Lucine's hand. "We cannot run. It is God's will."

Lucine's face drained and she walked as if in a trance. They drew closer to the entrance.

"Into the cave!" a gendarme commanded. "To work!"

The women at the front of the line stood still, and two of the gendarmes jabbed them with the butts of their rifles. They moved. Some of the women and children scurried backward, pushing and shoving. One of the gendarmes cracked his rifle butt into a woman's head, bringing her down. A wave of screams rose up.

"Now, Mihran," Lucine whispered. "Go!"

He looked at her and Makrouhi and then ran quickly to the left. He was not seen. One of the mounted gendarmes reached down, grabbed his pistol, held it high in the air, and pulled the trigger.

"Stop!" he said. "Stop, or I will shoot you all!"

The group obeyed, and the gendarmes restored order. They were herded into the cave. Lucine and Makrouhi walked forward.

"Move to the back!" the gendarme commanded.

Suddenly, a cart was pushed into place. A gendarme slashed the rope that held the hay bales and they fell in front of the cave. There were screams of protest from inside. Lucine and Makrouhi held each other's hands. The screams echoed off the cave's walls and Makrouhi crossed herself. Overhead, their muted screams could be heard through the shallow rock.

The Cetes were up there.

They had come into the camp during the night and had changed into gendarme uniforms. They stuck metal poles into the earthen top of the cave and then drove them in with wooden mallets.

Lucine looked up toward the sound, and as she did, pieces of rock and sand fell. She looked at Makrouhi. Shafts of light shone down, hole after hole opening, and the others looked up. They struggled, trying to get closer to the fresh air. As they did, streams of liquid began falling from the openings. They cupped their hands together, trying to catch the water. But as they did, the smell reached their nostrils.

"Move away!" Lucine screamed. "It is kerosene! Do not drink! Move back!"

The screams filled the cave. Lucine grabbed Makrouhi and they pushed their way through the others, trying to reach the entrance. The Cetes set the lit branches to each of the holes. Instantly, the shafts of light turned into flames, sending up a wall of fire. Two gendarmes stepped forward and dropped torches onto the bales of hay. They were dry, and they smoked instantly.

The screams were horrible now and Lucine felt Markouhi's hand go limp. She looked at the woman's ashen face as she fell to the ground. She bent over her, but it was too late. Lucine got to the front of the cave, but as she did there was a loud WOMF! and the bales flamed up. Lucine drew back, away from the heat. Behind her, the shafts of fire drew down. Trapped. Screaming. She began to cough. There was no air left. She looked at the wall of flame rising in front of her.

She fell to her knees, flat to the ground. There was air here. She could breathe a little. But it would not be enough. The wall of flames circled in on her. In moments, she was gone.

Outside the cave, the screaming grew louder and louder. The young gendarme touched his canteen and turned his head away from the cave, his face twisted. One of the older gendarmes grabbed him by the shoulders, spun him around, and slapped him across the face.

"Look! Look!" the gendarme said, shaking him. "You cry for these murderers?" He slapped the young gendarme again. "Look, I tell you!"

The young gendarme nodded and looked at the mouth of the cave. The flames burst out of it in a great WHOOSH! as the air inside exploded. The screams rose, horribly so, and then there was nothing.

PART SEVEN

CONSTANTINOPLE

Morgenthau shook his head. The reports from the consuls contained some of the most gut-wrenching descriptions of horror that he had ever read.

"God," he said softly. "There is no way I can save them... No matter what I do. There are too many of them."

Within twenty-four hours, Kitchener would carry out Asquith's orders and the evacuations from Gallipoli would begin. And at 0300 hours, on the eighteenth of December, the last of the soldiers left Anzac.

Asquith. Kitchener. Churchill. Each would carry a different burden. Churchill would leave government service and take a position on the Western Front. Kitchener perished in the icy North Sea waters, the German torpedo finding its mark on the Cruiser Hampshire. Lloyd George replaced Asquith.

It had been disastrous. Forty-six thousand dead, over a quarter of a million casualties. And as the sun came up along Gallipoli, at Dardanos, Kilid-Ul-Bahr, Sedd-Ul-Bahr, and at Anadolu Hamidie, the men slowly came to the realization that their fire was not being returned.

"We have won! We have won!"

"HUZZAH! HUZZAH!"

"God save them," Morgenthau said, pushing the papers away. "Now they'll think they're invincible. There will be nothing stopping them." He reached for the map outlining the different Armenian villages in the eastern sector, and began cross-referencing the numbers from the consul reports to the village locations. He worked slowly and methodically, careful to get the facts and figures correct. He was determined to leave a complete and accurate record.

Enver, Talaat, Von Der Goltz, and Von Sanders sat in Enver's office. Enver's aide, Hillmann, entered. He handed the cipher to Enver, and left.

"The shelling has stopped," Enver said. "The British and French have retreated."

The men looked at one another.

"What? Let me see that," Von der Goltz said.

'To: German-Turkish War Command. From: Merten at Sedd-Ul-Bahr. Allied shelling ceased, 1300 hours. Warships have commenced retreat. Silent evacuation undetected.'

"We have won, gentlemen! We have chased them off!"

The fire was burning and it made the room comfortable. Major Taylor and Morgenthau sat, nursing their drinks. The last few days had brought even more British and French citizens to the Embassy, all terribly concerned that they would be mistreated, especially in light of the Entente retreat at the Dardanelles.

"How bad is it, Major?" Morgenthau asked.

"Well, with the withdrawal, the blockade is going to get a lot worse. The goods will pile up with nowhere to go. Say what you will, but Wangenheim alone pulled this off."

Morgenthau paused. "I can't deny that. But Enver's been predisposed to Germany for years. "Well, it's gone now," Taylor said. "British, Bulgarians, Turks, Russians. I've heard estimates that Britain is planning for another three to five years."

"Five years!" Morgenthau exclaimed.

"Yes," Taylor replied. "There are also new machines being built; new tanks, new traction mechanisms, you name it."

"Five years," Morgenthau repeated. "My God, there will be nothing left!"

"The Armenians?"

Morgenthau nodded. Taylor looked at him and a few moments passed in silence.

"Every week I receive consul reports of terrible atrocities. Mrs. Morgenthau sends me the Times from the States. Thankfully, the relief societies are allowing us to draw up the orphanages."

"I think we will have to answer soon," Taylor said. "King George, Clemenceau; they won't sit and let us wait forever." He reached for their glasses and walked to the bar.

"I cannot save them now," Morgenthau said, whispering to himself. "In five years, none of them will be left."

OUTSIDE MOSUL

"Buzz on, buzz on, buzz buzzon," Sona said, quietly whispering the children's rhyme. In her lap, she rocked a small girl. Her name was Tamar; she had just passed her fourth birthday in the sands just outside of Mosul. Elise slept, and Sona gently put the girl down and covered her with a shirt.

She turned and as she did, the thick hand shot quickly from behind and clamped over her mouth. She screamed, but it was muffled. The gendarme grabbed her arm and twisted it behind her. He dragged her. She tried to struggle her energy was gone.

He pulled her into the surrounding bushes and threw her down. Her head hit the ground, stunning her. The sand flew into her eyes. She turned her head, trying to clear them. He jumped onto her, putting the bulk of his weight directly on her stomach. The air rushed out of her. He grabbed her arms and pushed down. He slid his hands from her forearms down to her wrists. He clenched them tightly, and the metal of her bracelet dug deeply into her skin, cutting it all the way around, leaving deep indentations. He felt the bracelet and ripped it from her wrist.

Sona shook her head and opened her mouth to scream. He put his hands together and swung from left to right, hard enough to shatter cheek bone. Her body buckled. She wailed, and her arms fell in a heap. Her mouth was filling with blood. She could taste it.

Her eyes watered and she could hear the rip of her dress. She tried to move her legs, but it was useless. She looked up at the clear night sky and saw the stars shining down on her. He spread her legs further apart and she felt him inside her. The air swirled around her face and her vision became cloudy. From her left ear, a trickle of deep dark blood oozed.

BAGHDAD

The late afternoon sun filtered in through the open barn door. Hagop walked about, and although he limped, his leg felt quite strong.

"Your leg has healed well," Salleh said, entering.

"It is very stiff, but I am able to put weight on it."

Salleh motioned for Hagop to sit.

"I know that it is your intention to go to Mosul," Salleh began. "But I... and now I speak not only of myself but for my family as well... if you wish, you may stay here and make this your home."

Hagop opened his mouth to speak. The man's generosity had overwhelmed him. He had not betrayed him and, despite danger to his family, he had hid him.

"Salleh," he said. "I am deeply in your debt. I will never be able to repay your kindness. But I must find out what has happened to my own family."

Salleh nodded. "Hagop," he said, putting his hands together in front of him. "I fear for what you will find."

Hagop nodded. "As do I."

"Then you must be very careful. Today there were many German and Turkish troops coming through."

Hagop nodded. Salleh looked at him opened his mouth to speak, and caught himself.

"What is it, Salleh?" Hagop said. "What has happened?"

Salleh paused for a moment. "When Al-Fulani came he told me something," Salleh said, looking at him. Hagop held his breath. "I did not want to say anything to you until I saw for myself."

"What is it?"

"The soldiers have brought in some children. There are only four of them, none more than five years of age. They are all Armenian. All girls."

"Armenian! From where?"

"I do not know where they are from," Salleh said. He looked at Hagop. "They are to be sold."

"Sold!"

"Yes," Salleh said. "That is the way it is done here."

Hagop looked at him and his face suddenly became hard. "We have to get them out, Salleh. We cannot let it happen."

"Yes, that is what I knew you would say if I told you," Salleh said.

"Where are they?"

"They are being held in Al-Fulani's barn. The soldiers have taken it from him to house their horses."

"Can we get to them without being seen? Are they guarded?"

"There is only the main entrance, two double wooden doors. At night there is only one soldier." Salleh paused for a moment. "But there is another way inside."

"How?"

Salleh picked up a stick and traced out lines on the ground as he spoke. "There is a door leading from Al-Fulani's home through a very narrow wall. It leads into the barn." Salleh looked at him. "From time to time, Al-Fulani does not trade in everything that is legal. You understand?"

"Yes," Hagop said. "Will he help us?"

"Yes. But if we are caught, he will claim that we are thieves." Salleh stopped, making sure Hagop understood. "Hagop, you know what the penalty for stealing is here?"

"Hands."

"Yes," Salleh said. "Your hands. But if it is you who are found, the punishment will be your life. Probably the bastinado for me."

"Then I alone will go," Hagop said.

"No," Salleh said, shaking his head. "Two men."

"When do we start?" Hagop asked.

"I have already started."

NEW YORK CITY
Christmas Day, 1915

It was a blustery Saturday in New York City, and for those who awoke to a tree laden with gifts and surprises, it was a cheerful day.

"Mom, can we go and play with our toys?" the young boy asked.

"Me, too!" his sister said.

"Yes, but help Mommy first and take your dishes into the pantry," the mother answered. The children complied, eager to return to the day's bounty.

Their father sat and unfolded the paper to the front page. He picked up his coffee cup.

"It's a damn shame what's happening over there in Armenia," he said gesturing to the front page.

"They're having a rally down at the school on Wednesday to raise money for them," his wife said. "I was planning on baking something."

"Good idea," he said, nodding. The Times had been providing coverage almost every day. He traced the headline 'The Starving Armenians', accompanied by a grainy black and white photograph of a band of refugees who were looking directly into the camera.

"A damn shame."

OUTSIDE MOSUL

Elise awoke and instinctively reached for Sona. The young girl, Tamar, was still sleeping. Elise stood, looking around.

"Sona!"

She walked, scanning faces. Nothing. She looked left then right, and noticed some clothes lying next to a small knot of brush. She walked towards it and as she drew nearer, she ran, frantic, her feet slipping deep into the soft sand.

"Sona! Sona!"

She was curled up, naked. Elise knelt down and turned her face toward her. She was badly bruised, and the welts were bright red. Sona recoiled, turning from her.

"Sona, it is me, mama."

Tiny whimpers left Sona's mouth. Elise gathered up the clothes and saw the blood on them.

"Everyone up!" the gendarme commanded. "Now! We must move!"

"Good God!" Elise said. They had to go now. If they hesitated, and they saw Sona like this, they would kill them both. Tamar and an older girl came over.

"Help us," Elise said.

The girls nodded, and they helped Elise put Sona's clothes on. Elise tied the torn ends together. She ripped a piece of cloth from her dress and used it to clean the dried blood on Sona's face. She turned her head and noticed the blood staining her right ear.

"Come, come my girl. We must go."

Sona protested, drawing her head away.

"Come, just for a while," Elise said. They lifted Sona to her feet. She moved on impulse only. They began walking, and soon joined the rest of the caravan.

"Her color is bad," the older girl whispered.

"We must keep moving," Elise replied.

"Where do we go now?" Tamar asked.

"We are close to Mosul," Elise said. "We will be there soon."

OUTSIDE BAGHDAD

He had made it this far. Now he had to be careful. During the last two days, he had seen Turkish and German troops in the area. He would wait until dark and continue moving. He hoped to find someone; did they know Hagop Melkonian or Souren Jamgotchian? He rested, closing his eyes, never really sleeping.

Hagop and Salleh quietly made their way to Al-Fulani's. It took ten minutes, and Hagop noticed how fatigued he was just from the short distance. By arrangement, Al-Fulani was not home. If anything went wrong, he could not be blamed. At the front of the barn, the soldier sat smoking a cigarette.

They drew to the back of the home and Salleh opened the door. He and Hagop walked along the left wall. The smell of dried meat filled the air, and Hagop looked up to see hanging strips of dried beef and peppers. Salleh moved a chair out of the way and he and Hagop stooped down. There was an outline of a frame, and Salleh pushed it. The door swung, pivoting on hinges.

"I will go," Hagop said.

Salleh nodded. "If anyone comes, I will close the door and hide. If you return and see the passage shut, wait until I knock before you come out." Hagop nodded. "Crawl through," Salleh said. "Then stand and go along the wall. It will be very narrow; it should be no more than ten meters. There is a latch on the door. Feel for it with your hands."

Hagop crawled into the opening. It was tight and dark but not as narrow as he first thought. He moved sideways and slowly made his way, feeling with his hands. Outside, the guard stood his rifle next to the barn door and sat on a wooden crate, bored.

Hagop reached the end of the passage and felt for the latch. It took a few moments, but he found it. He pulled the small metal hook and the door slid to the left. Hagop peered into the barn. He saw the four children sleeping on straw. He crawled out of the passageway and slowly walked to one of the older girls. He bent over and put his hand over her mouth.

In an instant, her eyes snapped open and she started to struggle. Hagop quickly reached his hand into his shirt and pulled out his cross. He showed it to her: Armenian. The girl relaxed. He put his left index finger to his lips and she nodded. Slowly, he took his hand from her mouth. She took a deep breath, taking in air.

"Hye-em. My name is Hagop. I will help you," he said, whispering.

She nodded.

"What is your name?"

"Miriam."

"Where are you from?"

"Kighi."

"Are any of the others from Palou or Bitlis?"

"No," Miriam said. "Just Kighi and Chemeshgezak."

Hagop looked away for a moment. "Did you see anyone from Palou or Bitlis when you came?"

"They were from all over," Miriam said, her voice anxious.

"Do not worry," Hagop said. "We are going to get you out of here. But you must do everything I say. Do you understand?"

Miriam nodded. "Yes, anything you say."

MOSUL

The caravan moved slowly through and then stopped. They were only a few meters away from the Tigris, and they could hear it flowing through the brush.

"We stop here!" the gendarme commanded.

Elise gently laid Sona down onto the ground and draped her shawl around her. She was ashen and weak, and the grayness in her face seemed to be spreading to her lips.

BAGHDAD

Salleh and Al-Fulani had traced the routes and Hagop agreed. It would work. They needed one guide and one carriage. The girls were small and could easily curl up inside. Hagop had told Miriam precisely what to do.

"If the soldiers come for you, pour water on two of the girls. Show them that they are sick, they are having sweats. The soldiers will not want to catch the sickness. They will leave."

Miriam nodded. "When will you come back?"

"Tomorrow night, if everything is ready."

Al-Fulani would take the girls up the mountain pass and into the hills. He, as did Salleh, knew families who traded with Europeans. With a bit of money, they could get the girls out.

"But promise me that you will get them to safety, Al-Fulani," Hagop had said. "Promise me that you will personally do it."

"This I will do," Al-Fulani said. "You have my word."

Atop the carriage were several large wooden boxes. They had slats for ventilation and were used for carrying animals. It would be cramped, but the girls could fit inside. Just in case he was stopped, Al-Fulani would carry chickens. Besides, it would be dark. The chances of anyone interfering would be small. Still, there were brigands, and he would be alone. He pulled back the material from his caftan, revealing the pistol that hung from his neck by a long rawhide strap.

"Because you can never take chances," he said.

Salleh nodded and looked at Hagop. "Did the girl understand everything?" he asked.

"Yes, it is going to work," Hagop said.

Al-Fulani sat atop the carriage. Behind him, the cooped chickens flitted about. Four empty boxes stood to the back. Once the girls were inside, the other boxes would be put on top, concealing them. Salleh walked past the front of the barn. The guard sat, reading a journal.

Hagop retraced his steps along the small passageway and reached the door leading to the barn. He felt for the latch and slid the door away. Miriam and the other three girls were waiting for him and, one-by-one, Hagop sent them into the dark opening.

"Follow the wall," he said. "Go slowly. When you reach the end, there will be a man. I will be right behind you."

It was dark outside and Hagop, Salleh, and Al-Fulani helped the frightened girls into the cages.

"Do not worry," Hagop said, bending down. "This man will take you to people who are friendly. Do as he says. You will not have to be in there long."

Al-Fulani looked at Hagop and Salleh. He nodded, and snapped the reins. In seconds, he was off.

"We did it, Salleh," Hagop said.

"Yes," came the weary reply. He looked at Hagop. "Come, let us get back."

MOSUL

"I am cold, mama," Sona murmured. "Very cold."

"Do not worry, my sweet one," Elise said. "I will stay close to you, to keep you warm."

Sona looked up, eyes swollen, and managed a slight smile. Elise choked back her emotions and stroked her hair. It felt good. Like when she was a little girl. Sona smiled and then her eyes gently closed. Elise felt her hand go limp. She stroked the hair of her youngest daughter and crossed herself. The tears flowed down and she silently wailed

"Sona... Sona..." she said, her voice trailing off.

BAGHDAD

Al-Fulani shook hands with the man and handed over the bag of coins that Salleh had given him.

"I have given my word," Al-Fulani said.

"They will be there in ten days," the man said. "Twelve at the most." Al-Fulani nodded. "Once they are delivered to the orphanage, my responsibility ends," the man said.

"Agreed. I thank you my old friend."

The soldiers had come and gone more frequently over the past days. There was little to do but wait until the area was clear of them. Salleh had been right. To move now would be too dangerous. Hagop wondered about the girls, but knew they would be safe.

He walked slowly around the barn. His leg was much better. He sat atop the soft hay, rested his head in his hands, and closed his eyes. The sound of marching boots flooded back and forth, and they took on a strange echo in the barn. They became distorted, swirling around him. The sound of women and children filled his ears. The slapping of whips, the braying of horses. He heard a rifle crack in the distance and the sound of boots marching away, fading from him. There was a high-pitched little girl's scream, and it moved in and out of his head. And then the thump, thump, thump of the boots rose again, this time coming toward him. The sounds built upon one another and grew louder and louder. He shook his head back and forth, trying to clear them.

"Hagop! Hagop!" Sona cried.

He heard her voice.

"Hagop!"

He shook his head. Through blurry eyes, his vision was distorted, and the sounds of the boots stopped. My God! They were here! The soldiers are outside the door! He stood up, backing into a corner. The door opened and in poured the stinging, blinding sunlight. He tried to shield his eyes. The soldier stood and pointed the rifle at him. Hagop shook his head back and forth, waving his hands in front of him.

"Hagop!" Sona cried.

The figure moved forward and the sun burst in further, creating a fiery ring around the man as he drew closer. Hagop stumbled, fell back, and then regained his balance.

"Hagop! Hagop!"

"No!" Hagop said, charging. He drew up his fists and began pounding the man.

"Hagop!" the man cried, trying to hold him back. "It is I! It is I! Armen!"

Hagop froze, and his hands went limp. He drew back and as his vision returned, the man stepped out of the shaft of light and became Armen.

"Armen?" Hagop said, drained. "Armen!"

"Yes, yes! Armen!"

Hagop rushed forward and they hugged each other tightly. "What...? Where did you come from?"

"I escaped," Armen said. "I have been going from village to village."

Hagop looked at him. He looked different. Older.

"I saw you two days ago," Armen said.

"You saw me? Why did you not...?"

"I could not get closer," Armen said. "There are soldiers here now. I had to wait."

"But how did you find me?"

"I was going to Ctesiphon. This was only to be a stop. In each place I asked if they had seen anyone."

"What did they tell you?"

Armen touched Hagop's shoulder. "They told me many things," he said. "Many horrible things." He paused. "I came here. There was a shop. The man gave me something to eat. A girl came in for supplies to treat a wound. I followed her to this place. I do not know why, I thought, I hoped it could be..."

"Iman," Hagop said.

"Who?"

"She is the daughter of the man who owns this place."

Armen nodded. He looked at Hagop. "Souren..."

"No," Hagop said, shaking his head.

Armen nodded, but said nothing. Hagop looked at him. "Palou..."

Armen paused for a moment, and his body began to tremble. "No," Armen said. "It is all gone."

Hagop nodded. He bit his lip. "My family..."

Armen looked at him. "They came, the Turks, and took your father, my father, Souren's father... and many other men. They tied us together. When we reached the edge of the village, they began shooting."

"My father..."

Armen shook his head, lowered it, and then looked into Hagop's eyes. "No. My father too. Souren's." Armen stopped, thinking. "I saw it all..."

Hagop shook his head, and took a deep breath.

"I escaped and hid," Armen said. "They sent everyone else away; your mother, Anahid, your grandparents, all of them. I saw them leave, but it was too dangerous to come out," Armen said. "There were soldiers and gendarmes everywhere." He looked at Hagop and his face began to shake and contort. "I should have come out!" he said, through tears. "I should have come to help them!"

"No. No!" Hagop said. "You were right to stay hidden. They would have killed you. They are killing all the men first so that we cannot fight back."

"Yes, I know," Armen said. "There are no men anywhere. Why?"

Hagop looked at him. "So we cannot breed."

Armen's eyes widened. Hagop looked at him.

"Sona?"

Armen shook his head. "I do not know. All from Bitlis and Moush are deported. They go through Mosul."

"But all must go to Deir-Zor," Hagop said.

"Deir-Zor..." Armen said, his voice trailing off.

Hagop looked at him for a moment. "We must go to Mosul."

"Hagop," Armen said, looking at him gravely. "We cannot. There are Cetes and soldiers everywhere."

Hagop said nothing, considering. Armen looked down for a moment.

"There is one more thing."

Hagop looked at him. "What is it?"

Armen said nothing, hesitating.

"What?" Hagop repeated.

"It is Anahid," Armen said. "I... I think that I have seen her..."

"Anahid!" Hagop exclaimed. He shook Armen. "Where? Where is she?"

Armen looked at him. "She is in Diyarbekir," he said, softly.

"Diyarbekir!"

"Hagop," Armen said. "I do not even know if it is she. I saw her this one day. I could not be sure. She wore a veil. Maybe it is not..." He paused for a moment. "She makes housekeeping in the home of a rich man."

"We must go to Diyarbekir!" Hagop said.

"But... but, listen to me," Armen said. He looked at Hagop. "She did not..."

Hagop stood, waiting.

"She seemed strange," Armen said.

"It does not matter," Hagop said. "We will go tomorrow."

Armen looked at him. "Hagop. There are orphanages now. Many people told me to go there at once. They are set up by the Americans. We can go to one," he said, his voice pleading. "Hagop, there is nothing left..."

Hagop shook his head firmly. "We will go to the orphanage. But first, we go to Diyarbekir."

"If you do that, then you will need these," Salleh said. Hagop and Armen turned towards the door. Armen glanced at Hagop, who motioned that it was safe. Salleh held up two caftans, and two keffiyehs.

"I did not mean to listen to your conversation," Salleh said. He looked at Armen. "I saw you enter."

"Salleh," Hagop said. "This is Armen. He is from Palou."

Salleh stepped forward and offered his hand. "I am happy to meet you."

"I am Armen Khatisian."

Salleh paused for a moment and then looked at them. "If you must do this, then listen to me. You must go by rail to Diyarbekir. It is the only way." He picked up a stick and drew a jagged line that snaked northward and then to the west. "You go from Baghdad to Tekrit to Mosul. And then from Mosul to Diyarbekir." He looked at them. "But you must be careful. There are soldiers everywhere. If you are asked anything, answer only in Turkish." He handed them the outfits. "You wear these. And take this as well." He held out a small white pouch.

"Salleh..." Hagop said, feeling the coins through the thin canvas.

"Do not say anything," Salleh said. "Just be careful. And remember what I told you: if you are spoken to, answer in Turkish or in French, nothing else. Do you both understand?"

Hagop and Armen nodded. Salleh looked at Hagop.

"Hagop Melkonian," he said. "Your friend is right about the orphanages. They can give you safe passage to Europe." He looked from Hagop to Armen. "After you go to Diyarbekir, do not hesitate. Near Diyarbekir the Americans and the British have made an orphanage. I do not know exactly where. I have heard it may be nearer to Severeg than to Urfa, but I do not know." He looked at them. "Find it. Make haste there. Or it will be too late."

BAGHDAD

Hagop pulled the white cloth close to his face and he and Armen made their way to the train. The tickets had been easy to buy: he held up two fingers, and uttered one word: "Diyarbekir."

The train was almost empty. It was stinging heat inside the car and after a half-hour delay, the train pulled away. Only moments earlier, they had heard the blaring siren of a military vehicle as it sped past. They had sat in fright, wondering if the transport had been meant for them. Within minutes, the train was snaking around the curving track, measuring its speed before its engineer could open her up.

The military vehicle pulled up outside Salleh's home. They had said that collaborators would be punished; that no Armenian should be harbored. Now Salleh would pay with his life.

TEKRIT

Hagop and Armen looked out the window as the old wooden sign marking Tekrit swung back and forth. They had gone almost one hundred fifty kilometers, but the train moved quickly past. It would not be a stop today.

NEARING MOSUL

"Mosul!" the conductor announced. "Mosul in five minutes!"

Hagop and Armen sat up. The train began to slow, and it drew to a prolonged stop. The shadows of trees played against the interior of the train. Armen looked through them and saw strange shapes. He motioned to Hagop, who peered through the window.

They were raised earthen mounds: newly dug, shallow graves.

"Mosul! Thirty minute stop!" the conductor declared.

"We should move our legs for a few minutes and then come right back," Hagop said.

They descended and Armen touched Hagop's arm, motioning to the right. There were some German and Turkish soldiers standing around, but they paid no attention to the passengers. Hagop and Armen crossed to the other side of the platform. There was a small coffee and fruit stand. There were many people and they would not be noticed.

"I want to see," Hagop said.

"Hagop..." Armen cautioned.

"We will be careful," Hagop said. "Remember, if we are spoken to, only Turkish or French."

They walked to the right and into the clearing. There were several rows of freshly dug graves.

"There are so many of them," Armen said.

Just in front was a small hill. Two soldiers appeared just over it.

"Hagop!" Armen whispered.

"Just keep walking. We cannot turn back now," Hagop said. "Keep your head down, and do not look at them."

They adjusted their keffiyehs and continued walking. The soldiers, engaged in conversation, passed them. They reached the modest incline and stopped in utter shock. Spread before them were hundreds upon hundreds of bodies strewn onto the open field. Here and there, nomads stripped the bodies of their clothes.

"My God," Hagop whispered.

"They have killed them all," Armen said.

They drew closer to a row of bodies. As they did, they drew their keffiyehs closer across their faces. The stench was unbearable. They walked past row after row: almost all of the bodies were those of either women or children. Where there were men, they were all old men.

Hagop shook his head. Some of them were on their backs, on their sides, on their stomachs. Some wore expressions of shock and disbelief. My God! The children. They seemed to be sleeping, dreaming, drifting. But they would never awake.

They crossed a series of rows. Here the bodies were in worse condition. Some were partially burned. Others had gunshot or stab wounds. Tiny white maggots crawled in the sticky, open masses while flies buzzed in and out of ears, mouths, and nostrils.

"We must keep walking," Hagop said. "Otherwise it will draw attention."

Armen nodded. They crossed another row. Hagop stopped.

"I know this man," he said, looking down at the lifeless body. "But I cannot remember from where."

Armen looked at the man's face. It was distorted, swollen from death. "He is not from Palou," Armen said.

"No. But I have seen him," Hagop answered.

"Yes. Yes, you are right," Armen said. "I have seen him too."

They looked at the man's face. Suddenly, Armen remembered.

"Hagop, he is the peddler! The one who sold your mother the silk."

Hagop looked at Armen and then down at the man. "From Bitlis!"

"Yes," Armen said. "From Bitlis."

They looked at one another.

"You take that row, I will take this one," Hagop said.

Armen nodded. Hagop began walking, slowly at first, and then more quickly, looking at the faces. He moved two rows over, as did Armen, and they continued, alternating rows as they went. As he increased his pace, his limp became more pronounced, but he was unaware of it. His heart pounded, eyes darting left, then right. Armen moved slowly, deliberately. If there were people here from Bitlis, there could be people here from Palou. They had to make sure.

Hagop looked up but Armen shook his head. Nothing. They changed rows. Some of the gypsies glanced at them, then returned to their business. Beads of sweat appeared on Hagop's forehead. He quickened his pace. He was close to running now and small red stains seeped through the cloth. The scabs were starting to open.

He looked at face after face. He and Armen moved to the next rows. And as Armen looked up, he saw Hagop halt, almost as if he had been frozen in mid-motion.

Hagop looked down and saw the face.

"Oh, no..." he said. "No! No! No!"

Armen watched him and Hagop seemed to collapse. His shoulders loosened, and he dropped to his knees. He looked at her face. It was swollen and bruised. She must have put up a terrible fight. He touched her left hand and saw the markings where the bracelet had been.

"Oh... Oh... Sona..." he said. The tears trickled down, leaving wet tracks on his dusty face. He bent over and held her close. He stroked her hair and kissed her. Then he gently laid her back down onto the sand. Across the rows, Armen dropped his head and began to cry.

The train steamed forward north toward Diyarbekir. Hagop sat, his eyes sunken deep, his hands in his lap. He looked out as the landscape rushed past, one blur after another. Armen sat next to him. They had hardly spoken a word since boarding. It had taken all of Armen's energy to get Hagop to leave her. They had gotten back to the train mere minutes before it departed.

"Hagop!" Armen whispered. He touched Hagop's arm.

"Hm? What?" Hagop said, stirring from his trance.

"I know it is bad for you," Armen said, looking at him. "But we must get out of here. You remember what Salleh told us. We must get to the orphanage. There we will be safe."

"First we go to Diyarbekir," Hagop said, his gaze fixed. "First Diyarbekir."

DIYARBEKIR

It was early evening when the train pulled into the station. As they passed by the homes, light from kerosene lamps flickered back and forth.

"I am sorry," Armen said. "I was here only the one time."

"It is all right," Hagop said. "We will find it."

They had been walking for some time, and Armen struggled to remember the direction.

"I think this way," he said.

Hagop nodded, and they trudged along, searching. They walked for several more minutes, and Armen stopped.

"That is it," he said. "That is the home."

Hagop looked past the wall to the home of Ahmet Salim.

"There?" Hagop asked. He tried to imagine Anahid inside.

"Yes," Armen replied. "I have seen her in that place."

"Then we go now," Hagop said, moving forward.

"Hagop," Armen said. He grabbed his arm. "It is very dangerous."

Hagop looked at him. His eyes seemed to blacken and Armen took a step backward.

"And if it was your sister?" Hagop said, measuring each word. Armen said nothing, and Hagop caught himself. "I know you are frightened," he said. "I am afraid also."

Armen opened his mouth to speak, but Hagop silenced him.

"I want you to stay here, out of sight. I will go."

"If that is what you want…"

"It is," Hagop said. "If anything happens, leave and do not come back. Make your way to the orphanage." He looked at Armen. "Promise me."

"I do," Armen said. "I promise."

Hagop crossed the street, nearing the fence surrounding the home. He reached over the gate door and pulled up the latch. The door gave, swinging lazily toward him. Hagop looked around and was immediately taken by the garden's lushness. There was a white marble fountain with carved figurines of doves and falcons.

He reached the door and paused. Armen watched him, wondering why he had stopped. Finally, he reached up and knocked.

Nothing.

Again he knocked. A few moments passed, and the door opened. She stood there, dressed from head to toe, her face veiled. Only her eyes peered through the slit of material, but, still, he knew it was she.

"Anahid! Anahid!" he said.

He reached out, unable to contain his joy, and grabbed her, hugging her tightly. She struggled, and feeling her fighting him, Hagop instantly let go. She drew her hand back and slapped him across the face.

"Infidel Dog!" she spat. "Pig! Leave your hands away from me!"

Hagop stood, his eyes widening, unable to believe the words.

"Anahid!" he said. "Yes em! Hagop em!" he said. It is I! It is Hagop!

"Leave this place now!" she screamed. "My Pasha is here! He will call for the police!"

Hagop took a step backward, as if he had been stabbed.

"Yeghbayruht em!" he said. I am your brother!

"I do not know you!" she said. She looked at him, disgust in her eyes. "You are like all the others! You lie to get food!"

"No!" Hagop pleaded. "No, it is…"

"Nazmine!" the female voice called from beyond the door.

She turned, attentive to the command. Hagop could hear footsteps approaching.

"No!" he cried. "Koo anoonuht Anahid eh!" Your name is Anahid!

He reached and grabbed her. She turned, but before she was able to yell, he spoke quickly.

"Your name is Anahid. Anahid Melkonian. You are from Palou..."

She looked at him, blankly, and then her face darkened.

"Enough!" she said, breaking away from him. "Go now!"

"I beg you," he said.

Two women appeared at the doorway. They looked at her and at Hagop.

"If you will not come with me, make your way to the American Orphanages," Hagop said. One of the women looked at him, then reached out and closed the door.

"I am sorry," Armen said. "She is too far gone now."

They had walked in silence for some time, winding their way through the darkness, towards the outskirts of Diyarbekir. Hagop did not know what to do. They would be arrested if they tried again. Now that he had shown himself, they would not allow her to come to the door.

"We stay away from the station, now," Hagop said. "We go to the west."

"How do you know?" Armen asked.

"To the west is Urfa," Hagop said. "Salleh said it would be closer to Urfa, near Severeg."

"No," Armen said. "He said he did not know. I remember what he said. He was not sure."

"I say we go west," Hagop said.

They found a small shelter amongst some fallen trees and stopped for a few hours, neither of them sleeping. Just beyond the line of trees, dawn was coming up. They were somewhere between Diyarbekir and Severeg.

"She did not know me," Hagop said, finally. "There was nothing in her eyes."

Armen nodded. "Come, my friend. I can hear voices beyond these trees. It is time to go."

Hagop nodded and they trudged along. They could only stare as two enormously long lines moved before them. Boys were to the left, girls to the right. There were so many of them, and yet the air was strangely silent. Hagop looked at Armen, who nodded, and managed a slight smile.

The smell inside the American Orphanage was a mixture of chalk, old books, and of boiled potatoes. Hagop and Armen passed a room where young girls sat on the stone floor, learning to needlepoint. Across the room, older girls stood at an upright wooden loom, learning to weave rugs.

They reached a dispensing table and each boy was handed a small blanket, a white shirt, and a pair of dark blue pants. They heard the voice of an older boy supervising younger ones. As they reached the doorway, they saw that they were making shoes. Souren flashed quickly through their minds. They glanced at one another, but neither said a word. English and French filtered from both sides of the hallway, and they saw nuns writing on chalkboards and children repeating the phrases.

Finally, they reached their room. Stretched over the floor were at least forty of the small blankets. They found an empty area to the rear and laid their blankets next to one another.

"It is not what I thought," Armen said.

"What did you think?"

"That there would be many soldiers."

Hagop nodded. They sat, wondering what would happen next.

CONSTANTINOPLE

It was a clear, crisp winter's day as Morgenthau walked up the steps to Talaat's office.

"Thank you for coming, Mr. Ambassador," Talaat said. "A drink?"

"No, thank you," Morgenthau replied.

Talaat reached for the bottle of raki. He took a quick whiff and poured the contents into a glass. He added some water and the mixture instantly turned a light, milky white. He took a sip, satisfied. He sat, picked up some documents and waived them at Morgenthau.

"Mr. Ambassador," he said. "May I ask you a business question?"

"Yes, Mr. Minister," Morgenthau replied, "what is it?"

"Do you have friends in any of the American insurance companies?"

"Why?" Morgenthau asked.

"Well, you see," Talaat said, waiving the documents. "We have these policies and we need the Armenian names."

"Policies?" Morgenthau said. "What kind of policies?"

"Insurance policies, of course!" Talaat replied. "There will be no heirs to collect, so the money will come to us."

Morgenthau sat, incredulous. "I cannot help you," he said, exasperated.

"That is too bad, Mr. Ambassador," Talaat said.

"Mr. Minister," Morgenthau said, leaning forward. "Why did it have to come to this? Completely defenseless women and children are dying every day."

Talaat rolled his knuckles back and forth over the desktop until they cracked.

"They are the ones to blame," Talaat said. "They want their freedom. They want rebellion as in Van. We have driven them out. Now we have to finish them. If we do not, they will have their revenge."

Morgenthau sat, sickened. He had heard enough. By the time the world's journalists could put together the pieces, the war would be over, the maps would be redrawn, and the Armenians would be forgotten.

But the war would go on long after Morgenthau had left. Long after both Enver, Talaat, and the others had escaped. It would push on, relentless, churning up blood and bodies. Millions would die. When the eleventh hour of the eleventh month came, the world would be a very different place. And the Armenians would be on the brink of their extinction.

"Mr. Minister," Morgenthau said, slowly. "You are destroying Turkey in the eyes of the world."

Talaat sat and returned Morgenthau's stare. "The matter is closed. There is nothing more to say."

MOSUL

Once her complexion had been that of fine, white porcelain.

Once her hands had spun the finest needlepoint in her village.

And once she had been alive with joys that rivaled even the richest of pashas.

But now, here in Mosul, she was surrounded in the most horrible squalor. Only Deir-El-Zor could rival it for that. Her skin was dark, wrinkled, dead. Her hands and nails were cracked and bloody. And her spirit, as much as she tried, was broken. They mumbled to themselves. They screamed at things that were not there. They dug at their skin, leaving blood red marks. And when they scratched at their scalps, clumps of hair came off.

Elise looked around, barely able to raise her head. The sun was overpowering and she slowly crawled to get into the shade. Around her, there were screams: people gone crazy, people going mad. But they were muffled. The sounds didn't reach her ears right anymore. Her eyesight had failed these last days, and the tiny rock overhang was blurry as she crawled forward. She reached it and could feel its coolness.

Once she had been afraid of the dark. Once she had begged her mother to leave the door open. To leave the candle lit.

The sounds began to fade from her and as her eyes began to flutter, she had the most beautiful vision of a woman who beckoned her close, close, closer.

"Mama..." she said.

And in the bright light of the desert, Elise Marta Khatchaturian, wife of Nishan, mother of daughters Azniv and Sona, exhaled long and deep and slumped against the cool rock.

OUTSIDE DIYARBEKIR

Armen held the framework as Hagop fitted the top into the cut slats. Within the hour the bookcase would be formed, each piece of wood carefully measured, cut, grooved, and fit into place. These were good skills to have. The sound of footsteps grew along the stone floor and they looked up to see the new group of refugee boys and girls pass by the open doorway. Hagop's face momentarily brightened, and then fell as he returned to the work at hand.

No Anahid.

CONSTANTINOPLE

Morgenthau sat in the study. He looked at the blank page and began writing.

'My dearest Josephine. My days here are almost over and I will be with you shortly. The last have been particularly troubling and most of my efforts to intercede on behalf of the Armenians have been thwarted. Oh, it is true that I have been able to save a few here and there, but in due course, they will all exist only in the desert. From there, they will certainly perish. Nothing lives there. What gives me strength is knowing that I am right and remembering your last words to me. If all I do is save one and make the world know what's happened here I have done something.'

He replaced the pen in the inkwell and sat back. He was tired. So very, very, tired.

OUTSIDE DIYARBEKIR

Hagop and Armen lay awake on their blankets. Around them, the others slept, some soundly, others fighting off imaginary demons.

"Are you sleeping?" Armen whispered.

"No. I am awake," Hagop whispered back.

"I cannot sleep," Armen said. "What happens to us now?"

"Do not worry," Hagop said. "We are safe."

Armen looked at him. "I will not go back. Nothing will make me go back."

"You will not have to. They will send us somewhere."

Armen's eyes brightened. "They will?" Hagop nodded. "To where?"

"I do not know," Hagop answered. "They will not send us back because it is too dangerous."

They were silent for a while and finally Armen looked at Hagop.

"I am sorry about Anahid," he said. "And Sona."

"Thank you," Hagop said. "Thank you, my friend."

He stretched out his hand and Armen took it.

"Now we should try to sleep a bit," Hagop said.

CONSTANTINOPLE
January, 1916

Document after document. Report after report. They lay there. Numbers. Just numbers now. The atrocities were too much. He had conducted so many interviews. He had sent so many reports. And yet, he could only work on the periphery, bartering and trading lives as he went. He looked at the papers on the table, stood, and angrily brushed them onto the floor. He walked into the bathroom and stared at the man who looked back at him. The eyes were tired and the face was worn. He would be home soon. Home to his family and to his work. There would be much to do. And he would be able to speak out against the injustices that he had seen here.

Morgenthau flicked open the straight razor and paused. He took the stiff brush and spread the warm lather onto his face. He lifted the razor and drew it once across his cheek, revealing clean, fresh skin.

DIYARBEKIR

Anahid stooped over, cleaning the floors. It was hard work and Ahmet Salim had a large home.

She had awoken after days. The fever and convulsions had almost killed her and Salim had sent for Hosnani, the family doctor.

"I am sorry," he had said. "Come, look at this." He pointed at her leg.

Salim looked at him and nodded.

"Yellow scorpion," Hosnani said.

"What can be done?" Salim asked.

"We will give her these roots," Hosnani said, opening his leather case to reveal small bottles containing dark brown, orange, and red substances. He withdrew five different bottles, and handed them to Salim. "From each, every two hours. The girl is young. If she fights, she will live."

"Ah, welcome back!" Salim said, greeting her.

It had lasted almost eight days, but she had struggled, soaked to her clothes from sweat, not more than skin and bones. She had asked where she was, who he was, and in that moment he had decided that to tell her everything would be too much. It would be better this way. If in the future the truth had to be told, he would tell it. It was his responsibility.

"Can you not remember?" he asked.

"No." She raised her head to look up, but she was too weak.

"You are my late brother's daughter," Salim said, resting his hand on hers. "Your name is Nazmine. I am Ahmet, your uncle. This is my home."

She had looked at him, strangely at first, trying to remember. She knew his face, but there was a hole that she could not fill.

"What happened to me?"

"You have been very ill," Salim said. He looked at her. "Your condition was very grave. But, for now, it is important to rest."

Over the next days she had eaten and her strength returned.

"Your job will be to clean these rooms," Salim's third wife Sabirah, said. "First, the walls, then the floors. Do not forget to clean behind the furniture."

Anahid nodded, listening intently to the woman's directions.

Now she moved about the room, mopping and dusting. If she hurried she would be done in time to go to the market with Sabirah. Her room was small. There was a bed and a large walnut armoire. She mopped down the walls. Then it was the floors, being careful to clean under the bed, pushing the broom into every corner.

The armoire was too heavy to move, so she cleaned behind it by wrapping cloth around the end of the broomstick. She pulled it back and it seemed to catch on something. She bent down, reached in with her hand, and pulled out a bundle of dusty silk cloth. She unfolded it and as she did, the golden links of a chain tumbled out. She flipped back the last fold of silk revealing the golden cross.

She picked it up and looked at it. It was Lucine's. And, slowly, she began to remember.

Everything.

CONSTANTINOPLE

The whirling wind threw snow left and right. Josephine had been gone for almost four months, but he would soon be with her. The exit meeting was a formality for all departing Ambassadors and as Morgenthau walked into the outer office, he saw both Enver and Talaat engaged in deep conversation.

"Mr. Ambassador!" Talaat said. "Good afternoon!"

"Please have a seat," Enver said.

"Thank you," Morgenthau said. "As you know I will be leaving shortly. Today is our scheduled farewell interview."

"Yes, and we are both sorry to see you go, Mr. Ambassador," Enver said.

"Thank you," Morgenthau said. "Since you flatter me, I know you will promise me certain things."

"And what is that?" Enver asked.

"I must put you on record," Morgenthau answered. "That you will treat the people in my charge with all due considerations. Just as if I were here."

"You have nothing to worry about," Enver said.

"Thank you," Morgenthau said. He looked from Enver to Talaat. "And the Armenians?"

"Oh, what's the use now?" Talaat said, waving his hand. "That is all over."

Morgenthau sat. Thoughts collided in his head. Images. Women. Children. Grandfathers. Grandmothers. Talaat. Enver. Turkey. Armenia. Germans. Bombs. Tanks. Guts hanging out, held in by a helmet. Back and forth. Too fast, too fast. He couldn't think clearly.

"Mr. Ambassador? Mr. Ambassador?"

"Yes? Yes?"

"Are you all right?"

"No. No. I am fine, thank you…"

And now Morgenthau sat at his desk, reading the telex from Jackson, the American consul at Aleppo. Jackson and the ancillary consuls were estimating that more than three hundred thousand had perished in the desert marches. He fitted the document into the report binder he had been keeping.

Occasionally, the men would go to the Club de Constantinople, Le Petit Club, where they would gobble up plates of yamourtas alla Turca, shish kebab, dipping the delicately roasted meat into a yogurt sauce. But Morgenthau always felt that Tokatlian's was the best restaurant in all of Constantinople.

Now Morgenthau sat at his farewell dinner, surrounded by members of his staff. As the dishes of a dessert of mulberry and fig sorbet were cleared, Mowbry stood.

"Mr. Ambassador," he said. "On behalf of the entire staff, we hope that you will have a safe journey back to New York. We have been enriched by your guidance and your humanitarianism."

"Here, here!"

"Speech!"

"Very well," Morgenthau said standing and allowing himself a slight smile. "I fear that if I do not Tokatlian there will have us thrown out due to your riotous behavior!" The staff broke out into cheers and applause.

"All right, all right," Morgenthau said. "It is I who am grateful for having had the opportunity to have worked with you during these last two years. This is an arduous time in the world, but the spirit that guides us will see to it that justice prevails. I ask you to continue your good work and may God be with each of you." They looked at him for a moment, and then burst into applause.

The train whistled, signaling it was ready to depart.

"Thank you, sir," Mowbry said, extending his hand.

Morgenthau ascended the steps to his car and then turned. "James," he said.

"Yes, Mr. Ambassador?" Mowbry replied. It was the first time Morgenthau had ever called him by his given name.

"Do not stay in Constantinople long."

Mowbry nodded. "Yes, Mr. Ambassador."

The train, the Balkan Zug, had just been completed and glistened with new, shiny black iron. As it pulled away, Morgenthau looked out, Constantinople reflecting against his face, merging, blending, and then drifting away.

Twenty days later, on the twenty-second day of February 1916, on the Danish Liner S.S. Frederick VIII, Morgenthau sailed into New York

Harbor. Josephine was there to greet him, and at just before seven-thirty in the morning, he stood on the deck, eyes bright, and watched America come back into view.

It was wondrous.

And thirty years later, the view would dim, fade, and recede from him. He had become nothing short of an apostle to the Armenians and they had always remained close in his heart. They had not been made extinct. What was that saying? "Where two Armenians meet there will be Armenia," he said, shaking his head, grinning.

The Great War had taken with it millions. It had destroyed. It had shattered. The politicians had come in and sliced up the pieces. And Morgenthau knew that it would only be a matter of time before Germany would boil to the point of explosion.

"They are killing Jews there," he said softly, reading the documents. "Just like the Armenians."

The little black lines of news type became trains carrying Jews, moving through the dense forests, breaking and cracking off tree branches that fell into the snow. And as the wheels swerved along the curving track the snaking train turned into shifting, moving people. Walking, in the desert. Lines of people. Lines in the sand.

"The children of the exiles must not enter orphanages. They possess information dangerous to the Empire. Make all attempts to intercede them. Talaat." He signed the document and ordered it sent.

OUTSIDE DIYARBEKIR

Hagop and Armen painted the small birdhouse they had built. Soon it would be time for dinner. Sister Rose was a Roman Catholic missionary who had been in the area for almost six years. She was American, but had spent the last ten years in Paris.

"Hagop, Armen," she said. "May I see you for a moment?"

They looked up from their work.

"Yes, Sister Rose?" Hagop said.

"I have good news," she said. "Armen, this is a letter from your mother's cousin in New York."

Armen and Hagop exchanged glances.

"I do not understand," Armen said.

She withdrew the folded letter from the envelope and handed a photo to Armen.

"Your mother's cousin, Nevart Ajemian, has agreed to support your passage to America."

"I do not know this woman," Armen said.

"Armen, the papers are correct. We record the names of every boy and girl who comes here. The Near East Relief Society publishes in American newspapers the names of children in these orphanages. Your mother's cousin contacted Near East in New York."

Armen looked at Hagop, perplexed.

"It is good news!" Hagop said. "You are going to America!"

"Hagop, you are going there too," she said.

The boys looked at one another.

"I...?" Hagop said.

"Mrs. Ajemian has also agreed to sponsor you."

Hagop looked at her. "I... Sister Rose, I cannot go. My sister is still here."

She nodded and folded her hands. "Hagop. Listen to me carefully, my boy." She looked at both of them. "There are many opportunities in America. If your sister is meant to join you, it will be God's will." She looked at them. "If you believe in this, you must go." She turned to leave. "Now, prepare your things," she said. "You both leave tomorrow."

Hagop and Armen looked at one another.

"Tomorrow!" Armen exclaimed. "To America!"

Hagop looked over to Armen, who was fast asleep. He got up and walked carefully past the other orphans. He opened the wooden door and walked down the corridor. The door to the staff office was open and a flickering light came from it. He peeked inside. Sister Rose was there, writing.

"Hagop. Come in," she said, softly.

"I am sorry to bother you."

"Oh, you are not bothering me at all."

"I could not sleep."

"That is understandable. I am sure you are very excited about tomorrow."

"I..." Hagop said, hesitating.

"Hagop. I know that you are worried about your sister, your family," she said. "I promise you that if they are found, they will know where you are."

"No," he said. He looked at her. "I believe God will bring my sister back to me," he said. "But I know that everyone else in my family is dead."

"Hagop, you don't know that for..."

"Yes... I... do..." Hagop said.

"But there is always a chance," she said. He shook his head slightly and they sat in silence for a few moments. "Hagop, what is troubling you, my boy?"

"I do not understand," he said, struggling. "You are American, but I see Germans and the British here as well. And there are Canadians and French..."

"Yes, that is right," she answered. "All of them are together here."

"But I do not understand," he said. His face was anguished, tormented in some way that she could not fathom.

"No one came to help us," he said, his voice cracking. "No one! And now, everyone is helping us! Why can I be in here when the rest are out there?"

"Hagop," she said, gently. "The people here are all Christian missionaries. They provide relief regardless of the war." She looked at him. "Here, come with me."

She rose from her chair, and Hagop followed her. They walked to the end of the long corridor and turned into the front hall. She pointed to a framed document and a photograph of the mission's façade. In the right hand corner was a small photo inset.

"This is how you are here," she said. Hagop drew closer and looked at the decree. It was written in ornate script, and he could not understand all the words. He looked at the photograph. The man was dressed in an elegant suit, an older man, with pince-nez glasses.

"What does it say?" he asked.

"This is a letter of proclamation," she said. "It says that the establishment of this orphanage is through the efforts of the Near East Relief Society, the German-Orient mission, and many others."

"Who is this man?" he asked, gesturing to the photo.

"His name is Henry Morgenthau," Sister Rose answered. "He assists these efforts, working with the Americans."

Hagop quietly backed away from the wall. He looked at her and she could see that he had so many more questions.

"Come, Hagop," she said. "It is late and you have a very big day tomorrow."

"Yes," he said. Suddenly, he was very tired.

He found his blanket next to Armen. He lay down, looked up at the red clay ceiling, and slowly closed his eyes.

The boys packed what few belongings they had in the small blankets and rolled them up. Now they sat, waiting to be called.

The group of gendarmes ran towards the trucks. They were under Talaat's orders to intercede. It did not matter that they were children. It did not matter that some of them could not even remember that they were Armenian. The order had been given. They would carry it out.

Hagop and Armen stood in line with the other children. The trucks would be there soon, and they would be taken overland to Kessab in Syria. From there they would travel to America.

The trucks careened around the corner, kicking up sand and stones as they sped toward the orphanage. They had to hurry. They had been informed that they would be leaving today.

"Faster!" the gendarme commanded.

Hagop and Armen squinted in the bright sunlight as three open-air trucks stood, waiting. The missionary workers began organizing the children into three groups. Those up to five years of age, boys and girls, went into the first truck; all girls over five into the second truck; all boys over five into the third truck.

Hagop and Armen shuffled along in the line and as they did, Sister Rose rushed up to them.

"Boys," she said, handing them two small packages. "These are your official papers. Do not lose them. There are also letters for each of you which arrived in last night's mail pouch."

She looked at them.

"God bless you both."

"And you," they said.

They stepped forward and she hugged them. They climbed aboard the third truck and took seats toward the rear. The drivers started the engines and as the trucks began to pull away, two trucks rushed in. Hagop, Armen, and the other children looked up. Sister Rose and the other missionaries stood confused.

The British lieutenant stepped out of the vehicle and walked over to two of the male missionaries. Hagop looked at Armen.

"Something is wrong," he said.

Suddenly, the two trucks containing the Gendarmes roared ahead in the distance. As they drew nearer to the orphanage, they slowed. The head gendarme saw the two trucks containing the British soldiers. He looked quickly from the children to the British Lieutenant who stood, hand on his sidearm, staring directly at him. The gendarme said something to the driver and both trucks quickly sped away.

Within twenty minutes, the children were off, escorted by the British vehicles.

VESSEL OKYANUS

The late afternoon sun danced just above the horizon line. The orphans were crowded together, hundreds of them. Most slept, others looked out into the water as the Turkish vessel Okyanus steamed along. They had been on the sea only hours and it would be another seven to eight days, depending on the weather. Some of the ships stopped in Gibraltar, prolonging the journey by three to four weeks.

Hagop sat, looking at the water stream past, his mind on so many things. Armen approached, carrying two tin plates of food.

"Hagop! Look! Food!" he said, attempting to cheer him.

"I am not hungry," Hagop said. "Give it to the others."

Armen put the trays down and sat. "When you eat, I eat," he said. He looked at his friend. "I know that you are sad now, but soon it will be much better."

"It will not get better," Hagop said softly. "It will never get better."

"I do not understand," Armen replied.

Hagop looked at him, and his face slowly twisted with the torture he felt inside.

"They have killed my father. They have killed my mother." The tears began to fall from his eyes. Armen sat, silent, not knowing what to do. "And now, my sister is lost to me," Hagop said, the words coming out staccato between sobs. "There is nothing left."

Armen paused a moment and put his hand on Hagop's shoulder. "But you have something now," he said. "You have something they will never be able to take away." Hagop looked at him. "You have your freedom," Armen said. "And with your freedom, you have your future."

It was later now. Hagop looked over at Armen, who had propped himself up against one of the lifeboats. He was fast asleep. Hagop felt inside his coat and removed the package that Sister Rose had given him. He looked at the envelope with the official seal: his entry papers. Beneath it was a small travel book; he could make out the title: Discover New York. On the cover was a cityscape of tall buildings, crowded tightly together.

Sticking out of the pages was a small piece of paper. He turned it slightly so that it would catch the moonlight and slowly read the note. "Hagop, for you to practice reading English. Sister Rose."

He managed a slight smile, and put the note and the book back in the package. His fingers hit something stiff, and as he pulled out the white envelope, he was surprised to see his name, written in Armenian script. He blinked several times. He knew that handwriting! He frantically opened it. He withdrew the single sheet of paper, unfolded it, and a gold cross tumbled out. He held it in his right hand and looked at it.

'My dearest brother. When you came to see me I did not understand who you were. Many days later, I began to remember. I saw many things. Things that I hope to never see again.'

Hagop could hear Anahid's voice now, and he trembled slightly.

'I have come to the American Orphanage, but I am held in hospital for quarantine. The sisters here took my letter. I pray it will find its way to you. They have told me they are sending many girls to Beirut and to Paris and then to America.'

Hagop blinked several times and air rushed quickly in and out of his open mouth.

'Hagop, our mother made many decisions to save me. One day I will tell you what she had done. This is her cross. When she gave it to me she told me to never forget who we are and what happened to us here.'

He looked at the cross and brushed his thumb and forefinger over the raised surface.

'All my love. Your sister, Anahid.'

Tears streamed down his face and as he held the letter in his left hand, he began to shake. The cross dangled down, swinging to the rhythm of the boat's motion.

It swung to the left, then to the right, and suddenly the tiny clink-clink-clink of metal being pulled through a hole echoed in his ears and brought him back. There was Zabel, tugging on the cross, beckoning him awake.

Hagop opened his eyes and as he did, saw that the late afternoon sun in Providence, Rhode Island, was coming down. He looked into the eyes of his great-granddaughter, scooped her into his arms, and took her inside.

The Armistice ending World War One was signed on 11 November 1918. In the years 1915-1922, 1.5 million Armenians, one-half of their worldwide population, perished.

Seventeen days before the Armistice was signed, Central Committee members, including Talaat Pasha, Enver Pasha, Djemal Pasha, Bedri Bey, and Doctors Nazim and Sakir fled on a German ship to Odessa and then to Berlin.

On 6 July 1919, a Turkish Military Tribunal tried, convicted, and sentenced to death in absentia Talaat Pasha, Enver Pasha, Djemal Pasha, and Doctors Nazim and Shakir. The chief charge was the deportation and massacre of the Armenians.

In May 1918, Soghomon Tehlirian assassinated Harootiun Mugerditchian in Constantinople.

On 15 March 1921, living in Berlin as a fugitive, Talaat Pasha was assassinated in Charlottenburg by Soghomon Tehlirian.

In 1922, the Bolseviks killed Enver Pasha in Turkestan during an ambush. The circumstances of his death were never fully substantiated.

In December 1921, Arshavir Shirakian assassinated Grand Vizier Said Halim in Rome.

On 17 April 1922, Shirakian and Aram Yerganian assassinated Dr. Bahaeddine Shakir in Berlin.

In July 1922, Stepan Dzahigian assassinated Djemal Pasha in Tbilisi.

In October 1922, General Mahmud Kamil committed suicide.

In 1926, Dr. Nazim was hanged for plotting to assassinate Mustafa Kemal Ataturk.

"It is generally not known that in the years preceding 1916, there was a concentrated effort made to eliminate all the Armenian people, probably one of the greatest tragedies that ever befell any group. And there weren't any Nuremburg trials."

U.S. President Jimmy Carter

16 May 1978

"Wer redet heute noch von der vernichtung der Armenier."

Who after all is today speaking of the destruction of the Armenians.

Adolph Hitler

At Obersalzberg

22 August 1939

In preparation for the Invasion of Poland